D1505413

O, Democracy!

O, Democracy!

Kathleen Rooney

FIFTH STAR PRESS

CHICAGO

for my parents

O, Democracy!

I will plant companionship thick as trees along all the rivers of America, and along
   the shores of the great lakes, and all over the prairies,
I will make inseparable cities with their arms about each other's necks,
         By the love of comrades,
            By the manly love of comrades.

         — "For You O Democracy," Walt Whitman

~

Colleen Dugan's coworkers still wonder, sometimes, why she got fired. But we never wonder. We saw it from the start. Her end could only be abrupt.

And although, from our remote and bodiless perspective, she cannot be identified as especially exceptional, we will now consider the story of Colleen Dugan.

By any fair measure, the intense but inexpedient passion with which Colleen applies herself is of questionable significance to the history of the nation. Yet we, the narrators of this tale, are interested in episodes like these.

Whenever any citizen—in addition to merely feeding, clothing, housing, and reproducing himself—possesses aspirations to take a role in the furtherance of democracy, we look in on them in much the same way one might detour by a former residence, just to see how the new owners are keeping it up.

We follow Colleen and others like her from a place outside the temporal world. We can claim little stake in these individual fates, and no capacity to affect them. Our perspective is akin to that of a group of relatives gathered at Thanksgiving watching football on television, which some of us did religiously.

In life we ourselves were anything but ordinary. Our victories and disgraces went unremarked upon by no one. We amassed power and prestige, or else power and prestige coalesced around us. Our names and likenesses were, and continue to be, known to even the most ignorant of our countrymen, propagated by schools and streets, cities and currency.

This is precisely why ordinariness like Colleen's is of particular concern to us.

~

THE CHIEF OF STAFF

Colleen Dugan was, to me, uncommonly pretty. Always. Even back when she was an intern, back when her short haircut made her look like a baby-faced dyke. I put her on the office softball team on the basis of that alone—the goddamn league was coed and we always needed women. She's got long hair now, or did the last time I saw her, Fall '08, but she was still tall, skinny, no tits to speak of.

Add to that she was an uppity bitch—quite the mouth.

But I thought I loved her, could love her, would always love her for that.

That and I never could abide a dumpy woman, and Colleen Dugan would never be dumpy. She was too vain. Too much like me.

And now I'll never see her again. That's almost certain. But I'll think of Colleen at least once a day till the day I die. The day I go from being a Senate employee of the managerial class to the Chief of Nothing.

COLLEEN

I've heard that every senator, when he looks in the mirror each morning to shave, thinks he sees the face of the next president.

But not my boss. Not *the* Senator, who looks in the mirror and sees not Mount Rushmore, but a plain-faced man who likes being who he is—the Senior Senator of the State of Illinois.

That's all. Or is it all? I'm not sure I know.

When my other boss, the Chief of Staff, looks in the mirror in the morning to shave, he sees a man handsome and impossible to resist. A man who runs the Senator's Chicago office like a pirate ship. What else? Two grandchildren? Another on the way? His legacy? Posterity? I don't know that either.

The Senator is nowhere near the bantering leading man the Chief of Staff fancies himself. He's a workhorse, a sparkplug—a drudge, not a gallant. Not dashing, not dapper, not flashy in any way. That makes him a super-okay guy to work for, and I've worked for the Senator, and therefore the Chief, on and off since I was nineteen.

I started as a summer intern in the Chicago office, back when I was sure—like every other Poli-Sci major—that this was the start of an illustrious career in public service. I got asked to return as a staffer the summer I was twenty because I could take a well-composed photograph, write a respectable sentence, and remain unfailingly polite when constituents were calling me, and the horse I rode in on, an asshole.

Also because the Chief of Staff found me attractive. I tried then, and try still, not to take that personally.

During that first summer as a staffer, I approached Gina Moretti, the press secretary, about the Chief's, "Um, attentiveness," I think I'd said.

"You're not the first to remark upon that, Dugan," she'd said, leaning across her desk, her voice low. "There are only two options, though, and they are as follows. One, if you can't tolerate it, you can find a gig somewhere else. Two, you can get used to it and stay. Please note that I am not expressing an opinion about this. I am only clarifying your situation."

The idea of quitting trotted across my brain as I processed what Gina was telling me. But I couldn't fathom walking away from a job I'd wanted so badly.

I thought it was my destiny. Or a stepping stone anyway. The great thing about this country, I'd learned back in elementary school, is that anyone can grow up to be the President of it. And I—of the gold stars, the flashcards, the student council, the speech team—had heard and believed.

No matter how much stupider and more unlikely this childhood goal gradually came to seem.

With guys like that in charge, how could I ever be President? But wouldn't quitting let guys like that win? And even if I never got to be Commander in Chief, couldn't I stick around and at least be something? Do something? Help somebody somewhere?

The Chief was the Senator's friend and advisor.

His treatment of certain women was accepted as part of the package.

Part of his charm.

In spite of myself, I did not find it entirely uncharming.

In the short time I'd worked there, I'd come to feel a kinship with the Chief, like we must be assembled from some of the same materials.

So I adapted, marveling at how you could get used to anything if you had to.

~

We were murdered in theaters. We invented bifocals. We owned slaves.

We were killed in duels.

We did not believe in God, or we did, or we pretended to.

There are many of us, and we never sleep, and we see everything.

The one attribute we all have in common which we do not share with the innumerable others who have died is that we retain an insomniac's awareness of the republic we have departed.

We remember our pasts the way we remember America's, but we are not individuals anymore.

Our triumphs and defeats, so consequential in life, retain no significance for us.

Where we are there are no longer any arguments.

~

THE CHIEF OF STAFF

I have a fantasy.

I've been falling asleep alone to too many noir pictures, reading too many hard-boiled detective novels single in my hotel double-bed, the wife downstate.

Colleen will read my obituary in some city newspaper, and she'll show up at my funeral in Decatur, snobby nose wrinkling at the sweet-stink from the global plant processing their infinite soybeans, their endless dog food. She'll be older than I would ever have known her, but still looking young, still thinner, still with more style, better dressed than anyone that town's ever witnessed besides me.

All in black she'll be. Black dress with long sleeves, a black hat, black net mesh screening that tantalizing face—sarcastic at rest and still, I hope, hopeful. She'll turn up graveside, silent as you please, and thud a single blood red rose against my casket as they lower me down.

She wanted to make a difference, and she did, and she suffered for that.

What will the Colleen tossing an absurd floral farewell atop my mortal remains have turned out like?

All I know is that the last time we spoke, she still hadn't realized.

Idealism is itself a form of violence against the world.

COLLEEN

When I look in the mirror in the morning, it's not to shave, and this morning it's the rearview of a rented sedan, and I see myself running late, running yellow lights, advancing the Senator, trying to beat him to Aurora.

When I glance to my right, I see Andrew Eckhart, my fellow Senate Aide, big hands clutching the armrest in a parody of white-knuckled dismay.

The clock in the dash reads 10:29, and although we're forty miles outside Chicago, the traffic remains vicious. In the backseat, Dézi Díaz rustles printed-out pages from two competing online map services which contradict each other about how I am to reach our destination.

1

Where there used to be Potawatomi and a sea of grass, there is now big box retail and a sea of cars. Just before Colleen, Andrew, and Dézi are supposed to make their left toward the dilapidated downtown, they see the yellow and puce sign of the Aurora Pancake House. A pony car disgorges an uncombed crew of guys in concert T-shirts who walk inside, tossing their shiny hair like horses.

It reminds Colleen of a movie that as a sixth grader she memorized every line of, that had featured two actors from a late-night sketch comedy program as the hosts of an improbably successful cable access show broadcast from the basement of a suburban home. The folderol for which she can muster nostalgia astonishes. She mentions this to Andrew and Dézi, tries out a catchphrase.

"Party time!" she says, pointing. "Excellent!"

"Yeah," says Andrew. "We're not worthy."

But Dézi was growing up in the mountains of Guatemala when the movie was released. She became a citizen two years ago, swearing the oath the same day as her parents. She promises to watch it soon, but Colleen says not to knock herself out.

The blue sky behind the Pancake House looks hand-tinted, and Colleen twists to snap a photo as they're stopped at a light.

"Don't tell Gina I did that," she says.

"Course not," says Dézi.

"Sure, Colleen," says Andrew. "Why would we ever let one of our superiors know you were taking personal photographs on the government clock?"

"Thanks, Dézi," says Colleen, ignoring Andrew, who spends spare moments in his cube studying up on contracts. He wants to stop being the Senator's webmaster and use his law degree to open a private practice.

"It makes no sense that Gina would care anyway," says Dézi. "Agnes shoe-shops for two hours over lunch and nobody says one thing. Steve sits in the Chief's office watching bartending videos all morning. But you can't take one photograph?"

"I like the way you think," says Colleen. "If only we could get you in a leadership role."

"Never gonna happen," says Dézi. "Unless somebody dies. Intern babysitter for life—that's me."

They pass the Hollywood Casino, one of the state's many riverboats-in-quotes, a mostly dry-docked vessel partly floating in the muddy shallows only inches from the Fox River shore—a twenty-first century caricature of nineteenth century grandeur. The downtown looks jilted. The underfunded stabs at revitalization give the impression of a neighborhood still gasping at the slight.

They are here in search of the Typical Gas Station Colleen had scouted out earlier in the week, at Gina's press secretarial behest. The Senator will stand next to it and hold a press conference, taking Big Oil to task for skyrocketing prices.

But somehow, Colleen has managed to get them a little lost—though only a few weeks back this was her turf, the county of Kane and the county of DuPage, allotted to her on the sole virtue of the many years' experience she had gathered growing up middle-class and white in the Western suburbs.

Her bump up—nothing so formal as a promotion—from regional outreach to press team came about when the deputy press secretary quit at the first of the month.

A stalwart non-drinker, fat and clean-mouthed—an office oddity—he'd been planning to join the presidential campaign of the Junior Senator from Illinois. But while waiting for that offer to finalize, he had responded to a posting on the website of Chicago's professional hockey team—media relations coordinator with strong contacts in Chicagoland and a solid knowledge of the game—and he went for the money, a bazillion times more dollars than he would ever earn as a civil servant, Colleen figured.

So why her?

Just like the time she was put in charge of environmental initiatives, expertise played no role.

Here, in the Chicago office, sheer enthusiasm won the day. From such zeal, all necessary skills would proceed.

And they did.

Which is one of the reasons Colleen likes the state office—because here, unlike DC, if a person decides she is interested, and is willing to become an expert, then those two forces can make it so.

Back at college in DC, the Young Republicans and the Young Democrats—claiming to be diametrically opposed but really all competing for the same dull goal, admission to law school—made Colleen want to puke.

And at her own summer staff job, she had started to make herself want to.

She spent her junior year in Paris. She fell in love with her boyfriend Walter, a Fine Arts major whom she never would have had the luck to run into in the States. He brought her by his studio one night, mentioned he'd had a hard time finding models for his paintings, and she volunteered.

After the first session, when she had put her robe back on, but not her clothes, they ended up fucking on the dais, sweating under the clip-on lights.

"I've never done that," Walter said. "I mean, I've done it, but not with a model. I try to be a professional."

"I hope you'll be as unprofessional as possible with me," she said.

All that year, when she was posing and when she wasn't, Walter listened with limitless patience as she talked herself into switching majors—to Photography.

In politics, one keeps working hard and showing up, and it's difficult to say what skills one is using; one rarely sees the outcome of anything. And because of the sclerotic political situation in America, the job seems to be less about accomplishing good than about stopping other politicians from inflicting harm: endless stalemate.

In photography, there is a tactile pleasure. A measure of control. Quick results.

So photography was Colleen's alternate plan. But it was also one, she figured, that would make her more suited for a job in an elected official's office, should she decide she wanted one.

Politicians always need photos.

Sure, Walter agreed, if you looked at it that way, it was like having web design skills, or knowing a language.

S till, much of what Colleen does is bewildered and improvised. She's driven them as far as the incorrect directions say, and the Typical Gas Station remains nowhere to be seen.

She pulls into a driveway and prepares to turn around when her phone rings.

"Those A-holes at the *Trumpet* have done it again," Gina is saying.

Colleen brakes, causing Andrew's travel mug to sling coffee from the cupholder. She mouths *sorry* as she listens to Gina, who's calling from outside the Senator's first event, a roundtable on helping troops with Traumatic Brain Injury at an American Legion post in the Fourteenth Congressional District.

The flag-wavers there have come down hard on the Senator for his original vote against the invasion of Iraq.

The Senator's opponent in the upcoming election happens to be a war hero, or at least a man with a military background whose campaign literature bills him as a war hero. That he's also a congressman in the United States House of Representatives from the Tenth District of Illinois is, as his campaign portrays it, secondary service.

This man, Congressman Ron Reese Ryder, walks as though he is wearing a chestful of medals, even when no medals are actually pinned on.

They ran the whole schedule!" Colleen can hear Gina pacing as she talks. "They put it on their site and it got picked up by the AP newsfeed, and now it's all over the right-wing blogs with calls to come demonstrate. This is the second time in two weeks those pricks have pulled this stunt."

The schedule Gina is referring to is the one Colleen sent out last night of the Senator's appearances today. Gina had instructed Colleen to emblazon the mass email and blast-fax with swarms of asterisks and the warning:

> *** NOTE: The times and locations of these events are for media planning purposes only and should not be published or aired in any form. ***

"They've got to be doing it on purpose," Colleen says.

"I know. I already called and ripped them. They took it down, but the damage is done. You have to find a new location, and you have to find it stat. Where are you?"

"Almost to the station," says Colleen. "We got a little turned around."

"We're running behind, too, so you've got time. I need you to find a new place nearby—like even a block up the street—and tell me where it is. I'll tell Steve so he can reroute, and I'll call the media who've said they're coming. Then I need you to swing by the original site and see what's happening, if anybody's there, who they are, and then get back to the new location. You need to tell the media to follow you and you need to not be followed by the demonstrators."

"Um," says Colleen. "Got it. So—"

"Okay, the boss just walked out. Gotta go."

K eep your eyes peeled for a new station," Colleen says, explaining to Andrew and Dézi, half to fill them in and half to get it straight in her own mind.

The neighborhood they're in is mostly residential—historic houses replaced by the occasional McMansion that eats up two lots instead of one, flashy, like gold-capped teeth in an old mouth, defying the character of their surroundings.

Every other yard has a Planned Parenthood BAD for Aurora sign, gold with navy letters, staked close to the curb.

They're almost to the original site and still haven't seen a single other station when Dézi calls out, "New Typical Station, three o'clock!"

And there it is—or there it goes—its yellow bivalve sign just visible over the crowns of ash trees. Colleen hangs a right turn from the left lane, tires squealing, cars honking, drivers giving her the finger. They get the address, and Andrew relays it to Gina.

Three blocks later, they arrive at the Old Typical Station. It's 10:55.

Blue skies, a breeze.

A lovely day for a picnic or a protest.

A handful of people mill beneath the oaks, clutching hand-lettered posters. *Support our TROUPES* and *More DRILLING, less PAYING* and *Jesus Saves.*

Colleen almost wants to help.

To tell them, "You're doing it wrong."

To instruct them on the importance of focused messaging.

Instead, she leaves the keys in the ignition, hops out, and walks toward the press massing on a patch of sidewalk.

S teve Moon Collier, who'd be advancing too on behalf of the campaign if he weren't driving the Senator today, has warned that from now until November, they'll be tailed at every event by a tracer from their opponent's office. Colleen sees that of the two video cameras here, only one is news. The other is a spy in the hire of Congressman Ryder.

Photographs of his freckled face have been circulated to the staffers in both the Chicago and the Springfield offices. Bumbling yet sinister, he wears a cropped blond haircut, khakis, and a powder blue shirt, and he's primed to videotape the Senator's every move.

The spy is such a douchebag that it shames Colleen to admit: she would thrill to the chance to spy on Ryder on the Senator's behalf.

She's suggested as much to the Chief of Staff, to hurry up and get her over to the campaign already. "You'd make quite the cinematographer, babe," he had said. "We'll see."

Andrew, too, wants to be reassigned. By law, the two operations must be separate, and the normal office gets boring during elections. That's why he's riding shotgun with Colleen, even though technically the only other person who should be is Dézi, who's staffing one of the later events.

Andrew's hustling makes Colleen imagine him as a contestant on a reality TV show, vying for the Chief's attention, yearning for the Chief to give him the rose, the clock, the immunity idol, dreaming of the moment when the Chief will look him in the eye and say, "You. I need *you*."

Colleen wants the same prize.

Colleen walks calmly to the members of the media. She fills them in on the revised plan, avoiding the earshot of the Republican secret agent. She slips back into the car and gives the thumbs-up to Andrew and Dézi.

Is about to pull away when she looks again at Ryder's guy and notices that his khakis are gaping.

She knows she should just go, but she can't help herself.

"Quick," she says to Andrew. "Roll down your window."

They rent American to please the unions, and cheap to please the taxpayers. Andrew cranks the handle.

"Okay, look out." Colleen leans across Andrew's lap and—in front of the cameras, the reporters, the protestors, everybody— yells, "Hey! XYZ!"

The Ryder spy looks up, confused. He points to himself and mouths, "Me?"

"Examine your zipper! Your fly is open!"

The guy looks down past his powder-blue polo to fumble his pants closed. He looks back up and sees the reporters heading to the vans. It dawns on him what's happened, but it's already too late.

Same for the protestors.

"Dammit, Colleen," says Andrew, but Colleen can hear in his voice that he's smiling.

Dézi waves from the backseat.

She can't stop laughing as Colleen peels away.

~

Those of us who look from beyond upon these happenings remember such moments as these.

Delicate seconds of lightness and grace.

We remember them more acutely than any battles won or treaties signed.

Months from now, after the elections and the unexpected death, after the scandals and the disasters, this will be one of the few episodes in her brief and misbegotten career that Colleen will be able to look back upon with genuine fondness.

~

"Colleen is my new hero," Dézi will say later, telling the story to Gina Moretti and the Senator, to Steve Moon Collier and Lo'kewell Benson and the Chief of Staff at the end of the press conference.

The Senator will laugh and say, "Come on now, Colleen, you didn't really say that," and Gina will shake her head in mostly mock disapproval, and Colleen will say, "What? It was. His fly really was down. Wouldn't you want to know?"

The Chief of Staff will kiss her hand and tell her, as they are about to head to their vehicles, "You know, for such a nice girl, you can be a real bitch."

"Takes one to know one," Colleen will say.

As she pulls into the New Typical Station, Colleen notes that she's managed to arrive before the Senator after all.

The media vans are parking, starting to unload.

Things look like they will work out for today. The long-term is less clear.

Colleen is 28, unsure whether she wants to stay in politics, go back to photography, or do something else as yet unspecified.

In her state of guilty exhilaration from her humiliation of the Ryder spy, Colleen wonders if this will be as successful as her professional life gets. Has all her childhood precocity been leading up to this?

They scramble out of the rental, Dézi putting on her suit jacket, Colleen and Andrew grabbing the camera equipment and the stack of press releases.

The spring air is honeyed with gasoline.

Colleen launches into her A.V. Club routine. She guesses she's more sentimental than she'd like to be, because every time she's about to record images of the Senior Senator, she recalls the first image ever recorded of her with him.

On Capitol Hill.

On a high school trip known for taking students to experience Washington, DC "close up."

At the conclusion of the constituent coffee the chaperones had taken them to.

Colleen had managed to wend her way to the center of the group photo, flanked on her left by the Senior Senator and on her right by the state's first and only black female Senator.

It hadn't been hard. She was back row material—gawky, tall.

After she received the nine-by-thirteen glossy from her social studies teacher back in the bland classroom in the bland suburbs, she had it matted and framed and hung it in her bedroom.

A visualization exercise, of sorts.

Like *One day I will be there again, in a chamber like that, getting my picture taken. Only I will be one of the senators.*

She was wearing a green dress and a ridiculous grin—a face she hates now and never makes in self-portraits.

But she had been so happy.

She pulls the tripod from its black canvas sling and wrestles with the legs. Their equipment is crappy and barely adequate.

As webmaster, Andrew has been asking for upgrades, using the fact that it's campaign season to shore up his requests, but the Chief of Staff is a self-identified cheap bastard, so this is what they get.

She raises the rake, untangles the cords which someone (Andrew, probably) has coiled into an electric bird's nest, and plugs in the mic. Lets the reporters know that they can do the same.

"They'll be here in five," says Dézi.

Two cameras have shown up, both from the press, both huge. The cameramen hoist them on their bulky shoulders, "spraying for B-roll"—a term Colleen finds faintly vulgar. Her camcorder is palm-sized and labeled like summer camp underwear, *Property of U.S. Senate*. She fixes it atop the tripod and wonders whether she'd feel emasculated if she were a dude.

The cameramen, macho and chivalrous, introduce themselves. "I can't believe this is the best a Senator's office can do," one says, gesturing at her camera. "Lemme jot you down some recommendations on newer models you guys might like."

Colleen doesn't much care, and the Chief, she knows, will care even less. The footage she is about to shoot is destined only for the Hot Topic page on the Senator's website. Among the site's tiny coterie of ardent followers, the Senator can be counted as the most so. But she thanks the Local News Service guy, opens her manila folder, and hands him a press release. Out of her stack of fifteen, she hands out only six.

And one is a repeat. The reporter from the radio station whose call letters refer to their old slogan, "We Must Ask Questions," has accidentally let his blow away.

Colleen's been raised to give a hoot and not pollute. The environmental staffer in her cringes to see the sheet alight on somebody's lawn across the street, a rogue albino leaf, but there isn't time for her to go get it.

The Senator will be arriving any minute. For the first time all morning, Colleen stops to realize how nervous she's been, how nervous she still is.

The turnout is barely mediocre. Two cameras, one radio station, a single newspaper.

"Suburban press is withering on the vine," Gina told the Chief at their last scheduling call. "There's less and less of them each time we go, so the boss wants to go there less and less."

Colleen misses the bygone power of the Fourth Estate. She remembers learning in a political communications class about how, after the turn of the last century, a newspaper magnate and pioneer of yellow journalism was almost single-handedly responsible for the direct election of senators by the states' citizens as opposed to the state legislatures.

These days, the *Daily Trumpet* and its cohort specialize in pictures of puppy dogs and children's birthdays.

"They're here," says Dézi. Colleen turns to see Steve Moon Collier parking the heavy black sedan.

Exiting first, Lo'kewell Benson—the unfolding of his hulking elegance making the town car resemble a clown car. At six-five, 260, a former defensive lineman for U of I, he is continually mistaken for Secret Service, but Lo's here today only because, as veterans' liaison, he staffed this morning's American Legion roundtable.

In any case, the Senator doesn't have bodyguards—doesn't see the need.

Next out is Gina, who slides across the middle of the leather seat, her curly brown hair shining in the sun—on the brink, it appears, as does Gina herself, of springing in every direction.

Now, the Chief, looking, as always, like a man who expects his entrance to be played back in lingering slo-mo.

Finally, the Senator himself appears.

Steve Moon Collier scampers to open the door, falling over himself as if to impress a date.

The Chief of Staff surveys the landscape before tossing his jacket over his shoulder like a model in a catalog, settling his shades in front of his blue eyes, striding to the knot of media. He's wearing a tie with red and gold stripes that makes him look, despite his graying hair, like a prep school boy.

He comes up behind Colleen, places his hand at her waist, his mouth to her ear. "Hey babe," he whispers.

Glancing through the viewfinder, he says, "Nice shot," brushes the small of her back, and wanders away to stand near Steve.

"Was that the Senator?" the radio reporter asks.

C olleen would have killed to leave the heart of the heartland after high school and see the East Coast, but eventually she found herself stranded on the West.

She and Walter moved there for a job Colleen had been offered, teaching photography at a small college in Tacoma.

Halfway through the year she felt like a shipwreck, washed aground in a sad backwater, surrounded by other derelicts, the action elsewhere.

It was December of 2006, but even at that early date the Junior Senator from her home state looked ready to announce his candidacy for the presidency.

The current president was an empire-building dictatorial maniac.

Her dad, an Army Reservist, had just found out he'd been assigned to a second tour of duty with a medical unit in Iraq.

She wanted to do something that mattered.

She wanted to be invited back.

T he Senator is the same height as Colleen—five-eight when she's not in heels—and he lumbers up like a small bear, offers a handshake to the radio reporter. "At your service," the Senator says, smiling a smile that reaches his friendly brown eyes.

Then he faces Colleen and says, "Colleen," a cue for his talking points.

Colleen has a moment of inner panic, but she keeps it off her face.

The Senator should already have them.

They should have been in the packet that Hannah the Scheduler puts together for him every night.

Steve should have handed him the packet this morning when he picked him up at his condo on Lake Shore Drive.

But Colleen is prepared. She has a copy, too. She hands it over.

The Senator scans the page for less than a minute, tosses it at Colleen's feet, approaches the microphones. God save anybody's ass if they haven't got the talking points, even if he doesn't really need them.

"Nice work, Dugan," Gina mutters to Colleen.

Gina is terrifying and a miser with praise. Colleen nods and tries not to beam.

Not that Gina would see her smile anyway. She has already revolved to the reporter from the *Trumpet*.

"Hey," Colleen hears her greet the reporter by name. "What's the big idea?"

"Excuse me?" the woman says, eyes widening.

"Publishing our media advisories even though they come labeled with instructions not to? Are you guys somehow worse at reading than you are at writing?"

But before the reporter can reply, the Senator has started to speak.

Colleen gets out her notebook as she watches, through the camcorder's eye and alternately her own. Gina heads up front with the digital camera around her neck and a handheld voice recorder in her pocket that she'll use to document any one-on-ones.

The Senator's voice is firm with a faint rasp. He pauses periodically to lock each set of eyes as he gestures with his square hands. He used to be a trial lawyer.

He begins by haranguing the Federal Trade Commission about their lack of oversight.

"The watchdogs watch idly while gas prices rise," he says. "They are letting this happen without even a whimper."

He has a way of resurrecting a dead figure of speech and reanimating it briefly. He takes phrases that Colleen saw on the talking points, bulleted and choppy, and weaves them into a whole garment, well-suited to his oratorical talent and even temperament.

"These companies are not only making more money than oil companies have ever made," he says. "They are making *more money than any business in the history of America*. The five largest oil companies in 2007 had profits of $103 billion—$2 billion a week in profits!"

He utters lines other politicians might make angry or outrageous, but presents them smoothly—with emphasis, yes, but allowing the words to work for themselves.

He speaks with a respect for his audience.

The Chief, who has a hard time standing still and an even harder time picking a single vantage, leaves Steve's side and saunters toward Colleen. He sidles up and gives her skirt—full and black, the bottom scalloped with eyelets above her black stockings—a whack.

"I'd follow you anywhere in that dress," he says, quietly as he can.

"Oh really," she says. "You'll need to have it altered before it'll fit you."

"The Duke's all fired up," he leans in to whisper, brushing her shoulder with his. "He's in a good mood today."

"You seem to be doing well yourself," Colleen says, as he moves away again.

One night, in Tacoma, when Walter was asleep and Colleen was insomniac, she emailed the Chief of Staff.

He replied immediately. "I've been thinking of you recently and your future and how I'd like a piece of it. I have reason to believe you'd be the perfect addition to our campaign team. You've got skills. We should use them. Let's talk on the phone."

They sorted out logistics. Colleen would return at the end of the school year—first to work in the Senator's regular state office, then shift focus to his re-election.

In his follow-up email after the call, the Chief had signed off:

"I'm excited about your return, and I'm not kidding. My life is better when you are near. I hope all this works out."

After filling up at the pumps, a few motorists park and get out of their cars to see what's being put on TV. The Senator's cadence indicates that he's wrapping up.

"We can have high-paying energy jobs," he says, "right here in Illinois, but more drilling simply is not the answer. Let's invest in new technologies, and make those jobs green!"

When they'd stand and recite it together in grade school, Colleen had to remind herself not to add "Amen" to the end of the Pledge of Allegiance. Similarly, she has to resist the urge to clap whenever the Senator finishes his remarks at a press event.

"Anybody have any questions?" he asks.

The woman from the *Trumpet* calls "Senator!" and asks, "Any chance the Junior Senator is going to ask you to be his running mate? And, follow-up, if so, what will you say?"

The reporter's question is idiotic—no modern presidential ticket would consist of two politicians, much less two Senators, from the same state.

But the Senator replies with dignity. "Well," he says, "I consider myself the designated driver of the Senate."

It is a leading line, a line he almost always uses when asked about the prospects of leaving his current office for positions ostensibly bigger and better.

Colleen makes eye contact with Lo, then Andrew, then with the Chief of Staff, and they all look at the asphalt to keep their faces straight. They'll be expected to laugh, but they have to wait for the punchline.

"What do you mean by that?" the reporter asks.

"I stay in my seat," he says, "and keep us on the right road when the people around me are getting drunk with plans for greater power."

The Senator smiles as he says this, so the reporter can tell he's not being critical of those others, but that he is taking his duty as the state's senior Senator with the utmost steadfastness.

On cue, able to look at each other again, the staffers laugh. So does the reporter.

"In other words, I've chosen to take a long-term leadership role in the Senate because I believe that's the best way for me to keep doing what's best for Illinois and for the country."

Most of the motorists who gathered meander back to their cars.

One, though, a middle-aged man in paint-stained jeans and a T-shirt for the Chicago football team—orange and blue on heather gray—walks up to Colleen. His face is red. She can't tell if he's embarrassed or sun-burnt.

"You work for that guy?" he asks her.

"Yes sir," she says.

"Is that the Mayor? Is that Hizonner?"

"Of Chicago? No. We're in Aurora, and they have their own mayor. That's the Senator."

"Of Chicago?"

"No. Of Illinois."

"The whole state?"

"Yes, the whole state."

"Can he help me find a job?" the man asks. "I been outta work for six months. I work construction, but there's nothing doing these days. I'm gonna lose my house. Maybe not a job, maybe he can help me just not get foreclosed on. I got three kids—"

Colleen hands the man her card, off-white with raised black lettering and the Senate seal embossed in gold leaf.

"That's a pretty card," he says, and puts it in his cracked leather wallet.

She tells him she's not sure, but that maybe they can open a case for him.

She tells him to go online and print out the Privacy Act Release form authorizing their office to look into the matter, and then to mail it to her attention at the address at the bottom.

She doesn't say so, but she doubts there is anything they'll be able to do. But if he does write, she will write back.

So little has changed since she was first a staffer almost eight years ago.

Colleen finds it hard to believe she ever thought she could become the first female president. As they prepare to leave, she just hopes she'll see a female president elected in her lifetime.

Only thirty-eight women have served as senators. Only six black people. Fourteen senators have also been elected President of the United States. The Junior Senator from Illinois hopes to become the fifteenth.

The Junior Senator happens to be black, but whether he's "black enough" or "too black" remains debated. A woman, the wife of the Forty-Second President, is also running. This woman hasn't conceded yet, but in recent days it has become clear that she will not be the first female president, either. This causes Colleen, a supporter of the Junior Senator, to have mixed feelings.

The Senator has held elected offices of various kinds for the final fifth of the twentieth century, for almost as long as Colleen's been alive, though he's only been a Senator since 1996. The Chief of Staff has been with him for the duration—fighting for their jobs, as they say—making sure the Senator gets reelected at regular intervals, first on the brutal two-year cycle of the House, and now the more leisurely one of the upper chamber.

They have entered the final months of the Senator's second six-year term, and he wants a third. But Ryder, the war hero who won't stop talking about being a war hero, wants a first.

So here Colleen is—here they all are—out among the People, buffeted by what one of us, her favorite Founding Father, called the "amazing violence and turbulence of the democratic spirit."

Colleen frequently finds herself fed up with the People, disgusted by the spirit, but she has never seen the Senator flag in his belief in both.

The *Trumpet* reporter has approached the Senator.

The Senator is shaking the reporter's hand.

Colleen bets he's asking her some questions about herself, personal enough to make her feel noteworthy, but not so personal as to be invasive—where's she from, where'd she go to school, how does she like working for the paper.

If he runs into her again, he will remember every detail with the warmth of an old friend.

Colleen can see the reporter begin to think that the Senator is a pretty good guy, which is what almost everyone thinks if they allow themselves to chat with him. In terms of motivating the *Trumpet* to stop trying to turn their own media advisories against them, this encounter will not hurt.

Gina hovers, recording the exchange.

All the staffers besides Gina clump like scattered beads of mercury, rejoining to become a single pool—Colleen, Andrew, Dézi, Lo, the Chief of Staff, and lastly Steve Moon Collier, eager to get behind the wheel.

The next event is a luncheon with the Painters and Allied Trades at their new union hall.

Per the Chicago office's system of assigning outreach based on social background and ethnic origin, Steve Moon Collier—half Irish-American, half-Korean-American—should have been an obvious choice for Asian-American community liaison, but he had resisted.

Allegedly, he chafed at the ethnic typecasting.

In fact, he viewed the position as a dead end.

Instead, he got suburban political outreach with a specialty in unions.

"Did you hear what our girl Colleen said to the Ryder bastard?" the Chief asks Steve.

"Yeah," Steve says. "Funny. Any chance we can get the boss to hurry it up?"

One bright Saturday morning the previous fall, Colleen had attended their union hall opening on the Senator's behalf. The facility was dazzling, containing not only offices, but also training stations where members could perfect their skills as painters, glaziers, and drywall finishers.

That's what the legislative affairs guy, beefy and crewcut, explained to Colleen as he toured her around.

Or rather that's what the guy said to Walter, who she'd brought with her. They were going to stop by her parents' place for lunch afterwards. And though it was Colleen's card he held in his hand, though it was Colleen who wore the nametag labeled Senate Aide, he spoke only to Walter.

Walter kept looking at Colleen and shrugging, *sorry.*

Her coworker Nia Bird later told her, "Yeah, I've been to those union things. They don't know what to do with women. And black women? Forget it. No eye contact. None."

But Steve liked working with the unions, the unions liked

Steve, and it would be easier for everyone if they didn't arrive later than necessary.

"Let me see if I can work my powers of persuasion," says the Chief.

This is how it goes, this is how it always goes, this is how it will go for the rest of the day.

When they finally make their way back toward the city, they'll have to call Hannah the Scheduler to let her know they are going as fast as they can, because the Senator is due that evening for a fundraiser.

After that, the Senator will head downstate to Springfield for the weekend to march in the Memorial Day parade, and the Chicago staffers will get a rare three-day weekend before reconvening Tuesday.

Colleen will follow the Senator's sedan down the clotted tollway, Dézi beside her tuning in public radio, Andrew in the backseat, reviewing estate planning materials so he can learn how to make wills. She will watch the back of everyone's head through her front windshield, their rear one.

They will keep living in the future in the months to come, anticipating changes that have not yet happened, but that they want to see happen very badly.

Colleen will think, *The Senator is an optimist. He wants to make the world over into what he thinks it rightly should be.*

Then, though the day has been a good one and she should be feeling hopeful, Colleen will find herself staring into Steve Moon Collier's brake lights, convinced that an optimist is one of the saddest things that a person can be.

2

Many offices are comprised of experts on baseball. The Senator's office is comprised of experts on history.

Colleen's colleagues have huge senses of it. And not just the standard, distantly-past kind of history most folks are vaguely aware of.

No, when it comes to history, her colleagues believe that they have helped make some of it and are presently in the process of making more.

It's June now, hot and hazy already in the morning, too humid for Colleen to want to bike in. Andrew texted her overnight, asking if she wanted to meet on the Lake Shore path and ride together.

She texts him back as Walter makes their oatmeal and she throws on a dress, "Sorry. 2 sweaty! Taking the train."

Walter isn't a jealous guy, but he doesn't like Colleen spending too much time with Andrew outside work. "It encourages him to harbor romantical yearnings toward you that you can't reciprocate," he says.

Colleen can't call his reading inaccurate.

"I know you've got to leave for work like five minutes ago," she says. "But so you're aware, I think I have fallen into deep despair."

Walter is washing strawberries to pack in their lunches. He cups his right hand beneath his nose and draws it down to make sure nothing's stuck in his coppery mustache, a habit he's developed since growing it last winter. It started as a joke and was meant to be temporary, but Colleen convinced him to keep it. She finds it sexy.

And it reminds her of her dad. Messed up, she knows.

"How can you feel despair in this election cycle of hope?" he asks, tapping the bumper sticker in support of the Junior Senator that's stuck with a magnet to the fridge.

"It's nothing to do with that," she says. "Mostly. Work yesterday was dead, so I was going through my zip folders of stuff I've shot recently to see what I have. It's all crap. It feels so bad to work so hard and be so mediocre in every area of my life. Some areas below mediocre. I've clawed my way to the middle, if I'm charitable, in 'politics'"—sarcastic fingers hooking around the word—"and what makes it all worse is that I thought I'd be succeeding by now. That I would have Made a Difference."

She speaks the last phrase in a tone that indicates self-critical capital letters, which she knows Walter will hear.

"Well, at least your job doesn't require you to actively make the world worse," says Walter. "Besides, the majority of people fail, right?"

"Yes. Or succeed on such a small scale that it is essentially failure."

"Maybe you need to quit being ambitious," says Walter. "Work on accepting that odds are against your succeeding regardless, and just be grateful that you have a routine to distract from the fact that the purpose of each day is to move us gradually closer to an unremarkable death. That's what I've done."

He gestures with both hands down the length of himself, tall and tie-clad, like a spokesmodel displaying a prize on a game show.

They stare at each other.

"Kidding!" Walter says. "Colleen, you always get this way when you haven't spent time on photography for a while. Why don't you take the weekend to shoot?"

"Maybe. And you could take the weekend and spend it painting?"

"Not this weekend. Your uncle's got me on liquor licensing. I can't get it done at work because I keep getting interrupted, so I told him I'd have it finished by Sunday evening."

"Fuck, Walter," she says. "Your lifelong dream is to be a painter, not a glorified secretary slaving seven days a week."

"I know. But don't start. It won't be this way forever. I've gotta go, okay?"

"Have fun among the municipals," she says.

"Please do the same among the feds," he says, kissing her.

Sitting in one of the backward-facing window seats on the Red Line, Colleen sees a front page headline that horrifies: "British Oil Company to Dump More Toxins in Lake Michigan."

"The Indiana Department of Environmental Management," the article reads, "exempted the oil company from state water laws to clear the way for a $3.8 billion expansion that will allow the company to refine heavier Canadian crude oil."

Then: "Under the new state water permit, the refinery in Whiting, three miles southeast of Chicago—already one of the largest polluters along the Great Lakes—can release 54 percent more ammonia and 35 percent more sludge into Lake Michigan each day.

And finally: "Ammonia promotes algae blooms that kill fish, while sludge is full of heavy metals."

She looks at her fellow commuters and can't believe they seem so calm.

~

When we walked the earth, we farmed, we gardened, we looked into the primordial forests and saw our dreams reflected.

We dispatched explorers to chart the fauna and the flora of our vast new territories.

Swimmers and sportsmen, hunters and stewards, we established a system of public lands and national parks, preserving and protecting sections of soil and mountains and rivers and trees on which we and our countrymen could pursue pleasure and leisure.

In our minds, nature and democracy were inseparable.

~

As the train lurches underground from the elevated tracks, Colleen hopes the Rapacious British Oil Company will get the Senator upset.

It's hard to predict why one news story will send him on a legislative crusade while another, equally within the realm of his interests, won't.

Why autism and not, say, Parkinson's?

Why puppy mills and not elder abuse?

Why food safety and not school violence?

The Senator's mentor—the economist turned legislator, for whom the Senator had interned in DC in the '60s when he was in law school—was a proto-environmentalist who fought to save the Indiana Dunes, south of Lake Michigan.

When Colleen was herself an intern, the Senator had told her a story of his own internship.

During World War II, his boss had had the nerves in his left arm severed by machine gun fire. One of the Senator's jobs had been to sit with him in the late afternoon while he signed correspondence.

"The sun would sink behind the building," the Senator had told her, "and I'd get up to turn on the light. He was determined to sign every letter. His right arm was fine, but he needed help holding the paper steady."

The train arrives at Jackson, and Colleen climbs the stairs and hurries through the subterranean pedway, borne back into the daylight of Federal Plaza.

The red-orange stabile of a giant flamingo reveals itself to her right, and the Tuesday farmers' market fills the expanse between the long low Post Office and the clean black steel of the Kluczynski Building. A German architect, one of the fathers of modernism, used the maximum amount of glass to suggest transparency—the connection of the government to the people it governed.

A compelling concept, but the building is cold in the winter, hot in the summer, and hardly a day goes by without the Chief of Staff goddamning the architect's name.

Colleen and the chatty GSA employees clutching their donuts ride the elevator to their respective floors.

She gets off at thirty-eight, the second-highest. The thirty-ninth contains the office of the Junior Senator, though he's almost never there due to the demands of his campaign.

She walks through reception, says "hey" to the interns, then heads to the kitchen. The Chief of Staff is standing at the sink, surrounded by flowers and curvaceous vases half-full of water. Each Tuesday, he buys new cut plants from the market.

"Morning, Colleen. You're looking lovely this lovely June day. How are you?"

"Pissed off at Big Oil," she says.

"You've seen the front page, then? So has the Duke, and he's on the warpath. He's already called in to say he expects to be standing on a beach on Friday."

The Chief's nickname for the Senior Senator is the ironic kind, like Slim for a fat man.

The Senator is not regal—not ducal. He is salt-of-the-earth, a guy you could run into on the bus. You might see him in the seat next to you and think *nice suit*, but that's about it.

Which is the opposite of his good friend, the Chief, who has a kingly air mixed with a touch of the court jester, ribald and motley.

"He doesn't mean in trunks with a drink in his hand, presumably," she says.

"No. He wants a news conference where he gets to hand the oil company a chunk of their own ass." He shifts a stem slightly to the left. "Gina's not in yet, but we'll talk about it on scheduling call."

Colleen reaches past him through the maze of glassware to pull her favorite mug from the drain tray and fill it with coffee.

The Chief stands back to watch.

He compliments her shoes.

She replies that they are comfortable, both because they are and because it is a neutral thing to say.

"That strikes me as surprising," he says.

"Why's that?"

"Because the way they complement your doe-like foot makes me think that to look that beautiful, they must cause pain."

"How," Colleen says, taking a sip, "are you ready with so much bullshit so early? I'll talk to you at ten."

"Wouldn't miss it," he says.

The Chief goes back to arranging his gladioluses. The flowers trumpeting from their stems, fleshy and thrusting, seem suggestive to Colleen—over-compensatory.

The coral petals pick up the accent color in his tie.

Their office occupies the east side of the building, meaning an unimpeded view of Lake Michigan's watery stretch to the horizon. This morning it's chopped with tiny waves, the sun rising over it dappling each one. She feels a voluptuousness looking out at the sparkling like a glitter curtain hung across a stage.

She goes back to the padded gray cubicles across from the Chief of Staff's office where she works in a cluster with Lo Benson, Steve Moon Collier, and Andrew. Aside from the Chief and a few interns, Colleen thinks she is the first one to arrive, and she jumps when Andrew emerges from his cube. He is wearing bike shorts and sneakers, and struggling, bare-chested, into a dress shirt, buttoning it up.

"Geez, Colleen, let a man get decent. Haven't you ever heard of a thing called privacy?"

"Haven't you ever heard of a thing called a bathroom?" she says.

"Good point," he says.

Andrew is so big, so blond, so All-American—with "All-American" in quotes, like he knows it and is winking—that it's hard to discern how much distance there is between what he is saying and what he is thinking. He shrugs his shoulders to get the shirt to sit right, his broad back quarterbackish and wholesome. He is open-faced, like a sandwich.

"Did you hear—"

"About the Lake?" he says. "Yeah. On the radio. While I was eating my toaster pastry."

"The Senator heard, too," she says, "and we're going to try to stop them."

Andrew pulls a tie from his panniers and starts to put it on without the aid of a mirror. After a couple tries, he gives up, picks up his pants, and steps toward the Senator's office, where there's a private bathroom open to staffers whenever the Senator's not around.

"I think it's great you want to save the Lake, Colleen," Andrew says, walking away. "But I don't think it's going to work. The oil company is legally allowed to do this. The dumping's within the confines of federal law."

Though he's officially on the press team, Andrew graduated from a private East Coast law school and passed the Illinois bar. He does pro bono for a volunteer legal services agency, but has never worked in a firm.

Colleen isn't sure why not, and she hasn't asked.

She does know that he went to undergrad with one of the Chief's three kids—his youngest daughter, Nora—and that it's through this connection that Andrew, an autodidact of HTML, came to be working as the Senator's webmaster.

She also knows she likes him less when he talks like an attorney.

"I hate it when the law stops being about justice and starts just being about the law," she says to Andrew's retreating back.

"Have it your way, Colleen."

Working for the Senator has fouled Colleen's language and dimmed her outlook.

But she still has the impulse of idealism that brought her here. She wants Andrew to still have this impulse too. She spends more waking hours in his company than she does with almost any other person.

Her first week back, having lunch with him on a granite bench in Federal Plaza, she'd complained about an editor who still owed her 250 bucks for a photograph he'd used months earlier on a website.

"Did you have a contract?" Andrew asked.

"Of course," she said.

"Then we can get him. C'mon, Colleen. Nothing says 'I hate you' more than a lawsuit."

He had offered to send a letter via certified mail, threatening small claims court. She didn't take him up on it, but she admired his élan.

She could tell he was interested in her, or at least in finding a girlfriend, but she had Walter, and she let him know this. Still, Andrew had invited her to parties and bars, and sometimes she'd gone.

But he always seemed downcast whenever she showed up with Walt.

Just before she got switched over to the press team, Colleen and Andrew had been sitting in a basement cafeteria eating their lunches and working the Sunday crossword. Colleen was describing her aggravation at doing outreach.

"It's always the same," she said. "Rent a car that's conspicuously American, drive to some suburb that looks identical to every other suburb, go to the office of whatever person you're having a meeting with, who has maybe a fifty-fifty chance of understanding why you're meeting with them, sit across the table from them while you explain that the Senator cares about their needs, and then get asked for money. Money that isn't there. You shake their hand and promise to look into it. Repeat, repeat, repeat."

"Everything seems tinged with futility doesn't it?" said Andrew, filling in 21-across. "But that's work sometimes. Pointless and depressing."

This morning, work has the potential to be pointed. Colleen has an hour and fifteen minutes before scheduling call, which they hold each Tuesday at 10 a.m. CST for the state offices in Chicago, Springfield, and Marion, 11 a.m. EST for the two DC offices—regular and leadership.

She turns on her computer and sets down her coffee mug. While she waits the two minutes for it to boot up, her eyes wander to the chart Andrew made entitled "Descent into Winter Darkness." It marks how the days will grow incrementally shorter after they pass the summer solstice.

This hangs above a photo of her and Walter pretending to dance, posing, Walter dipping her, her head thrown back, jaw sharp and dark hair shining down her back, her uncle Tom Dugan's kids running behind them holding tennis racquets.

"5up3rPh0t0graph3r," she types—the password Andrew helped her set.

I am in a holding pattern, Colleen thinks.

As a member of the press team, press would normally be all she would do. But the office has been far from normal lately.

Two of the top staffers—Palmira Guzman, the Chicago Director, and Nia Bird, the Director of Casework and Constituent Services—are pregnant now, both due in mid-July. This will put them on maternity leave during the height of the election season.

Adding to that confusion, those in charge can't decide whether to hire new people to cover for them or to work on the campaign against Ryder. Steve Moon Collier is supposed to be in charge of restructuring, but Steve is wrapped up in the campaign and lacks follow-through.

So Colleen is still doing casework and issue-specific outreach on housing and the environment, but what she really wants is for the campaign to wrap her up, too.

That's why she came back.

But the Chief of Staff keeps telling her to sit tight.

"It's all in the timing, babe," he says, and says, and says again, whenever she asks.

She's jotting down the callback number for the seventh of her voice mails when reception rings her.

"Colleen?" It's Sudha, one of the interns on the first phone shift. "You've got a constituent who says you're helping with her case? Or more like, you didn't help enough?"

Colleen looks her up in the Capitol Correspondence system. As she suspected, a foreclosure.

Some of them have been predatorily lended to via subprime mortgages, and these she refers to the Attorney General's office. The rest, though, while not totally hopeless, are not cases the Senator's office is getting involved with. They have neither the resources nor the expertise.

But even though Colleen has crafted a two-page letter detailing the policy ins and outs of the crisis, and even though she includes fifteen pages of information in both English and Spanish about where to seek help, constituents feel brushed off when they receive their packet with the news that their case is, as far as the Senate is concerned, closed.

She pictures them in the kitchens of their soon-to-be-lost homes, throwing the envelopes in the trash bins under their sinks and picking up their phones to scream at her.

"Tell them that the word 'mortgage' comes from the French for 'death pledge,'" said Andrew last week, after she'd hung up from an especially abusive caller. "Tell them they dug their own graves with their thoughtlessness and greed, and now they're going to have to lie down in them indefinitely."

"Do you want me to put her through?" says Sudha.

"'Want' is such a strong verb," says Colleen, "but yes, please do."

When Colleen was growing up and her mother accused her of "talking back," she would say to her daughter, "It's not what you say, Colleen, it's how you say it."

Colleen hates to admit that this has proven true.

Whenever a constituent acts ignorant or crazy or rude, she's perfected the technique of repeating what they say back to them, as if she were taking notes, or asking a series of innocent questions in an attempt to understand.

She becomes a dumb echo of their own dumb words, so they can see objectively how unreasonable their behavior really is.

Usually it works.

Occasionally, she's rewarded with a "You're a nice girl, sweetie, and it's a shame you work for a man like that."

And then, there's today.

"Good morning, this is Colleen, how may I help you?"

"That's the whole problem," says the raised female voice on the other end of the line. "You don't wanna help me."

"Per our records, you should have received a list of housing counselors late last week."

"That's all you people do? That's what you call help?"

"I'm sorry, ma'am, but due to the fact that we're not trained housing counselors, this is the best course of action."

"But my husband is a veteran."

"Thank you for his sacrifice."

"He fought in Vietnam."

"Vietnam, I see."

"He's about to lose his leg!"

"His leg—I'm sorry."

"To diabetes! And this is all you're going to do for me?"

"According to your letter, Wells Fargo is your lender. Unfortunately, we are not in a position to tell privately held banks what to do with the loans they hold. We only get involved in instances where predatory lending has occurred or where Fannie Mae or Freddie Mac, the two federally held financial institutions, hold the loans."

"Well, how the hell do I know if Freddie Mae or Fannie Mac holds my loans?"

"You sent documents indicating that Wells Fargo holds your loans, ma'am."

"You only help when you want our vote!"

As the woman meanders, Colleen's mind wanders.

Often the same callers who rave that it's "a disgrace that our Federal Senator can't help with our house" are the ones who are against "government takeovers" or "handouts" or "socialism." Steve Moon Collier had looked up a couple of callers who threatened "never to vote for the Senator again" and discovered they weren't even registered.

"Fine," the woman on the other end of the phone says, finally. "Can you take a message for the Senator for me?"

"Yes, ma'am. I'd be happy to."

"I want you to give him my number and I want him to call me."

"Okay, ma'am, I'll pass that along."

"I don't bet that'll happen, though, will it?"

"It is unlikely that he will call you, ma'am."

"Listen. We're white. We are white Americans. My last name is Mexican but my husband and me are both Caucasian. My husband and me—we were born here."

"We'd provide you the same guidance even if you weren't born here, ma'am," says Colleen. "Good luck to you both."

She hangs up the phone and exhales.

Steve Moon Collier saunters by on his way to his cube.

The clock at the bottom of her screen reads 9:40.

Lo follows, leisurely, at 9:45.

Colleen finds it infuriating that the majority of her male co-workers practically make a point of not working as hard as she does.

Sudha flashes past Colleen's cube in a marigold blouse, waving at Colleen with the pink message slip in her manicured hand. Colleen thinks of a bird with pretty plumage. Sudha is tall and slender and walks around the office with a sheepish look, as if she is always apologizing for being so beautiful.

"Steve?" Colleen hears her say when she knocks, and it sounds awkward. Steve Moon Collier believes he deserves an office, and has fashioned his cube into a makeshift one, removing a panel that would have been against the wall and using the spare piece to create a smaller entrance. All he's missing is a door.

"This guy from the Carpenter's Union says he's left you several voice mails over the past couple days," Sudha says. "He asked would I please give you a paper message instead. He also says your email inbox is full."

"Look," says Steve. "Give a guy some time to settle in before you jump all over him."

"Um, okay," says Sudha, "I'll be sure to do that," and shrinks back to the front desk.

"It's almost ten o'clock, Steve," says Andrew. "Kind of time to be settled."

"And you came in through the back door," says Lo, from his cube in between Steve's and Colleen's. "That girl has no way to know how long you've been in."

"Look," says Steve. "Andy, Lo'kewell. Whose side are you on?"

Steve has developed a habit—imitative of their upstairs neighbor, who's now running for President—of saying "look," the verbal equivalent of sticking his fingers up the listener's nostrils and dragging their eyes to the item he want them to see. Steve realizes he's been rude and tries to joke. "C'mon. Is that any way to talk to the Mayor of Cube City?"

"Mayor McMean-to-the-Interns, you mean?" says Andrew.

Colleen usually tries to stay out of Steve's way, having written him off as kind of a dick, but today she can't take it. "You were an intern once, too, Steve," she says.

"So? So were you."

"That's why I'm nice to them. You don't even learn their names."

"They need to learn their place," he says.

"Sudha knows her place," says Andrew. "She's a great intern."

"You're only saying that because you think she's hot," says Steve, who has difficulty believing any woman could be valued for her skill set alone.

Then he's on the phone, presumably with the guy from the union, parroting wise sayings he's picked up from the Chief of Staff.

Though Steve sounds hollow reciting aphorisms like, "Look, the thing you need to remember is that there are basically two types of candidates, Danny, incumbents or insurgents."

When Colleen returned last summer, Steve had been friendly. They noticed they both brought in music they thought the Chief of Staff might like in hopes of convincing him to play it on the stereo, which all of Cube City could hear when he turned it up, which was always. They burned each other CDs.

Steve was on the short side, but decent-looking, with dark black hair from his Korean mother and freckles from his Irish-Amer-

ican dad, and he had the habit of imitating the Chief of Staff
in his style of dress. Colleen almost thought he'd been hitting
on her. She didn't even know he had a girlfriend, an elementary
school teacher named Elsie, until she overheard him mention her
to Andrew in the context of "Elsie won't stop nagging me about
moving in together."

These days it is definitely clear he is not hitting on her. Steve
has come to consider Colleen a stuck-up bitch. A bitch—that's
what he calls any female person, including the Female Presidential Candidate who has recently conceded—who has ideas.

Colleen hears Steve hang up as Hannah the Scheduler emerges from her cube, boxy conference-station phone in hand,
and walks through the Chief of Staff's door. Colleen closes her
browser—where she's been scanning a semi-scurrilous lefty blog
that she likes to read despite or perhaps because its contents are
so gossipy and unfiltered—and joins the others.

Hannah takes her place at the front left of the Chief's desk to
punch in the conference code. Her wavy black hair is still damp
from the shower. Normally she's the queen of boring corporate
fashion, but lately she's been dressing like every day is casual day,
a consequence of being so busy scheduling for the Senator and
planning her wedding to an attorney who works across the street
in the Monadnock building. They first met at Jewish summer
camp, he a counselor, she a camper.

Gina sits on the far left of the overstuffed black leather sofa,
next to Nia and Palmira, who appear equally pregnant.

They do not seem, to Colleen, to be feeling particularly mirac-
ulous. The doubled chins, the spider-bellied stances, the webby
intricacy of varicose veins across their calves.

To Colleen, pregnancy looks parasitic.

Palmira is carrying a girl, and the thought of a small, screaming female body being expelled from a larger screaming female one seems to Colleen uncanny.

That almost no one else in the office will acknowledge this grotesquerie only enhances Colleen's alienation. Everyone except Dézi treats her as monstrous if she expresses misgivings about the violence of childbirth or the drudgery of motherhood, so she's learned to act excited about the prospect of getting knocked up herself one day.

Hello, expedience.

Colleen sits in the next chair over, directly facing the Chief's desk. Dézi nestles herself on the radiator. The sun beats against their backs through the floor-to-ceiling windows.

The chair where the Former Deputy Press Secretary used to sit now contains—but barely, not because she's big but because she's so irrepressible—Sylvia Eltibani, draped with semi-precious beads from her jeweler days. She came to the Senator's office as an intern in her early forties and is having a blast at her second career. She calls the Senator Papa Bear behind his back.

Lo, Andrew, and Agnes Lumley never come to scheduling call since it's not critical that they be there. They'll get the rundown from Hannah's email afterwards.

Steve Moon Collier wheels in his leather lounger, pushing through the threshold and pulling the door closed behind him.

The gang's all here," says the Chief of Staff.

"Hail, hail!" says Sylvia, bouncing.

"How are you today, sweetheart?" the Chief says to Nia, who's slumped at the center of the sofa, shoes kicked off, feet swollen.

"Present," says Nia.

"Well, I guess that's all I can ask, isn't it? That you just . . . be here."

Hannah dials in.

Colleen looks over her shoulder out the window at the Lake and the factories on its lower rim where Chicago smudges into Northwest Indiana. The refineries line the southern curve like silty backwash at the bottom of a cup. A gray veil of particulate haze hovers above them. Driving by, it's hard to tell which refinery belongs to which oil or steel company, their pipes and ducts blending. The parks and trails, beaches and greenways on the Chicago side give way near the state line to the tyranny of industry.

Springfield joins the call, and the voice of Lizzie Leipzig—also pregnant but not due until Thanksgiving—pipes in high and cheery, "How's everybody in Chicago?!"

"We're okay," the Chief says, "but I'm sweating my ass off here, thanks to that bastard Ludwig Mies van der Rohe." He gestures to Colleen to flip on the oscillating fan in the corner.

Washington has joined the call, too, but Ryan Slattery, the DC Director, is still in a meeting with the Senator about the Lake and the Rapacious British Oil Company. Even when he's not detained, Slattery likes to leave them hanging, emphasizing how secondary the State is in comparison to the District.

You can't tell it from his voice—nasal and staccato—but Slattery is a resentfully short man with a weak chin and cheeks like a baby, though he's over forty.

Dead blue eyes like those in the book Walter got Colleen for her most recent birthday—a collection of images by a Wisconsin photographer in the 1890s, in and around a community unduly plagued by crime, mental illness, suffering, and disease.

It is morbid and beautiful.

She's read about why blue eyes look so creepy in those old photographs. Emulsions were blue-sensitive then, meaning such blue things as human irises and cloudless skies were always overexposed, sinister and white.

Slattery's eyes look like that in person—pale and depthless.

He began, like Colleen, as an intern, but did so when the Senator was only a rep, the better to climb the staff ladder, going out of his way to step on people's fingers on his journey up.

Or so she's overheard the Chief of Staff say.

It's hard to reconcile a man as mean as Slattery being in the employ of a man as mild as the Senator. But then again, that's exactly why he's there.

The Majority Whip needs a hand to wield the whip, and Slattery is precisely the sadist to do this.

A s they wait for Slattery, the Chief turns to Gina. "So this weekend we know we're having a beach party—"

"About that," says Gina, pen behind her ear, yellow legal pad on her lap. "I had already arranged for the boss to do an ed board, and—" She looks at the Chief's face and sees she won't win. "All right. I don't like it, but I'll reschedule."

"As I was saying," says the Chief, "this weekend is spoken for. But next weekend, what's this question-marked Dot Family Reunion business?"

"Dorothy asked me to save that Saturday and Sunday because her side of the family's having some picnic in Missouri," says Hannah.

The Chief of Staff always refers to the Senator's wife, as "abnormally normal." Colleen is not sure what kind of attachment the Chief has to his own spouse, but it does not resemble the Senator's to Dot. The Chief lives in a hotel near the old Water Tower, the one that didn't burn down in the Great Fire, and his wife resides at their house in Springfield. Colleen has met her and noticed that she, like the Chief, does not wear a wedding band.

"Maybe we could have him do some things in Metro East before and after?" suggests Lizzie.

"We'll have to get permission first, now, won't we?" says the Chief. "Too bad the Duke loves his wife so much. It really complicates life for the rest of us. Let's pin that down as soon as we can, Hannah."

Hannah nods and makes a note. Of all the people Hannah will have to follow up with, Colleen guesses Dorothy will be the most pleasant. Since taking over as scheduler, Hannah has become one of Dorothy's biggest fans. A couple Fridays ago, Dot called Hannah mid-afternoon to ask when she thought the Senator might be home. She was trying to decide if she should fix a pot roast for dinner.

"She's so cute!" Hannah had squealed to Colleen over the wall of her cubicle.

The Senator and his wife are private people. Colleen only recently learned an odd medical fact, something she's not even sure all her fellow staffers know—that Dorothy was born with only one lung.

When Andrew casually mentioned this a few weeks ago, as was his habit with information he gathered from the Chief's daughter Nora, Colleen wondered if the Senator was so careful to schedule around Dorothy because she was delicate.

Then Colleen saw her at a fundraiser, where she appeared perfectly strong, and realized that Dot's condition had little to do with it.

He just really loves her.

And Dorothy really is loveable. She reminds Colleen of her own mother—down-to-earth, Midwestern, obviously intelligent, but self-effacing as a matter of course.

Slattery joins the call from DC.

"Just got done with my one-on-one with the big guy," he says from the Whip office. "Sounds like all the reps whose districts touch the Lake are outraged over this. Except Ryder. His silence on the matter is deafening."

"God, what a weasel," says Gina.

"True story," says Slattery. "We'd want to hit the ground running regardless, but that's all the more reason. The boss has already put a call in to the oil company's CEO, but we're not holding our breath on a callback. And he absolutely wants a lakeside presser on Friday."

"Damn right," says the Chief of Staff.

"Personally," says Slattery, "I think we ought to hold off. Give the company some time to respond, so we don't seem like knee-jerk attack dogs."

"I'm looking out the window at the goddamn Lake right now," says the Chief. "I can see the factories. The fact is, he wants do this, and it should be done, and it's up to us to make it happen."

The Chief always gets restless during scheduling call, and now he's begun prodding the water-stained tile in the ceiling with a golf club, gardening in the terracotta pot on his desk with his fountain pen. He brings a leaf to his lips—arugula—and eats it.

"We need to draft a letter, too," the Chief says, "because this telephone song-and-dance is going nowhere fast. Why in the hell *would* they ever call back? We should get the letter out today or tomorrow so the Duke can share it with the press on Friday."

"I'm on the case," says the voice of Lisa Niedecker, the Legislative Assistant on Energy and the Environment—one of the few non-jerks in DC who doesn't assume that whatever's happening in the Capital trumps anything happening in-state.

"Hey babe," says the Chief. "Didn't know you were on the call. We need to get that letter in front of the eyeballs of Lord Asshat of Manderley, or whoever, and let him know we're serious."

"That guy's not the CEO anymore," says Lisa. "He stepped down last year in a sex scandal. It's a new guy, now. Less titled, but equally slimy."

"Sex scandal?" says the Chief. "Racy. Why didn't anybody tell me? Anyway, whoever needs to get the letter needs to get the letter. I want a draft by this afternoon."

"Okay," says Slattery, "but we've got a lot of stuff on our plates out here."

"Us, too," says the Chief. "So how about we let each other go. Good chatting. Talk soon."

He punches the button with his middle finger and the call disconnects.

"Ryan needs to remember that we need to work together," says Palmira, as Hannah winds up the cord. "The two control centers can't compete. They have to work in synch."

"We're not separate entities," says Colleen. "We're like a dinosaur with two brains."

"And DC treats us like we're the brain in the ass," says the Chief. "All right, everybody out. We've got a huge multinational corporation to smack down and a lake to rescue."

3

The sun slips behind a skyscraper, and the streets below darken. The avenues look as though they should cool like canyons, but Colleen knows they'll be steaming when she goes back down. The Mayor keeps promoting green roofs and alleys, but the city still becomes a heat island on days like this one. Colleen pushes her sunglasses from in front of her eyes to a headband position.

"So in addition to everything else," she says, "the Chief of Staff has me drafting a letter to Donovan."

She and Ethan are at Happy Hour on Thursday evening at a roofdeck bar overlooking the Loop. Colleen stares past Ethan's bony face at an elevated train rumbling over the tracks by the public library below, its gargoyles supersaturated with golden light.

The magic hours.

Diffuse and photogenic.

An even better composition with Ethan at its center, looking like a skate punk painted by a Pre-Raphaelite. Ethan's mother was a model, and he inherited her jaw line, her glossy black waves, her cherry lips. Even clad as he is in a threadbare T-shirt, he looks like an image you'd paste on a flashcard if you wanted to provoke the response "male beauty."

She and Ethan have—have always had—a total absence of sexual chemistry. When Colleen's out with her other guy friends, servers and cashiers tend to assume that she and whomever she's with are together, but if people assume anything about Ethan, it's that he must be her brother.

The bar is hosting a reception for incoming students of the third-rate law school over on State Street. Colleen and Ethan did not know this when they made their plans, and somehow, although they wear neither halter-top floral sundresses nor pleated-front khakis, they must have been mistaken for 1Ls by the waitstaff, because complimentary gin-and-tonics keep appearing before them.

"Donovan?" says Ethan, squeezing a lime between languid fingers. "The folk singer?"

"The very same. You know his song about trying to catch the wind?"

"To feel you all around me, / and to take your hand, along the sand?" sings Ethan, who used to be in a band. "Sure. Pretty song."

"The oil company thinks so. It's part of their greenwashing campaign. They use it in TV ads that fake an interest in wind power. They've been branding themselves as 'environmentally sound' for ten years, but they're one of the biggest polluters on the planet."

"Repulsive," says Ethan.

"We can only hope that Donovan will agree."

They met in high school in Downers Grove. Ethan had been photo editor of the school newspaper their senior year, and he was forever asking Colleen to take assignments. "Come shoot the quarterback for this story on Homecoming," he'd say, and nine times out of ten she'd be all, "Nah, I'm going to go to the darkroom to develop some still lifes." She said yes just often enough to be able to list "newspaper" under the "activities" section of her college applications.

Colleen has always admired how Ethan uses available light and composes on the fly, how he prizes what's there in the world more than what can be crafted in the studio. Lately she's gone from admiration to imitation, stealing street shots when she's out in service of the Senator.

Dark circles ring Ethan's eyes, which are mossy green. He is nocturnal when left to his own devices, and early-morning shoots mess up his natural sleep pattern. His pale skin is immaculate otherwise. Perspiration pocks the foreheads and upper lips of the servers and law students, but Ethan keeps cool as an alabaster statue.

"I'm going to guess," he says, "that reaching out to Donovan isn't the major thrust of your save-the-lake strategy. What else have you got planned?"

"We're having a news conference at North Avenue Beach at 1:30 tomorrow. You might want to come shoot it. If you can get your skinny ass out of bed in time."

"I've been awake in the morning a lot lately," he says. "Business is booming."

Colleen envies Ethan for making a living with his photography. A freelancer, Ethan does some work for the major daily that publishes in a tabloid format, and some as a stringer for papers on the coasts. But his bread-and-butter comes from the Graduate School of Business at the University of Chicago—grip-and-grins and frontal portraits of ugly talking heads paid-for generously from their generous endowment.

Friendly jealousy aside, she tries to throw jobs his way when she can.

"The Senator is interested—which means Gina is interested—in having a sympathetic photographer come along to document campaign-trail stuff as the election gets closer. If you get some hot shots tomorrow, it could help you be that guy."

"All right," says Ethan, inking the details on the back of his hand. "I'll be there."

"How's your other project going?" says Colleen.

"'In the Dumps'?" Ethan says. "Every day I wake up and hope it's gone viral. I'm expecting I'll get to take a self-portrait while we're here, in fact."

A photojournalist by training, Ethan has taken to producing

his own creative work. His latest project: self-portraits in the act of using the stalls of public restrooms—nothing too explicit. He's been posting the results on his blog—has developed an online following, of sorts.

"How's Walter's painting going?" Ethan asks.

"It isn't, really."

"Sucky," says Ethan. "I love how old-masterly his style is. How it's got all those ironic art-historical references. His paintings are so learned. They school me."

"Yeah, he's gotten way less conceptual," she says. "When he paints at all anymore. Somehow, he keeps improving his technique, but he's making these enormous, accomplished paintings that don't really say anything except 'I am a good painting.' Mostly he's completely absorbed by the minutiae of working for my uncle."

"Understandable, I guess."

"Kind of. But if you're going to act indispensable, you should be making six figures. If not, take the modest paycheck and make some art when you're not at the office, you know? Actually, I'd rather not talk about it."

"Dwindling ambition does seem to be a turnoff for you, doesn't it?" says Ethan. "Maybe that's what feeds your weird love-hate thing with Andrew. Is he still all lovesick after the incident in Iowa?"

"Hm," says Colleen. "That topic's not any better. How about we drop it?"

"Okay," he says, "third time's the charm, then. How's your photography? Still kind of secret?"

"Yeah, I can't mention anywhere in my photo materials what my day job is. Nobody at work thinks nude self-portraits are risqué, but they're afraid our conservative enemies would have a field day."

"I bet," says Ethan, finishing his third complimentary drink. "'Senator consorts with live nude girl.'"

Colleen's been twisting and untwisting the two wrappers for the straws the waitress brought for their waters. Ethan reaches across the table, putting a hand atop hers to stop her.

"Lay off with the externally manifested agitation already," he says, although even now, when she's allegedly driving him crazy, his movements refuse to hurry, remaining as fluid as if he were under water.

"Sorry," she says, crumpling the paper and dropping it to the bottom of her empty glass.

"Some happy news, though, is that nature calls. Mind waiting a few while I create some great art, and then we can leave?"

"Not at all," says Colleen. "Hope everything comes out all right."

She watches him slink through the dowdy crowd with the grace of a big cat.

E ntering their apartment, Colleen is surprised for a moment that it does not contain Walter.

Calls his name.

Remembers.

He's at their friend Chuck's studio in Wicker Park.

Chuck calls the poorly-insulated second-story above a plus-sized lingerie shop a "live-work space," but the "live" part is viable only because he's willing to shower in tepid water from a hose, and to do the math such that hotplate plus electric teakettle plus mini-fridge equals kitchen.

Chuck has gallery representation and an increasing number of shows. He has quit jobs for his painting, broken up with girl-friends, gone hungry, been so broke he couldn't buy a belt and had to hold up his pants with a piece of white rope, but neither she nor Walter have ever heard Chuck say any of this sacrifice might not ultimately be Worth It.

Chuck's gallerist sold two of his paintings last month, and Chuck is flush with cash, so he proposed to Walter that they go in together on hiring a model. At Colleen's pestering behest, Walter had agreed, and that's where he is—working on a four-hour pose with Chuck.

It's been so long since Walt has done any significant painting that Colleen had forgotten.

Walter's painting had been stunning when she met him in Paris, and had gotten even better when they were getting their MFAs at a small college in Boston. Even if he hadn't been her boyfriend, Colleen is pretty sure she'd consider him one of the most gifted artists she'd ever encountered.

But he'd become casual about applying his gift.

He worked as a barista while Colleen was teaching in Tacoma so he could have a flexible schedule and time to paint. But when they'd headed back to Chicago, her Uncle Tom—worried about Colleen's ability to support herself, owing to her being a woman and all—let them know he needed a new executive assistant in the suburb that he managed. "Get Walter to turn in a résumé and we'll have him come in for an interview," her uncle had said.

Of course, Walter got the job, and Colleen had to admit it was comforting for him to have a salary, like an authentic adult.

So she should be rapturous.

Instead she's annoyed.

Walking through the living room, taking off her work clothes, leaving the lights off so no one outside can see in.

Irked, because this means she too should try to get some photo stuff done.

She doesn't have to hire anyone to pose. She's usually her own model, a common enough strategy in the work of the photographers she most admires: one who casts herself in starring roles in stills from films that don't exist, one who made blurry black and white images of her naked body melting into tumble-down interiors before jumping out a loft window to her death at twenty-two.

Colleen has never photographed Walt aside from snapshots. They've never talked about why.

Drunk-hungry, Colleen stands in the kitchen in a black lace slip, microwaving herself a quesadilla and trying to psych herself up to do a shoot. It's almost worse to have a little bit of free time than to have none at all. It reminds her how she doesn't have the wherewithal to work the way she wants to anymore.

Better to be busier with Senate shit.

I n Tacoma it was easy.

She rented a studio for next-to-nothing in one of the cruddy industrial buildings by the waterfront in the sad downtown, and she'd used some of her college-professor salary to buy her own lights, though she sold them before they came back to Chicago, fearing they'd get destroyed in the move. She'd intended to upgrade anyway, but she's never gotten around to it.

In Tacoma, she dug into a groove of making images that looked like they were happening in real domestic interiors, not an empty warehouse. She had crafted these interiors with obsessive control.

She and Walt would borrow a pickup truck from one of his coworkers and drive around the inappropriately nicknamed City of Destiny, scavenging choice detritus from trash piles, sometimes commercial, sometimes residential: clawfooted bathtubs, chiffoniers, wallpaper, lamps, safes, beds, stuffed elkheads, building blocks, jacks-in-the-box, electric ranges, mounted fish, license plates, baby dolls, cash registers, a taxidermied pheasant that reminded her of her dad and his hunting, televisions, cribs, radios, sofas, mirrors, ladders, a carousel horse, one time even an air rifle. With which she would make fake living rooms, bedrooms, kitchens.

Then she'd make up stories about the people who lived in them, stage fraught scenes in which she played all the parts, usually nude. In grad school she would hire fellow students as models, but in Tacoma nobody could be bothered. Too Vitamin-D-deprived, too Pacific-Northwest-private.

On their first foray into aesthetic dumpster-diving, Colleen found a bolt of material you'd use to make sheer drapes—translucent and dingy, but so much the better for her purposes.

She set all her scenes behind them, achieving vaporous effects, like the photographs were a window and you were a peeping Tom. What you saw looked put together like a ship in a bottle, with tweezers and tools snaked in from beyond by an unseen hand. Like instead of Colleen's studio, you were looking into a dollhouse, this trompe l'oeil perfection disrupted only by the presence of Colleen's body in the tableau—her pale torso revealing that the setting pictured was not to-scale, but just scale.

This exhibitionist angle came naturally to Colleen, who has always felt as though she is being watched.

Maybe by ghosts, she's frequently thought—though her watchers are neither scary nor benevolent.

Just sort of curious, sort of keeping an eye on the score.

S mearing salsa on the quesadilla, taking a bite, Colleen thinks how much effort all that old work required and feels exhausted. But when she was doing it, she felt satisfaction, or better yet, felt nothing.

Had forgotten herself in the flow of getting it done.

Outside, the darkness has completed itself.

She pours herself a whiskey, puts on an album by a singer-songwriter who stabbed himself in the heart, and turns on her laptop, named after an apple and favored by Creative Types.

Colleen's not sure she still qualifies.

She's wallowing, she knows, but what's to stop her?

Looks back through her Tacoma portfolios. Very composed, very stagey. She's sold quite a few of those images, and used them to get an artist's grant from the state of Washington, but she's not even sure she likes them anymore.

It's like they were taken by someone else.

She feels simultaneously irritated by and protective of her former self.

Next she flips through the images she's snuck during her nine-to-five. Their energy—covert and dynamic—pleases her, but little else about them does. The boys walking into the diner in Aurora, looking like horses—that's nice, but so what?

She starts color-correcting a few—a mindless-enough chore—while she thinks of other ways to alter them, to make them more illustrative.

But illustrative of what?

She hates this fucking feeling—unsure and dry.

Keeps at the task through three more LPs. The albums the singer-songwriter made were short, like his life.

Saves her work, brushes her teeth, crawls between the sheets.

She hates going to bed without Walter, but he won't be home for a while, and all Colleen wants is to be unconscious. She sucks even at this lately—the simplest human act of falling asleep.

She hears Walter's key in the door, him walking in then sliding the deadbolt home. Hears him listening to see if she's there, and if so, whether she's awake.

She calls out, "Walt."

She smells him before he touches her, the velvet scent of linseed oil, the topnote of turpentine. He sits on the edge of the bed and tells her that his night of painting has been productive, and she says this makes her happy, even though her night of not-quite-photography hadn't been.

"It's hard now, I know," he says. "But it's smart you're moving in a new direction. Your old work is amazing. It's prize-winning. But operating under that kind of fanatically-detailed control is a) not possible with your present lifestyle, and b) maybe a little too reflective of your larger difficulties at accommodating yourself and your expectations to the disappointments of reality."

Rational and wise, Walter knows her so well.

When he's gone to get ready for bed, she stares straight ahead in the dark and thinks how she needs him so much, but could also punch him in the mustache sometimes.

She adjusts her attitude as he climbs across her to his side of the bed. Lithe, fox-like, gently pawing the edges of her body. She tells him she loves him, because she does, and that she's glad he painted, and he falls asleep.

After a couple more hours of lying alongside him, grainy and wired, she does, too.

4

At 12:45 on Friday, Colleen, Andrew, and the Chief of Staff stand outside the Federal Building in their suits, carrying the A.V. equipment and hailing a cab. She and Andrew are here to advance the press event. The Chief's coming along because he's so keyed up.

They slide out of the pine-fresh taxi at North Avenue Beach and set up on a concrete platform next to the Beach House. The red-white-and-blue structure is built to resemble a ship, atop which sits a restaurant called Castaways that plays songs about towns named after drinks and the bittersweet disappearance of the boys of summer.

The news teams arrive and frame their shots. The nearest beach-combers bunch up and shove closer, like fish in a koi pond attracted by the breadcrumb cameras.

A pudgy boy in red swimming trunks, zinc oxide smeared across his ski-slope nose, walks up to Andrew and asks, "Are you the news?"

"Yes," says Andrew, and the boy seems satisfied.

Colleen hands out copies of the Senator's polite but firm letter to the CEO of the Rapacious British Oil Company, to which, predictably, the CEO has yet to reply.

She greets the representatives from the Alliance for the Great Lakes and the Environmental Law and Policy Center who will be joining the Senator to speak. She has met the director of the former organization half a dozen times, and he greets her with warmth befitting this history.

"Gina!" he says, giving Colleen a double-handed handshake. "So good to see you again!"

"Colleen," she says, and just in case he's a visual learner who will be helped by seeing Colleen Dugan floating on an off-white rectangle next to an embossed golden eagle, hands him a card.

He apologizes.

"No harm, no foul," she says. "Gina will be here momentarily."

Out in the field, Colleen gets mistaken for Gina, an Italian-American, or Palmira, a Latina, or Hannah, a Jewish girl, or Sylvia, whose family immigrated to the Land of Lincoln from Palestine.

Colleen is interchangeable with all of them because she is so unimportant, and because they are all expected to cultivate a grace by which they recede into the background behind the Senator, like a pleasant shade of paint.

Colleen does not really look like any of them—none of them really looks like each other. Palmira speaks Spanish half the time and is pregnant, and Colleen is taller by a head than all four.

The Senator tells them apart, of course. "How's my shutterbug?" he'll say to Colleen whenever he hasn't seen her for a while. But Colleen knows she is viewed by most constituents—and much of the time by the Senator himself—as just one of a fleet of generic brunettes. Andrew is the only blond in the Chicago office.

"To what do I owe this display of pulchritude?" the Senator had said recently, as Colleen, Palmira, Gina, and Sylvia sat arrayed in a minivan one morning, picking him up at his condo for a full day of site visits.

"What the hell does that mean?" Gina had said, sotto voce, to Colleen.

"It means he thinks we're pretty."

"Very good vocabulary," the Senator had said, like a schoolmarm, buckling up and smiling over his shoulder.

Colleen had smiled back, but said nothing.

The only reply she could think of involved wondering whether *pulchritude* was better or the same as *baby doll, princess, hot lips, Trixie.*

Whether the Senator was really that dissimilar to the Chief of Staff.

Differing degrees, she decided. *Same kind.*

"This is the best press conference ever," Andrew says from behind his mirrored cop shades. "Check out the bikini babes. Be sure to get some pics for the Hot Topic page."

The Chief of Staff stands in a semicircle of tawny girls in two-piece bathing suits. Colleen shoots stills with the Senate-issue camera, wishing for a 24-70 zoom but making do with the macro she's got, while Andrew handles the video. The girls giggle and pass around the Chief's sunglasses, posing with them on.

"Hot Topic" is right.

Hanging the office camera around her neck like a tourist, she pulls her own camera from her bag and takes a few pictures for herself while Gina's not here to catch her.

Someone taps her on the shoulder, and Colleen's sure, as she turns, that she's got a guilty expression on her face.

It's a reporter, one she's never seen before.

He introduces himself as the new guy from Chicago Public Radio, and Colleen gives him a press release. He is younger than her, still in J-school at the Big Ten university in Evanston, bearded and earnest. His sleeves are rolled to mid-forearm, and she sees the bottom of a black tattoo.

"What's that?" she asks.

He rolls the cuff over his elbow to show her: the empty outline of the Prairie State.

"I've lived here my whole life," he says, "but the tat has made me learn a lot about the place. You know, so I can live up to it."

Her phone rings and it's Dézi, this week's driver. They're almost there.

"Nice camera," the reporter says, as Colleen waves, phone

sandwiched between shoulder and ear, cramming the camera in question back in her purse.

As Colleen and Andrew cross the Lake Shore bike path to greet Gina and the Senator, Andrew does a falsetto mockery of the public radio guy's voice.

"Oh, Colleen, I know so much about your beloved home state. I ride a fixed-gear bike and like alternative pursuits. Oh, Colleen, tell me more about your artsy photography."

"What's your problem?" she says.

"You're both here to work," he says. "He's being unprofessional."

"Tell that to the Chief," she says. "Tell that to your bikini babes."

The bikini babes hoot at the Senator's arrival.

The Senator stands behind the mic and gathers the Alliance and the Law and Policy guys to his left and right.

Colleen spots the Ryder spy.

He snakes up next to her and starts recording with a handheld camera. He wears the same khakis he had on in Aurora, fly closed this time.

"Nice pants," Colleen whispers, as the Senator starts to speak.

"Just you wait," mutters the spy.

The Senator's comments on the need to preserve the integrity of the Lake are music to the beach-combing crowd, and unlike at most press events, he gets spontaneous applause.

Her pocket vibrates with a text from Ethan. He overslept and isn't going to make it. His loss, Colleen thinks. The Senator is in top form.

She's somewhat more annoyed to see a couple of satellite vans from local TV stations, just now pulling up as the speech is winding down.

"This is the third-largest global oil company—the fifth-largest company in the world, period," the Senator says. "They are spending almost $4 billion to expand so they can add new technology to refine more oil? Why not use some of that to add new technology that can reduce pollution? I think it's worth it. And I know the people of Illinois"—he gestures to the crowd, where the bikini babes cheer on cue—"think it's worth it to take steps to keep from poisoning a resource"—he gestures to the Lake, which remains silent and beautiful—"that you simply cannot put a price tag on."

The Senator fields questions from the already dispersing press. He shakes hands and poses for photos with members of the masses.

Unlike most politicians, the Senator does not keep his eyes roving over the crowd, like a shark that must keep moving or die, in search of someone more powerful to speak to. He looks *at* you. Listens *to* you. Which itself is a quiet power over you which inclines you to do what he wants you to.

Colleen orbits around him as he does this, taking more photos. He asks the bikini babes where they're from, and they answer Monmouth—the western part of the state, practically Iowa.

"What made you come all the way to Chicago and choose this beach?"

"Because we heard you'd be here, Senator!" they say, and, "As soon as we can vote, we're coming to work for you!"

Minutes ago they were asking the Chief *Who is he?* and *Is he a Republican or a Democrat?*

Gina rolls her eyes and says, "This is all we need."

Hold up there, Trixie," says the Chief, pointing at a black SUV skulking across the bike path and coming to rest yards away. "*This* may actually be all we need."

Colleen tracks the vehicle—spots four of Ryder's henchmen

down the beach, setting up a portable PA and a microphone rack. The reporters who hurried away from the Senator's event are huddling there now, and mixing with them are five or six people wearing yellow work shirts bearing the logo of the Rapacious British Oil Company.

"You have *got* to be kidding," Gina says.

The SUV spits out Congressman Ron Reese Ryder, blunt and twerpy, from its passenger side, while the Rapacious British Oil Company CEO—the mop-headed Englishman who would not deign to speak to the Senator all week—expels himself from the back.

They advance toward the microphones in a flurry of victory signs and friendly waves.

"Ladies and gentleman of the press," Ryder says, his reedy voice rising, "I know you folks are busy this fine Friday afternoon. But if I can beg a few moments, I'd like to present my respectful and rational disagreement with what you've just heard from my opponent."

The mop-headed CEO is ruggedly handsome in a way that suggests long hours spent outdoors, all of it on boats and horses. He places a fatherly hand on Ryder's shoulder in a gesture of support. Ryder sports his trademark leather bomber jacket.

The Chief of Staff sidles next to Colleen, following her line of sight. "Because faux-populism-meets-folksy-militarism is always in fashion," she says.

"Thank you," Ryder says, attempting a smile at the reporters. "I appreciate your fairness. Your balance. For as you folks know, one of the traits that makes this nation great is that here we are free to see that every story has two sides."

"Free," says the Chief, "to see this guy perpetually distinguish himself as a whackass prick."

But instead of booing, instead of turning away and leaving, the crowd, to Colleen's dismay, stays and listens.

"Now I'll break it right down for you, and I'll keep it brief. My friend here has come all the way from England as a show of good faith. He and I have just had a productive conversation about this great lake. A very productive conversation. He's not going to make a statement today—you can look for his press release in the morning—but I'm here to tell you what should already be clear. The company this gentleman represents is a major employer for the Tri-State Region. And that's a fact."

"I don't know," says Gina, warily. "It looks like he may have finally got some brains behind his operation."

"But you know what else is a fact?" Ryder says. "Not all scientists agree that dumping industrial byproducts into the lake is a categorically negative action. There are organisms—completely natural organisms—that actually use these materials for food. That's a fact for you. And what the Senator here failed to tell you just now, and that I am very pleased to announce, is that I have worked it out with my friend here that his company will offset its actions—actions which, as you know, are perfectly legal under federal and state law—with windmills and solar panels and other such things, that are green and that create jobs. Because that's the future."

Ryder runs a hand through his short haircut, bushy and bristling, like an old-fashioned shaving brush. He looks pleased with himself. He shoots a glance at the mop-headed CEO, who looks pleased with him, too.

"Excuse me, Congressman," the Chicago Public Radio reporter says. "I have to ask the rather obvious question. Will the Oil Company agree not to dump toxins directly into the Lake?"

"No," says Ryder, "of course not. Because they are well within their corporate rights to do so. You be sure to get this down. If someone wants to tell the hard-working men and women of Illinois and Indiana that they're not going to get a paycheck anymore just because some college professor up in Evanston doesn't like the smell when he's strolling along his fancy beach, then be my guest. But to me, that smell is the smell of jobs. It's the smell of prosperity. And I, Congressman Ron Ryder, will never, ever say to the working people of this state, 'Sorry, no job for you, no paycheck for your family.' I won't say that now, and I won't say that when I'm your Senator. Thank you."

The reporter begins again, his call echoed by the other reporters gathered on the bike path, but Ryder's press secretary blockades the mic. "The Congressman has said what he needs to say. It's simple enough to understand. No further questions."

And with that, Ryder and his entourage reinstall themselves in the black SUV, leaving tire treads in the sand and incredulity in the air.

G ina and the Chief are ushering the Senator into Dézi's waiting car, and to Colleen's astonishment, he's going willingly.

The reporters take their leave for real this time, and the Chicago Public Radio guy comes up to Colleen as she's folding the tripod.

"I get the impression," he says, "that the Ryder campaign didn't notify you that they planned to piggyback on your presser. Am I right?"

She looks him in the eye just long enough to answer his question without answering it. "Better not comment on that," she says.

He hands her his card. "Hope I'll see you around," he says.

Andrew hollers from the backseat, "Pile in!"

Colleen crams next to the Chief, who is crammed next to Gina who is crammed next to Andrew, and slams the door of the rental sedan.

It's quiet inside as Dézi pulls through the underpass onto Lake Shore Drive, and Colleen is aware of a soft interior voice warning her to keep her mouth shut.

"So," she says, "why didn't we respond to Ryder's response?"

The Senator turns toward the back seat, displaying his less-than-classic profile. "That kind of grandstanding rebuts itself, Colleen."

"When we want your advice on strategy, Dugan," says Gina, "we'll ask you for it."

"Gina, it's all right," says the Senator. "Make no mistake, I'm furious. But the truth is more eloquent on its own at this point. Who in his or her right mind is going to believe that piping poison into the city's drinking supply isn't deadly and bone-headed?"

Colleen wants to answer that probably about fifty percent of the people in the country will believe it—that the press will report on the issue as if both so-called sides were equally valid. The headlines will not read "Poisoning Water Supply Stupid, Evil," but rather "Views Differ on Toxicity of Toxins."

But Gina—who will get her ass handed to her as soon as they return to the office for not knowing in advance about Ryder's press conference hijack plans—already sees her as insubordinate.

"Nobody, Senator," Colleen replies. "Not a soul."

~

Weeks in the Chicago office cycle by like the summer weather we used to know back when we still had bodies. Doldrums broken by storms both bracing and routine.

Each typically begins with Colleen and her colleagues putting the Senator on a plane and bon-voyaging him back to DC.

He'll return with equal force on Thursday night or Friday morning.

Of course, they try to anticipate his path, but his unpredictability renders their estimates inaccurate.

Maybe he'll come to Chicago, maybe downstate.

Maybe the bill they've been planning a press conference about passes, maybe it dies on the floor.

Subnormal calm settles over them from Monday afternoon through Wednesday evening until the crescendo recurs.

A repetitive posture of reactive near-chaos.

~

5

Palmira has called an all-staff meeting for today, Thursday, at 2:00 p.m. sharp. On the agenda: the upcoming Fourth of July parades, just eight days away. Also, staff reassignments that will occur because she and Nia are giving birth within the next three weeks.

If Colleen hadn't worked here long enough to know that the last minute also happens to be their favorite minute, she would marvel that they'd neglected the parade plans until barely a week before go time. Independence Day is any politician's most important parade date, especially in an election year.

Gina values parades from a press perspective because they earn the Senator coverage merely for marching.

The Senator values parades because he and the People can encounter each other in the flesh. Not him as a talking head on TV, not them as part of some pollster's sample.

The staff sits around the dark wood conference table, fluorescent lights off, waiting.

Nia says the vibrations give her headaches now that she's super-pregnant. Palmira is always late, and since she's been pregnant it's gotten worse.

Colleen's insomnia has been ferocious lately, and she shuffles truisms to stay awake.

If Hollywood is like high school but with money, and if politics is like Hollywood for ugly people, then politics must also be like high school for ugly people with money.

But conventional wisdom does not apply to the Chicago office.

Though the income disparity between high-level and lower-level workers is extreme, none of them are wealthy, per se.

And all of Colleen's office mates are qualitatively good-looking—fit and attractive and improbably multicultural, like drawings of people in foreign language textbooks. They are all under thirty-five.

All except the Chief of Staff, who has not yet arrived, and Agnes Lumley, a career bureaucrat who's worked in the Chicago office for as long as the Senator has had one, and for his bow-tied predecessor for years before that.

But the Chief is as trim as anyone in the room, and Agnes Lumley was grandfathered in.

A gnes likes few people, and few people like Agnes.
She handles Social Security, Medicare, Medicaid, and a handful of issues with the Department of State, including international adoption, upon which she frowns: Why can't people satisfy themselves with a homegrown baby?

She is never so happy as when she's unhappy.

This reminds Colleen of her maternal grandmother and any number of other female relatives, so she goes out of her way to be kind to Agnes. This impulse usually winds up backfiring. Agnes whines to her about not getting her fair share—of money, of vacation, of intern help, of comp time—baring her teeth, mossy and coffee-stained.

But sometimes it's worth it.

Colleen's Uncle Tom Dugan, her father's youngest brother and Walter's employer—he once worked for the Senator's predecessor—he still knows Agnes.

And before he served a tour of duty in Afghanistan right after September 11 and came back an arch-conservative, derisive of the Senator's peaceful progressivism, he had encouraged Colleen to try for a summer internship. He liked to do favors he could crow about for years, and which positioned allies in places where they stood to pay him back.

And so it was that winter break her freshman year, Colleen put on one of the suits she wore for Mock Trial and took the train to Union Station—walked through the Loop to the Federal Building for an interview with Palmira, who was then the internship coordinator.

The city grid pulsed thirty-eight stories below, muffled whitely by snow.

Colleen knew she had an in, albeit a minor one, but as she sat across from Palmira, she suddenly found herself wanting the internship more than she'd thought it possible to want anything.

This view, this perspective, this chance to have a hand, however small, however unpaid, in the office of a man who was himself just one in one hundred.

Colleen has never stopped feeling this way.

To be part of this world, an indispensable part, but knowing she can never can be.

She feels that way now, with the Senator's reelection campaign gearing up, about to leave her behind.

At that first interview Palmira was gracious, active in her listening, but Colleen figured she probably acted that way with everyone. After the interview, when they had risen so Palmira could walk Colleen out, she had no idea whether she'd be accepted.

Agnes, short hair dyed a rusty shade, thin frame stashed in a frumpy suit, had peeked from her cubicle as they passed. She had shaken Colleen's hand.

"Tom told me you'd be coming in today," she had said. "You seem like a very nice young lady. I hope we will get the chance to have you come work with us."

"Thank you," said Colleen. "I hope so, too."

"Be sure to tell your uncle that Agnes says hello," she had added, and looked at Palmira.

When the acceptance letter arrived in her dorm mailbox, Colleen knew that Tom had helped her get the yes. She appreciated this, but resented it, too. She felt sure she was qualified, but so were dozens of college students, ones who didn't have such uncles.

Still, she liked Agnes for stepping up for her, and also for Agnes' memory of Tom before he changed.

Ten years later, Palmira is the Chicago Director, Colleen's on the press team, and Agnes remains in the same cube with the same habits.

2:15 and no sign of Palmira.

Everyone chats, amiably wasting time, except for Agnes, who sits sighing in the farthest chair, and Gina, who's reviewing talking points. Gina's smartphone, named after an aggregate fruit, rests dormant, face-up on her yellow legal pad, a sleeping pet, a sinister hamster ready to wake and demand attention.

Palmira waddles in.

"Sorry I'm late!" she says. "But great news. The obstetrician thinks they won't have to induce!"

The baby will be Palmira's first, and Palmira is wild about having an all-natural pregnancy and an undrugged childbirth.

She has eaten only organic food for eight-and-a-half months.

She will refuse an epidural.

She is determined to breastfeed.

She brings in clippings for Nia, including one on how deli meats should be avoided unless they are heated to steaming due to potential bacteria. *Listeria monocytogenes*—a name Palmira mispronounces even after Colleen has taken pains to say it correctly—which can, in vanishingly rare circumstances, cause premature labor or stillbirth.

"Nia, is that a cold ham sandwich?" says Palmira, lowering herself into the leather chair at the head of the table. "The USDA—"

"Palmira," says Nia, who sips a single glass of white wine all night when they go out after work on Fridays, and who already has a thirteen-year-old daughter. "People in the ghetto do not pay attention to the recommendations of the USDA or the AMA or the-whoever-the-whatever. You've been to the West Side. Nothing's stopping those folks from having plenty of healthy, full-term, bouncing black babies. Same on the South Side. I'll be fine. Back me up, Lo."

Nia flips an imaginary card from an imaginary deck on the table in front of her—her I-am-playing-the-race-card gesture.

"It's true," says Lo.

"What'd I miss?" says the Chief of Staff from the doorway, late, too, from an overlong lunch meeting. "Nia's giving somebody another ass-chewing?"

"Just enjoying my ham sandwich," says Nia.

The Chief walks around Colleen's side of the table.

He strokes her hair—in curls that the teen magazines she used to read would have called "romantic"—as he passes.

Her coworkers have grown used to this. He always has a Favorite. They barely react.

The ones who do, do so with their usual mix of irritation and gratitude—that the Chief doesn't do it to them. The Chief, the thinking goes, needs to be amused.

Agnes and Andrew roll their eyes.

Palmira and Gina avert theirs.

Steve Moon Collier smirks. By doing her hair, by wearing lipstick and dresses, she's effectively Asking For It.

Part of what makes the Chief likeable is that he moves and acts like a much younger man.

But he also behaves—and gets indulged—like a child.

The Chief sits in the last empty chair, next to Steve, who copies him in styling his clothes to match his personality. Cool and almost free of color. Blue at best, otherwise gray. Never trying too hard. Closed and opaque.

Palmira glances at the Chief, who nods.

She begins to speak.

Sitting in the half-light has made Colleen sleepier, making her mind watery in a way she wishes it would be at night.

"As you all know," says Palmira, lapsing into the vacuous manager-speak she uses to assert her authority, "we've called you together to touch base on our plans for the months leading up to the election. We want to be sure everybody's on the same page going forward."

Colleen re-crosses her legs and sits up straighter in the leather chair.

"But before we get into the bigger changes, we have a few new rules we'd like to institute before I go on leave. The first one isn't a rule so much as a reminder: we need to be thoughtful about how we dress. This applies to everyone, because we represent the face of the Senator. But it applies to the ladies in particular. The officials we meet with tend to include older men more often than not, so, you know."

Palmira trails off.

Colleen ponders the implications.

It is never up to older men to exercise self-control. Obviously. It is up to younger women not to entice them. Sure, that clearly works.

Colleen has no poker face, so she looks past Palmira, out the window at the Lake, dotted with white sailboats, careful stitches in cerulean cloth.

"The next rule has to do with what we can and cannot post outside our cubicles."

Her use of *we* is disingenuous. Palmira has a spacious office, as do the Chief of Staff, Nia, Gina, and Sylvia.

"We can't have this place looking like—"

"Like a college newspaper office," the Chief says.

"Yes, like a college newspaper office anymore. When visitors walk past to meet with the Senator, it needs to be clean. Everything posted inside needs to be in a frame. No more clutter."

"Let me make sure I've got this," says Andrew, who has a robust poker face, and who is taking exaggerated notes. "Instead of a college newspaper office, it's going to be like a high school locker inspection?"

"That's not our goal, smartass," says the Chief. "We're going to be reasonable, but if you're not sure what we mean, ask."

"That leads me to the last rule," says Palmira. "Language. We have to clean it up. Stat."

The office lexicon tends toward profane exuberance, largely owing to the Chief of Staff's virtuoso cursing—colorful filth and compound swear words.

"Some of us have been lax about this in the past," Palmira says. "But all of us—and we do mean all of us—need to eliminate the worst words from our vocabularies."

"No more f-bombs?" says Gina, looking up from her legal pad. "How the—how on earth do you expect us to communicate?"

"That's it exactly, Gina," says the Chief. "If we can't break our verbal habits entirely, then we'll have to find clean substitutes."

Andrew, on Colleen's left, writes her a note in the corner of his steno: *Did you know swears make up 0.3 to 0.7 % of the average person's daily language? 50 of the 10,000 words said per day.*

Colleen read the same story in the trashy free newspaper during her commute. *Yes,* she writes. *And 2% of all words on social networking sites are swears.*

Good facts, he answers, then scratches the conversation out.

"All right," says the Chief. "Moving the fuck on."

So," Palmira says, "Nia and I are both planning on working as close as we can to our due dates, but then we'll be mostly out-of-pocket. Sylvia is going to step into Nia's shoes and oversee casework during those twelve weeks or so, but we're still going to need extra coverage. This being the case, I am pleased to an-nounce that Mary Dodge and Nasrin Shalabi will be joining us temporarily from DC."

"Nasrin!" says Sylvia, applauding. "My nice Nasrin is coming back to me!"

Mary Dodge is one of the legal experts in the Whip office—Nasrin's J.D. is newly minted.

Colleen has never met Mary Dodge, but she feels like she has from her stream of matter-of-fact emails on Senate rules and ethics—when to accept a gift, when to refuse it, when to speak to a lobbyist, when to shy away.

Colleen has met Nasrin only once, out in the Capital late last fall shortly after she was hired by the DC office, and found her to be cheerful, well-read, and sincerely supportive of everyone and everything. They spent maybe half an hour together, but Nasrin still leaves encouraging comments on the wall of Colleen's social networking profile about her photography and Walter's painting.

Colleen likes her very much, but not as much as Sylvia El-tibani does. Sylvia grew up the youngest of seven on a farm downstate, was raised Christian but identifies with her Palestinian father, and with anyone who, like Nasrin, also happens to be Palestinian-American. Sylvia performs her work as Asian Outreach Liaison with consistent jubilance, but she dotes on the Arab-American community, or "my A-Rabs," as she lovingly calls them. Five bright gold bracelets—a decades-old gift from her grandfather—angle on her tan right wrist, a daily show of solidarity for the displaced people of what she calls the Motherland.

"Yes," says Palmira, "Mary and Nasrin will join us after the parades. They'll split their time between here and crossing over to help with the campaign."

"What's going on with the campaign anyway?" asks Sylvia. "Seems like that squirrelly Ryder's having a tough time finding his feet out of the starting gate."

"I'm glad you bring that up," says the Chief of Staff. "He was. It was like he was using *The Asshole's Guide to How Not to Run a Serious Statewide Campaign*."

He feels Palmira's gaze.

"I know, I know—language," he says, and then, "But Ryder's

been stepping it up lately, and we're prepared to step it up, too. It's looking for now like we won't run a very extensive offense—our bearing's going to be defensive."

He pauses.

"I don't think this is anybody's first tractor pull, but it bears repeating: we have to keep our campaign activities separate from our regular governmental ones. We've got the campaign office set up over at Grand and State. The rule here is, you have to spend at least one full day per week in the state office to remain on the Senate payroll, otherwise you're considered full-time campaign staff. At this stage, nobody's going to be full-time campaign, although you may see some of us less and less, and then we may really be gone."

"Who's us?" asks Andrew.

"We're going to staff it with a skeleton crew at first. Those skeletons will include the Duke, of course, yours truly, Gina, Mary, Nasrin, and last and definitely least, the dumb boy-wonder to my right."

"Your eye's gonna be wondering about the blunt side of my fist if you're not careful," says Steve Moon Collier, obviously pleased at his own inclusion, and at the exclusion of so many others.

Colleen is barely listening now to her co-workers' questions about the trivial particulars of this latest shitty development—about the ethical ins-and-outs of who will take turns in the driving pool.

She feels sick, disbelieving.

How can she not be helping with the campaign?

She can't let go of the elation that resides in that word: *campaign.*

Martial and military, with a whiff of danger and noble privation.

Laying down your self, and, if needed, your very life for a cause.

That is what the workers on the presidential campaign of the state's Junior Senator make it sound like.

That is what, in a smaller sense, it had felt like when she phonebanked and canvassed in high school, before she could even vote, for whatever doomed Democratic House hopeful hazarded a run in her home district, the unlucky Thirteenth.

That is what she and Andrew had felt for a day in late December when they went to Ames to knock on doors for the Junior Senator prior to the Iowa caucuses.

Colleen wants badly to have this feeling again—of giving your whole petty personality over to something much larger.

She moved herself and Walter back to Chicago on the basis of the Chief of Staff's promise—implicit, but still—that she could take part in this.

She tries to catch his eyes. But they alight everywhere in the room except on her.

As her colleagues talk across the ovoid table, she feels beset by a bout of what Ethan has diagnosed as chronic FOMO.

Fear of Missing Out.

The affliction, he claims, is endemic to humans, but Midwesterners are superbly susceptible to the sense that whatever's happening to them, something of greater consequence is happening elsewhere.

She looks out at the skyline. The red CNA building, the skyscrapers and smokestacks, the train tracks and rail yards crisscrossing to the south by Chinatown, the trains bound to the coasts.

She allows herself to feel melodramatic.

Chicago is her city, but it is the Second City.

The senator she works for is not the one running for president.

And though her senator is a member of Senate leadership, he is second there, too. The Democratic Whip, not the Majority Leader.

Colleen realizes she is making a face like she smells a bad smell.
She knocks it off.

She will talk to the Chief after the meeting.

W hat about the parades?" says Dézi. "I need to give the
interns the scoop, so they have no excuse for not being
there."

Each year, the changing of the intern guard. Between Summer
Session One and Summer Session Two. The Fourth of July.

The outgoing interns and the incoming ones are all expected
to swell the ranks of supporters marching behind the Senator.

They usually do at least two parades, but this is an election
year.

"We're marching in three," says Palmira. "Or rather, you all
will be. Nia and I get out of it. No marching for the mommies!
We'll be doing Elgin first, then Glen Ellyn, and ending up in
Northbrook."

"Do all of us have to go to all three?" says Agnes. "Because
Glen Ellyn is so close to Lombard, I could go home after that
one, and—"

"Your choices on this are slim and none," says the Chief of
Staff. "And slim just took the train out of town. Everybody who
isn't knocked up better be there."

"I don't see why he likes parades so much," Agnes says. "He's
been doing them for thirty years, and it's always the same."

"He gets a unique sense of how the voters are feeling, based on
how many people give him the finger," says the Chief. "Plus he's
not miked up when he's marching, so he can speak directly to the
average citizens."

"Dézi, I'm putting you and Colleen in charge of parade plans,"
says Palmira. "Dézi because of the interns, and Colleen because
it's kind of a press thing. Okay?"

Colleen and Dézi look at each other, then back at Palmira, and say "okay," because there's nothing else to say.

Dézi unironically likes parades.

So does Colleen, when she gears herself up to like them.

"Stimulating as it's been talking shop," says Gina, "can we wrap this up?"

"I've said my piece, so I'll excuse myself, too," says the Chief, who never stays for the duration of any staff meeting.

He dons his suit jacket and walks off, breath mints clicking in his pocket.

Gina follows with bow-legged swagger.

B efore we all go," says Dézi, "These interns haven't had their meal with the Senator yet, and tomorrow will be their last chance. Can we make that happen?"

Each set of interns gets to have coffee and donuts or sandwiches with the Senator.

Between bites, they go around the conference table like the teen stars of a variety show named after a cartoon mouse, introducing themselves by turns, then hearing the Senator hold forth on how he got to be where he is today through persistence and hard work.

They get their photographs snapped next to the man himself. These photos are eventually signed, suitable for framing. Colleen still has hers sitting atop a bookcase in her childhood bedroom at her parents' place in the suburbs.

Though Andrew was never an intern, he has one, too, atop a bookcase in the apartment he shares with his yoga-instructor roommate, next to snapshots of himself holding a baby nephew whose name is Colton but who Andrew refers to as "the perfect chick magnet."

"Hannah," says Palmira. "Can we fit that meal in?"

"Yes, if we do a breakfast and not a lunch."

"All right everybody. That's it," says Palmira. "Let's get on it."

They push back their chairs.

They rise.

And away they straggle or stride.

T he Chief of Staff is plucking dead leaves off the oxalis he keeps in a green glazed ceramic pot in his office when Colleen goes to see him.

It's a shamrock, he's told her, but a false one, not the real thing—*Trifolium dubium*, symbol of Ireland.

His Irish-American heritage is of great importance to him. As is hers—to him, not to her.

Like so many people she's encountered in Chicago politics, he compliments her often on her good Irish name.

Colleen has never been moved by the mania in America for saying you're Irish, though she understands the appeal. As her father likes to mention to anyone who will listen, the Irish were a very oppressed group, and through grit and determination, they fought their way to the top.

Okay.

Colleen will drink green beer and cheer at the Chicago River flowing emerald on Saint Patrick's Day, but she considers herself just American, whatever that means.

The Chief, meanwhile, has gone so far as to send a lock of his hair for DNA testing in a lab somewhere.

To confirm his belief he's descended from Irish kings.

He calls her Princess. She knocks on his open door.

"Hey, Princess," he says.

"You must have me confused with someone else," she says. "That's not my name."

"It ought to be," he says. "You could certainly be one. You have such charm of manner. I thought you might stop by. Come on in, and you can close it behind you."

She sinks into the black leather sofa and waits.

"So," he says. "The campaign. There's so much about this that I couldn't have foreseen."

"Sure," she says, wanting to disagree but acting sympathetic.

"Everybody getting knocked up, for instance," he says. "Listen. I'm glad you're here, and I'll never be sorry to have you, but we need you more in this office than over at the old Hotel Grand. These Ryder bastards are starting to have a little fight in them. And it *is* more fun when you're getting shot at all the time. But for now, I want people with more experience on the campaign."

"I know," says Colleen, trying to convey eagerness without desperation. "But I came back prepared to do for the campaign whatever needs done."

"I've never doubted that," he says.

"I just hope I'll get a chance to prove it."

"You will," he says, "but not right now. I know you know, but this whole thing's a team effort. At the moment, the governmental office is where you're needed."

Colleen's mother sends her clippings. Among the last batch was an article about how women are often meek at making requests that will advance their careers, and how subsequently they do not advance.

At least she has asked.

But are her ambitions too high, or not high enough?

In this morning's edition of the trashy free newspaper, there was a shallow profile on a Russian model. When asked if she was content or if she would rather be a supermodel, she responded with what she claimed was a Russian proverb: *Only a bad soldier doesn't want to be general.*

Colleen had to admire the model—or the model's publicist—for that answer.

Ordinarily she'd bring this article up to the Chief. He'd find it amusing, or at least want to see a picture of the model. And half her whole job, any of their jobs, is to keep him entertained.

But she doesn't feel up to entertaining.

She looks through the window beside the closed door and sees the football helmet atop Lo's cubicle, the one he'll have to take down now that the rules deem it unprofessional.

"Right," she says, and quotes Lo's favorite saying from his defensive line days. "Teamwork makes the dream work."

She stands to leave.

"That's my girl," says the Chief of Staff, putting his arm around her shoulder. "For what it's worth, I've found that in this line of work, stick around long enough, and you might get a battlefield promotion."

She nods and puts her hand on the door handle.

"Just a sec," he says. "About this Lake stuff. I'm going to be meeting with the Pipefitters Local next week, on account of they're bent the hell out of shape thinking we care more about the water than we do about eighty temporary jobs at the refinery. Now, they're right—we do. But the Duke needs us to go see if there's some way we can make everybody happy."

"You want me to tell Collier to come talk to you?" she says. Unions are Steve's turf.

"Normally, yes. But water and the earth are more your territory, right? So why don't you go give him the heads-up that you'll be taking this one with me? How's that sound?"

Her consolation prize. But Colleen knows that meeting with the Pipefitters is all she'll get at this point, so she decides to let herself be consoled.

"I'll let Steve know," she says, imagining how pissed he'll be and trying not to let her smile get too wide.

"Thanks, babe."

"One other thing," she says. "I'm about to go meet Dézi to talk parades. If there's room in the vans, is it okay if I invite my friend

Ethan? He's a photographer, and Gina was mentioning maybe wanting to get him on board for some campaign coverage."

"I have my doubts about Gina's desire to have another shutterbug around when you're already such a handful. But any friend of yours is a friend of mine, Colleen. Go ahead and bring him."

"Thanks," she says.

Sometimes a soldier is all you can be.

6

Whenever the interns had their much-anticipated meal with the Senator, staffers were expected to cover the phones. This morning—box of coffee in one hand, box of donuts in the other—Dézi had materialized in Colleen's cubicle.

"Nobody's here yet," she had said, jerking her head to indicate Steve Moon Collier's cube, "and even if they were, they'd tell me they're too busy. Could you please, please, please do reception? It'll only be for like an hour."

So here Colleen sits, alone, red pen in hand, pink message slips at the ready, wondering how so many people have time to call the Senator's office at 9:00 a.m. on a Friday.

The Chief of Staff tells every batch of interns to treat each caller with the patience they would afford a grandparent, even if said grandparent is up to their eyeballs in misinformation or racism or misogyny.

The most vitriolic callers have become, for her, part of a competition with herself to see how much crazy she can take.

The Chief walks in at 9:45, crisp in suspenders and a bespoke summer suit.

"And how's the girl of my dreams this morning?" he says.

"If I see her, I'll ask," says Colleen.

She craves the glow of his regard, feels it when he laughs. He walks around the desk and joins her. She takes another call as he pauses to catch a strand of her hair between his thumb and forefinger, rubbing it like he's testing its authenticity.

The Chief of Staff considers his charm something of an atomic weapon, and as such does not see the phones as beneath him. It's a competition for him, too.

He takes a seat in the empty ergonomic chair next to her and helps for the next twenty minutes.

Hanging up, he exhales like a whoopee cushion deflating and turns to Colleen.

"Some a-hole just informed me that the Senator's going to hell for supporting a black presidential candidate. Specifically, he said, 'The Senator is going to smoke a turd in Hell.'"

"Did you ask him what brand of turd? One of the fancy Cuban ones, I hope."

"Such a bitch," the Chief says, taking her hand in his. "You must have to bite your tongue all the damn time up here."

"'Til it bleeds," she says, drawing her hand away.

~

The fact that the nation we loved and served has come to be "governed" by individuals who spend all their time and energy simply consolidating their power is repugnant to us.

What should have been clear to us during our lifetimes seems incontrovertible now: one does not serve democracy by showing up every day in one's suit to answer telephones in the hope of being assigned to some high-profile detail that will lead to future higher-profile details that will eventually permit one to garner a flake of power that can be leveraged to propel one's ascent through the rank and file of drudges and rapscallions to some still greater position of authority.

One serves democracy when one does almost anything other than that.

The system by which our nation has come to be run does not reward—or make particularly beneficial use of—those whom one among us famously called the best and the brightest.

Colleen will learn this the hard way, but Colleen will learn.

~

At last the two interns, Sudha and Bobby Peacock, arrive to relieve them.

Bobby is a rising senior at a prep school and has well-connected parents. He has interned on and off in the Senator's office since he was a sophomore. In his limited spare time, he runs marathons and travels to Africa to help AIDS victims.

When he gave Dézi an updated copy of his résumé earlier this summer, she came over to Colleen's cube to say, "This kid makes me feel like a loser!" Under the newly added Hobbies & Interests heading, Bobby had written: *Subscriber to, and dedicated reader of,* The Economist, The New York Times, The New Yorker, News-week *and* Sports Illustrated. *Constitutional law, American political history, and the United Nations. Indianapolis Colts football, Duke University basketball, and Chicago Cubs baseball. Playing any sport.*

Colleen admitted that if Bobby were not so genuine, she would not be able to tolerate him.

This morning was Bobby's third intern meal with the Senator, so by Colleen's reckoning he has partaken of coffee and muffins, Chinese takeout, *and* Chicago-style deep-dish pizza with the man.

But he's sincere when he answers the Chief of Staff's "How was it?" with "Brilliant, as always."

Colleen felt the same after her intern meal. That first impression has a lot to do with why she's still in the Senator's sphere.

"He's such a great guy," says Sudha. "Seriously, this office has spoiled me for ever wanting to work anywhere else."

"I thought my ears were burning," says the Senator, appearing in front of the desk to face them all crowded behind it. "Now I know why."

"Senator, hi!" says Sudha, standing up straighter behind Colleen's chair.

"Thanks for the good questions this morning, kiddos," says the Senator. "And for the special guest phone coverage. Colleen, a little bird told me you're helping organize the parades."

"Was the bird's name Dézi?"

"Might've been," the Senator says. "Chief? A moment of your time?"

"For you, I can spare at least five," says the Chief of Staff, and they scatter at the force of the Senator's impact, like pool balls to their respective pockets.

The Monadnock Building is a proto-skyscraper, the last built in Chicago using load-bearing wall construction.

Colleen learned this on an Architectural Foundation field trip for the interns that she helped Dézi chaperone. To support its own mass, the walls at the base are six feet thick.

This morning Palmira, almost too pregnant to move, directs her husband to use the ledges that lead to the deep-set windows to set the coffee and donuts they've brought to see the Fourth of July paraders off.

Everyone mills along the building's west side, across the street from the office, near three boxy white rental vans. Colleen and Gina review the intern-made parade signs with Sudha. Done in mixed media—marker, crayon, highlighter and glitter pen on multi-colored posterboard—the signs are cute, especially the one in text-speak: "Interns <3 The Senator." The pencil lines used to keep the inked letters flush show faintly beneath the hot pink handwriting.

"Guys, I hate to say it," says Gina, "but I've got to ixnay this one. I know this sounds silly, but it's potentially controversial. Thanks to that rep from the great state of Florida and his page scandal, nobody wants to be seen as 'hearting' or being 'hearted' by his interns too much."

Wearing white shorts and wielding a clipboard, Dézi looks like a cruise director as she checks everyone in and tells them what van to sit in. She'll give the lists to the drivers so nobody gets lost.

Steve and Sylvia load dozens of bottles of water into red, white, and blue coolers so nobody gets dehydrated, and the Chief of Staff tosses out yellow-and-blue T-shirts bearing the Senator's name to anybody who isn't already sporting one, mostly the new interns from Summer Session Two.

"Turnout's awesome," says Dézi, walking over to Colleen, helping herself to coffee.

"Everybody made it?"

"All except one. She's the one I was most worried about anyway, so no surprises. She just texted to say she'll be in on Monday for orientation."

"Which one is she again?"

"The former Luvabull."

"Oh," says Colleen. "Right."

When the applications for the summer were flooding in, Dézi would show her the most outrageous.

A former professional basketball cheerleader, this applicant had enclosed, unbidden, a headshot along with her résumé.

As big as her résumé, in fact—an 8½-by-11 glossy of herself in what appeared to be her uniform.

She has just graduated from the third-rate law school on State Street, and interviewed well enough, so Dézi hired her.

Andrew's parents are in town from Wisconsin. They like the Senator even better than the senators from their own state, so they're marching, too.

They stand near the second van wearing visors and tennis shoes, chatting with Ethan. A little pod of people who don't know the other people, yet.

The Senator approaches them.

Colleen hears him performing his signature move: making sure the newcomers are settling in, but commanding them each in turn before they're fully settled to "Tell me something about yourself."

Cheap but effective—knowing how people love to tell their stories to someone, all the better when that someone is powerful. Palmira orchestrates a group photo.

Her husband snaps it with their camera while Ethan pops off several shots with his.

They all climb into the vans.

Palmira and her husband wave as they caravan toward the Expressway, past the inner ring of urban suburbs that bloom around the city, wreathing it like the head of a horse who's won a derby.

Tree-plus-geographic-feature, the classic suburb-naming technique. Oak Park, Elmwood Park, Evergreen Park, and so on.

A perquisite of being a parade planner is getting to arrange who's in your van, and Colleen has stocked hers like a well-appointed liquor cabinet: Lo in the driver's seat, the Senator beside him, Andrew and his parents after that.

Then herself, Ethan, Gina, and the Chief of Staff, and the back row full of interns, including Sudha.

Minimal traffic under a cotton candy blue sky.

"Too bad we're not marching in DG," says Ethan.

Downers Grove, the suburb where he and Colleen went to high school. His parents still live there.

Colleen grew up in Woodridge, one suburb over, and her parents still live there, but nobody's ever heard of it, and the ones who have look down on it.

Most ardently, the Downers Grovers. Woodridge kids go to Downers Grove high schools, and Woodridge has many more "under-resourced"—code for Black and Mexican—residents.

The local nickname for Woodridge when she was growing up was "Hoodridge."

She gathers this is still the perception.

She disliked both towns equally when she was a teenager in

them, but these days when she is asked where she hails from she tends to say Downers Grove—or more often, because she tries not to lie outright, "I went to Downers Grove North High School."

Any time she does this, for that extra scrap of recognition-plus-expedience, she instantly feels dumb.

This is America, so it's supposed to be possible, but can anyone ever truly overcome the accident of her birth?

At any rate, even Ethan seems to have forgotten her Woodridgean origins.

"Yeah," she says. "Too bad we won't get to stomp on the old stomping grounds."

~

We miss parades. We had not expected to, but we do.
In life we marched in so many—military and otherwise.
On horseback and afoot.

The dates of our births and deaths still sometimes occasion them. We rode in so many processions, most of them uneventful, certain others ill-fated.

To put the powerful within reach of the common citizen is a risk, but a necessary one.

Pageantry is more important than many people realize.

~

E lgin will be the best parade of the day, and it will be over too quickly.

Elgin is a real city, albeit a small one, the eighth largest in Illinois, and the one Colleen's fondest of in Kane County for its location on the Fox River, its diversity, and its giving the Senator a hero's welcome.

A breeze ruffles the highest leaves in the oak trees spanning the route, making a sound like distant applause.

Ethan has never been to Elgin, and as they take their place in the lineup, he takes photos of the painted scrollwork of the Victorian houses, of the russet donkey belonging to the local Democratic party, of the guys dressed in clown suits and themed costumes, many of them intended to suggest the styles and fashions of our own bygone eras: powdered wigs, pantaloons, stovepipe hats.

Colleen studies how Ethan works and thinks of a moth—silent in the air, blending in with whatever surface he lands on. He causes subjects to behave as if they are unobserved, getting the images he wants without his own presence spoiling the moment.

Colleen can't imagine being so invisible, or wanting to.

Ethan takes pictures of the boy interns, each of them ogling the Elgin High School Drill Team, the shimmering pantyhose that encase the girls' shapely legs catching the sunlight as they practice their high kicks.

L eaving Elgin, they get a little lost.

"Let's get there by horseback," says the Chief of Staff. "Let's get there by tilt-a-whirl, let's get there by rollerskate, whatever the hell, but dammit, let's just *get* there!"

He bangs the ceiling with his open palm.

Bobby Peacock, in the lead van, thought to bring a GPS, so Andrew manages to call him and get Lo back on course. As Col-

leen does portraits of everyone in their seats, the Senator plugs
in his portable media player. There's a vapid feature today in the
broadsheet paper on candidate playlists. The Junior Senator, Ron
Reese Ryder, the Senator, and the rest of their ilk have offered
their Top Tens.

"Or had their communications directors list them. Right,
Gina?" says the Chief, winking.

"I'll have you know, I chose my own songs," the Senator says.
"Well, Dot may have suggested a couple. What can I say? My
wife's got good taste."

Gina pulls the paper from her backpack, and they try to guess
which songs were chosen by which politicians.

"All Elvis, one through ten," Colleen guesses for the notoriously erratic Elvis-loving Governor, who idolizes the late King
because he believes himself to be one.

"Correct," says Gina. "But the real stumper is, which of these
distinguished candidates listed 'Baby Got Back' among his al-
leged favorites?"

"Rumor has it Ryder likes back," says Andrew.

"*Andy,*" says his mom, shushing him.

"Uh, correct, actually," says Gina. "That's his track."

"No way!" say the interns in the backseat. "He didn't really say
that."

"What else is on there?" says Andrew. "The Pet Shop Boys?
George Michael? Cher?"

"What a colossal jackass," says Gina. "I can't believe Ryder'd
let his people phone this in for him. Compare that to the presidential candidate's thoughtfully composed list."

"Senator?" Sudha says, raising her hand.

"Sudha," says the Senator. "You can just talk. Don't wait to be
called on."

"Could you play your playlist?"

"Angelique Kidjo" and "Jack Johnson" and "Cannonball
Adderley."

"Emmylou Harris" and "Van Morrison" and on up to number
ten.

The Senator announces each track as they make their way down US-20.

The interns car-dance as the sun beats in.

"Lo, crank the AC," Gina says.

"You're making me sweaty just looking at you," says the Chief.

"Be sure to drink lots of water. It's in the cooler behind you," says Colleen.

Ethan leads the interns in making choo-choo motions to the rhythm of a song about forming a train made of love. By Glen Ellyn Road, five miles to go, everyone needs to pee. "Train in Vain" frolics through the speakers, but the interns refrain from making another locomotive.

"Once I get us where we need to be, I promise I'll find us a bathroom," says Lo.

"What would Joe Strummer say?" says Andrew, shaking his head.

"I could try to keep bouncing," says Sudha, black hair head-banged askew, "but I'm afraid you'd wind up with a disaster on your hands."

The Senator deals so often in abstractions that it can be easy to forget about earthly needs. When they arrive at their designated parking space in Glen Ellyn, on an elm-lined street a few blocks from step-off, they need to pee so badly, the Senator included, they can no longer concentrate.

"Excuse me," says Lo, taking the keys from the ignition. "I'll be back for the rest of you, but I have to go right now—in the woods."

"The woods?" says Gina, eyeing the sparse stand of trash-trees opposite the van. "A vacant easement with a fireplug in it is not 'the woods.'"

"The woods sound good enough for me," says the Senator.

The staffers and interns giggle, thinking he must be kidding, but he's unfastening his seatbelt and shambling after Lo.

"He's a real no-frills guy, the Senator," says Colleen.

"Never could tell him anything," says the Chief of Staff.

Their blue-and-yellow-clad figures angle away from the van into some low shrubs, their backs leafy but visible.

A red-white-and-blue bedecked family hangs bunting on their historic home across the street. If they look over, they will have an unobstructed view of the urinating twosome.

Gina is freaking, a vein in her forehead Colleen has never noticed before protruding as she raises her voice to plead, "Oh my God. Pee faster. Jesus."

"It's like it's happening in slow motion," says Ethan.

A police car cruises by.

Gina is thinking aloud of potential election-costing headlines.

"Illinois Senior Senator Indecently Exposes Himself to Young Male Staffer in Suburban Woods," she says.

"Not punchy enough," Colleen says. "Senior Senator Caught with Pants Down—Literally!"

They all laugh, including Andrew's parents, not so much because it's funny as because it's a relief.

The Senator has emerged from the undergrowth, tucking his shirt in, and Lo trails behind, both looking refreshed.

The Senator sets out to mingle with the crowd, and Lo drives the rest of them to a chain coffee shop in a little strip of upscale suburbanoid restaurants and boutiques along Main Street. Ethan diverts from the group when he sees a bank of portable toilets: "Can you believe I don't have any Porta-Johns in my 'In the Dumps' collection yet?"

They meet back at their parade slot in time to eat sandwiches from a chain sandwich shop that Steve Moon Collier will not let people forget he has provided.

Nia shows up, too, with a construction worker's lunchbox-sized cooler full of melon cubes that she's soaked overnight in bourbon.

"I felt bad missing you guys downtown," she says, "but I could not get myself out of bed that early on a day I didn't have to. I thought you'd need these more than donuts anyway."

They each have a couple before Nia leaves.

"On my way to do some outlet shopping for last-minute baby supplies," she says. "Can't tell me the suburbs aren't good for anything."

They line up behind the Congressional candidate they're here to support, a Retired Female Army Colonel and mom who's attempting to unseat the current Rep, an Ultra-Conservative, Evangelical Personal-Injury Lawyer.

The Challenger is not going to win, they're all pretty sure, but she is making a dignified run for it.

Just ahead of the Retired Female Army Colonel's red convertible are still more drill teams, hands manicured, torsos sequined.

Ahead of them are the marching bands, and ahead of them the VFW and the American Legion.

Colleen's father was Post Commander of the Legion in Downers Grove before he got activated to go to Iraq. If he were home, he'd be marching, too.

And he'd be carrying a sign for the Junior Senator, because he hates the war and the way the Republican Party thinks they have a monopoly on patriotism.

Colleen looks at the Legion guys in their ribbons and medals and hats, glad she's wearing sunglasses because of the tears in her eyes.

"You okay?" says Andrew.

"I think it's just the whiskey," says Colleen.

Resolved to imitate Ethan's grace, Colleen takes out her personal camera and busies herself taking pictures.

Of the sun glinting off the drill-team abdomens.

Of the teacup Chihuahua in a God Bless America shirt.

Of the bite-marked watermelon rind glistening in the gutter.

"Watch what you record there, Dugan," says Gina. "You're on the clock today."

"I'm just soaking up the Americana," says Colleen.

"I'm just soaking up your relentless pursuit of your own interests on government time," says Gina, kind of joking, but in that Freudian truth-at-the core sort of way.

"When I'm famous, I'll dedicate my first coffee table book to you."

"You damn well better not," says Gina.

The Retired Female Army Colonel climbs into her car as the parade pitches forward. Her vehicle is bedecked with campaign regalia, but riding like that is a rookie mistake.

Better to do as the Senator does and walk the routes, to be among the people, even if many of them—especially here amongst the richer and more fearful—dislike you.

They pass three lemonade stands operated by children with cornsilk hair, straw-haired mothers hovering above them, regarding their entrepreneurial offspring with pride and passersby with wariness.

The windows of palatial houses look out on the parade with affluent, jingoistic eyes of a kind Colleen would not have believed existed were she not here to see for herself.

But among the political propaganda—bearing the names of the evangelical personal-injury lawyer, of Ron Reese Ryder, of the Republican presidential candidate—are the usual For Sale signs.

Nowhere is totally safe.

Some of these people, too, will have to take a loss.

Three years back, the Senator read an FBI report about the interrogation tactics used by American soldiers on prisoners at Guantanamo Bay. He read aloud from this report on the Senate floor, quoting the first-person account of an FBI agent:

> On a couple of occasions, I entered interview rooms to find a detainee chained hand and foot in a fetal position to the floor, with no chair, food or water. Most times they urinated or defecated on themselves, and had been left there for 18–24 hours or more. On one occasion, the air conditioning had been turned down so far that the barefooted detainee was shaking with cold. On another occasion, the [air conditioner] had been turned off, making the temperature in the unventilated room well over 100 degrees. The detainee was almost unconscious on the floor, with a pile of hair next to him. He had apparently been literally pulling his hair out throughout the night.

The Senator publicly observed that if you heard such cruelty described without knowing who was responsible, you'd be inclined to guess it was perpetrated by the Soviets in their gulags, or the Khmer Rouge of Cambodia, or even the Nazi gestapo. But not by Americans.

After the Senator's speech, the Texan President's pig-faced chief of staff accused him of treason, the media promptly crucified him for his failure to support the troops, his un-Americanism—and the Senator apologized.

To Colleen's disappointment.

The Senator's detractors, with no other material to work with, dig up his remarks, dust them off, and put them on display on occasions like this one.

And toward the end of the route, near the Colonial-style Glen Ellyn train station, they come upon the requisite knot of protestors carrying signs that indicate that the Senator "hearts" terrorists and "disrespects" the American military.

They wear Ryder T-shirts and jerk their hands back when the Senator offers to shake.

Their facial expressions say, *I have chosen stupidity.*

They boo the Senator's back, but he breezes past, equanimity intact, which only serves to make them madder.

"How are you doing today, Colleen?" the Senator says, coasting up.

"All the world loves a parade," she says.

"You and Dézi did a good job with this. Thank you," he says, and cuts crossways to work the opposite side of the street before the route concludes.

H omestretch!" says the Senator as they pack themselves into the vans one last time to drive up to Northbrook.

"Enemy territory, you mean," says the Chief.

"Northbrook," Colleen explains to Ethan, "is actually *in* Ron Ryder's current Congressional district."

Step-off for the Northbrook parade is at three, and they have their best placement yet. Colleen and Dézi wrangled them a spot toward the front so they could be done sooner, and go their separate ways, catching whatever barbecues might still be going on and seeing the fireworks that evening, if fireworks are their thing. Walter will be waiting to take Ethan and Colleen home, so they don't have to ride all the way back downtown.

Lo parks at the cross streets Colleen has given him, but when they walk over to their slot, they find it already occupied with throngs of marchers in Ryder gear.

"What the hell?" says Gina.

"Excellent question," says the Chief. "Come on, babe, let's see if we can't get this straightened out."

He and Colleen find a parade organizer directing traffic on the sidelines.

"It was our understanding," says the Chief in an even voice, "that Slot Twelve over there was supposed to be for the Senator."

"It was," says the woman in a fluorescent Park District polo, "until you sent your staffer to say you were running behind, and wanted to be moved to the back. We did our best to be accommodating. Although I should say that honestly we prefer people not to demand changes on the day of the parade."

"Wait," says Colleen. "What staffer?"

The woman shades her eyes with her right hand and points with her left, "That gentleman over there. The one in the khakis, holding the video camera."

"This is not your fault," says Colleen, "but so you know, that man is not on our staff. He works for Ryder, and I think they lied to you."

"Oh dear!" says the woman. "Well, now, shoot. It's almost three and I don't see how we can get them all to move without making a huge production—"

"Don't trouble yourself," says the Chief of Staff. "It was an honest mistake. On your part, that is. We'll just take the other spot."

"Everybody, let's move it back!" says the Chief. "We have been made the victims of some unforeseen circumstances."

Steve Moon Collier starts to walk toward the Ryder henchman.

"Cool your jets," says the Chief. "I want to do the same thing, and this is pretty bad, but take a closer look at Ryder's butt-boy over there. He's videotaping us, so let's not give anybody the satisfaction. We do not let pissants like them see class acts like ourselves get mad."

"All right, kiddos," says the Senator. "Change of plans."

They about-face and trek to the back of the parade. Ethan turns to snap a few pictures of the Ryder guy.

"I'll call these 'Portraits of a Total Douchebag as an Ugly Young Man'," he says, then grabs Colleen and says, "Wait a second. Who the fuck is that?"

"Ow! Who's who?"

"That guy dressed up like Maverick from *Top Gun*."

Colleen turns to see Ryder himself.

Short but domineering.

Carrying an American flag.

Aviators nestled atop his bushy hair.

As usual, he wears a leather bomber jacket despite the 90-degree heat and greets his supporters with upraised hands.

He high-fives his henchman and the crowd around him cheers.

Colleen does not understand how anyone could look at this group and not see what she does: a mob full of itself and of terrifying bullshit.

"Um, don't you ever look at the news?" Colleen says. "That's Congressman Ron Reese Ryder, real American hero—enemy of Lake Michigan, and our gallant opponent."

"Holy shit," says Ethan. "I didn't know that was him. I—"

"Right. Well, it is. And he's an asshole. Now you know that, too. Come on. We're losing our group."

Colleen takes Ethan's wrist and leads him away.

They take their places directly behind the Northbrook Police Department's equestrian corps.

"This stinks," says Sylvia. "I mean, it really does."

"Everybody careful where you put your feet," says Dézi, and they're off.

The Chief of Staff is walking charisma, an influential man with a famous-looking face. People are always assuming he's the Senator, then trying to place him when they are told that he is not. Sometimes he gets taken for the mononymic lead singer of a reggae-inflected British rock trio popular in the late '70s and early '80s.

The Senator, on the other hand, is lower-profile—both because his style of manner and his style of face. He blends in at first, but then you notice his distinctive slow burn. You may not remember exactly what he looks like, but you will remember the way he looked at you.

Like you were the only one on the parade route.

Like he cares about you, and it's okay with him if you do not care in return.

The Senator and the Chief work the crowd like champions, in the tag team they've perfected over almost three decades. Even here, in Ryderland, even with a parade placement that is literally shitty, they pick their way around the horse turds, shaking hands and kissing babies, and melting most people's reserve as they do so.

But some remain unmeltable.

Squat and closed off, they remind Colleen of houses encased in winter ice.

B locks from the finish, the Senator's wife Dorothy sneaks into the end of their group.

Colleen sees Sylvia see her, and Sylvia's about to exclaim, but Dorothy puts a finger to her lips and walks up behind the Senator.

She does the trick where you tap the person on the opposite shoulder of the one you're closest to. He looks left and misses her, then looks right, and smiles an open-mouthed smile.

"Dottie!" he says. "To what do I owe this pleasure?"

"I wanted to be sure you got home in time to make it to the cookout," she says. "I brought the car. I can drive us."

Their steps synch up and she puts her arm around his waist as his falls in place around her shoulder.

Colleen is touched at Dottie's doing the same sweet thing as Walter.

Hannah the Scheduler elbows Colleen and makes they're-so-adorable eyes.

Colleen can't hear the rest of what they say, and then the Senator is bringing Dottie back and forth across the hot asphalt with him, introducing her to the crowds as "my lovely wife."

Because of her single lung, she can't walk as fast as he's been, so he slows his pace.

Ethan takes pictures.

The following week, when he sends them to Gina, she will remark to Colleen how glowing they both look, and will say it's a shame they don't need the photos for anything official.

In the car, Colleen tells Walter all about their day, pausing to let Ethan chime in, but he supplies none of his usual snark.

"Ethan, did you get sunstroke?" says Colleen, reaching to hand him a bottle of water which he waves away like a mosquito.

"No. I don't know. I feel weird. But, like, emotionally."

"Yeah," says Walter. "When I did the parades with Colleen last year I felt like they gave me a lot to think about. Just seeing all the ways the American flag gets worn, even. Star-spangled bras and striped bikini tops, red-white-and-blue boxers, socks, cell phone holsters, dog sweaters, ball caps. Beer cozies and fanny packs. Lots of people express how they feel about our country very differently than I do."

"I guess it's something like that, yes," says Ethan.

Walter and Colleen make peripheral eye contact. Walter glances at Ethan's face in the rearview.

"Maybe you *should* drink some water," he says. "You have two perfect, round, rouge dots on your cheeks. You look like a Goya. If I weren't driving, I'd want to paint you."

Ethan does not respond to the teasing. When they drop him off at his place, he's so quiet that Colleen asks if he needs them to come up. He says no, he'll be okay. But as Walter parallel parks in front of their apartment, Colleen's phone rings, and it's Ethan.

"I'm super-sorry to be so spazzy, but can you guys come back? For a minute?"

"Oh god, I knew it," says Colleen. "You're sick."

"No, no. I'm fine. Physically. I've just got something I really need to show you. It's about this guy Ryder."

"Ryder? What is it? Don't be coy. Tell me!"

"You of all people should know that a picture is worth a thousand words."

"One thousand thirty-seven, I believe, is the current estimate."

"My point is, I can't describe it. I'll show you, okay? You have to let me."

"Ethan, Walter and I are going to go watch fireworks at his coworker's place," she says—figuring Ethan will get the message, knowing how hard she's been trying to be a better girlfriend these days—then adds, "With work and all, I only see Walt awake and alone for a couple hours every day. I can't come back now."

"Can you come over tomorrow, then?"

"Maybe," she says. "I want to! But I'm supposed to go to this cookout tomorrow afternoon."

Walter is taking the keys out of the ignition, and she can feel his shoulder blades rise, tense, willing her not to bail.

"Okay, you know what? Walter's here now, obviously, and I can tell he really needs me to go with him to this thing tomorrow. It's at my Uncle Tom Dugan's place."

"But it's *his* boss," says Ethan.

"Sure, but it's *my* family," says Colleen. "Honestly, the soonest I can come back over is probably like, twenty-four hours from now. Tomorrow night. Does that work?"

"I wish it was sooner."

"I wish you would just *tell* me what the hell you're talking about. You're acting like it's the end of the world."

"Okay, fine. Tomorrow. Like eight? Tell Walt he can come, too."

"Yeah," says Colleen, "I will."

They hang up, and she fills Walter in. He's intrigued, but also grateful that she'll still be his wingman at her uncle's party.

She doubts he will join her at Ethan's.

He likes his alone-time, and said this morning that he might try to get some painting done tomorrow night.

But she knows he'll probably just look at—and make hyper-literate comments on—art blogs.

She tries not to be offended at the way he squanders his talent, or to blame herself for making him take the job that consumes him, working for her uncle out in the suburbs.

Hadn't that technically been patronage? she wonders. Sleazy, like who's-your-daddy?

No.

At worst, it's just a little unsavory.

Besides, Walter himself is an honest citizen, upright as a piano. She loves him. Everyone loves him. There's nothing not to love.

Tomorrow night, when Colleen finally watches what Ethan wants to show her—a couple of minutes of shaky video— she will retroactively correct him in her mind.

It's not exactly a picture, though it is worth many words.

When she views it, it will not feel like the world is ending, though she'll know why Ethan was acting that way on the phone.

The end of the world—finite, interpretable, game over forever—would be easy compared to what she sees.

7

"Of all the things we own," the Senator is fond of saying on the floor of the Senate, as preamble to berating the banks over the foreclosure crisis, "the most important is our home."

And though Colleen's uncle Tom Dugan deplores the Senator every chance he gets these days, on this point he would agree.

Driving back into the city from her uncle's enormous house on the North Shore—crammed with kids and steaks—Colleen and Walter feel a little alienated, a lot hungry, and somewhat satisfied they fulfilled their obligation.

Aside from her camera and assorted equipment, Colleen does not own anything popularly considered to be important, and as she walks toward the back of their six-flat, this is a relief: to be a renter.

Walter parks the car in front, and Colleen comes through the alley to take out the blue bag—now full of empty cans and bottles—she had brought to Tom's, knowing he probably wouldn't bother to recycle.

The landlady's hung a flat metal sign on the gate that says *Warning! Security Dog* in red letters which frame the simple outline of a canine—a Doberman?—and Colleen hitches the latch behind her to maintain the illusion that something lives in the yard, dangerous and protective.

She climbs the wooden stairs.

The windows of the first-floor apartments display placards printed with blue block letters, *We Call Police,* the same kind you see in the restaurants and liquor stores just north, along Devon.

At a recent barbecue to welcome a new tenant, one of her neighbors told Colleen that he sees her walking through the alley at regular intervals and worries for her safety. "My mom," he had said, "she was tiny like you. She liked to change it up. Not take the same walking route each day, just in case. You might try it."

Colleen doesn't see being small as a liability.

At dinner the other night Walter observed that his coworkers keep getting bigger and bigger, and she agreed that she notices it too—not her coworkers, but the people they encounter while working—that humans are, on the whole, getting fatter, like goldfish—eating until there's no more food in front of them and expanding to fill their gargantuan fishbowl-windowed homes.

Nearing the top of the stairs, Colleen passes their tomato plants, staked up in five-gallon buckets and tied with strips of white T-shirt. She started them indoors, from seeds, the way her dad did when he was not in Iraq.

Walter's in the kitchen when she comes in, chopping up vegetables and preheating the oven.

Their place is cozy. If someone tried to break in through the back door, it would echo through the entire space.

She and Walt have talked about buying a condo, but neither really wants to. The thought of owning something so permanent makes them both claustrophobic.

Walter doesn't even decorate his office.

"I like to convey the impression that I could vanish without warning," he says.

Howdy, Pardner," she says, stepping into the kitchen and giving him a kiss.

"I couldn't wait to get out of there," he says, taking down a nine-by-thirteen dish and pouring some olive oil into it. "Sorry it took hours to do so."

"It's all right," says Colleen. "It would have sucked less if there'd been some food there that wasn't wrapped in bacon, but we knew what we were getting into."

"Yeah, hardly a lunch break goes by that I don't get to hear about how vegetarianism is socialist," says Walter.

They're making a potato salad for dinner, but with sweet potatoes instead of white and cilantro-lime dressing instead of mayonnaise. The sweet potatoes have to cook for forty minutes, and she and Walter have sex while the vegetables are roasting, a routine of theirs. They didn't set out to establish it—it just happened. They'd been waiting for something to boil, and what better way to make the cook-time pass?

They shed their clothes by the light of the sunset and the heat of the oven.

Afterwards, she gets up to pee. The bathroom window opens onto an airshaft, topped with chicken wire to keep out pigeons, squirrels, leaves, and in the summer, you can hear what everyone else in the building is up to, if they're up to it in their bathrooms. High-density living and its accidental intimacy enchants Colleen—hearing another tenant blow her nose, flush the toilet, gargle, talk loudly through the door to a significant other.

On her mother's first visit, she had come out of the bathroom remarking that she would hate to have so little privacy.

Colleen tried to explain that she found the arrangement reassuring.

She liked waking up in the middle of the night from a bad dream and knowing that her neighbors—Troy and Hailey, with their pet iguana and their pot plants; Pat and Elisa, with their bonsai and their ukulele—were all there, too.

Her dad had said he wouldn't like it, either, but he understood that she and Walter were doing their thing.

After dinner, she invites Walter to Ethan's, but he declines, tells her to bike safe, and that he'll see her later tonight.

"Happy painting," she says.

"We'll see."

It is not quite dark, and the coppery hairs on his arms catch the porch light.

"Look, it's twilight," she says, reluctant to leave him. "I like it."

"Me too. But *twilight's* such a cheesy word."

"Yes, but it's just right for the atmosphere," she says, breathing in. "The air is one part oxygen, two parts tristesse."

"You're a weirdo and I love you," he says.

"I love you, too," she says, and descends the stairs.

At the gate, she turns to wave, but he's gone.

When she starts to ride down the alley, the wind in her ears sounds like words whispered into a sound-system.

She can't make them out.

Colleen is chaining up to the wrought-iron fence in front of Ethan's building.

She thinks that if she were the main character in a movie—a political thriller in which people exchange lines like *This thing goes all the way to the top*—and a friend had asked her to come over right away to see something important but she'd come over hours later instead, then she could be reasonably sure, upon arrival, of finding her friend murdered in some gruesome way and the important thing missing.

That's silly, but she's still a little nervous as she rings Ethan's bell.

The front door buzzes without delay. Ethan's stairwell smells like Catholic church—incense the first-floor tenants burn to cover up their pot smoke. When Ethan meets her at his door, Colleen expects him to rush right into the big reveal, but instead, he's sheepish, barely letting her into the foyer.

"Thanks so much for coming over," he says, in a tone that sounds like she's doing him a huge favor by being here.

"Um, of course. Why would I not, especially since this has to do with Ryder?"

"About that," he says. "Now that I've slept on it, I think maybe I was overreacting. I mean, you already know so much about the guy, since he's the Senator's opponent. You don't need me to tell you anything more."

"Have you lost your mind?" she says, slipping past him. "I'm not leaving until you show me whatever it is that freaked you so far out yesterday."

Ethan remains in the doorway, his back to her, looking down the stairs. He seems to be checking to see if she's been followed, or thinking about making a break for it, leaving her here. "Yeah, okay," he says. "Okay. So—I was going to cut straight to video. But now I'm thinking some background may be in order."

"Video?" says Colleen, following him to the kitchen, where he insists on mixing them both drinks.

"Rusty Nail?" he says.

"Sure," says Colleen. "You have Drambuie?"

"Between me and the roomies, we've got everything."

"Where *are* the roomies, anyway?"

"Out for the night, luckily, so we can conduct our business in private."

"Cheers," she says, clinking his glass and taking a sip. "Here's to you telling me what you're talking about already."

They each pull up a chair to the kitchen table, a hand-me-down she recognizes from his parents' rec room in Downers Grove. They face his laptop. He rubs his palms on his thighs to wipe off the condensation from their glasses, and, she guesses, the nervous sweat.

"So," he says, "you know all about 'In the Dumps.'"

"Sure. Self-portraits every time you shit in a public restroom. It's unforgettable."

"Right. So. God! This makes me sound like a total perv, but—okay, sometimes, when I'm on the can in a public place, I'll hear noises. From the next stall, usually. And a lot of times, it'll be couples. Making out. Getting it on. Two guys, a girl and a guy, whatever. And sometimes I'll figure, 'Hey, as long as I'm in here, and I've got this great camera, and these folks are too busy to notice, why not shoot a little footage?'"

"Seriously invasive voyeurism," says Colleen. "Why not?"

"I know, I know," says Ethan, drinking half his Rusty Nail in one swallow. "But I never intended to *do* anything with these. I never intended to *show* them to anyone. I never even watch them again in the comfort of my.own home. I just like to *make* them. It's more about videotaping the act and not getting caught, you know?"

"I don't," says Colleen, "but that's okay."

"A long time ago, like maybe a year. Last summer. I was down-town after a portrait assignment in the Loop. I had to go, and I was right by the Palmer House Hilton, about to jump on the Red Line, so I figured, what the heck, I haven't got an 'In the Dumps' shot in the bathroom of the Lobby Bar yet. So in I go. I'm doing my thing, I'm feeling relieved, I've got some quality shots. Then I hear these smacks and moans one stall over. And this is the part I'm going to have to show you. And you're going to wonder, 'Ethan, why didn't you show me this a year ago when you first shot it?' And that will be a good question. But I didn't know until we were amid all that David-Lynch-meets-Norman-Rockwell pageantry yesterday what Ryder even looked like or who exactly I'd filmed. But okay. Enough. On with the show."

Ethan flips the light switch. The kitchen is dark except for the glow from the screen. The shadows make the hollows in his cheeks look even more famished, otherworldly.

The audio comes up first.

The loudest sound is Ethan's fumbling to position the lens over the top of the stall and angle it down into the next one, but the telltale grunts and slappy sounds are sharp in the upper register.

Colleen gathers that this kind of lavatory tryst happens all over the place on a regular basis, but this particular hotel—named after a robber baron who made his fortune buying up properties for cheap even as they burned during the Great Fire of 1871— is still a shocking venue. The bathroom is so upscale, the act so lowdown.

Ethan's hand comes away from the viewfinder.

Colleen sees one middle-aged white man standing up but looking down—sweating, khakis around his knees. Below him, another middle-aged white man. Kneeling. Blowing him. She can mostly see the standing man, very drunk, very out-of-it. But the kneeling man—she can just make him out.

United States Congressman and real American hero Ron Reese Ryder.

Ryder wears a pair of blue latex gloves.

The standing man sports a pale red condom.

Apropos colors, thinks Colleen.

She thinks, too, about who the standing man might be—a traveling businessman, perhaps, the bar is mostly tourists. She pities his family. He's wearing a wedding band. She can see it flash sometimes as he thrusts his groin forward and grabs the back of the toilet above the handle to brace himself.

She imagines he's from some faraway state and travels occasionally to Chicago for work—is essentially unaware of Illinois politics, politics as a whole. Just not on his radar, aside from hating taxes. Ryder, she presumes, must target guys like this— married, no strings attached—from immense hotel bars where the selection is large and anonymous.

The sucking and slurping go on and on, and Colleen is about to tell Ethan, okay, he can fast-forward, she's gathered the gist, when the standing businessman comes, not without violence, and she can hear Ethan gasp in the audio as he struggles to get the camera down, back into his stall.

Ethan is opening his door, still filming, camera held in front of him, clutched against his abdomen. He's standing at the sinks, aiming his camera at the mirror.

The stall door to the left swings open. Ryder steps out.

The real money shot.

His face lit up in the mirror like an actor's as he peels off the gloves, walks toward the reflection. Tosses them away, not stopping, turning back out to the bar.

A few seconds later, zipping up, the businessman follows, lathers and rinses his hands, sighs, and walks out as well.

Neither man looks at the other. Nor at Ethan.

Neither man utters a word.

F*ini*," says Ethan.

Colleen feels like she should wash her hands.

Not sure what to say, she says, "What kind of camera were you using?"

Ethan tells her the brand and model number.

"You'd expect a video like this to be blurry," she says, "but the quality's compellingly high. It's a little red, but otherwise—"

"Yeah, they came out with a new version of it this year. It's worth checking into. The auto white balance under low light can be a little kooky. I think your camera gravitates to a more bluish image—"

"Especially without flash—"

"Which makes sense," he says, "because your work is more moody. Artsy-fartsy."

"Whereas your project is just fartsy," Colleen says.

They fall silent.

Colleen flips the light on and the room is yellow again, warm and lemony.

A Lake breeze riffles the lace curtains like gills, like the room is breathing.

"The Chief likes to say Ryder's queer as a three-dollar bill," she says. "But no one can prove it."

"The man can turn a phrase," says Ethan. "Now *we* can prove it."

"We've got the smoking gun."

"Or the smoking pole, as the case may be."

"This does lend some insight into the quiet divorce Ryder's been going through. Gina's predicting the documents will be sealed. Seeing this, I wouldn't bet against her."

"I've burned you a copy," says Ethan, handing her a DVD. "So you can show this to your bosses or whatever, and you can nail this jackass to the wall. Am I right, or am I right?"

Colleen imagines the video being dissected by the helmet-haired anchors of the local networks, preceded by warnings of mature-content.

She imagines the screen-captures printed in the papers.

She imagines the links cropping up across political blogs.

She imagines the internet, hurtling with emails.

O kay," says Colleen. "So, bracketing whatever this project says about your own sexuality for a moment, I'm afraid that the course of action here is not crystal clear."

"What are you talking about?"

"For starters, explaining how exactly we laid our hands on this would be complicated."

"Can't you do the anonymous tip thing?"

"I don't know."

She puts the DVD back on the table, on top of a wrinkly issue of a photo magazine. She looks at the address label. Ethan appears to have lifted it from his dentist's office.

"Can you make me another drink?"

"Yeah, sure. I figured we would. I thought we'd feel celebratory.

I thought we'd toast our victory over the forces of bigotry and faux family values."

"I need to think for a sec."

Ethan is quiet, back turned, booze mixing, ice clinking.

Cicadas cycle through their clicky song in the trees.

Colleen sees her eyes reflected in the DVD, closes them, and imagines more screenshots analyzed on cable by righteous talking heads.

Sees Ryder getting pilloried, here and in DC.

Opens them and sees Ethan's back in its black T-shirt, shoulder blades moving as he stirs the cocktails, supple and sure about his proposed plan of attack.

Colleen feels disgusted and disgusting.

By the video and by her own reaction to it.

By what Ryder did—cheating on his wife back when he was still propping her publicly at his side like a cardboard standee of the perfect marriage—and by what Ryder is doing—lying to his constituency while decrying the Senator for not "defending traditional marriage." And by what she is thinking. Which is, *Holy fucking shit, I now have the magic amulet. I went from totally marginalized to I-get-to-decide-the-election in like fifteen minutes.*

She takes a deep breath.

Ethan brings her fresh drink over.

The room smells nostalgic to Colleen, like when she was little and pressed her nose against the squares of window-screen to look out into the dark, where all she could see were fireflies.

She hasn't seen any this summer.

Whatever happened to the fireflies?" she says. "It's probably us. Something terrible that humans are doing without anyone even knowing it."

"Um, am I mixing these too stiff?" says Ethan. "Will you show this to the Senator right away, or will other people have to take a look first?"

"Why were you almost not going to show this to me tonight?"

Ethan opens his mouth, then stops. He looks, as he sometimes does, like a jack-o-lantern, outsized features eerily prominent. Beautiful people can be so grotesque. His Adam's apple bobs and he tries again, "Because you've already got so much on your mind? And this'll make your insomnia even worse?"

"Ethan," she says, putting her hand on his arm. "You can't bullshit me. You've had this video forever. It's from right after he declared for the Senate. I understand that when you recorded it you had no idea it was a celebrity blowjob. But when I got here, you didn't even want to let me in. Why?"

Ethan picks up a utility bill from the table and starts tearing the envelope into jagged squares.

"For one thing," he says, "I had to psych myself up to expose my voyeuristic tendencies. And for another—promise not to be mad?"

Few phrases make Colleen madder, but she promises.

"You know how everybody we went to high school with— maybe not everybody, but all the 'gifted' ones we were in the same classes as—you know how they're all making tons of money in lucrative professions? And how the, I guess, *less* gifted ones maybe aren't, but they at least seem to be wasting their twenties in interesting ways?"

"Yeah," she says. "I know what you mean."

Colleen tries not to view other people's success as indicative of her own failure, tries not to perceive other people's interesting lives as a sign that hers might be boring.

She's heard that one girl has become a poet, but otherwise the Class of '98 is being sensible. Doctors. Lawyers. Programmers. Consultants. Traders.

Colleen always hears it first as "traitors."

Most of their friends are pursuing careers befitting their expensive degrees and their costly orthodontics.

Colleen, meanwhile, is not living up to her potential, not earning the maximum she could earn in a year, is in a job her former teachers tout with pride but to her feels like a fraud.

Not a "career."

Impostor, she thinks.

Feckless.

Dispensable.

So," says Ethan, "when I realized who I caught in this video, I thought I could make some money. Serious money. By trying to sell it to Ryder. But I couldn't see myself as a blackmailer. So I thought, maybe I can sell this to a TV station or a newspaper. But then I couldn't see myself as a paparazzo. So, okay, no dollars for me."

Ethan picks up his glass and puts it back down again without taking a drink.

"Then I thought, maybe I could just *give* it to the media, and then when they did all the stories, they'd mention me and my photography and I'd get incredibly famous. I think it's a Midwestern thing? Like I have all this ambition, but don't want to be perceived as ambitious?"

"Yeah," says Colleen. "Too self-congratulatory."

"Anyway, none of that felt right either. But I'd been obsessing all day, so when you showed up, I almost wanted to keep it to my selfish self. Then, when I saw you, and I thought about how weaselly and anti-gay you're always saying Ryder is, I knew I couldn't hide it, and that I don't really want to profit by it. What I want to do is something heroic, even behind the scenes. I figured you'd know what to do. How to do it."

He leans back in his chair.

Colleen can't tell if he looks relieved that the burden is off him and on someone else, or if she's just imagining.

Colleen has always been impressed by people who, when asked a direct question, don't provide a direct answer, but instead tell a story. Her dad can do it. So can Walter and the Chief of Staff. She decides to try it.

"Back in grade school," she says, "I loved it when we had tornado drills. We couldn't have done them more than twice a year, but in my memories it's like we did them constantly. Sit cross-legged facing the lockers. Tuck your head, clasp your hands behind your neck."

She remembers the musty smell of the carpet and the pattern it made on her forehead.

"In front of the entrance, where we lined up each morning, there was this super-realistic, life-sized metal sculpture. It was called 'The Hero.' It was this little girl shielding an even littler girl, putting her duck-and-cover over the smaller duck-and-cover. And there was this funnel cloud behind them, hurling debris."

Ethan's staring at her face, but his eyes don't quite seem to focus. She can't tell if he's really listening.

"The plaque said it was based on true events, that this girl really did save the other girl. She got hit in the temple by a brick, and she died."

She shrugs.

"It's embarrassing, but I was jealous of the dead girl. I wrote about it in my diary. I never got a chance to be a hero. I mean, it would have been hollow anyway, because I would have been a copycat, and I didn't really want to die. But I did want that chance."

She looks at the fridge. There's an *Indiana: Flat but Fun!* magnet on it. He bought it at a gas station on their way back from the

Dunes, where they went after prom with a bunch of their friends to stay in his parents' cabin.

"There are so few opportunities to truly be a hero," she says.

"Yes!" says Ethan. "This is that opportunity."

"No! That's not what I'm saying!" Colleen thinks maybe she's not suited to this technique. "Your heart's in the right place, Ethan, but it is not an act of heroism to reveal somebody's clandestine sex tape."

"But he's a liar who deserves—"

"Listen," Colleen says. "You're pro-gay rights. I'm pro-gay rights. So is the Senator. Ryder isn't, although he clearly ought to be. If we circulate this tape, Ryder will lose a lot of votes not because he's a bad person who lies to his constituency, and not because he votes against interests that should be his own, but just because he's gay. He would lose largely because of the fact of his sexuality, pure and simple. That's gross."

She lifts the DVD to her face and sniffs it.

"Beyond that, I'd bet you a million dollars that the Senator wouldn't go for it. He's sharp, but he's not a win-at-any-cost, ends-justify-the-means kind of guy."

"You know that if Ryder got his hands on something like this, he'd throw the Senator to the wolves," says Ethan.

"But being as brutal to your enemies as they would be to you isn't heroic either. It's not the Senator's style. It's not *our* style."

Okay," Ethan says, "I'm being an asshole. Fine. I get it."

"Ethan, I didn't say that. I'm just not sure what to do. Steve's always joking with Andrew that it'll be all over for Ryder once somebody digs up his secret boyfriend. And they're right. We just never expected we'd be the ones to dig him up. Or, worse than a boyfriend, that it would be multiple intoxicated, anonymous sexual encounters."

"Good point," Ethan says, and smiles.

"You've basically broken the story of the year. I just don't know if and when we should break it to anyone else. I need to contemplate. It's barely July. We've got some time until November. All right?"

"All right. But take the DVD with you. Just in case?"

Colleen tucks it into her bike bag.

If she were to send this to the Semi-Scurrilous Lefty Blog she reads every morning, it could be all over the country in a matter of hours. Always ready to post some linkbait, totally comfortable saying *This is just something we've heard*, she bets they wouldn't even vet it.

She pushes in her chair.

"You're not leaving?" says Ethan. "Stay and have another. We don't have to talk about the video anymore."

"Nah. I've got a two-drink maximum when I'm on my bike. I should go."

"Okay. I hope I haven't made things weird."

"You have," she says, "but I'm glad you did. It was brave of you to show me. And I don't think you're a perv. Thanks for doing this, and I'll let you know when I come up with a plan."

"Terrorist fist-bump?" says Ethan.

This is the way they've taken to saying good-bye ever since the Junior Senator and his wife did the dap at a campaign speech in Minnesota and conservative news organizations were set ablaze with speculations about the gesture's hidden meaning.

Their balled fists meet sidelong in midair. Hers small, his big, like two-thirds of a passed-out snowman.

She reaches for her helmet.

The ride home is balmy and full of people. Dining late, al fresco, drinking on the sidewalk patios of bars, making the most of the warmth as only residents of a city where it's winter seven months of the year can.

When at last she rounds the corner and approaches her own alley, she fishes out her cell, still pedaling, and calls Walter, and he comes down to carry her bike upstairs. She could do it herself, but likes that he doesn't mind.

They stand in the kitchen, and she doesn't ask if he painted.

She kisses him, and he asks about Ethan's news.

She pours herself a glass of water from the pitcher in the fridge and tells him.

Shows him the DVD and offers to play it.

Nah, he says, he gets the picture.

Colleen wishes she could call Andrew—talk to him at work on Monday and get his opinion—but her instinct is against it.

She saves the footage to her hard drive and then to a jump drive.

"I think you did the right thing," says Walter, who does not make statements like this blithely. "It's important to know about this, but the best plan is to sit tight. The Senator's in the lead, so what would be the point? That's not how you guys operate."

It's only eleven, but feels to Colleen like the middle of the night.

They make their way bedward. Lying there, it is too hot to touch, and they both sweat lightly, motionless as they are.

The ceiling fan spins above them.

Usually that does the trick, but tonight Colleen feels stuck under lukewarm water, like the fan is a propeller, sending wave after warm wave.

Walter begins to snore, a low rumble, almost like a rock tumbler, but too erratic to function as white noise.

Resentment flutters up and brushes Colleen's nerves like the greasy feathers of a rank black bird.

Irrational envy of his ability to stop being conscious.

She stares at the sodium glow shuffling through the drawn

blinds, and she hates everyone everywhere—including urban wildlife, including all housepets—for being asleep when she can't be.

The swollen air and the gingery light from the street remind Colleen tonight of DC.

W ho is she to expose Ryder? Or anyone?

She'd read recently that even the Sixteenth President had probably had syphilis, had probably given it to crazycakes Mary Todd.

Colleen feels fucking horrible.

For all the bad things she's ever done, and for all the bad things she'll ever do.

She tries to calculate what doing something with the blowjob video would entail. It would involve DC, for one—DC, where the real work gets done, where the big decisions get made, that swamp of power, that murk of ego.

She thinks about how the District office—which is to say Ryan Slattery—would react, when usually she tries not to think about the District office at all.

When she finally drops off, she has anxiety dreams.

Literal, obnoxious, populated by coworkers.

She sees the Chief of Staff sitting at his desk during scheduling call, making graphite circles with his mechanical pencil around the bottom of his coffee mug, summing it all up.

"Here's what we know," he says. "Nothing."

8

The gray-eyed woman standing before the front desk wears a powder-blue suit twenty years out of date. The seams are singed like a mock treasure map, the skirt sewn with naked baby dolls. She's draped chains over her padded shoulders and dipped her hands and face in fake blood.

She stares at Colleen.

The pocket of protestors behind the woman holds signs bearing grainy color photographs of aborted fetuses.

They shift from foot to foot, superior and waiting.

Behind Colleen are the dozen Summer Session II interns, and Dézi, who has asked Colleen to help with this portion of their training. Today is their first day.

Another woman, older, also draped in wool with a gold-plated crucifix, has brought out a camcorder. She pans the faces of the interns and intones, "Lo, how he uses innocents in his murder of the innocents."

She trains the lens on Colleen.

Colleen decides that matter-of-fact bemusement is the best course of action. She addresses the baby-doll woman as she might a perplexing trick-or-treater.

"And who are *you* supposed to be?" she asks.

"I'm the Senator's good friend, the Speaker of the House. I'm a baby-killer. That's why I'm burning in Hell for eternity."

"I see," says Colleen. "And how can I help you?"

"You can tell your boss that he's going to pay. We'll see him burning in Hell, as well."

"I'll pass that on," says Colleen. "But I have to ask. Are you threatening the Senator, ma'am?"

"No more than that man is threatening the unborn," the woman says.

"Okay, then, I'm going to have to ask you to leave," says Colleen.

She knows they will not depart on their own.

"We're not leaving until your boss comes out here."

"I'm afraid he's in DC, ma'am, so it might be a while."

"We're staying put until he promises to cease his slaughter of the unborn."

The baby dolls quiver as she speaks. The protestors behind her murmur their assent.

"All right," says Colleen. "Then I'm going to have to notify my supervisor, and probably also the Capitol Police."

Colleen hates having to concede.

This is what they want. To get arrested. To suffer publicly for their beliefs.

She feels the camerawoman zoom in as she rises and walks to Palmira's office. She hears Dézi tell the interns to go back to the conference room so they won't be videotaped.

At least my hair looks good today, she thinks. And, I wish I had my camera.

Pro-life protestors usually target the DC office. They have not shown up on the thirty-eighth floor since Palmira's been pregnant. Colleen tries to prepare her, but when Palmira steps, belly-first, into the waiting room, it's clear she's not ready for the posters.

The Virgin Mary clutching the infant Jesus.

The miniature beating hearts and hands and feet.

The smeared roadkill mess of the twig-limbed fetus on an anonymous white sheet.

Definitely not ready for the blue-suited woman to say, "Do you agree that your unborn baby is beautiful? You should be on our side."

Nor for the group to erupt in a chorus of slogans. "Abortion is murder" and "Down with radical feminism" and "Tell the Senator it's a child not a choice."

Palmira repeats what Colleen has already said, to no avail.

The blue-suited woman makes her face both flinty and smug. She steps toward Palmira.

She raises her voice and her bloodstained hands as though in a pulpit.

"Since 1974," she says, "we have been living in the midst of a national atrocity. You—of all people—are one of the ministers of the Culture of Death."

Palmira looks about to cry.

Colleen wants to correct the woman and say *Roe v. Wade* was decided in 1973.

"This office is a den of lies!" the woman says. "We need to rip off the mask of 'choice.' Do you think your baby is a choice? Do you?"

Nia's office is closest to reception. She's heard the commotion and steps out next to Colleen, in front of Palmira. "In the interest of courtesy," she says, "I need to inform you that the Capitol Police are on their way up. If you leave now, they'll let you go."

The blue-suited woman gapes at Nia's stomach. She can hardly believe the fecundity and hypocrisy she is now facing off against.

The baby dolls dangling from her outfit are all white, but she takes this opportunity to show she does not discriminate. "We are simply trying to save unborn babies like yours," the woman says, gesturing at Nia. "All babies. All races. All are beautiful in the eyes of Jesus. He's watching you. Both of you. Don't think He doesn't see. Don't think He won't remember who you worked for here on Earth when the Day of Judgment comes."

Three officers push their way into the knot of protestors as Palmira slips back out of sight.

The protestors lie down on the cadet-blue carpet and pretend to be dead.

Colleen has witnessed this trick before.

It's a common tactic of the antiwar demonstrators who try to force their way into the office each Tuesday in the summer, the same day as the Farmers' Market in Federal Plaza, the better to garner maximum publicity.

They puzzle her even more. The Senator voted against the War. His stance is their stance.

Their feigned deaths are unconvincing. They call out from where they lie, "Lord, forgive these sinners, not for what they do to us, but for what they do to your unborn lambs."

Vituperative, sanctimonious, they put Colleen in mind of her Catholic relatives, her grandmother, her aunts, even her mother, who fixate so singularly on other people's bodies and sexual practices that they lose the capacity for rational discussion of anything but "baby-killing."

Looking down, she imagines kicking the blue-suited woman, ramming the pointed toe of her high-heeled shoe between the wool-clad ribs inches from her feet.

It would be so easy.

As with the war protestors, the Capitol Police alert the mock-deceased pro-lifers that they have the right to walk away, or else prepare to be dragged.

Now that the blue-suited woman is supine, Colleen notices that the baby dolls on her skirt are the kind with glass eyes that open and close.

Inert, the protestors opt to be lugged.

As the police slip their leather-gloved hands beneath the protestors' armpits and scud the heels of their shoes softly down the hall, the protestors glow, alight with the ecstasy of righteous martyrdom.

"Will we have to be handcuffed?" asks the woman with the camcorder as she's tugged around the corner at the bank of elevators.

Colleen hears the hope in her voice.

Colleen shuts the glass door adorned with the blue Senate seal decal, and turns to fill out the threat assessment form. Palmira stands with one hand at the small of her back and the other over her belly. She is shorter than usual now that she has to wear flats because her spine aches. Her fingers look puffed, like sausage links.

Like Colleen, Palmira was raised Catholic. Unlike Colleen, she still believes. She wears a small Virgin Mary bracelet, as she has done every day since she started showing.

She looks directly at neither Colleen nor Nia. "What on earth possessed you to let those people in here, Colleen?"

"They let themselves in. The door was open, like it always is, except for Tuesdays. It's Monday."

"I know it's Monday, Colleen. I don't care what day of the week it is. Tell the interns that from now on that door needs to remain shut. Visitors must be buzzed in. It needs to stay that way until I say otherwise, or until I go on maternity leave. That was uncalled for."

"It was," says Colleen, "I agree," and is about to add that it was also sort of hilarious, and that the other protestors must have been jealous of the blue-suited woman, like *Goshdarn, why didn't any of us think to dress up as the Hell-bound Speaker of the House*, but Palmira has stomped away.

They hear her office door slam at the end of the hall.

Nia too started wearing a cross when she found out she was pregnant. As she drops into the chair behind the front desk and picks up the threat assessment form, it taps against her chest.

Colleen clung to religion as long as she could, but by high school it seemed completely made up.

Childish superstition and OCD ritual.

Her grandmother's rosary collection.

Her mother's praying to Saint Anthony to find a parking place. The bumper-sticker comfort her aunts found in the phrase "Let go and let God."

"Don't worry, Colleen," Nia says. "Those people were ridiculous. Nobody could have stopped them."

"Thanks," says Colleen. "You don't have to do that. I can file the report. You should go back to your office in case they come back."

"No, I can fill it out. I hope they do come back and see me," says Nia. "Bunch of psychopaths. You go help Dézi do damage control with the interns so they're not overly traumatized."

C olleen!" Dézi says when Colleen walks into the conference room. "I was just telling them how unusual that kind of disruption is, and how most of the walk-ins will be much less troublesome."

Colleen knows Dézi needs her to concur.

And Colleen wants to believe that these people are the fringe.

Maybe it's just because it's an election year, and they can feel their time of power dwindling, but their anger seems to be swelling. People like them have been showing up more often.

Like maybe an American fascism is becoming the new normal?

But she can hear Walter's voice in her head telling her not to overstate the situation in a ludicrous way.

And she'd never say any of this aloud, certainly not in front of the interns. Nor will she mention her suspicion that everything up to and including the protestors' forcible removal will shortly be available for viewing on the video sharing website whose motto is Broadcast Yourself.

"Totally," says Colleen. "It might get so boring that one day you'll wish we could invite those guys back. Although sometimes when you're doing your phone shift, you might get the sense that you're talking to people who only feel alive when they're hateful and angry."

A few of the interns take this down as a note.

"Speaking of which—Sudha? Can you go up and help with the phones? Nia's there by herself."

Sudha walks out and Andrew walks in, high-fiving her as she passes.

Staffers will be introduced to the new batch of interns throughout the day. Most prefer not to spend too much effort on it. Andrew, though, loves to get the interns to love him through sheer affable cheer. He reminds Colleen of a golden retriever.

"Am I in time for the icebreaker games?" he says. "I was told there would be candy."

"Just in time," Dézi says. "It'll be great if you and Colleen can play with us."

"Can I rejoin you after you've broken the ice?" says Colleen.

Juvenile, these games remind her of high school, when her mother forced her to attend a Catholic youth group on Sunday nights. Dingy beige carpet, faux wood paneling, abstinence-only speakers and scared-straight films in a dank church basement.

"Aw, come on, Colleen, it'll be fun!" says Dézi. "Right guys?" and the interns, eager to please, agree.

"What you need to know," says Andrew, very serious, "is that Colleen is a contrarian. A contrarian is like a librarian but with dismay instead of books."

Dézi passes a package of fruit-flavored, cube-shaped taffies around the table. She has each intern take a couple. Andrew takes a handful. Colleen takes none. Dézi explains.

If they have a red one, they say something fun they did over the weekend.

Orange means they name a pet peeve.

Yellow and pink mean other things, but by now, Colleen's stopped listening.

She looks around the table and wonders how this crew will do.

Whenever they go through a round of intern-hiring, a certain number of applicants are flagged, meaning they have a connection, strong or tenuous, to the Senator's office. Maybe their parents are generous donors or maybe they've interned before in DC.

A former flagged intern herself, Colleen cannot be categorically opposed to this practice.

She remembers talking with the Chief that summer almost ten years ago about how, since her uncle Tom Dugan put in a word for her, her getting the internship was, literally, nepotistic. The Chief had studied Latin decades before at his Catholic high school downstate, and he told her that the root word was *nepos*, meaning *nephew*.

She was obviously a niece, he said, rubbing her back, but you got the idea.

"Being here is so fun, the word should be nepo-*tastic*," she said to make him laugh.

A s the game winds around the conference table, the interns talk with great interest and candor about themselves.

Colleen thinks of an article she ripped from the free trashy newspaper earlier that morning.

The piece had criticized the Berlin Zoo's handling of a polar bear named Knut. A former media darling owing to his being the first baby bear in thirty years to survive being born there, animal experts feared the young-adult Knut had been raised to be a sociopath addicted to human attention.

She had thought of her own pursuit of nude self-portraits.

She had thought of Ethan's "In the Dumps" project.

But now, half-listening to the interns, she wonders: maybe *they* resemble the polar bear?

She and Dézi talk sometimes about how much hand-holding the interns require, how poorly they take criticism, how they expect praise incommensurate with the completion of minor tasks. The phrase *kids these days* pops into Colleen's head as she looks at these kids—who are definitely kids. Eighteen to twenty-two.

Except for one, the one talking now, who must be close to thirty and is saying her name in a Southern accent. Silken and thin, she wears her bottle-blonde hair in a half-ponytail bouffant. "I'm Jennifer Whitlock," she says. "But my friends call me J-Lock, so that's what I hope y'all can call me. I'm originally from Alabama, but I just got my law degree right up the street. Since I've got a little yellow one here, a fun fact you might not know about me is that I used to be a professional cheerleader for the Chicago Bulls. Since I've got a pink one, too, one of my hobbies is to take long walks in the woods. It gives me such a sense of the holiness of creation."

Instant dislike toward Jennifer Whitlock.

Colleen tries to stop herself, but can't.

Jennifer Whitlock tosses a lock of processed hair over her shoulder. She has a baked-on tan and breasts that sit on her chest like snowglobes.

"Thanks, J-Lock," says Dézi.

Colleen stares out the window at the sunlight refracting off the Lake.

"Colleen, you're the last one left—your turn to share."

"I haven't got any candies."

"Just tell us one fun fact about yourself?" says Dézi.

"Okay," she says, "when I'm not working on the Press Team, I do photography. I got my Master of Fine Arts in it."

"Oh my god! I *love* photography," says Jennifer Whitlock. She smiles a smile that shows both rows of teeth, the two in the top front overlapping slightly. "I used to be a model!"

Jennifer Whitlock is pretty, but not supermodel pretty. More like pretty enough to pose for the Sunday circular of a mid-range department store. Colleen can see that she has put a lot of time into making herself look like a generalized concept, that concept being Every Man's Fantasy.

Her beauty is surrounded by air quotes.

O kay," says Dézi, "any questions before we move on?"
      "Actually, yes," says Jennifer Whitlock. "Dézi is such an exotic name!" She is mispronouncing Dézi—saying it like the first name of the famous Cuban-American musician and actor—and Colleen is about to say so when Jennifer Whitlock goes on, "Were your parents really big on *I Love Lucy*, or what?"

"It's a long story," says Dézi.

"We've got time, Dézi," Colleen says, pronouncing it correctly, looking at Jennifer Whitlock. "You should tell it."

Colleen's own name doesn't mean much. Just "girl" in Gaelic, a New World name given as a show of pride for the old. But Dézi's story is fresh and tragic.

"All right," she says. "I was born in Guatemala in 1983. Some of you might know that Guatemala was in a civil war from 1960 until 1996. The longest civil war in Latin America. The whole thing was really bad, but in 1982, the Guatemalan government was taken over by a military dictator."

She tucks a strand of long black hair behind her ear.

"But I'm getting ahead of myself. I was named in honor of my uncle, my mother's younger brother. One summer in the early 80s, he went to work in the States, and he ended up as a ride operator on the boardwalk in Cape May. He had an American girlfriend. She worked in one of the concessions. But at the end of the summer he had to go back to Guatemala. He always wanted to return to New Jersey so they could be together, and when my mom was pregnant, he kept trying to convince her to name the baby, if I was a girl, after this girlfriend. My mom and dad

kept saying no, no, they wanted to give me a traditional name."
The interns have stopped rustling their candy wrappers.
"After the coup in 1982, there were forced disappearances. Most of the people killed were indigenous like my family. Afterwards, the Commission for Historical Clarification found that most of the brutality was perpetrated by the Guatemalan Army. Which, by the way, was trained by the American Army, the Green Berets. When Bill Clinton was president, he said he was sorry for that, but it was kind of too late. A lot of people fled to Mexico—Chiapas, Tabasco—but my family stayed. My uncle was one of the people who went missing."

Like Colleen, Andrew has heard this story before, but he still sniffles—once, at this detail—beside her.

"We're sure he's dead. My parents decided, okay, we'll name her according to his wishes, in his memory. And I guess his girlfriend's name was Daisy, like the flower, but my uncle's English wasn't great and at the time my parents' was non-existent. So they spelled it phonetically, and ended up with D-E-Z-I. I never thought it was strange until we came to Chicago when I was thirteen."

Dézi looks down at her clipboard, then up again.

"So, no, none of us especially love Lucy."

Jennifer Whitlock looks like a robin that's bashed into a clear glass window, if a robin could look less injured, more ashamed.

The other interns take contemplative sips of their beverages.

"Anyway," says Dézi, "I think we can break for lunch. We'll give you an hour and a half today so you can explore the Loop. Thanks, everyone!"

Each day at lunch break, whenever Andrew is not scheduled to appear in court for one of his pro bono cases, he and Colleen take theirs together.

Each day, from the carvery in the basement cafeteria of the

nearby bank building, Andrew buys a roasted half-chicken, skin-colored and glistening.

And each day, Colleen brown-bags it because—it's cheaper and because restaurant portions are vast.

Before he got sent to Iraq, Colleen's dad would walk the three miles between Union Station and his job at the VA Hospital and back. But that thirty miles of weekly walking, he used to say after family dinners, wasn't his most effective exercise. That distinction, he would then demonstrate, went to a simpler action.

"You push both hands firmly against the table, and send your chair and yourself away from your plate."

Yes, Colleen would think, even though she'd seen it a million times.

She still thinks of it every morning when she and Walter pack their lunches.

In his latest email, her dad wrote,

> It is depressing to be here, Colleen. It is so hot, you sweat all the time. You lose weight. I'm back down to what I weighed my senior year in high school.

He's been gone since February of 2007, could be there until February of 2009.

He wrote,

> The bees must be working hard these days. Are the boys at the Legion taking care of the hives? I worry the little guys won't have enough honey for the winter. Speaking of food, the Iraqis make tasty pistachio ice cream. Those of us with the most weight loss have to eat it after lunch every day. A painless cure, I guess.

Colleen hopes and hopes he'll get sent home sooner.

Each day when they return from lunch break, Agnes Lumley asks Andrew what he ate and makes the same joke about how he must have a tapeworm.

Each day, they laugh.

And each day, as they are doing this afternoon, they ride the elevator back up to the thirty-eighth floor, Andrew sucking his fingers clean of chicken oil like a barbarian because he knows it grosses Colleen out.

What he has no way of knowing is that today it turns her stomach in a specific way. A Ryder-sucking-off-the-businessman kind of way.

She opens her mouth to confess the video.

The words after "Andrew" stick behind her teeth.

Instead she says, "I need to grab my mail from the staff mailboxes."

So they return via the intern room. The pit, Andrew calls it. Central and windowless.

The interns are gathered in a raggedy horseshoe around one of the communal computers, and Nia sits in front of it, training them on casework.

"Hey, Andy," says Nia, looking up from the screen. "I was just showing them CapCorr and explaining they'll have to be patient because it's a little buggy. If they have any serious problems, they can check in with you while I'm away, right?"

"Oh yeah, happy to help," says Andrew, and then to the interns, "Our affectionate nickname for the Capitol Correspondence system is CrapCorr."

Colleen reaches into the cubby for the usual packet of letters and manila folders.

"Hold up a sec, Colleen," says Nia. "I just put a live one in there, and I wanna have a teachable moment."

"Be my guest." Colleen passes the stack to Nia, who pages through them.

Andrew and Colleen cross the room to the wall containing the Intern Board, cork-covered with a rickrack border and a layer of construction paper cutouts done in a beach theme, atop which are tacked a layer of fresh instant-film photographs labeled with the interns' names, hometowns, universities, and the staffer to whom they've been assigned.

Colleen sees that the Chief of Staff has done the honors—his way of getting to know the interns. Stand them one by one in front of the American flag, climb atop a leather-covered chair, loom over them with the camera. Holler, firing-squad style, "Ready! Aim!" and pop the flash. A sound technique, Colleen admits—the flattering angle of looking down on your subject, the semi-sneak attack ensuring that faces rarely have that flat mugshot affect. The man has instincts.

"Okay, listen up," Nia says. "'Dear Senator,'" she begins,

> Thank you for forwarding my letter to the Attorney General's office. You indicated they would reply directly. Unfortunately this has not occurred. I would like to say I fully understand that this is a small-potato issue in comparison to the huge complex situations you have on your plate presently. However, a potato is a potato, and this particular potato that is on my plate is actually both monetarily and emotionally destroying my life. This is a no-brainer.

The interns giggle.

Yes, Nia agrees, it's funny. Cases often are.

"Think," she says, "of the problems you or your parents may have encountered in your lives. When in the course of those human events did it ever occur to you to write to your Senator for help in solving them?"

The interns shake their heads. A few say, "Never."

The Chief of Staff wanders in to make a copy, sees Nia's on a roll, lolls up next to Colleen to listen.

"Right. So what you have to remember is these people are desperate, and a lot of them are not sane. They'd be writing to Bozo the Clown if he was still on TV."

She pauses.

"But what you also have to remember is that this correspondence represents the substance of people's lives. Strange as it seems, there is often a chance we can help. We must always be responsive, and we must always be timely."

The Chief picks an object from atop the table—one of those glossy ovoid coin purses that pucker like lips. He puckers it at Colleen. She gives him the side-eye.

"What I'm getting at with this guy," says Nia, "is that if you're a casework intern, or even if you're just on the phones, you need to read carefully and you need to listen. You'd go into CapCorr and look him up and see that, okay, yes, we did send a letter to the Attorney General's office back in May, and we sent him their response telling him he needs to seek legal representation. We can also see he's called almost every week since, and that he doesn't like that answer. We know all this because Colleen and her interns have used the 'Notes' section. From this day forward you need to do that, too, so we can see at a glance what's been done and what hasn't."

The interns nod with what seems to Colleen a strangely winning combination of nervousness and arrogance.

"Some constituents will tell you they were promised the moon, and you can understand why they'd say that. But if our records are thorough, we can know for sure we've taken the right steps. Bottom line: take everyone seriously, and be polite, but don't let yourselves be pushed around. Got it?"

Jennifer Whitlock enters, breathless. "Sorry I'm late, y'all. I had to run to my apartment over lunch and the train was delayed."

"You've missed the whole presentation on constituent services," says Dézi.

"I'm real sorry," says J-Lock, without a hint of apology.

She gawks past Dézi toward the Intern Board.

Her brown eyes alight on the photograph containing her face.

She shuts them, mascaraed lashes battening her lids as if she can't bear to look. "Dear Lord," she says, "I cannot believe y'all would put that thing up!"

She plucks the photo from the board, dashes across the room, and slices the picture into strips with the paper cutter, sharp elbow working the blade like a farmer at a hand-pumped well.

She shivers as she flutters the scraps into the trash and pulls a new photo from her handbag, push-pinning it into the empty space. "There," she announces. "Much better."

Jennifer Whitlock stares at her handiwork.

Everyone else just stares.

The picture, torn from a magazine, the paper cheap and pocked, not glossy.

In it, J-Lock stands against a red backdrop in her cheerleader tank top, clenching a long-haired white lapdog to her chest, pointing the creature's shiny black nose like a revolver, only cuter.

If the room were a social networking page, its mood would be set to "Aghast."

Colleen feels the Chief of Staff tensing next to her and knows he has decided that he can't abide J-Lock.

He picks his photocopy off the machine and stalks away.

Horrified, yet transfixed, Colleen tries for some small talk. "Darling dog," she says. "What's his name?"

"*Her,*" says J-Lock. "It's a girl. Her name is Hillary. Cuz she's feisty!"

This strikes Colleen as wrong in a number of respects—the foremost being that since the Female Presidential Candidate sadly conceded a month ago, the dog's functionality as a trendy accessory is now compromised by its association with a loser.

"Funny," says Colleen. "Is she a Shih Tzu?"

"I beg your pardon," says J-Lock, putting a hand to her tan sternum. "I am a lady, and where I come from, we do not swear. We refer to that particular breed as a Sweet Sue."

9

During her uncontrollable googling of J-Lock that follows, Colleen sees what about the photograph must have set her off.

The left side of her face.

All the pictures in her image search—J-Lock cavorting in a basketball jersey without any pants, J-Lock sporting face paint, J-Lock in a spangled evening gown, J-Lock hugging the canine Hillary and making a face, both their tiny pink tongues sticking out—feature her right, the side she has internalized as her Good Side.

The Chief of Staff took her photo from the left.

Colleen has a good side, too, also her right. She poses for herself and for others with it forward when possible. But she has never had a full-on public freak-out about a photograph of the left.

Colleen does not want to commit woman-on-woman crime by despising J-Lock.

But annoyance rushes at her in waves, like nausea, as she visits the website of the local pro basketball franchise and reads: "The Luvabulls are synonymous with talent and beauty, glamour and glitz, as well as hard work, dedication and commitment."

The pictures—Luvabulls flexing their orange thighs in black vinyl boots, Luvabulls thrusting their well-groomed pelvises in hotpants—make them look synonymous with kitschy self-exploitation.

Ditto the explanation that "Luvabulls must be at least twenty-one years old and have full-time employment or be full-time students. Selections to the group are made based on appearance, personality and dance ability."

Colleen notes that J-Lock hasn't been one of their number since 2002.

In the intervening years, she's taken stabs at careers such as "beauty pageant consultant" (she once held the title of Miss Cotton Princess) and "actress" (in projects which required her to writhe on the hoods of cars in music videos for a rock subgenre that was dated and regressive even when it was in vogue twenty-five years ago).

The back door slams—Steve Moon Collier returning from a two-hour lunch.

Andrew pops out of his cubicle like a prairie dog to greet him. "Have you gotten a load of the interns yet?"

"No," says Steve, setting his briefcase on the overstuffed recliner he keeps in his cube sweet cube. "I'm in no hurry to."

"Oh my God," says Colleen, wheeling herself into the aisle. "Did you read Dézi's email? Miss Crazytrain USA has been assigned to the Press Team."

"What are you talking about?" says Steve, as the Chief of Staff emerges from his office.

"Nice of you to rejoin us today, Collier," says the Chief. "I believe Colleen is referring to our new intern Jennifer Whatsherface, who just hacked up the glamour shot I took of her like an expired credit card. Aren't you, babe?"

"She's beyond obnoxious," says Colleen.

"Colleen's just jealous because she doesn't have yellow hair," says Andrew to Steve.

The Chief of Staff takes this as his cue to put a hand on Colleen's shoulder and sing the first lines of an Irish air he's shared before. "On Raglan Road of an autumn day / I met her and first knew / that her dark hair would weave a snare / that I might one day rue ..."

"She doesn't really have yellow hair either," says Colleen, unable to believe that not even half an hour ago she'd been ready to divulge her secret to Andrew. "I question her long-term viability."

"What?" says Andrew. "She's an attractive girl. If she doesn't like a photograph it's her choice to take it down. It's not like she killed somebody."

"Sure," says Colleen. "But it concerns me that she's obsessed with making sure everybody knows she used to be a professional cheerleader, as opposed to, for example, learning what she'll have to do to work here. I don't want the Press Team associated with that behavior."

"Don't worry, Colleen," says Andrew. "There is no danger that anyone would ever mistake you for a former Luvabull."

Colleen is insulted that he expects her to find this insulting. "Right," she says. "And it's a trade-off, because nobody will ever accurately be able to use the expression 'hot box of crazy' to describe me either."

"A palpable hit, Colleen," says the Chief. "But get in here a minute."

She pushes her chair into her cube and follows the Chief into his office. The lights are off, but afternoon sun washes in through the wall of glass. It is indirect.

"That dress, by the way, is everything a dress could be and more."

"You're looking jaunty yourself," she says. "I think it's the *mouchoir*."

She says it snotty, because that's how he likes it, but the pocket square in his pocket, the pose of it, is perfect. He has a calculated romantic look, glazed with an ever-present mild disdain, but Colleen has learned that this act masks a profound concern.

He looks at her, saying nothing.

She looks around the room, at the tacky trophy on a fake marble base for Park District summer softball—"2nd Place in

League, 2007"—and at his heavy wooden desk, big as a bed. Atop this desk rests the metal skewer he uses to keep track of pink paper message slips, run through like roast pigs on a pike. He reaches to remove the topmost.

"The Pipefitters finally gave us a time to meet about this Lake business," he says. "Call and tell them this Friday at ten is fine."

"Okay. I'm with you. But won't that be a press conference time slot?"

"Always on top of it, you," he says. "But not this Friday. I talked to Gina, and she's booked the Duke some studio to make radio ads. We're keeping it simple and sticking close to home since Nia's the driver and she's ready to pop."

"As medical doctors like to put it."

Palmira said months ago that pregnant women could remove themselves from the driving pool at their earliest discretion, then immediately proceeded to do so. But Nia insisted she was "knocked up, not handicapped," and would keep her name in until the bitter end.

"I'm going to be in the campaign office for the next few days," the Chief says, "but Friday morning we'll meet up here, and I'll drive us over to the union. Be sure to wear something nice."

"Thanks for the free advice," she says.

She stands to take the pink slip from his hand, which he does not stretch out, so that she has to come close to grab it.

"While I'm at it, Colleen, don't let the cheerleader bring you down," he says. "And don't let Andy drool over her too much."

"Right. Got it. Brother's keeper."

B ut Andrew does not feel like her brother, exactly.
     On the Senate-sealed wrist-rest in front of the keyboard in her cube sits an index card with a pearl-topped stickpin woven in and out. Above the stickpin, Andrew has written in his curly,

feminine hand, "This pin is for Colleen because she likes pretty things."

Below it, "Had to run to court, see you later—leave at 5:00 and bike together?"

White as snow, the top of the pushpin reminds her of Iowa in December.

Andrew and Colleen went there ahead of the caucuses to canvass for the Junior Senator.

The man they really wanted to go for—the peacenik from Ohio who had a beautiful English wife and an admitted belief in UFOs and who followed a vegan diet, a practice perhaps stranger to most voters than extraterrestrials—had no real presence in the state and was unelectable. They'd heard on the radio that only a teensy sliver of Iowans voted in the caucuses anyway, mostly because of the time commitment and the evening schedule. They couldn't get away from their jobs or afford childcare.

Andrew and Colleen could only go on the weekend themselves—they'd have to use vacation or comp time, otherwise—and Colleen had arranged for them to spend the last Sunday night of 2007 in an apartment in Ames, at the dull center of the state. The apartment was being rented by a grad-school friend of Colleen's, Janka, now a photojournalist covering the presidential race for an East Coast newspaper.

When Colleen called her up to see if they could crash, Janka said fine, she wouldn't even be there. She'd been assigned a Republican event on the Nebraska border.

"It's a firetrap shitbox," Janka had said. "Freezing cold. That's what you get for $250 a month, even in Iowa. Dress in layers and bring sleeping bags because I don't have a bed. It's all so temporary, it's not worth furnishing."

In the days leading up to the trip, despite being in the same office only cubicles apart, Colleen and Andrew chatted online about their plans. If they talked out loud, Steve Moon Collier would want to join them.

> **Andrew:** we can have ever so much fun! you bring the cookies and i will bring my ipod. you bring the water and i will bring the conversation topics. you bring the ____ and i will bring the maps. i couldn't think of a third one.
>
> **Colleen:** I'll bring some conversation topics too. and my camera (duh). have you mapped the way to ames?
>
> **Andrew:** i am doing it now 5.5 hours it says.
>
> **Colleen:** so we should leave by 6am. they are going to be so excited to have us!
>
> **Andrew:** 6 am is early but we can so handle it
>
> **Colleen:** it is exciting
>
> **Andrew:** our excitement will keep us going. rock out with your caucus out!!!
>
> **Colleen:** I get it. It's funny cuz it's sexual.

They both sat low in his black two-door, so compact that even with the seat back as far as it could go, Andrew had the steering wheel practically between his knees.

From Lake Shore Drive they took Lower Wacker, the city below the city, making excellent time on their way out of town. Andrew had two huge cups of coffee from a 24-hour donut shop in the cupholders and an album about feeling the Illinoise on the stereo, and they were well along I-88 when the Pulaski Day song came on, the one about her favorite Illinois holiday, in honor of the father of the American Cavalry.

The Senator was forever trying to pass a Congressional resolution granting the man posthumous American citizenship. He was forever being blocked by Republicans, not because they believed the Polish national did not deserve a reward for his sacrifice—"He got shot in the balls for democracy for Chrissakes!" as the Chief of Staff says—but because they hated the Senator.

A mysterious fog was rolling over the highway, pouring up from the ditches like a dry-ice special effect. Andrew kept flicking his headlights to see which setting was best. Colleen mentioned the suburban legend she'd heard growing up about how you weren't ever supposed to courtesy-flash anybody with their highbeams on or with their lights off entirely, because those cars were driven by gang bangers doing an initiation that required them to kill the first motorist who did so.

"The moral of that legend is that suburban people are dumb," said Andrew.

They stopped at the ominously named Bloody Gulch Road, at a gas station owned by the Rapacious British Oil Company which would eventually become the principal villain in Colleen's professional life.

They listened to a podcast about an Alabama woman's refusal in 1955—the same year as the Mississippi murder of a black boy from Chicago—to move to the back of the bus, and how these days racism was just as evil, but more amoebic and vaporous.

What to do?

Snow sanded the trees at the roadside like those lattice cookies dusted with powdered sugar. Flat and white, it was hard to spot the horizon line where the sky began and the ground ended, as if someone had penciled it in, then smudged it out.

They arrived in Story County, which would be their home for the next 24 hours.

Before they reported to the Ames headquarters for the Junior Senator from Illinois, they decided, per a tip from Janka, to swing by the Giggling Goat in Boone to watch a campaign stop by the boyish Southern Populist with the burnished hair and the smooth drawl and the message that the two Americas—one rich, one poor—had to be united, and also the cancer-stricken wife, on whom it would be revealed within the year he had been cheating.

The staffers at sign-in assumed they were media, because Andrew and Colleen—thin, young, stylishly dressed, and, in Colleen's case, toting a professional-quality camera—did not look From Around Here. A DC guy in a suit said to Andrew,

"Full house, huh. We've stopped doing hard counts anymore—no point. We do know we had 100 RSVPs for today, but at least 160 people are here. Been like that everywhere."

"Awesome," Andrew said, thumbs up, "but we're not press. We're just here to watch."

Shunted toward the front right of the stage beneath an enormous American flag, they waited in a crowd of mostly older people, all of them white. They guessed the Goat must be a dance hall normally by the icicle lights and the hardwood floor. A perky blonde walked the aisles, handing out signs bearing the slogan Tomorrow Begins Today.

"We can't hold these," said Colleen, after the woman had passed. "We're not here for this guy."

"Right," said Andrew. "But we want to be on TV to prove we were here."

"But I'm going to take a million pictures to prove we were here."

"You don't understand anything about how to be famous, Colleen."

A local luminary, the first female candidate for governor in Iowa—unsuccessful, Iowa being one of twenty-seven states which had never had a female governor—took to the stage to warm up the crowd for "the man who will be the next President of the USA!"

The throng outside began hooting. This let everyone inside know he was walking by.

Diesel fumes from the campaign bus and cries of "Go, John, go!" drifted from the wide-flung side door.

His cancer-stricken wife entered, looking pretty—so fresh even from off the bus, as all the ladies in the vicinity noted to Colleen.

Wearing tight sweatpants and a Navy blue cardigan, the cancer-stricken wife marched to the mic to the strains of a song that proclaimed her an American Girl.

Colleen felt stiff and road-weary, in need of yoga and coffee and non-preservative-laden food, and she and Andrew had only been traveling for half a day. She didn't know how the campaigners managed it—it had to be exhausting. Then again, she wanted to be exhausted. She felt slightly jealous of the cancer-stricken wife who got to live her days with such purity of purpose, to focus all her endurance on a cause for which she was prepared to let go her life.

Then the Southern Populist himself was striding up the aisle, like a pro wrestler on his way to the ring, stopping at every other person for a handshake and a hug, wearing the round-cheeked grin of a man who believed his own bullshit.

Janka worked the room.

She took a picture of Colleen and Andrew—shiny-eyed and simply composed, like a propaganda poster—against the enormous flag ("For my blog," she said, grinning) then made her way back to the center to snap a shot of a singer, formerly known as "Cougar," singing "Our Country," as the candidate's little kids trotted back to the bus, dismissed to play video games while their parents gave speeches.

Colleen took pictures from where she stood. Self-conscious, conspicuous. Not part of the press corps. Envious that Janka was.

The Southern Populist's eldest daughter, twenty-something and wearing a red sweater, stayed and sat at her father's side.

Andrew kept trying to get Colleen to take her picture—an average-sized girl with brown hair polished and sleek as the grain of expensive wood.

This irritated Colleen, but she reminded herself—as she did when the Chief of Staff fawned over another woman—that it was none of her business to care. She had Walter.

"Think that's her boyfriend?" Andrew said, elbowing Colleen and pointing with his chin at the back of the glossy head of the young dude next to the daughter.

The Southern Populist began speaking before Colleen could answer.

The photographers mobbed like they were pigeons at his feet and he was throwing them popcorn.

The Southern Populist talked about CEOs making hundreds of millions of dollars in profits, how it was anti-American to concentrate wealth into the hands of a few.

The Southern Populist overused the word "literally."

Then the Southern Populist concluded, "Enough is enough!" and a clutch of photographers riffled through the aisle like a lump in a cartoon pipe.

An older lady to Colleen's right said, "Ain't there more cameras here than you seen in your whole life?"

Colleen fantasized about what life might be like if she were one of their number.

"Gotta dash," said Janka, "Following their bus. But here's the key. Put it under the flower pot by the front door when you leave, okay?"

B ack in Andrew's car, a man's voice on the radio started a local commercial with, "God is great, but sometimes life ain't."

They headed to the Ames headquarters for the Junior Senator from Illinois, in the basement of a building—metal and black glass—that looked like it was new in the early '80s.

Back when I was new, thought Colleen.

Beneath the darkened suites of dentists and eye doctors, the headquarters buzzed with harried young people. A nasal girl from New England printed their list of households from the neighborhoods they'd be canvassing, plus brochures to give to undecideds. Canvassing for the caucuses sounded as though it wouldn't be as thorny as for the actual election. The people on the lists were all registered Ds, so she and Andrew could assume a baseline of shared beliefs—as opposed to knocking on all doors, which meant likelier confrontations with racism, sexism, and fanatic free marketeerism.

In the first neighborhood, Colleen suggested that she and Andrew each take one side of the street, then meet at the end for the sake of efficiency. But Andrew said it was too dangerous for her to go by herself. "Just because Iowa appears wholesome and bucolic doesn't mean they don't have perverts, Colleen," he said.

More importantly, he would get too bored alone.

They stuck together, crossing off each neighborhood as they completed it, then driving to the next. They arrived at a snowy cul-de-sac, and Colleen observed that she'd learned at an outreach meeting that people who live on circles are an average of six pounds fatter than those who live on through streets. The cul-de-sac-y neighborhood was full of cute single-family homes—somewhere between suburban bland and those build-your-own ceramic towns people decorate with at the holidays.

It almost made her want to own a home.

Here she could probably come close to affording one someday.

The only drawback being—she'd be in Iowa. Andrew moved with goofy grace along the shoveled sidewalks.

Watching him work, easy and glad-handing, she remembered how, the other week, she and Walter had driven past the university in Evanston. As they passed fraternity row, she had mentioned that Andrew had gone there, and had been in one of those frats. "That must be where his insincere sincerity comes from," Walt had said.

"Go slower," said Andrew, when she walked at her normal pace. "We can't all be so quick and light, especially those of us with powerful, meaty haunches."

"Get a longer stride," she said. "Come on. Change we can believe in!"

Asking strangers who stood stocking-footed in their foyers, "Do you already know how you're voting?" and "Can you tell me who for?" had to be finessed. It felt like asking "What's your religion, and why did you pick that one?" or "How much money do you make?" or "What do you like to do when you have sex?"

They reported back to headquarters around five as the white sky faded to blue-gray, then black. The campaign worker from New England had been replaced by a kid with a beaky nose who handed them tickets to a rally for the Junior Senator being held in Des Moines that night.

"We've got the gol-den tick-ets!" Andrew sang, in the style of a classic film about a boy's visit to a chocolate factory, as he drove them to the edge of Ames where Janka's apartment complex slouched, squalid, on a dead-end road.

The interior contained a sprinkling of items for barely one person. Toothbrush, washcloth, phone charger, secondhand desk. It was deathly cold. They threw their sleeping bags on the dingy tan carpet and got back on the road for the rally.

The event was billed as Stand for Change, but the staffers commanded them to sit for it. The latest arrivals had to crouch on the puddly gym floor, avoiding melting boot-snow.

Compared to the Southern Populist's event that morning, the music was less nostalgic, and the attendees took up more space, threw more elbows.

Klieg lights everywhere.

A cranky woman in a sparkle-snowflake sweater and a purple beret sitting on the lowest riser of the bleachers made Andrew and Colleen pinkie-swear they'd stay seated when the Junior Senator took the stage so they wouldn't wreck her view.

"Obviously, we need this guy to win," said Andrew, "but let the record reflect I'm sick of all this superstar bullshit. Why does everyone here have to be in *love* with their candidate?"

Colleen zoned out, studying the multitude, diverse in gender, age, and race.

Lots of people looked, like she and Andrew did, as though maybe they were not from around here. The press was not permitted to roam the room as they had been that morning, but were confined to two banks of risers at the free-throw line. The gym was hot and highly secure. Colleen wondered how the hard-faced Secret Service agents lining the perimeter had resolved that, yes, they would definitely take a bullet for the Junior Senator.

She took pictures of their stony profiles.

Then, the din in the gym grew deafening, and everyone's camera flashed at once.

"Quick—get a picture of us together!" Andrew said, leaning back so the Junior Senator, behind the podium, was distantly next to him, over his shoulder. Through the viewfinder, Colleen could see that even the Junior Senator's details—his collar, his cuffs, the conspicuous absence of an American flag pin—seemed to have details. His nails were buffed.

Chic and willowy, the Junior Senator waited a long while for the cheers to die. Colleen felt like she was in a tunnel with the wind rushing around her as the noise subsided.

When he was able to speak, he did so calmly, making a few light jokes, nothing too funny. As always, his messaging was flawless as he cited the Fierce Urgency of Now. Like the Southern Populist, he told a few stories about the people he'd met on the campaign trail, like the girl from his hometown of Chicago, in college full-time with a sister who suffered from cerebral palsy who she managed to take care of and still earn straight A's, all while surviving on three hours of sleep per night.

"I don't believe that story," said Andrew.

Colleen pretended she didn't hear him.

Plenty of people had implausibly difficult lives.

She wanted to believe that the Junior Senator would help that girl, would help her, too, would help everyone in the gym.

Would and could help all of them, everywhere.

When it was over, the crowd rushed from the gym, and the icy air refreshed Colleen's flushed face.

The day had been like attending a music festival. The Boone stage, the Ames stage, the Des Moines stage, the concessions. It was still early, 9:30, and neither Colleen nor Andrew were in a hurry to retire to Janka's.

They decided to find a bar, ended up drinking at a pizzeria billing itself as "Chicago-style."

The room was ringed with TVs broadcasting sporting events, interrupted by caucus commercials, mostly of the spiteful attack variety.

Andrew ordered a whiskey and a beer because "Why not get a little lit? This fucking place. Chicago-style? Even Iowa doesn't want to be in Iowa."

Andrew prided himself on his amiability, but sometimes a darker mood brooded. Colleen liked to look through the cracks between the two and wonder what caused the contrast.

"I am ninety-nine percent open," Andrew had told her once when she asked about these gaps in his temperament. "But I am one percent secrecy."

The waitress botched Colleen's order, bringing her the wrong beer, and she was about to take it back to the bar and dump it, but Andrew stopped her. "I can drink the mistake," he said.

"Cheers," said Colleen.

They locked eyes and smashed their glasses together.

When they were ready to leave, Colleen was not drunk. She pointed this out and got the keys from Andrew.

The snow on the ground echoed the starlight as she drove the flat, straight highway, then the curvy residential streets to Janka's. Andrew sang along to the bubblegum on the radio, making up the words he didn't know to an emotional ballad by a Canadian singer whose name meant April in French. "I'm standin' at the bridge / I'm laughin' at the rain / I'm wondering whyyy you're dummmmb."

"Don't make me laugh so hard," said Colleen. "I'll crash your car and kill us both."

"Scientists have discovered that one hundred percent of human lives conclude in death," he said, then kept singing.

Back at Janka's, Colleen put on the pajamas she had packed: gray flannel pants with black leopard print and a satin ribbon at the waist that had seemed campy when she stuck them in her overnight bag, but which now seemed illogical, and a long-sleeved black T-shirt that said in faded silkscreen that in 1998, her senior year of high school, Colleen had been a double state champion in speech and debate.

"Oh my God, Andrew. Don't look at me," she said when she came out of the bathroom after brushing her teeth.

He had already changed, too.

She'd taken out her contacts, so the lines of his face looked imprecise, like a photo taken in a dim room with no flash, but she could see his teeth as he started to laugh.

"I know," she said. "This outfit makes no sense. And I have hat hair."

"I like a girl who's a little bit vain," he said.

His voice was slurred, like he'd gotten drunker, or like he was laying the groundwork for excuses he might need later. He moved his hand to ruffle her hair, then changed his mind and sort of smoothed it down and tucked it behind her ear.

As his fingers moved down her jaw she tried to think of anything to say back, but then she didn't have to, because they were making out. Standing up, then down, on the sleeping bag, then in it.

His breath smelled like wintergreen toothpaste, and under that, whiskey.

He hadn't shaved that morning and his chin prickled.

It was so cold they wriggled out of their clothes under the covers, and it occurred to Colleen that in the zippered bag they must look like creatures—something precious, she pictured kittens—grappling in a trap.

She snickered, and he asked what was so funny, and looked hurt.

"Nothing," she said.

She thought of Walter again—was thinking of him in a low-grade, back-of-the-mind way the whole time—and felt sad.

"Don't go away," Andrew said.

He got up, began pulling items out of his messenger bag, casting them aside, airplane pens, mittens his mom had knitted, the Compact Latin Dictionary he always carried.

Finally he found his wallet, and in it the condoms.

Andrew was big, rough-and-tumble, and he was not too drunk to make it last a decent duration, and they both got off.

And when they were done, Colleen felt sincerely what-the-fuck about it.

She had never cheated on Walter. Had not had sex with anybody else since before they moved in together, back when it wasn't clear how exclusive they were being.

She certainly had never intended to sleep with Andrew that weekend.

If anything, she'd expected that she'd have to reject him once and for all—had been steeling herself for it since they began planning the trip, had been idly plotting how to put him off, had even rehearsed her refusals.

She was now mildly surprised that she hadn't used any of them.

Outwardly untroubled, Andrew told her she was athletic, then modified "and pretty," then fell immediately asleep, his gold hair pointing in the silver moonlight.

So bright in the country, thought Colleen.

She pried his arms away and got up to pull down the crumply mini-blinds.

She wanted the room darker, totally dark.

Then she crawled into her own sleeping bag and lay awake, curled away from him, eyes open for a very long time.

~

None of us can say why Colleen did this.

Then again, neither do we recall why we did the many regrettable things we did in life.

It is likely that we did not know this even at the time.

Why did we dally with French whores who gave us the pox? Why did we father children by our slaves, then decline to free them? Why did we drop the second bomb on the second city, when the first had proved itself more than sufficient? Why did we enlist men to break into the opposition's headquarters, though we should have known that we were all but certain to be caught and that the election was already in the bag?

There is, perhaps, a shadow cast by the desire for a more perfect union.

The desire for any perfection at all.

Which is an unwillingness to be satisfied.

~

The next morning the light was weak and watery, the apartment so chilly they could see their breath. Colleen showered, even though she had to use Janka's towel, which she was sure was filthy, since washing would make her feel marginally better.

When she came out, Andrew was helping himself to the dregs of a graham cracker cereal directly from the box. The only bowl and the single utensil sat in the sink, where it looked like they might have rested for weeks. A rust corona encircled the spoon.

"Graham?" said Andrew, proffering the cardboard box.

"No thank you," said Colleen. "We can get some coffee on the way out of town, right?"

"For you, Colleen? Anything," he said.

He stuffed another handful into his mouth.

"So," he said. "Like, last night."

"I don't want to talk about it," said Colleen. "I mean, it was awesome and all, aside from the fact that I live with someone, but I think it should never have happened, and that we should try to pretend that it didn't, and sort of never talk about it again."

"But I thought—"

"Don't think about it. Are you ready? Let's go. It's supposed to snow—maybe we can beat it."

She could picture him crying then, and imagine reasons that he might.

Andrew put the empty box in Janka's cabinet where he'd found it and slammed the door, but he didn't try to say anything more.

They spent the better part of the last day of 2007 together in his car, very close but not touching.

The snowstorm accosted them at the Illinois border.

From Mile Marker One on they had to remain in the slow right lane, because the left was unplowed, and both were treacherous.

At Dixon they saw the first car of the day—a blue one whose

slogan said it was built like a rock—glide into the ditch below the sign denoting the museum for the Fortieth President.

Slithering into the snowbank, the car reminded Colleen of the time her mom and dad had taken her and her younger sister Bridget to a touring ice skating show, and the skaters had been dressed as cartoon creatures who were three apples high and blue.

They passed a flock of sheep in the snow, difficult to see because of the snow.

Colleen looked at Andrew's profile.

She turned the podcast down, then off, so he could concentrate. He was biting the nails of his left hand and steering with his right, staying cautious as other cars whizzed by. Colleen was grateful for his positivity, for his saying, "Whatever. Screw those guys. We don't need to hurry," and when a few more of those cars slid into the ditch, for saying, "We're gonna make it."

More than his patience, though, she appreciated that the snow gave them something to think about besides whatever else they might have been thinking about.

At least we probably won't die, Colleen thought.

Though maybe we should.

She imagined perishing in a massive car pile-up, crunched bumper bashed into crunched bumper like grisly dominoes.

Walter would be sad to lose her, sure, but then she wouldn't have to worry about keeping any secrets, and he'd probably end up meeting someone less selfish, with more willpower.

"The snowflakes are falling like rabbit fur," said Colleen.

"The sadness is falling like a lead piano," said Andrew.

They fell mostly quiet for the rest of the trip.

For a while after that, the awkwardness—at work, at home—the weird mixture of sadness-plus-comedy in the improbable way that she never confessed to Walter and never spoke to Andrew about it again, made Colleen think her life lately had felt like an independent movie.

Not one she'd necessarily want to see.

Not one she'd necessarily pay money for.

She and Andrew unlock their bikes from the metal fence at the base of the Federal Building. The air is gauzy, hot. They've been talking about the anti-abortion protestors.

Andrew is always faster, stowing his lock and reattaching his front wheel before she has a chance to undo both her U-Lock and the chain one.

She's wrapping the latter around the crossbar when the Chief comes up behind her and palms her helmet. He never wears one.

"She's on her bike," he says, "and I couldn't be more in love. Ride safe, you two."

He walks to the opposite side of the fence to get on his own bike and ride away, spruce in the same suit he's been wearing all day. He looks like an archival advertisement for an upscale men's clothier.

"Anyway," Colleen says. "I don't know why they get so hung up on making sure everybody else has as many children as possible. I don't want any kids ever."

"What about Walter?" Andrew says.

"He's right there with me," she says.

"Okay," he says, "but what if it was an accident? Even the best goalies in the world let one slip by every once in a while."

He pulls ahead, around the building, and onto the street.

At the first stoplight, Andrew says, "I want them some day. Kids."

"I don't think I'll ever be ready," says Colleen, "Whatever that means. I'm still immature enough to snort when my horoscope tells me 'Uranus is urging you to go crazy.' I cannot fathom being responsible for another human life."

"Immature people reproduce themselves all the time, Colleen," he says as the signal changes.

At the longest light before the Lake Shore path, Colleen shares a fun fact she learned last fall when she visited her sister in Philadelphia, where she's studying to be a physical therapist.

She and Bridget had gone to a museum of medical oddities. "Andrew, did you know that the birth canal of an average human female pelvis has a thirteen-centimeter diameter, while the average fetal head is ten centimeters, so there's almost no room for variation? Babies slash up your lady-bits."

Andrew is watching the light, inching into the crosswalk. Colleen does the same.

"Colleen, you're being gross and insane," says Andrew as the light changes again.

"When I learn things like that," says Colleen, "I'm not sure it's me who's crazy."

On the path, she changes the subject.

North of Wacker, near where the Chief of Staff lives, they pass a shining silver-blue building that soars above the river. Its spire in the clouds gives it the appearance of a mythic creature, a unicorn maybe.

She knows the answer, but says to Andrew, "What's that building?"

He tells her it's the new tower that a self-aggrandizing New York developer and reality TV star built and named after himself.

"It looks like a narwhal," she says.

"That's what it's designed after. He had one as a pet when he was a child."

They round a dramatic curve in the path where the Lake cuts in, and Colleen can't resist looking back.

The hot air balloon stationed for rides near Navy Pier has a helicopter hovering behind it, and in her backward glance, it looks to Colleen like it might fly right into the balloon, a scary airborne fertilization.

They keep biking north, talking as they go.

The sun hits that point where, after it's been slipping slowly, it sinks out of view suddenly, like an egg dropped in boiling water.

It's gone behind the buildings, and now Andrew's going too, through the underpass toward Lakeview, his neighborhood, raising a hand to his helmet and saluting farewell, and Colleen's left by herself, miles to go before Edgewater, keeping one eye on the path and the other on the last, best part of the sunset, the shreddy orange clouds traffic-coning the sky.

10

Two of Colleen's favorite words are "Let's go," and on Friday morning, the Chief of Staff says them, pushing the door of his convertible open for her.

His auto's brand name means the People's Car, and he uses it to cruise around in furtherance of the People's Work. The top is up. "Don't want you to get a sunburn, babe," he says.

She can't see his eyes behind his shades, but she knows they rake her up and down. The air inside is cool. He squeezes her left thigh above the knee as she buckles her seat belt, and it is like a reflex test in reverse.

She is not supposed to kick.

A dead female country and western singer croons from the stereo.

Crazy, she says.

Colleen considers for the infinity-th time whether or not she is crazy for putting up with the Chief of Staff.

At the Fourth of July parades, Ethan had been floored by what he regarded as the Chief's unambiguous harassment. Sure, Colleen said, she could see how it might look that way. But to her it felt more sporting. "A distasteful but still mesmerizing competition," she had said, "like boxing."

Driving them home from the parades, Walter observed that the Chief's behavior had been going on for so long—years—that it was obviously an end in itself. Far from moving sexward, his flirting is a surrogate, outrageous but chaste.

"Everybody knows that the people who talk about it the most

do it the least," Walt said, and Ethan had said, "I see," in a voice that made it clear he didn't really.

Over the River and over the Expressway, on their way to the Pipe Fitters Association to discuss the actions of the Rapacious British Oil Company, Colleen reminds herself that it's not strictly about *her*, per se, this attention the Chief pays.

Weeknights in bed, she and Walter read before they fall asleep.

Before Walter falls asleep, rather, since Colleen's insomnia refuses to let her.

She lies next to Walter, who snores slightly despite the nose strip that, its brand name explains, is supposed to help him breathe right.

Colleen has been reading an old French novel. Last night she came to a passage where the narrator said, "It is not a woman I want—it is all women. And I seek for them in those around me, one by one."

That is what the Chief of Staff is like, she'd thought.

She read the lines aloud to Walter's sleeping back.

S he wants this, too.

Not all women, but the seeking.

The experience of more than one life.

Everything, everywhere, all the time.

The way she dreamed she could have when she was young.

The way kids like her from the middle of the middle of the fucking middle class are raised to believe. That you can be and do and have anything you put your mind to.

Which, of course, is not true.

Eventually, sooner than you think, you stop becoming and find you've become.

She feels naive for thinking it could be otherwise.

Feels herself weighing decisions—politics? or photography?—

but without the faith she once had in her general fortunes rising stratospherically through sheer ambition and hard work.

Maybe they will, but if they do, it will be as attributable to luck as to ability.

Meritocracy, schmeritocracy. At best it's an arbitraritocracy.

Where the attributes that you think matter—the noble ones you strive to cultivate—matter less than where you started in the first place and who likes or dislikes you.

For reasons largely outside your control.

The Chief of Staff is wearing one of the ties in which Colleen thinks he looks best, wide swaths in muted tones of pink and white and gray. They put her in mind of Neapolitan ice cream, if Neapolitan ice cream contained a gray stripe.

She reaches into a zippered pocket in her purse to confirm that the jump drive with the Ryder blowjob video is still safely inside.

"Penny for your thoughts, Princess," he says. "You're quiet today."

"Where are the pipefitters at, exactly?" she says.

"Across from Union Park, over on the Near West Side."

"So Union Park isn't just a clever name," says Colleen.

"Not evidently."

Before long, they're buzzing in to the headquarters—low orange bricks, tall American flag, a sign saying Pipefitters Union in black block letters with the word *Local* and the number squiggled below in blue script.

Not retro, just old.

The business manager greets them, shaking their hands and boasting as he does that they represent not just pipefitters, but sprinkler fitters, welders, and HVACers, that they have an apprenticeship program, that they've gone eighty years without a strike. He ushers them into a glass-walled conference room and seats them around a rectangular table with other men who resemble him—pinky rings and slapdash haircuts and synthetic suits in impetuous patterns.

The American labor movement and the eight-hour workday are convincing to Colleen.

The struggle against injustice!

The fight to end the exploitation of less powerful people at the hands of more powerful people!

She maintains an admiring familiarity with their Chicago history.

The Hull House Riot. Bug House Square.

The Illinois and Michigan Canal.

Haymarket.

But often, the union guys she meets strike her as thuggy thugs, smaller bullies in the face of larger ones. Her heart is on labor's side, but she's not sure how labor feels about her. This, she figures, is part of why Steve Moon Collier likes working with them. His style of doing business is to treat the bureaucracy of which he is part as a kind of thugdom by other means. He knows he gains power by his ability to say no, to obstruct.

He knows if he says yes and things go smoothly, he becomes invisible.

As it is, Colleen is the one who has become invisible upon crossing the conference room threshold.

Some people simply consider her a waste of their time because she hasn't got a dick. These people can be of either gender. The new intern, for instance—Jennifer Whitlock—is much more eager to get to know Andrew than she is Colleen.

This is because Colleen can never be her boyfriend.

Colleen feels like a spectator at a tennis match, the business manager whacking a statement at the Chief of Staff, the Chief lobbing it back.

"The discharge amounts allowed under the oil company's new permit are at or below federal guidelines," the business manager says.

"But public outcry says that's no longer acceptable," says the Chief. "Dumping fifty-four percent more ammonia into the Lake every day is not going to fly."

"The creation of eighty new jobs, plenty of them for our guys, is," says the man with a salt-and-pepper brush-cut seated at the business manager's right. "Indiana state law trumps anti-pollution rules if a company offers economic benefits. That's what we're looking at."

"A lot of people," says the Chief, "the Senator included, think eighty jobs is not worth thirty-five percent more sludge crudding up the city's drinking water. The House just voted 387–26 to approve a resolution urging Indiana to reconsider the permit. The Senator's working on the EPA to put the permit on hold while we get the company to consider additional upgrades to make a cleaner plant. That could mean even more jobs, and a safer Lake."

"Listen," says the business manager, setting his hand on the table so hard his wedding band clacks. "The Senator's been a friend to us in the past. I wanna keep this cordial. But to put it bluntly, people can go crying like little girls to the EPA all they want—"

Here Colleen kicks the Chief of Staff's Oxford under the table, and they make sidelong eye contact.

"—but that doesn't change the fact that the oil company is within the law. In this economy, if they want to make more jobs for our guys, we're not going to be happy with people who get in the way of that."

"We're not saying you can't have jobs," says the Chief. "What we're saying is that maybe it's possible to have both: more jobs and a safe Lake."

Colleen watches the Chief, comparing him to the other men. He dresses to kill, and back at the office he hums with an unseen nervous energy, but his public manner is unfrilled and nimble in its economy. No movements wasted.

The debate tapers.

"May I add something?" she says.

Everyone, including the Chief, looks surprised she has spoken, but the business manager says, "Sure thing, sweetheart."

"When I was in high school," Colleen says, "two of our history teachers, this husband and wife, took us to see important labor sites here in the city. One of the places they took us was the old gate to the Union Stock Yards. They read to us from *The Jungle*—slaughterhouse workers falling into rendering vats, getting ground up and sold with the sausage. So I appreciate what you guys, what unions, were founded to do."

A couple of pipefitters shift in their seats, slacks rustling against the vinyl cushions.

"But after the gate, they had the driver take the bus over to the Thirty-Fifth Street Bridge. You know, the South Fork of the South Branch. Bubbly Creek. They told us how at the height of the stockyards, they ran 500,000 gallons of river water a day through to clean them up, but that it all washed right back into the River. I threw a rock in and it bubbled up black. You guys must know this, too. That's why they reversed the Chicago River in 1900, to keep the slurry and the sewage from running all the way into Lake Michigan and poisoning the drinking water, even though the River was already wrecked."

She pauses.

"Now the city's spending millions of dollars trying to restore it. What our teachers were trying to show us was that workers shouldn't suffer, but neither should the environment. It seems kind of sad that over a hundred years later, we still haven't realized that we shouldn't treat our waterways like open sewers, and we're still letting industry force us into these false alternatives. Doesn't it?"

Colleen's hands are shaking.

She rests them under the table in her lap.

She has never spoken like this in a meeting.

"Miss—" the business manager says, studying the card she handed him on the way in. "Dugan. You got a good grasp of history. But your grasp of how the world really works is gonna have to improve."

Colleen wants to tell the business manager to stick it in his ass.

Instead, she decides she will send some information to the email address on his card. About an alliance, recently founded, between blue-collar industrial organizations and environmental ones.

And before she can decide how to reply, the Chief of Staff is standing up.

He is saying, "Okay, well, thanks for having us, and we'll be in touch."

Colleen is following his lead.

"But it does seem," the Chief says, getting the last word in as he shakes the business manager's hand, "that the best way to clean up the Lake is to not keep dumping more crap into it in the first place."

W hat the hell got into you, Dugan?" the Chief says as they get back into his convertible.

It's another hot day, windless this far inland, and she scrunches her nose at the hanging smell of exhaust.

"I couldn't listen to it anymore," says Colleen. "Sorry if I was out of line."

"No—you're cute when you're mad. Besides that, you're right. And they'll come around," he says, fumbling with his phone. "Their continued existence depends on it. Green jobs and all that. For now, they've just gotta flex. But what really fries my ass—"

Colleen gets ready to add that what really fries hers is how it seems that people haven't learned anything, *anything* from their past mistakes, when, phone to his ear, he says, "Shit."

"What?"

"Gina's voicemail. The Senator is on his way to the hospital."

Colleen's stomach clenches. A woozy, skydiving feeling. She tightens her grip on the door handle.

"What happened to him?" she says. "Or maybe ... it's Dorothy?"

"Goddammit, she didn't say."

The Chief is calling Gina, driving one-handed, weaving in and out of traffic. Colleen feels herself going pale with concern, with a vivid awareness of how much her and her colleagues' livelihoods all depend on the health and safety of one fierce, avuncular, slightly roly-poly man.

At the same time, the beginnings of a thrill creep at the edges of her dread.

For once, something is different, something is happening.

The Chief of Staff gets Gina on the first ring.

Colleen takes off her sunglasses and watches his face. It takes thirty seconds but feels like forever.

"We're on our way. See you back at the ranch."

He hangs up, puts both hands on the wheel. "It's Nia," he says. "*Nia* needed the hospital. The Senator's fine, and so's she, but she had the damn baby."

"Excuse me?" says Colleen.

"Nia picked him up from O'Hare this morning and was bringing him straight to the ed board, where Gina was going to meet them. Then, whaddya know, Nia goes into labor. Bumper-to-bumper on the way downtown. They stop, swap seats, and now *he's* the driver, trying to get her to the hospital. He's using his much-vaunted knowledge of shortcuts, but right there on Lower Wacker the baby shows up. The Duke used his goddamn shoelaces to tie the umbilical cord. Turn on the radio."

Colleen feels queasy contemplating the logistics. She finds the AM station that gives traffic and weather on the eights, and after they are told that the traffic is awful and the weather oppressive, the announcer announces the "news time, 10:39," and then the breaking story.

Of how the Senior Senator of Illinois delivered a staffer's baby by the side of the road.

"What a mess," says the Chief.

"At least it was a rental car," says Colleen.

When the Deputy Press Secretary left to work for the hockey team, Gina gave Colleen a crash course in Communications 101.

"The biggest question we should always be asking ourselves in terms of messaging," Gina had said, "is 'What would it mean for the middle class?'"

Colleen sat in one of the chairs next to Gina's tabletop Zen garden, full of rocks and sand, taking notes, numbering as she went:

1. The Senator as a man who is a hard worker!
2. The Senator as a man whom circumstance and showing up every day have made a national leader! (But who is always thinking of the greater good, not just for Dems, but for everyone!)
3. The Senator as a man who really does deliver for his state, not just talk about it! He brings federal dollars back to Illinois and does lots of heavy lifts on legislative language!

Colleen used the purple pen that Andrew had given her to punctuate each note with an exclamation point, not because that degree of emphasis was required, but because it helped her stay awake.

Insomnia again.

"The Senator is known nationally as either a partisan asshole or an idealistic champion, depending on where you're sitting. We'd never put this in a press release, but he also does a lot—"

Gina pauses to search for the right words.

"—not of backdoor dealings, but—let's just say there are ways to get things done besides obtaining sixty votes on the floor. Stuff that's more—"

"Behind-the-scenes," Colleen supplies.

"Yes," Gina says, hedgingly. "Not secret. Just not with a lot of fanfare."

When Colleen's been the driver, she's heard the Senator get on the phone.

Heard him crack the whip, so to speak.

Collar his colleagues to get on board.

Heard him more than once employ the phrase, "You can take the credit," and mean it.

"It's not a function of being sneaky," Gina continued, "but of his not requiring that particular variety of ego stroke."

Gina paused to grab a strand of curly hair from somewhere on the back of her scalp, twist it around her index finger, and yank it out. It was a gesture of hers, habitual and mindless, but every time she did it, it gave Colleen the shivers.

"And that dovetails, actually, with the central theory of the kind of PR we do around here. The game plan is that we target at the middle ground. Independents, on-the-fencers we can tip to our side. Persuadables."

Grab, twist, yank.

"We don't worry about the five or so percent who are as bleeding-heart as he is, deep within his own semi-secret bleeding heart. Left to his own devices, the Senator would talk about do-gooder causes of great importance to him personally. But the Chief absolutely will *not* let him, or us, talk about any of those issues in-state. No ACLU, no global AIDS, no climate change. None of it."

Grab, twist, yank.

"Almost everywhere we go in the state, people feel for him. Except the rabid five or so percent on the opposite end of the spectrum who compare him to Hitler, name-call him a traitor, a baby-killer, a commie, et cetera."

Grab, twist.

"Aside from those headcases, most people perceive the Senator with vague fuzzy feelings of goodness and dependability. A fighter for middle-class families, plus likeability."

Yank.

"There's our message."

Behind Gina was a stair-step of framed black-and-white photographs of three of us: Great American Presidents.

The Depression–era one who went by his initials, riding in an open-topped car, hatted, bespectacled, grinning with his weak-chinned and crusading wife grinning too.

The Catholic one, also known by his initials, resting his feet on his desk, a hand to his temple, backlit like he had a halo.

The one from Arkansas, prematurely white hair feathered above a pair of eyes that conveyed an empathy that almost made you believe, "Yes, this man really *can* feel my pain."

Three great American philanderers, also, Colleen thought, and marveled at how devoted the Senator was to Dorothy. Swore again to continue her renewed fidelity to Walter.

"Downstate," Gina continued, "they see the Senator like Santa Claus showing up with a sack of gold slung over his back because he's so good at helping specific towns get money."

Town$. Colleen pictured the word as Gina said it. She flipped the page of her steno.

Gina told her she didn't need to recall all this verbatim.

"I know," Colleen said. "This is just how I remember. Visually."

She did not add that it was also an aid against falling asleep.

"You shutterbugs," said Gina. "Long story short: your job, when you are coming up with wording for media advisories and press releases, is to identify where the traps are so you can tiptoe around them in the writing. No walking over minefields. Questions?"

Colleen knew she was not expected to have any, but she couldn't help asking: "Do we ever reach out to the major political blogs? Write any guest posts, or add any bloggers to our media lists?"

"Blogs," said Gina, "are an unvetted, inaccurate no-man's-land. We don't waste our time."

Colleen thought about talk radio.

How it was so conservative because progressives missed their chance to capitalize on that format as it was getting off the ground.

How the Left ought to take the opportunities offered by the blogosphere.

But her job, as she has been reminded tacitly every day since she started, is not to volunteer opinions. Just to do as you're told.

"Got it," said Colleen, flipping her notebook shut. "Thank you."

"Wait a second," Gina said. "Lemme find you something."

Gina printed a press release from the share drive and handed it to Colleen.

From November 2006, after the last midterm elections.

It began by stating that the Senator "was today reelected to the Senate's second highest ranking leadership post, Assistant Majority Leader, also known as Majority Whip. This marks only the fifth time in history that an Illinois senator has served as a Senate leader."

"The leadership stuff isn't something we harp on here in the state," said Gina. "It's a bigger deal in DC. We're honestly just happy if Illinoisans can identify the Senator as the senator."

Gina reached for another hair.

Colleen rose from her chair.

"But you should know this for your own edification. Plus, it's one of the late great Deputy Press Secretary's finest pieces. Enjoy."

Colleen headed for the door.

"And try, if you can," Gina said, "to be as good as he was, okay?"

The late great Deputy Press Secretary's press release really was well done.

Neither the position of Whip nor that of Majority Leader, he had written, is mentioned in the Constitution.

The title "whip," he had continued, comes from "whipper-in," a fox-hunting term for "the person charged with keeping dogs from straying during a chase."

Even holding a higher opinion of Congress than the average woman-on-the-street, it was easy for Colleen to picture the legislators as a pack of slavering beasts.

Easy, too, to picture the Senator as the sane man with the firm hand necessary to tame them.

Colleen would try to hew to the standard the late great Deputy Press Secretary left as his legacy.

She also knew, even then, that most releases wouldn't be as memorable, as fun.

Except for the one she's about to write.

She and the Chief are back in the office, the front-desk phones are ringing off the hook, and Gina is saying, "We may as well go with it."

It being the out-of-control interest in the Senator's level-headed heroism on Lower Wacker.

It's harrowing, Gina says.

It's heartwarming.

Plus this is the first time in months that people are more curious about the Senior Senator of Illinois than the Junior Senator.

Colleen is to write the release while Gina calls the hospital and clears them to hold a news conference on the sidewalk outside the emergency-room entrance. Waiting for her computer to boot up, Colleen wonders what she would do with the rest of the day following a morning on which she had helped a woman deliver a baby in a rental car.

Go home, clean up, have a drink, something?

But no. The Senator is in his office, door open, returning calls, checking emails, catching up, waiting until it is time for the Next Big Thing.

She hears the back door open and Steve Moon Collier walks in. He rounds the corner to Cube City and runs into the Chief of Staff. "How'd it go with the pipefitters?" he asks.

"If you'd been there," says the Chief, "you would have wilted like a cut flower in the heat, but not Colleen. She very politely handed them their own asses."

"I'll hand you yours if you keep it up," says Steve.

"Back off, jackoff. You're a day late and a dollar short. The newest news is that Nia's a proud mother for the second time in her life, and the Duke did the honors of dragging the baby kicking and screaming into this degraded but still salvageable world."

When she checks her email, Colleen sees the Senator has already replied-all to a message from Nia's husband, announcing the backseat birth of a bouncing baby boy.

"Hooray!" the Senator typed, "Another Democrat!"

Colleen will adapt this joke into one of the quotes in the release.

These are never from the mouth of the man himself, but they sound like they could be.

Colleen can do a dead-on written impression of the Senator.

Colleen's father was, no, *is*—Colleen corrects her morbid reflex to speak of him in the past tense since he's been in Iraq—both a hunter and a lover of birds. Out in the woods, he taught Colleen and Bridget how to spot them when it looked like none were there, how to identify each by name, by their calls, by their plumage.

Writing the release, Colleen thinks *mockingbird* when she gets to the spots—two of them, per the formula—where she is to say what the Senator "said."

When she first joined the Press Team, Colleen had tried too hard to perfect her work.

Nobody wanted it perfected.

"They just wanted it fected," Andrew had said.

~

Democracy is not the exclusive province of a specialized class.

Or rather, it is.

In our own eras, it was open only to wealthy white men, and as we regard Colleen's story we can discern that not much has changed.

But democracy should not be conducted this way. Anyone who is taken with the notion of being a good citizen, but who is not set upon doing so as a career politician, we in turn find ourselves quite taken with.

And so we watch.

Among low-level participants in politics, Colleen is an unusual specimen, in that she insists on maintaining outside passions and pursuits.

That hers specifically involve art and photography is of no importance to us. Our own hobbies ranged widely in life, from the performance of music to the design of buildings to the penning of satires to the rigorous analysis of American football.

But we are heartened by the fact that she has them at all. The business of state is best conducted by those who possess limited interest in conducting it.

We are not rooting for Colleen as such. We know how Colleen's idealistic infatuation with politics will end.

Suddenly, badly.

Or does it end "badly"?

We are still considering.

~

Outside the emergency room, ambulances glide by, sometimes loud, sometimes silent. Colleen hands out releases, Gina directs traffic, and Andrew sets up the video camera amid the fawning ministrations of his new assistant.

The Press Team rotates through their three interns, taking them to events to provide hands-on experience. Andrew has chosen J-Lock to take the first one.

In spite of the heat, J-Lock is wearing pantyhose—unbreatheable nylon. The rest of her skin *looks* like pantyhose—satiny, a particularly unnatural shade of nude. Her floss-blonde hair catches the sun, and as she hovers around Andrew she looks misplaced, like a brass button that's fallen off somebody's coat.

Colleen is interrupted in her hating of J-Lock by a tap on the shoulder from Ethan.

Colleen had tipped him off. Maybe, she had suggested, he could sell a photo of the Senior-Senator-cum-baby-deliverer to a magazine somewhere, since this was shaping up to be such a popular story.

Ethan's photojournalistic sensibility—off-kilter, carnivalesque—has, he likes to say, made him "big in Germany," where a couple of newsweeklies periodically pick up his more off-beat images.

Colleen wishes she could whip out her camera and do the same—she could use the paycheck—but Gina, who earns over twice what Colleen makes, would flip her shit.

"So?" Ethan says, raising one charcoal eyebrow and leaving the rest unspoken.

"I haven't shown the video to anybody yet," Colleen says, as the Chief of Staff, Nia's husband, and the Senator emerge and head toward the rake, every slot of which contains a mic, a rarity. "So don't even ask. Talk to you after."

The hospital behind them is the finest of the fine. It is where Palmira hopes to have her baby. Though, Colleen muses, *in* the hospital, not on the way to it.

The Senator steps to the microphones.

He tells the story of what happened in the rental car that morning, in brief and with modesty.

"I feel humbled to have been able to help in the way that I did," he says, "but my staffer Nia did the real work. She and her new son are healthy, well, and resting comfortably in the building behind me."

He gestures.

"They can't join us, but Nia did tell me it would be okay with her if I took a moment, as long as I have you all here, to say a few words about a different but related subject, specifically obstetric fistula. Now it's not a pleasant subject, but it's worth knowing about, in order to prevent it. If you'll allow me to be clinical."

The Senator gets clinical.

He talks about how obstetric fistula is a condition that can afflict a mother, usually after a prolonged labor or a delivery during which adequate medical attention is not available.

He talks about how what happens is that a hole—a fistula—develops either between the rectum and the vagina or between the bladder and the vagina, leading to great pain and embarrassment to the woman in question.

He talks about how, through no fault of her own, this condition leaves her an outcast in her community.

Nia's thirteen-year-old daughter, Dahlia, comes and stands next to Colleen, dressed, as has been her habit of late, all in black, her T-shirt emblazoned with a silver lamé skull, goth and funny.

"Gross," she whispers, holding up her phone to video the Senator.

"Tell me about it," says Colleen.

"This condition," the Senator says, "used to be common across North America and Europe, but it's easily preventable, and treatable through a simple operation. In the developing world, it's a different story."

His brown eyes lock with those of individual reporters in turn.

"Genital mutilation, the early marriage of very young girls to older men, and lack of access to obstetric care means the condition is still common there. That is why I'm one of the sponsors of a bill currently before Congress to help improve the health and education of women in the developing world. To provide access to treatment, and to provide education so that the practices that lead to this condition don't continue."

Dead silence.

"I thank you all—and Nia thanks you—for your support and interest in the birth of her baby. But I also hope that with this small reminder, we can keep thinking of others, too, and that we can keep raising the standard of living—and the respect for all human life—for everyone, everywhere. Thank you."

The reporters call out, "Senator, Senator!"

They ask their questions.

Not one of which inquires further into the ins-and-outs of obstetric fistula, genital mutilation, or the plight of women in the developing world.

E than ambles up.

"Do I look visibly impressed?" he says. "Because that was impressive. Disgusting, but very classy. I think he just became my favorite senator."

"Yeah, he's mine," says Dahlia, putting away her phone.

She introduces Ethan to Dahlia. "The new big sister," Colleen says. "Congrats, Dahl."

"I've got these blue bubble gum cigars," says Dahlia, taking a cellophane-wrapped box out of her black messenger bag, onto which she has sewn a patch of a bloody red heart surrounded by a crown of thorns that reminds Colleen of Catholic Sunday school. "My step-dad told me to hand them out. Here."

Colleen takes one.

"Can you *name* more than one other Senator?" she asks Ethan.

"The way he took this chance to be a publicity hound," says Ethan, "and used it to fight for the underdog? I don't care who the other Senators are. I bet they wouldn't do that."

Colleen thinks he may be right.

B ack in the office kitchen, Colleen watches Andrew and the Senator unwrap overstuffed paper packets containing steaming Italian rolls dripping *jus* and piled with brown shreds of roast beef, thin as wood shavings. The Senator was hungry after the press conference, so they swung by an eatery known for purveying "Chicago's #1 Italian Beefs."

Giardiniera and hunks of sweet green peppers give the glistening sandwiches a Christmasy look.

"Bite?" the Senator says, proffering half the soaking sandwich to the Chief of Staff.

"Looks dee-lish," he says, "but I couldn't possibly. You gotta hand it to the Eye-talians, though. The Beef is a sterling example of working class ingenuity. They invented it during the Depression—stockyard workers slow-cooking undesirable cuts of meat to make them tender."

"Drenching them in broth to give them more flavor," says Andrew.

"Cutting the beef thin to make it go further," says the Senator.

"They served them at weddings to feed a lot of people for cheap," says Colleen.

"It's a damn fine sandwich," says Andrew. "As a tragic vegetarian, Colleen will never know this. But see how she relishes the relish."

The Senator insisted on getting her something when they were in the drive-through, so she sits at the table with a small waxy cup of green peppers in front of her.

"Sandwiches are just a platform for condiments anyway," says Colleen.

The Chief sits beside her and grabs one of the peppers, slurping it up. The Senator is asking him if he was raised in a barn, when Gina stomps in and throws a sheet of paper on the table.

"Assassins," she says. "Sorry to interrupt your meal, but this makes me sick."

The paper contains a press release put out by the Ryder camp.

"Representative Ryder's Statement on Today's Special Delivery by the Senior Senator," with the subhead, "Congrats in order, but not votes."

The Chief of Staff wipes the oil and spit from his fingers, clears his throat, and reads aloud:

CHICAGO, IL — U.S. Representative Ron Ryder (R-Ill.) issued the following statement today congratulating the great state of Illinois' Senior Senator on his impromptu delivery of an aide's baby boy on Lower Wacker this morning: 'I extend my congratulations and prayers to the family and its newest member. But considering that today's star is just one of society's many tiniest and most vulnerable members, I would be remiss if I did not also state: One single act of so-called heroism, or, if you will, quick thinking, does not a family values candidate make. In the wake of this sensational story, it is important to remember for November who the real pro-family voice for Illinois is, and it is Ron Ryder. My track record in Congress proves what I am willing to fight for, and it includes:

• Defense of traditional marriage between a man and a woman
• Opposition to so-called "hate crimes" legislation that seeks to advance the gay agenda
• Abstinence as the only true "safe sex" in sex education
• Shielding the unborn against abortion advocates and so-called "choice"

These are but a few of the issues on which it's clear that the ultra-liberal Senior Senator and his party are out of touch, and need to be out of office. Also, while obstetric fistula is an unfortunate affliction, worrying about women in other countries when women right here in ours need protection from making poor choices is cockamamie. In short, one convenient accident does not overshadow the Senior Senator's long career of anti-family votes.

The Chief hands the release to the Senator, crumples his napkin, and arcs it into the trash next to the fridge.

"Nothing but net," he says, pumping his fist, then, "That's our boy, alright. Short and stupid."

"He does manage to walk the knife's edge between mean-and-scary plus completely ridiculous," says Colleen.

"He's shooting himself in the foot with those bullet points," says Andrew. "Illinois is a centrist state."

"Infuriating, indecorous, and totally inappropriate," the Senator says, shaking his head, jowls swaying a bit. "Quite a shot across the bow, isn't it?"

"It's a kick in the groin," says Gina.

"Right?" says Colleen. "I mean, 'women need protection from their bad choices?' Really?"

"And *cockamamie*? Quite the word choice," says Andrew. "How about the hypocrisy with all the anti-gay stuff?"

"He's clearly baiting us," says the Chief.

"And we clearly will not take the bait," says the Senator.

"God, I know," says Gina. "But it's so tempting. It's only 4:00. We have time to issue a counter-statement. Very succinct."

"To dignify this turd," the Chief says, folding the release into an airplane, "with a response of any kind is to risk making his foolishness look legit. I vote no."

"Language, Chief," says the Senator. "And, ironically, this office is not a democracy. But I say no reply is the best reply in this situation, too."

Colleen has seen this non-attack-as-plan-of-attack strategy deployed before.

Last summer, the week a Republican senator from a Western state famed for its potatoes had issued a guilty plea for disorderly—downgraded from "lewd"—conduct in a Twin Cities airport, Colleen was on driving duty. She sat behind the wheel with the Senator beside her and listened as he received a call from the Majority Leader.

The hypocrisy inherent in those circumstances, too—a politician whose voting record garnered a ninety-six-percent positive rating from the American Conservative Union arrested in a sting for soliciting gay sex—made it enticing to pursue censure, or even impeachment, through the Ethics Committee. But after some banter about the Republican's "wide stance," the Senator and the Majority Leader concluded, "We should stand back and let his own party throw him under the bus."

"You know what our problem is, buddy?" the Senator ended the call with, "We're too darn nice."

"Well, that's that," says the Chief, throwing the paper-airplane press release toward the trash.

"All right," Gina says, intercepting the plane and smoothing it flat again. "I don't like it, but we'll let it ride."

"I'm going to call it a day," says the Senator. "All this excitement? All these insults? All this beef? I just want to go home and tell Dottie about it."

"How do you want to get there?" asks the Chief. "Steve Moon Collier drove in today and parked somewhat illicitly in the federal garage. I'd like nothing more than to tell him he has to give you a lift home since Nia is indisposed."

"Nah," says the Senator. "I'll take the subway."

Colleen is riding the subway too—the Red Line—the same line the Senator rides when he rides it.

She gets a call from Ethan, but she's too deep underground for her phone to hold the signal, so she lets it roll into voicemail. When the train climbs, roller-coaster-style, back above the streets, she listens to the message.

"Doogs! I know you said we could talk more about the video later. And you press people have your finger on the pulse, so I'm sure you already know all about the disgusting things Ryder said about the Senator. But I am appalled. The Senator is a stand-up dude, and Ryder—I can't even explain. I can't believe what a two-faced slimedog he is. Now could be the perfect time to retaliate. Call me, call me, call me, okay? Bye."

She doesn't particularly feel like calling Ethan back.

But she will, later, when she's not on the train.

At the Lawrence stop, overlooking the brick exterior of a music venue decorated to resemble Moorish Spain, she sees a sound guy with a pierced ear, lip, nose, and eyebrow sitting alone on a zigzag of fire escape, smoking and texting.

He looks like a demon, Colleen thinks, then figures it's probably just her mindset.

The train rolls forward again. An ugly rhythmic scrape sets her teeth on edge.

The other day, Colleen and the Chief of Staff were discussing the destruction wrought by the Rapacious British Oil Company, and how it always feels like the world is ending.

How everything is in a decline, impossibly steep.

How maybe every generation feels that way, but the world keeps going, and so do they.

How it's always already too late somehow, but they, the People, keep acting as though it's not.

And on they go.

11

The fourteen-by-forty-eight-foot face of the Senior Senator of Illinois looks down over the outbound lanes of I-55.

Any public relations firm will tell you that sales increase with outdoor advertising. This is as true for humans as it is for products.

Thus does the Senator—up on high with the paternity tests, the radio stations, the car dealerships, the places of worship, the fast food joints—gaze like a minor god across the land he represents and wants to keep representing.

They are in a rented minivan, bound downstate. Andrew at the wheel, Colleen riding shotgun, behind them Ethan and Sudha, and finally, in the third row, Bobby Peacock and two other interns.

They are, all of them, encountering the billboard for the very first time. The interns go off like a car alarm, squealing when they see it.

"Don't make me stop this car and come back there," says Andrew.

The Senator's light brown eyes, almost green, are creased in thought.

The Lake shines behind him.

The blue skies echo his casual but dressy shirt.

Pastels, almost furry, like a flannel suit, more flattering to the Senator than the jewel-tones they'd been getting indoors.

His fleshy cheeks frame his face like plump steaks.

In fact, as Colleen remembers, the photographer's studio was in the meatpacking district. The studio belonged to a grad-school acquaintance.

In the heart of Fulton Market, among the fishmongers and the meat-stink.

Among the butchers in pink-stained aprons next door to upscale night clubs.

Among the loading docks and the lockers, the forklifts and the bacon and the pallets and the pork rinds.

Among the bricky streets lined with still-operational wholesalers and the converted gallery spaces and the men pushing handcarts who whistled as she walked by.

The sun beat on signs that read Meat-Packing for America's Lifestyle and Sausage: Pizza Supplies. Colleen was joining the Senator, Gina, and the Chief of Staff there. They had come from some luncheon, and she'd recognized the place by Sylvia's uneven parking job.

Colleen rode the freight elevator up and arrived in time to chime in on which tie the Senator should wear for his official portrait. "The green one," she had said. "It conveys, *I care about the earth* and *I am for saving the Lake.*"

Gina agreed, so green it was, although the Chief had fussed that the kelly shade clashed with the flag draped behind him.

An assistant fluttered in and out of the frame, futzing, and the work of a Brill Building songwriter from Kansas City played for the purpose of sounding soothing. Coffee-table books and candles and Scotch dotted the assorted brushed-steel surfaces.

The Senator grumbled—not because the shoot was going poorly, but because he disliked being the center of attention in any way he considered vain.

Gina and Colleen had foreseen this problem, so they'd arranged to go to the Museum Campus afterward for some outdoor shots. Colleen found herself holding a clear plastic freezer-bag full of neckties in one hand and her high heels in the other as they ran around the grassy expanses near the aquarium, trying to catch the best light.

The aquarium's vice president of governmental affairs was there to escort them through locations not open to the public, and she marveled at what a sweet man the Senator was, even on the day of such a major undertaking.

She was sort of right.

Watching him shuffle over the manicured knolls, it occurred to Colleen that the Senator was kind of hippolike. Cute and easy to underestimate, but ferocious when pressed, and moody.

But at that hour on that day, in the less unnatural setting, the Senator had relaxed, joking about how much trouble they were having over so little hair as the photographer smoothed his flyaways with a small wax stick that resembled deodorant. The Senator was not bald, or even balding, as were many men in his demographic, but his hair was thin and hair-colored, an indefinite brown going slowly gray, like a field in November.

"I know," he had said to the photographer and to Gina, "that this has to look good looming over highways and byways. So I want to apologize in advance for giving you so little to work with."

They had hastened to correct him. "No, Senator! You look great."

"You're no supermodel," Colleen had said. "But it would be weird if you were, wouldn't it?"

This is why, she had told him, she had advised Gina to schedule the shoot for early afternoon, since if they'd done it in the morning, he'd have guaranteed bags beneath his eyes and a puffy face.

"Unavoidable among people of a certain age," were her exact words.

"At sixty-four, I suppose I qualify," he said.

"I cannot tell a lie," she said.

He seemed to appreciate the lack of bullshit.

Then she referenced the reality TV series about aspiring fashion models and told him not to grin so much, but to smile with his eyes.

They did the shoot in May, and in mid-July Colleen had helped Gina and the Chief pick final photographs for the billboards in top market areas, like the one they are passing now, and the one on I-290, and the one on the way out of Springfield toward St. Louis.

All this rattles around Colleen's brain, but nothing rattles her more than this: it is the middle of August, and she has come nowhere near the campaign since.

She has remained glassed inside the main office.

She has kept the papers immaculately pushed.

She has obsessed, the entire time, over the Ryder blowjob video.

They are on their way to the Illinois State Fair. Tomorrow is Governor's Day—aka Democrat Day, because the Elvis-loving Governor happens to be a Democrat.

Like the interns, Colleen can barely contain herself, so excited is she for a break in the dog days. They pull past the billboard, and the squealing subsides.

"The other one's on the Ike," says Andrew. "Right, Colleen?"

"Yep, inbound. Not far from the Hillside Strangler."

"That always sounds like a serial killer!" says Sudha.

"It is," says Colleen. "It technically refers to the bottleneck through the suburb of Hillside, but the first usage of 'Strangler' was during the late 1970s serial killer media frenzy."

"Which one is the Ike?" says Bobby Peacock, who does not drive. "Why do they call it that?"

"The Ike is the Eisenhower," says Andrew. "So named in honor of Dwight D., the man with the plan for the nation's highway system as we know and drive it."

"The original stated purpose of the system was the transport of troops and military equipment," says Colleen.

She thinks of her dad.

The Iraqi insurgents, he wrote in his latest email, *get sent here wounded, and they can't believe it. They can't understand that we'll fix them up. But we do. Tom can talk all he wants about the guys he thinks he took out, but I see the other end of it. I won't ever forget.*

"I-290," says Andrew, "Chicago's only Republican expressway."

"What about the Reagan?" asks Sudha.

"That," Colleen and Andrew say, almost in unison, "is a tollway, not an expressway."

"And what's this one's nickname?" says Bobby.

"The Stevenson," says Andrew. "After Adlai E., former governor and failed presidential candidate."

"He never won the presidency because he was portrayed as an 'egghead,'" says Colleen. "Somebody once told him he was sure to get the vote of 'every thinking man,' and he was all, 'Thanks, but I need a majority to win.'"

"I didn't realize I'd been assigned to the dork van," says Ethan, as Andrew deftly avoids getting crushed by a semi.

The Senator is a train man, advocating higher speeds and newer tracks and passenger cars manufactured in his own home state. Both his parents worked on the railroad. That's how they met.

Colleen had arranged for the office to take the train down to last year's State Fair, but they found out the hard way that rail in the Great Midwest is neither very new nor very high speed.

Switching problems on their way out of Union Station.

The iron horse motionless on the first bridge above the Chicago River, a hundred-year-old vertical lift.

Gazing torpidly through the ancient Pennsylvania steel into

Chinatown, the water dull below, the banks dotted with willows. They stood, suspended, for an hour, an affectless voice on the intercom providing unhelpful updates, the irony of the Senator's support for rail and their increasingly likely lateness lost on no one. They eventually moved again, of course, and Colleen couldn't help feeling it was a little romantic, the sun dappling through the leaves of the shimmery trees onto low-slung warehouses and auto graveyards.

Then Joliet, with its infamous prison, former home of the busiest electric chair in the state, built with local limestone and convict labor, designed by the same architect who designed Chicago's Water Tower, Springfield's Capitol—the prison that, in the movies, had held one of the two so-called Blues Brothers, and that, in real life, held the two would-be supermen who had committed one of the Crimes of the Century of the previous century.

Town after town glimpsed over other prisons.

More concertina wire.

They couldn't see the prison where the serial killer who dressed as Pogo the Clown had died, but they knew it was there.

Another prison in Pontiac, maximum security for males.

Another in Lincoln, medium security for females.

Final stop, Springfield.

This year Nasrin has assigned them to minivans, and they fit into three.

All except J-Lock, who was resolute about driving herself and Hillary, about getting her own room, which she'll have to pay for with her own money.

"It's worth it," she said. "Not to spend a single night away from my baby."

J-Lock's behavior does not seem designed to get attention, but rather to manage and deflect attention of an unwanted kind.

Image control via the destruction of a bad photograph.

Not bothering her roommates with the presence of her Shih Tzu.

Yet she seems not to realize that she attracts negative attention by this very behavior.

Colleen can remember wanting to be noticed when she was an intern, daydreaming ways to catch the Senator's approval, but she never did any of them.

It would have been like streaking, or laughing in the middle of a funeral. Compelling, but in poor taste.

J-Lock lacks a gauge to sense how irritating she's being.

That or she doesn't care.

A ndrew drives them by fields of corn and soybeans where they can see the rural way of life obsolescing.

Colleen's dad grew up in eastern Nebraska, and for years he talked about purchasing his family's forty-acre farm from Colleen's grandmother. He finally did it before he left for Iraq, although he doesn't intend to ever farm it himself. Instead he rents it out, worrying aloud that each year it'll get harder to find tenants.

No one makes money anymore, except in factory farming.

Even then, as Colleen has learned each time the Senator helps reauthorize the Farm Bill, the huge operations require subsidies to prop them up.

The Senator is a downstater through and through, born in East St. Louis, a resident of Springfield.

Adept as he is in the city, he allies himself, he jokes, with machinery like tractors, not with any long-standing Chicago political machine. He's expected to prove his commitment to maintaining the state's agricultural strength via subsidies and tax breaks.

Gina says you know you have written a suitable press release when, even if you suspect a bill to be crap, you find yourself stirred rereading your work.

Whenever Colleen writes material for downstate ag events, she comes away believing in her heart that the Senator has taken the best action for the farm families of Illinois, while knowing in her brain that whatever good the bill does will only permit the supposed little guys to stagger on a tiny bit longer.

Colleen finds her heart and brain pacing off for a duel more often than she'd like.

Walter says that giving hope to constituents, rural or urban, is not of negligible value.

But when Colleen writes the releases, she imagines the space breaks as chasms dividing the ideal from the real.

The inevitable gap between the purity of ideology and the necessity of pragmatism.

The distance you have to cross from what you know is best to arrive at a place where you can get something—anything—done.

I-55 is an ugly highway, and boring.

The interns say as much, and amuse themselves by singing along to songs on the radio about getting high like paper airplanes, dancing by making aircraft with their hands—about being a girl, kissing a girl, and finding you like it. Ethan shoots a photo in the rearview so they can all be in it. Eventually, the interns tucker themselves out and close their eyes, leaning their heads on each others' shoulders.

"Let's turn the radio down," Andrew whispers. "Our little princesses are sleeping, Colleen."

Closer to Springfield, traffic coagulates and the interns awaken.

"You can't even go down to the edge of town anymore," Colleen says, "because the towns don't have edges. They just bleed out."

"This used to be a vast and trackless prairie sea," says Andrew. "But for now, I just want the exit number, please."

They pull up in front of the hotel where they always stay when they attend the Fair, rising like an air traffic control tower above downtown Springfield.

Luggage dropped off, key-cards in hand, the staffers decide to find a late lunch and some drinks.

Ethan's never been to Springfield, and the interns are under-age. It's over ninety in the shade, and on a day like this Happy Hour at lunchtime does not appeal to Colleen, especially since this evening they'll have the usual barbecue and kegs at the home of the Downstate Director, so she volunteers to help Dézi take the under-twenty-ones for some historic sightseeing.

Andrew says they should wait at the hotel to make sure J-Lock makes it.

Colleen says it's a small town.

He can wait and catch up if he wants.

Later, on the social networking site the Senator likes to call MyFace, browsers will be able to see Colleen, Ethan, Dézi and the interns—minus J-Lock—frolicking all over the Old State Capitol, site of the Sixteenth President's announcement of his candidacy in 1858 and of the Junior Senator's announcement in 2007.

They will be able to see the interns learning that the Sixteenth President had only one term in Congress before he ran for the highest office, same as the Junior Senator has had in the Senate.

They will be able to see a table like the one at which the Sixteenth President wrote the "House Divided" speech, though at the time he was not an abolitionist.

"He just wanted slavery contained."

They will be able to see the tour guide, who just said this.

Colleen saw these sites on a family vacation when she was a little girl, and the memories blend with the present. She thinks of stepping outside and calling her dad, but catches herself. She can't call Iraq.

So instead, she stays on the tour. Cool air, dim lights, volunteers who keep repeating phrases like "This piece is, in fact, original to the building."

A century-and-a-half ago the room would have been hot and smoky, full of flies, and the cuspidors would not have been decorative.

"This is like a field trip," says Ethan.

"This is like a film strip," says Dézi.

A map the size of a projector screen hangs on the wall, a reproduction of one from 1845 when Illinois was considered the Western Frontier. Another, from 1857, shows that America had manifested its destiny from sea to slowly-warming sea. In a dozen years, Illinois had become what it would remain: the American Middle West.

Their guide resembles a certain actor with a cult following known for his reptilian countenance, deadpan delivery, and fancy footwork. He tells about the Eighteenth President, who got his start right here in the Capitol, mustering men at a makeshift desk under the stairs on the second floor.

"Times have changed," says the tour guide, guiding them. "This area would literally," he says, "literally," he repeats, "have been packed with hundreds, even thousands of men trying to get into the Union Army. A lousy farmer, a failed businessman, a drunk, and a highly corrupt president, it turned out that the one thing at which the Eighteenth President was truly gifted was being in the military. Or perhaps not even that. At West Point he graduated twenty-first in a class of thirty-nine. But the thing he was most good at was the fight to save the Union."

Sometimes, when Colleen thinks of history, she can almost feel history thinking back at her.

The glass is so old the windows look watery.

The guide reaches the tour's crescendo. He must have delivered it hundreds of times, literally, but his eyes tear up when he reaches it.

"April 14, 1865," he says. "Good Friday. The day our Sixteenth President was killed."

He pauses.

"74,000 people saw his body lie in state here that May."

Another pause.

"And *Now,*" he intones, "*he belongs to the ages* is writ o'er his tomb. Thank you."

The interns and other tour-goers clap as the guide bows, a lock of hair falling like a curtain across his forehead.

"That's a quote from his Secretary of War," says Andrew behind her, and Colleen jumps. "And it might have been *Now he belongs to the angels.* No need to be alarmed, though. It's a nice epitaph either way."

W here's J-Lock?" says Dézi.

      "At the hotel," says Andrew. "Getting her nails done."

Colleen can think of nothing nice to say, so she walks ahead.

Outside again, they watch as Sudha discerns from a life-sized statue that the Sixteenth President would have been difficult to kiss, requiring a stretch and a rise to the tiptoes.

The brochure the concierge handed them on their way out of the hotel tells them they will enjoy the many quaint shops, cozy bistros, and vibrant nightlife downtown Springfield has to offer. It's only 3:30, so they can't say for sure about the nightlife, but most of the quaint shops appear to be closed, and the tavern-themed casual dining chain at the base of the hotel—fern bar, fake Tiffany lamps—looks to be neither cozy nor a bistro.

They cling to patches of shade, searching. Colleen is determined to find something quaint.

And she does—a florist's with a vinyl banner reading "Free

Freshcut Flowers to anyone whose name begins with __ (ID required)." The letter "C" has been pasted into the blank. They enter.

Colleen picks hers from a bin labeled "Cherry Red Love Rose."

The Korean woman behind the counter cuts off the thorns and tells her how to make it last.

Andrew sings a power ballad from the '80s about how roses have thorns in the same way that nights have dawns and cowboys sing sad songs.

Back at the hotel, Colleen sticks it in the ice bucket after following none of the woman's instructions.

"We're only going to be here a day," she tells Ethan, who's sharing the room. "And it's not the rose that matters as much as the gesture."

"Only in a small town," says Sylvia in the lobby, when Colleen tells her and Gina.

They are waiting for the minivans to take them to the barbecue.

Colleen doesn't see that the flower has to do with the size of the town so much as her good luck—that out of twenty-six letters, the florist would be on hers during the one twenty-four-hour period of the entire year that she would be here. But she doesn't bother explaining.

I do tend to think of you as my good luck charm," says the Chief of Staff, mixing her a gin and tonic in the kitchen of the home of the Downstate Director.

Sports knickknacks and Prairie State bric-a-brac abound, and bottles of liquor surround them on the counters. Colleen has answered the Chief's, "How was your day?" with the florist story, and now he is saying, "Wondrous things seem to happen when you're near," and introducing her to his wife.

His wife's hair is short and fluffy, dyed a light blonde, and she wears a button-up blouse tucked into wide-hipped, high-waisted denim.

Mom jeans, thinks Colleen, then thinks, Don't be mean.

"I remember you," his wife says, keeping her hands at her sides as Colleen offers hers.

Colleen is not sure what to make of this. Does she just mean that yes, she remembers they have met before? Or something more?

Cup in hand, Colleen walks through the screen door to the deck, where the party unfolds in drunk little chunks.

The Senator and Dorothy have yet to arrive. They are dining with the Governor of New Mexico, whose name is being tossed about as a prospective vice-presidential candidate.

But everyone else wastes no time waiting, on their way to getting wasted.

The Downstate Director mans the electric grill, and Lizzie Leipzig womans the gas one, her pregnant abdomen covered by an apron silk-screened with the head of the Sixteenth President.

Only a handful of the DC staff are here—the ones from Illinois who have reason to visit during the August recess, plus a few from elsewhere who want to see the land they help their boss represent and to do so on the federal government's largesse. They congregate near the picnic tables covered with side dishes, marveling at the plenty provided by the Springfield staff.

BLT salad, deviled eggs, three types of coleslaw (one vinegar, two mayo).

Mostaccioli, cheeseburger salad (possibly taco), mandarin orange slaw, baked beans.

Two potato salads (one vinegar, one mayo), three bean salads (two vinegar, one mayo), two ramen noodle salads, some kind of bean stew in a crockpot.

Two one-gallon vats of kosher dill spears, one vat of sweet gherkins.

Three forty-four-ounce fridge-door-fit ketchups, two thirty-ounce containers of classic yellow mustard, one gallon of BBQ sauce from a Chicago company whose motto is *The Sauce is the Boss!*

Six bags of potato chips from a Chicago vendor whose mascot is a snackbag wearing sunglasses and playing a saxophone (plain, sour cream and onion, tangy cheese, salt and sour, sweet and tangy BBQ, and cheddar and sour cream ridgetts), a tray of watermelon wedges.

Infinite casseroles.

Nasrin stands at the head of the table like the docent of a museum explaining the displays, next to Mary Dodge, the legal expert in the Whip office who's come over to join the campaign.

Mary was once listed as one of the Fifty Most Beautiful People on Capitol Hill in a newspaper named after Capitol Hill.

Colleen and Andrew read that issue religiously. They study the pictures. Having lived in DC during undergrad, surrounded by sleazy and interchangeable men with confidence well out of proportion to their looks and talent, she always wondered how the paper managed to hunt down fifty.

The female interns, all in sundresses though it is twilight and there isn't much sun, are clustered by the keg clutching red plastic cups, taking turns getting served by Steve Moon Collier, Lo Benson, and Andrew.

Steve is wearing boat shoes and looking preppy, feet wide apart, as if the patio were his yacht, gently swaying.

As it is, the air is dead and still. It feels emulsified, almost colloidal—the individual water particles floating suspended.

No sea breeze.

Colleen joins them on the flagstones. She wears a sundress, too—it is too hot for pants. Ethan roves, taking the last pictures he'll be able to get without a flash, which he hates to use. Colleen is almost to the keg when her path is crossed by Jennifer Whitlock.

Over the past month, Colleen has been trying to relate. They are, after all, both on the Press Team.

But J-Lock's personality is a hard-to-navigate minefield of high self-love and low self-esteem. She presents herself alternately as just a li'l ol' pageant winner from smalltown Alabama and a tough-as-nails steel magnolia who's seen it all and survived it. Interacting with her is like trying to run on sand. Colleen cannot get traction.

The first hit single by a female pop star who got her start at the age of ten on a game show whose stated mission was to search for stars and who lately has been better known for her repeated breakdowns comes over the stereo.

"Classic jam," says Colleen, and feels mundane.

"My family was friends with her family," says J-Lock. "She's a schizo."

"Mm-hmm," Colleen says. "That seems clear enough."

"*No*," says J-Lock, sighing and sipping white wine not from the standard issue red plastic but from a long-stemmed glass. "She is literally schiz-o-phrenic." She enunciates each syllable as though Colleen is an idiot. "Like, she is certifiably schizo according to the DMS-III."

"The DSM-IV?" says Colleen.

"Whatever, Colleen. That girl is *sick*, is my point. People don't understand it. She's from Mississippi, you know, which is close to Alabama, and it's just a fact that everyone who grew up around her is aware of."

"Yeah," says Colleen. "Okay. I need to go powder my nose. Excuse me."

She doesn't really need to pee, and goes instead to the kitchen to fix another drink. She's squeezing a lime into a fresh gin and tonic when the Senator and Dorothy walk through the front door.

The Senator has reached the threshold between the living room and kitchen when the Downstate Director's chocolate lab, Nestlé Quik, recognizes him, stops barking like a hellhound, and moseys over to have his head scratched.

The Senator speaks to the dog, some private subject of doggy interest, and Nestlé shakes his ears and rattles his tags, heaving himself to the floor to offer his belly for rubbing.

Back in Chicago, the Senator is forever ducking out of Susan Scheck's fundraising office. He hates asking people for money.

Instead, he sneaks over to pet puppies at the shelter up the block.

How he loves the lovelorn canines. How they seem to laugh when they see him coming. How this drives the Senator's staff batshit.

The Senator's line about Susan is that "She knows where the bodies are buried and she knows who can write the checks."

Incredibly expert at her job, Susan commands tremendous esteem in the field. But esteem is not a quality she offers others. Not if these others do not happen to be loaded, potentially plenteous sources of Democratic funds.

Wealthy patrons, Susan cultivates.

Coworkers and underlings, she denigrates—when she speaks to them at all.

Time, to Susan Scheck, is, literally, money, and if you do not relate directly to dollars, you are, literally, not worth her time.

Whenever the Senator pulls his vanishing act, Susan Scheck will call Hannah the Scheduler demanding to know where he is, and when Hannah tells her, she refuses to retrieve him.

Susan Scheck hates dogs.

The Senator and Dorothy would probably have a dog, but neither of them stays in one place long enough. Colleen wonders, too, whether Dorothy's medical condition might be a factor.

One more belly rub for Nestlé, and the Senator straightens up.

Dorothy enters, slower as always, assisted tonight by the Governor of New Mexico.

Colleen is in the habit of telling people who say her job must be fascinating that it really is. "Each day," she tells them, "I get to go do something new. It is never the same day twice." This is the kind of optimistic self-deceit a lot of people spout about their jobs, but in her case it's also true—was, at least, until she wasn't invited to join the campaign.

"Sure beats having a real job, doesn't it, Colleen?" the Senator had once said to her before a press conference.

"With a stick, Senator," she had answered.

"How's work tonight?" the Senator asks, gesturing to her drink.

"Beats having a real job," she says, and follows them outside.

O n the patio everyone glows with a film of sweat, illuminated by porch lights.

Colleen watches as the Senator leans like a ship's figurehead from the deck to address the crowd. There is a moment at any event like this—be it private party or fundraiser—when the man himself makes a speech.

These points are pivots. People hold out for them.

The ones who are not staying leave shortly thereafter, having gotten their money's worth. The others who are can then let themselves go.

Colleen has heard this speech—thanking them for being there, describing what, politically, is at stake—countless times, so she doesn't listen, watching it instead like a TV with the sound down.

The Senator puts his arm around Dorothy, and Colleen thinks how rarely the two of them get to enjoy a so-called normal life.

When you are the driver, you take care of every little thing for the Senator. You pick up his newspapers, bring him his coffee, swing by his neighborhood dry cleaner so he can dash in for his and Dorothy's clothes.

She remembers this past spring, before she joined the Press Team, when she'd arranged for him to attend an after-school cooking class for underprivileged kids at an upscale grocery store that Walter refers to as the Food Hole. Colleen was the driver that week, but the Senator told her that since it was such a beautiful day, he'd walk there himself. He left a half-hour early, but didn't show up to the class until it was about to begin.

Nobody knew where he'd been: lost and aimless in the endless cheese aisle.

Looking, looking, thinking about cooking.

Finally, out of some urgency none of the rest of them understood, he had bought a pint of organic, low-fat curds and whey.

This, cold and sweating, he had handed to Colleen before joining the kids in learning how to make hummus.

She hadn't known what to do with it, so she drove it around—the container rolling at the feet of the people in the backseat—until the end of the day, until after she'd dropped the Senator off at his condo on Lake Shore Drive, when, emptying the car of papers and latte cups, she discovered the tub of cottage cheese, spoiled, and tossed it, too.

When the Senator got in the next morning and asked about it, she didn't know what to say.

The Senator looked off into the middle distance and said, very sad, "I suppose that grocery stores are something a man who has chosen my profession does not get to enjoy."

The Senator looks to be enjoying himself now, though. Here he is, introducing the Governor of New Mexico, the crowd going swoony.

Their own state's Elvis-loving Governor is such a jackass, and this governor—former ambassador to the United Nations, former Energy Secretary under the last, still-popular Democratic President—seems knightly in comparison.

Also, they suspect, they may be looking at the next Vice President of the United States, and so feel privileged by association.

Although "He's kinda chubby," there is, Mary Dodge says to Colleen, "something about him."

The Governor of New Mexico loosens his tie as he descends. His appearance, partly undone, makes him look like an invitation, a blank to fill in. Lizzie hops into the space he vacated, calling out logistics about getting their T-shirts for tomorrow, but no one is paying attention. They all want their picture taken with the Governor of New Mexico.

Ethan obliges.

The Governor of New Mexico strolls to where Colleen and Mary are standing next to Dézi and Sudha.

"My people!" he says, and starts speaking Spanish to Dézi and Sudha, who is Indian but does not correct him.

Ethan tells them to cram together, and the Governor of New Mexico grabs two handfuls—Colleen's hip and Sudha's shoulder. They all smile into the flash.

And on he goes to the next group of admirers.

Before long, he's gone. The Senator and Dorothy make their exit, too.

The pivot has pivoted.

Half the party departs.

The rest are in it to win it.

E than shows them his handiwork.

"The Governor of New Mexico is looking tan, rested, and ready," says Colleen.

"He's Mexican, silly," says Dézi. "He always looks tan."

"You know what I mean," says Colleen. "He looks like a man who might want to be VP."

Mary Dodge agrees, observing that his normally doubled chin looked single.

"He was certainly *acting* single, wasn't he?" says Andrew, looking over Ethan's shoulder.

"Poor Andy," says Mary Dodge. "Did you want the Governor to rub your back to see if you're wearing a bra, too?"

"Is that what he was doing?" says Sudha, refilling her beer. "Suave."

The Downstate Director invites the party-goers not to leave until they're ready.

Their hair gets larger. They forget themselves. Time telescopes the way it seems to when she's drinking.

When Colleen next looks at her watch it's nearly eleven, and all the senior staff besides the Downstate Director have left.

The rest of them pour themselves into the minivans and head to one of the two bars in downtown Springfield that haven't already closed.

Beer-reek and neon and no one requesting ID.

J-Lock sits at the edge of the bar, the strap of her sundress slipping, head nodding like a wilted tulip as Andrew brings her her umpteenth chardonnay. She sets it on the bar so half sloshes over the rim. They start to make out. From across the room, the rest of them watch.

"Avert your eyes!" says Colleen, cupping her hands over Sudha's as if she were a child.

"Whoa," says Bobby Peacock. "Correct me if I'm wrong, but doesn't that constitute a *don't?*"

"What happens in Springfield stays in Springfield," says Steve Moon Collier.

"I guess," says Dézi, compiler of the *Dos and Don'ts* in everyone's internship packets.

Ethan feeds more quarters into the foosball table and challenges Colleen to a rematch. She doesn't feel like playing, but the duration of the game will allow her to pound two more drinks.

The only way she'll sleep.

Ethan beats her, and she tells him to walk her back to the hotel so the coming obliteration can synch up with her fall into bed.

Tomorrow, they will put on their T-shirts, fronts emblazoned with the names of the Senior Senator and Junior Senator, backs with, "I [big yellow bovine head] IL" because, since 1922, the state fair has featured a life-sized cow sculpture crafted from eight hundred pounds of unsalted butter.

Tomorrow, Andrew will pull the minivan into the circle drive and step out, his blue T-shirt covered with fine white hairs, the hairs of a Shih Tzu.

"You spent the night with her?" Colleen will say.

And he will say, "I had to. Lo came in hammered and couldn't find the bathroom. He super-soaked his bed before I could stop him. The place smelled like piss, and I had to sleep somewhere, so I gave him my bed and took myself elsewhere. What was I supposed to do?"

"Um, not go straight to J-Whit's room, maybe?" she will say.

"It's not J-Whit," Andrew will say. "It's J-Lock." Then, reaching, "You slept in the same room as Ethan."

"Ethan is not an intern," she will say. "Ethan's my friend."

"Yeah, well, you can be pretty friendly when you want to," Andrew will say, and for the rest of the day, Colleen will feel like she's got a sprained personality.

Tomorrow, they will sit in a refrigerated hotel ballroom and listen to the delusional speech of the Elvis-loving Governor of

Illinois, who toes a delicate line between venal and stupid, and whom 59 percent of voters say they want impeached. His hair will be swept into a feathery and blow-dried cascade over one eye, will look to be a separate, sentient entity, like maybe it leaves his scalp while he sleeps and goes out into the night to commit crimes. "I hear he requires each staffer to carry a comb," Mary Dodge will whisper. "In case he has an emergency."

And tomorrow, they will stand outside at the fairgrounds and find it's like being wrapped in the cotton batting from a crazy quilt that's been dipped in a horse trough. Not only oppressive, but also smelly. They will clap half-assedly through more boring speeches. The acrimony between the Governor and the Illinois Speaker of the House, seated on opposite ends of the metal risers behind the microphones, will be so bitter that the Senator will decide to forgo his speech.

And the billboard with the Senator's fourteen-by-forty-eight-foot face that they saw on their way out of Chicago will be blank and white on the side they see on their way back into Chicago.

This has to mean something, Colleen will think.

But tonight, face washed, teeth brushed, she lies in the queen-sized, thinking of people she wants to talk to but is not calling.

Walter, Andrew, her dad, her sister Bridget, the Chief of Staff. She awaits the coming erasure.

She would want to call Ethan if he weren't already here, but he is, on top of the spread of the other bed because the AC's broken. Colleen is glad she is cold, tucked and neat beneath the sheet, because she's read there's usually semen all over hotel comforters.

She'd tell this to Ethan, but she's got the spins.

Too bad. It had been a decent party up to a point. Party, party,

party she thinks. From *partir*, to divide. A word with a political sense, meaning a side. A word meaning *person* in addition to *a gathering for social pleasure*: dinner party, hunting party, drinking party. Party as verb. Used in a sentence, *I, Colleen, have partied too hard*.

The party is over.

She left the party without saying good-bye.

Party pooper, she thinks, followed by *shut up shut up shut up, brain, please*.

12

Nobody got anywhere in the world by simply being content.
This bromide, attributed to the prolific author of American Westerns whose last name means *the love*, runs like the message on an LED reader board behind Colleen's eyes.

Her dad used to quote it to her mother when Colleen and her sister Bridget were little, when he kept moving the family all over the country to various shithole towns with veterans' hospitals to advance his career. Colleen has just dropped a book of these quotations, assembled by the late author's daughter, into the bin at the post office next to the Federal Building, addressed to her dad, care of his APO in Iraq.

Whenever Colleen gives a book as a gift, she reads it first. Tacky, yes, but the recipient can't tell, and she's a fast reader.

She couldn't finish this one, though.

The bedecking of one's speech and writing with such snippets of wisdom—concise, devoid of context—strikes her as pretentious and ingratiating, a ham-fisted signifier of learning and authority, in much the same way that chocolate-covered cherries—syrupy, embryonic—were a sign of refinement in her family growing up.

Embarrassment rises in her as she rides the elevator to the office on the thirty-eighth floor, then embarrassment for feeling embarrassed.

Colleen is trying to be content, and getting nowhere.

Career-wise, anyway.

She is trying not to care, but it isn't working.

And she is trying not to worry about her dad, but that is impossible, and it makes her begrudge all the people who do not have to care, who do not have loved ones "over there," who think it strange that an older, educated man of her dad's professional standing would have to participate in a war.

So déclassé.

She doesn't talk about it with other people much.

Just Walter.

Sometimes Bridget on the phone.

Not her uncle Tom Dugan, who'd love to talk about it (too many flashbacks, too much exaggeration of his own service) and not her mother, who wouldn't love to (too much talk about the hands of God, into which the situation must be placed).

Imagining God's imaginary hands does not comfort Colleen. It fills her with anger.

So Colleen contains.

Which was especially hard when she was still doing outreach to the counties, where *everyone* was asking for federal money, and she had to swallow the impulse to contrast the price of the wars with what these people could accomplish with a fraction of that cash.

She pictures flag-shrouded bodybags piled atop moneybags.

Hears the robotic Vice President cackling his dry laugh.

Sees him smiling that thin-lipped rictus which never fully reveals his crooked teeth.

For the past week, each day has started off befogged and gray. Even after the sun has burned through and she knows time has passed, it doesn't feel that way.

From her cube Colleen can't see the sky, and the light inside remains unchanging.

Worse, she has no reason to go into anyone's windowed office this week, because almost no one with a windowed office is here. They're all in Denver for the Convention.

No Chief of Staff, no Gina.

No Steve Moon Collier.

No Nasrin, no Mary Dodge.

No Palmira and no Nia, both still on maternity leave, though Palmira has gone to Denver on her own, bringing her baby with her.

Lo Benson is there, too, with the Congressional Black Caucus.

No Hannah, even, who didn't want to go, though as scheduler she had to.

Colleen would have gladly gone in any of their places, but she has no experience scheduling, no stylish Democratic baby. Nor in the long term does she want either.

That leaves only Andrew, Agnes Lumley, Dézi, Sylvia, and the interns.

And tucked away on a flash drive in Colleen's purse, Senate hopeful Ron Reese Ryder and an unidentified companion, in a stall in the men's room of the Palmer House Hilton's Lobby Bar.

W e'll all have to suffer in our jackets and ties then," Andrew said last Friday, when Colleen refused, at first, to be persuaded to ask the Chief of Staff to declare a casual week.

"Just go tell him that since no one will be in the office, no one will care if we're dressed appropriately," said Colleen.

"We need someone cute," Andrew said, gesturing at her, "to ask."

"I think *you're* cute, Andy," said J-Lock, sorting press clips.

"Cute and female," said Andrew, not looking at J-Lock, but looking pleased.

"Go ask Agnes," said Colleen.

"Come on, Colleen. Loose the noose," said Andrew, tying his tie around his forehead like a bandana—like the character in the 1980s movie saga about a vengeful and post-traumatically stressed Vietnam vet, played by an actor known as the Italian Stallion—until she finally gave in.

Colleen rarely participates in casual week. To her, nonfunctional dressy clothing serves a function. But she asked the Chief, and he conceded.

"I'm sorry I won't be here to see what you'll wear," he said.

"I'm sorry I won't be wearing it in Denver," she had said, and received no answer.

Colleen stares at the phone in her cube.

She's sick of chatting with little old ladies with voices like sugar who call because they're lonely.

Sick of her frustration at being left out of the campaign action—the constant secret calls and Grand Avenue office meetings—that covert, clubby feel that is the epitome of exclusive.

Of Andrew trying to comfort her about not being invited: "The Vice President doesn't go to meetings either, Colleen. He goes to the meeting *before* the meeting."

Sick, especially, of having to sit and sit and sit around the regular office and do her best to look busy while despising this willful confusion of activity with productivity.

Her work email is empty save for the automatic news service messages—all stories on the DNC—so she turns to her personal account. 'Tis the season when witty friends send fundraising emails:

From: Ariana Zimmermann
Date: Mon, Aug 25, 2008 at 8:18 AM
Subject: Thirsty?... For Change?
To: Ariana Zimmermann

What's a better combination than good drinks, great company, and a fantastic candidate? Nothing, that's what. (To those who would argue that winning the lottery would be better: you will undoubtedly be hounded by me for $2,300 shortly after your check is cut.)

Yep. I'm asking you (I know—again) to support my favorite Democrat running for Congress this year, Henry "Hank" Czyzniejewski—and have some fun and drinks at the same time:

• Email or call me and tell me that you're coming to this awesome event.
• On Thursday, September 4th, get in a car, bus, cab, train (or similar) and arrive at Zella from 7–9PM
• Set $30 of your money aside and write a check to Henry Czyzniejewski for Congress or make a credit card contribution (yay miles!) on the internet.
• Enjoy the heck out of yourself!

Here's the niftiest part: I'm asking you to participate, then you ask all of your friends. It ends up building a huge base of support and brings in a ton of awesome people and we get to have an extra-super fundraiser. It's kind of like a pyramid scheme, but better, because this way it's called "civic engagement" and it ends with you going to a party instead of into crippling, sleazy debt.

Please do let me know if you can make it. I'm REALLY looking forward to seeing you! Also, if you're sick of getting hit up, just remember. It will all be over soon / in November.

Ariana works for Susan Scheck in the Friends Of fundraising office.

Susan's in Denver—the better to be near the moneyed—and it makes Colleen happy in a misery-loves-company fashion to see that Ariana has been left in Chicago, too.

Colleen replies that next week is her week to drive the Senator, so she can't commit.

She doesn't add that she wouldn't go anyway.

She likes when she and the other staffers get to go for free, as part of the fill-the-room-crowd to make a candidate look popular among the young professional set—but she doesn't want to donate. The paltriness of her Senate salary makes giving money away seem mad, plus she figures she gives so much to the political process as it is, that her efforts add up to more than cash. Steve Moon Collier is always quoting the Chief of Staff's maxim that canvassing and word of mouth are more important than voting. Colleen doesn't know if they are more important than donating, but she thinks they might be.

She is free, too, of the symptoms of Fear Of Missing Out for this event, because she has another one to look forward to on the following night—the Democratic Senatorial Campaign Committee Fundraiser.

So there's that.

Colleen fixates on the phrase "all over soon / in November."

She does not know if the world that follows Election Day will be better or worse than this one, and no one else has come in yet, aside from the interns, so there is no one to hear her say out loud, "No matter what happens, it is probably too late for the Oughts to amount to anything but the stupidest and most disappointing decade of this new century."

Idly, she searches the Internet.

First up, Ron Reese Ryder.

She thinks of the video, what the fuck she'll do with it. Whether anyone else has broken the news. How Ethan's still so worked up about it that she's afraid she'll have to bodily restrain him from marching over and telling the Senator himself next time they're in the same place. She looks up "Ryder homosexual" and "Ryder gay rumors" and "Ryder incriminating photos" but aside from unsubstantiated comments scattered here and there—the kind she might find about any candidate—she comes up dry.

Next, the Convention—at a convention center named after a soft drink formerly known as "the choice of a new generation," where the Junior Senator will accept his party's nomination at a sports arena formerly known as Mile High Stadium, presently named after an investment management company incorporated in Bermuda.

Next, herself.

The site that Andrew has helped her revamp and add a blog to.

Not that she ever blogs, out of fear of the trouble she'd get into with Gina for calling too much attention to herself or, heaven forefend, to her connection to the Senator. "You have to have a passion for anonymity in this business," is one of many sayings the Chief of Staff is always saying.

Colleen is not sure she has this passion.

She turns away from the screen and takes out the book-length essay Walter got her to help cheer her up about feeling so B-Team.

The author describes Chicago as a city on the make. "Once you've become a part of this particular patch," he writes, "you'll never love another. Like loving a woman with a broken nose, you may well find lovelier lovelies, but never a lovely so real."

The city-as-woman metaphor reminds Colleen that even fifty-seven years after the author wrote this, it's still largely a man's world.

That aside, Colleen identifies with the author's landscape of "nobodies that nobody knows."

S udha knocks on the frame of Colleen's cube.

"Sorry to interrupt," she says. "I know you must be busy, but there's a whole crew of magazine people here who say they're scheduled to do a shoot with Bobby Peacock?" Her voice suggests a question, though what she's said is a statement.

Colleen sits puzzled for a beat. No one has told her anything about this.

"No one has told me anything about this," Colleen says. She's considering how to continue when Andrew appears over Sudha's shoulder, followed by Bobby. "Have you heard anything about a photo shoot?" she says to Andrew.

"Oh yeah, Gina sent an email on Friday," he says, taking out his phone, forwarding the message.

"Not to me," says Colleen as the email pops up and she sees everyone who's in the office this week in the "To" field except her.

"I'm sure it was just an oversight," says Andrew.

"I apologize, Colleen," says Bobby Peacock. "I should have told you personally."

"It's okay," says Colleen, skimming the email, the subject line of which is "Photographer in office":

> Want to let you know that a Chicago mag photographer will be in at 8:30 to take pictures of Bobby Peacock in action. Bobby was selected for a piece on eight students under 18 that have very bright futures. Lest you think Bobby is getting a big head over this, he apologized profusely for the shoot and said he tried to get them to do it somewhere else. See you next Friday.
>
> —Gina

"Story checks out," says Colleen. "Go ahead and let them in."

Sudha returns to reception, and Andrew high-fives Bobby. "You're holding up well under the media scrutiny," he says.

"It's absurd, I know," says Bobby, turning his hands skyward. Colleen notes how large they are for his puppyish frame.

"It's reductive," Bobby says. "The feature is 'Eight Teen

Dreams,' and they do it every year. They pick eight high-schoolers and assign them stereotypes—like one is the beautiful ballet dancer, one's the daydreamy writer, one's the science whiz, one's the basketball star. It's like they go, 'Talk about your hopes for the future, but only as they relate to this one category.' I really like basketball, too. And I know the science guy, and he does all these humanitarian, political kinds of causes. But that can't go in the article, because we all rep one type of kid."

Four magazine people have herded themselves into the intern room. The photographer sets up lights, umbrellas, and his assistant affixes cords to the floor with gaffer tape.

If I were a magazine photographer, Colleen wonders, would I get an assistant?

"Ready for hair and makeup, Robert?" says a blonde woman carrying a tackle box.

"I think she's talking to you," Colleen whispers.

"Oh. Uh, as I'll ever be. And please, call me Bobby," he says, as she and a woman carrying a garment bag flank him.

"Anywhere you'd recommend we go to prep him?" the makeup woman asks Colleen.

She directs them to the main conference room, then turns to the photographer.

"You might want to put your backpack on the base of that light stand," she says, knowing how wobbly they can be from doing portrait work in the apartment. "The intern room can be kind of high-traffic. Wouldn't want it to tip over."

"Thanks," he says, propping his pack across the feet of the stand. "We'll try to be in and out pretty quick."

Colleen says something polite about taking all the time they need, then she and Andrew head back to Cube City.

What must it feel like to be so young and full of promise?

Not merely equipped with a scrappy desire to make a difference but with parents who are wealthy and well-connected?

An almost guaranteed life of fun and profit if you just try a little bit and don't fuck it up?

"That Bobby Peacock is really going places," says Andrew, "so long as he keeps up his positive and over-achieving attitude, isn't he?"

"Why are these *Here Are Some Kids Who at Seventeen Are More Successful Than Most of You Readers at Home Will Ever Be* features so perennially popular?" says Colleen. "Is it like, 'Hey older people, you may be losing your edge, but there's still some hope for the damaged future?' What kind of emotions are they supposed to evoke?"

"Hatred and envy, I presume," says Andrew. "But I guess it's like reading about rich people in general. Or travel or architecture magazines. Places you can probably never go or be."

"It's all an illusion," Bobby will say later, after the article has come out, accompanied by an image of him standing in the intern room with the Interns <3 The Senator sign on the wall behind him—after the Chief has said, "Sharp tie, Red."

"It wouldn't lay right," Bobby will say. "The makeup lady took a pair of scissors and cut off the back half. They let me keep it. It looks perfect in the photograph, but it's totally unusable."

They will post the article in the break room, and they will continue to follow the career of Bobby Peacock with interest, the way they might pause to track the contrail of a passing jet while stuck in traffic on the expressway.

That afternoon, Colleen and Andrew sit in his black two-door, making exquisite time on Lake Shore Drive, having left the office at three. Who's to stop them?

Since he and J-Lock started sleeping together, he's been biking less, driving more. J-Lock requires that he squire her around, and would rather drop dead than squash a bike helmet atop her own helmet of blonde.

J-Lock had called in sick today, though, because she'd had a chardonnay-only dinner the night before, Andrew says.

Colleen shifts in her seat.

Her high-heel crunches into something on the floor. She reaches down and finds a portion-controlled bag of dark chocolate cookies—a brand typically sandwiched around a layer of "crème," but here consisting only of a "thin crisp" version of their black exterior.

"Since when do you not just eat regular cookies?" she asks.

"J-Lock subsists off those," says Andrew. "That's a calorie pack. Whenever I'm over at her place, she's always foisting them on me. 'Calorie pack, babe?' That's what she says. 'Calorie pack?' I'd be a rich man, Colleen, if I had a dollar for every time I heard her say that. Instead I have a bunch of calorie packs."

Colleen is not sure why she said yes when he offered her a ride.

"So," she says, despite not giving even one single fuck about sports but knowing he's obsessed with his alma mater's team, "college football starts this Saturday. How 'bout them Wildcats?"

"Not great, but not bad," he says. "This year I'm less interested in how the team's going to do than I am in football as a signifier of the changing season. The way the fight song carries in the cooler air. The first smell of wood smoke. Falling leaves and rotting pumpkins. Shorter days, longer nights."

"Longer nights do me no good," she says. "I'm so tired, but I can't fall asleep."

The night before, lying in the darkness with Walter log-like beside her, thinking about the campaign, her country, herself, she got a total of two hours' sleep. Today her focus and serotonin feel askew.

Your age is showing, she thinks, looking at her puffy eyes in the visor mirror.

She flips it up.

Andrew twists in his seat, arching his pelvis to reach into his pocket, bashing one hip against the low steering wheel.

"Are you in distress?" Colleen says as he pulls out a baggie.

Inside is a white pill, oblong and scored at the middle. He hands it to her.

"What is this?" she says.

He says the name of a popular prescription-only sleeping pill that sounds like the word *ambient*. "From the Latin," he says, "meaning *existing or present on all sides*."

"Where did you get it?"

"J-Lock," he says. "She's anxious. Can't sleep without them. I tried to get her not to take one last night on account of the liquid dinner, but she did anyway. Hence her absence from Cube City today."

"You stole a sleeping pill from your tanorexic girlfriend to give to me?"

"Dammit, Colleen, she's not my girlfriend," says Andrew. "I also stole the baggie."

"Have you tried it?"

"Yes," he says, "and I trust you'll find it delightful."

"How do they work?"

"They erase your short-term memory. Turn off the electrical activity in your brain cells. At first it seems like nothing's happening. You're lying there, not sleeping, like usual, when bam! Out. Then you sleep like a cherub on heroin."

"Is there a hangover?"

"Nothing a cup of coffee won't clear up."

She thanks him, putting the baggie in the zippered pocket of her purse.

Normally she's averse to medication, but this she knows she will take tonight.

She is that desperate to sleep.

And she is obliged to Andrew for knowing this.

~

We love science and medicine still, as we loved it in life.

We love the materials of the natural world and the forces visible and invisible which appear to govern it.

We designed estates according to the principles of classical geometry and farmed our crops with the latest agricultural methods.

We flew kites in lightning storms to pioneer human understanding of the properties of electricity.

We used scientific metaphors in our political writings.

We were true citizens of the Age of Reason. We wanted to know of what the world was made and how these substances operated.

We are still wondering.

But we are not interested in politics and history as a series of abstractions.

America is 300 million people acting mindfully each day. Or it should be.

This, perhaps, is the chief lesson death has taught us: that everyone, every day, in everything they do, is responsible for democracy.

That the blank slate is ours to fill, or to be filled for us.

~

After dinner that night, when Walter suggests they finish the bottle of red they opened the previous evening, Colleen declines, not wanting to mix it with the pill that Andrew has given her. After remarking on the weirdness of Andrew's lifting it from J-Lock, Walter agrees that she should try it without booze, at least the first time.

"I hate to require chemicals for something so basic as sleep," says Colleen, "but I don't know what else to do. If I don't get some rest soon, I am going to lose my ever-loving mind."

"Don't think of it as a drug," says Walter. "Think of it as a tasty mint. I can fold back the sheets and set it on your pillow if that helps?"

He does, and it does help, even though you don't put a mint on your tongue, then swallow it unchewed with a whole glass of water before lying down on your side and waiting for oblivion.

13

Colleen feels so well, she decides to take a sick day.

The sleeping-pill sleep was not as refreshing as the natural kind—her distant memory of the natural kind. But it was far better than no sleep.

The sleep was thick and dreamless—oily, almost, dark and viscous. No interruptions.

It's a Thursday—the day Walter puts together agenda packets for the weekly village board meetings—so he has no choice but to go, but he's all for Colleen not bothering.

"Everyone's still in the Mountain West, right?" he asks. "What would be the point?"

They make plans to watch the Convention tonight—particularly the speech in which, after being introduced by the Senator, the Junior Senator will accept the nomination.

Walter tells her she should stay in bed until she can't get any more sleep, and she lets herself be convinced. When she wakes again a couple hours later, she sends her I'm-feeling-under-the-weather message to the Chicago list.

At the desk in her apartment, she feels as though, overnight, she has regrown her sense of perspective. Checking her Senate inbox, she finds it is easier to get emails from people who assume she's where the action is. "I know you probably won't be able to reply to this until you get back from Denver, but…" they start.

She still doesn't correct them, but she cares way less.

Birds chirp in the maple trees. Colleen feels like she's inside a child's crayon drawing. She half expects that when the sun rises high enough to clear the buildings between her and the Lake, it will sport sunglasses and a face.

She turns on her favorite public radio station and spends the morning catching up on photography work she's let slide: updating her portfolio, revamping her CV, searching online for Chicago galleries. On a blog she hasn't checked in weeks she sees a post about a photo collective starting and sends the woman who's organizing it an email volunteering to help the next time they set up a pop-up gallery.

Around lunchtime she grabs her camera, walks to the Lake, and takes a bunch of pictures.

Treasuring her aimlessness.

She photographs the rocks, the sunbathers, the students soaking up the days before the semester starts next week, the refugee families from Africa that faith organizations have been resettling.

What a strange shore this must seem to them.

B ack at the apartment, uploading the photos, Andrew is online, too, and they chat.

He always pretends to be confused when she's not in her cubicle, even though she never forgets to account for her whereabouts.

> **Andrew:** Colleen, OMG. Where are you? are you okay?
> **Colleen:** is your email broken?
> **Andrew:** you're not really sick, are you?
> **Colleen:** not exactly. but I am experiencing my fake-sick day personality.
> **Andrew:** WTH does that mean?
> **Colleen:** I'm feeling kind of sad today. I think my real emotions are returning. Work makes me a flat, unfeeling automaton sometimes. It's the constant expedient suppressing of my true thoughts and reactions. know what I mean?

Andrew: unfortunately

Colleen: it is nice to feel like myself again.

Andrew: you like being sad? why?

Colleen: it's kind of wistful and unsatisfied and full of hopeless longing. It's a creative feeling

Andrew: colleen, you are like a seventh chord. you have so many overtones that it is hard to know where your tonal center is.

Colleen: thank you?

Andrew: maybe you lack testosterone? I heard a piece about that on the radio this morning.

Colleen: I heard that piece too, but I think I'm just a naturally kind of sad person. but also happy.

Andrew: maybe you need a shot of "t"?

Colleen: i hate how you reduce everything to chemicals. It's boring.

Andrew: sometimes chemicals are the best thing to reduce everything to. speaking of: how was your sleep?

Colleen: I dreamt that a gigantic Senator appeared from a cloud and told me to "Explore"

Andrew: for realsies?

Colleen: No. I had zero dreams. But the sleep was magical. Like being let back into a kingdom from which I thought I'd been banished. did J-Lock notice a pill was missing?

Andrew: no. she got shitfaced last night and we had a huge fight and she ended up passing out quite naturally.

Colleen: can you bring me a couple more? I need to make a doctor's appt so I can get my own, but in the meantime I can't live without these.

Andrew: sure. I confessed the theft to J-Lock this morning and she says you can have as many as you want until you get your own supply. She really wants you to like her.

Colleen: Well, that is very nice of her.

Typing this, Colleen wonders whether there's an emoticon for a fake smile.

> **Andrew:** it is. Life is too short, she says, to not get any sleep. She says she wants you to sleep like an angel right up in heaven.
> **Colleen:** she wants me dead, you mean?
> **Andrew:** no. she is a very godly person. She believes in heavenly rest and peace.
> **Colleen:** too bad there's no such thing. You just take a dirtnap. dirtnap forever.
> **Andrew:** yeah well anyway, gotta get back to work
> Colleen: enjoy that. See you tomorrow.
> **Andrew:** cu

Colleen flips the radio on again as she sends a few queries about some old photo projects that might still be of interest to galleries and magazines.

A story comes on about how this is the hundred-year anniversary of the lengthy loserdom of the Chicago baseball team named after baby bears. They have not won a World Series since 1908, but they're fielding a better team than usual, so people have started to think that this might be The Year.

The fans have grown so fanatical for their Boys in Blue, the story says, they're gaining notoriety for unsportsmanlike behavior.

There have been incidents.

There was the time a group of fans attacked an opposing player who got too close to the seats trying to field a routine foul ball.

There were the two fans, now standing trial, accused of beating a rival fan in his home stadium in Milwaukee.

There was the fan, chest painted blue, face painted half blue and half red, who dumped an entire coolerful of water onto a very blonde, very attractive freelance reporter doing interviews outside the ballpark entrance. "Welcome to Chicago," he is heard to say on the cellphone video his friends were taking.

There was, of course, the long-standing tradition of tossing the ball back after an opposing player hit a home run, but the balls have become more numerous—one dozen, two dozen, three dozen—the delays in gathering them more lengthy.

The radio story cuts to men on the street.

None of the four men interviewed seem particularly bothered.

The reporter asks, "Which would you rather have happen—your team win the World Series, or the Junior Senator win the presidency?"

All four men say, "World Series."

Only yesterday, this would have annoyed the hell out of Colleen. Today she thinks, Whatever. Those are honest answers, and they are probably correct in their assessments of how happy or not happy each outcome would make them.

Sick days make it easier for her to come closer to understanding how most of the population feels—shut out, uninvested—when it comes to politics.

She and Walter normally never watch television, but Walter gets home in time to figure out how to jack into the cable of their downstairs neighbor so they can eat their dinner to the Convention speeches.

They watch one by a former Vice President best known for speaking about how the globe must be stopped from warming.

They watch a particularly boring one by the Governor of Virginia.

And then they watch her boss, the Senator, calm and short behind the wooden podium on the enormous stage. They cheer at the TV as if he were an athlete who scored big.

"This is basically my Super Bowl, you know?" says Colleen.

"I do," says Walter, holding her hand.

The Senator does not once turn his gaze toward the teleprompter. He is, Colleen judges, the most organic speaker of the convention. His warm and offhand tone leads Colleen to imag-

ine that he's just been walking down the street with the Junior
Senator and happened upon some friends he thinks the Junior
Senator should meet.

Like, *Hey, America, got a minute? Because this is my pal, the Junior Senator. He's a great person you should really know about.* Then
everybody shakes hands, sincere and relaxed.

~

We were once capable of oratory like that: calm and informal and oddly magnetic.

Or we were known as poor extemporizers whose fumbling constructions suggested a troubling lack of intellect.

Or we were as polished and stentorian as the finest stage actors, pulling the people toward us with our every hand gesture.

We spoke of terrible losses sustained in battle.

We spoke of fear itself as the most fearful thing.

Or of the military-industrial complex, which even in its infancy we knew was monstrous.

Or of self-sacrifice, by way of rhetorical questions in the rhythmic ribbon of chiasmus.

Ask not for this, *we demanded, and then demanded,* Ask for that.

Now we can no longer remember how our individual voices sounded, and when we speak, our voices are no longer ours alone.

~

The Senator yields the podium to the Junior Senator, who begins by weaving his own story "of the brief union between a young man from Kenya and a young woman from Kansas who weren't well-off or well-known" with the "promise that's always set this country apart."

He defines that promise as the "hard work and sacrifice" through which "each of us can pursue our individual dreams, but still come together as one American family, to ensure that the next generation can pursue their dreams, as well."

He pauses, then, punctuating the air with his left index finger, and declares, "That's why I stand here tonight. Because for 232 years, at each moment when that promise was in jeopardy, ordinary men and women—students and soldiers, farmers and teachers, nurses and janitors—found the courage to keep it alive."

Colleen thinks it would be hard for her to feel more moved were she actually in the stadium.

"Our government," says the Junior Senator, "should work for us, not against us. It should ensure opportunity, not for just those with the most money and influence, but for every American who is willing to work. That's the promise of America—the idea that we are responsible for ourselves, but that we also rise or fall as one nation; the fundamental belief that I am my brother's keeper, I am my sister's keeper. That's the promise we need to keep, that's the change we need right now."

Walter looks over at Colleen and notices that her eyes are welling up. His are too.

"It's good we're not there," he says. "This whole thing is produced in such a way that it's meant to be watched by 38 million people at home, on a screen. Who needs Denver?"

Colleen is tempted to say "Me," but almost agrees.

Friday morning and Colleen's inbox is awash in emails from friends and colleagues about seeing the Senior Senator on national TV. "I know you were probably there, but your boss was great. I didn't realize how cool he was!" and so forth.

Some of the messages are from people in the art world, people she hasn't seen in years.

Everyone who actually was in Denver is returning today, but not until late morning at the earliest. It's Colleen's driving day, and it promises to be a long night with the fundraiser, so she's taken a page from the Steve Moon Collier playbook and not arrived in her cubicle until after ten.

No one says a thing.

The cab-loads of staffers coming back from Denver arrive from the airport shortly before lunch, just in time to catch the breaking news that the Republican presidential candidate has picked as his running mate the unknown first-term governor of Alaska, a woman who describes herself as "just your average hockey mom."

Gina, an early supporter of the female Democratic candidate, leaves her luggage at reception, races to her office, flips on the TV. "What a pandering motherfucker," she mutters. "This is disgusting. He picks a woman—but not a strong one? Some goddamn unheard-of sexy librarian Stepford wife?"

"She sure does fill out that suit, doesn't she, boys?" says the Chief of Staff, watching the screen while resting his chin on Colleen's shoulder.

Colleen elbows him in the stomach, softly enough to show that she's kidding, hard enough to show that he's being an asshole.

"And those red shoes?" says Steve. "With those open toes?"

The Alaskan hockey mom pays lipsticked lip service to feminism without actually saying the f-word, declaring that before she dropped out, the female Democratic candidate "left eighteen million cracks in the highest, hardest glass ceiling in America."

Then, in what strikes Colleen as one of the most cynical co-optings of an opponent's words she has ever heard, "But it turns out the women of America aren't finished yet, and we can shatter that glass ceiling once and for all."

The crowd before her in Dayton, Ohio is not all for this.

In the audio a few women are cheering, but low-pitched groans and boos underlie them.

Colleen can't believe that this is only the second viable female running mate in US history, after the one who ran in 1984, twenty-four years ago, when Colleen was four.

Hannah comes in to tell Colleen that the Senator's flight from Denver arrives at 1:30, so she'll need to go soon. "Here's this afternoon's schedule," she says, "and the speech Meg wrote for him for the DSCC tonight. Not that he'll use it, but I'm sure he'll ask."

"How does the rest of the weekend look?"

"Empty for you," says Hannah. "He's flying to Wyoming to campaign for you-know-who. But he'll use the car service. Monday morning he flies back to DC, but Dot volunteered to take him to the airport, so you're off the hook."

Colleen resists the urge to pump her fist in the air. Everyone loves light driving weeks, but it's best not to show how much.

Even though the fundraiser will be a reception with drinks and a sit-down dinner, Colleen keeps referring to it simply as *the thing*. "You're still planning on coming to the thing tonight, right?" Colleen says to Andrew and Dézi. "I hear it's going to be pretty major."

"Wouldn't miss it," says Dézi.

"The kids don't say 'major' anymore," says Andrew. "They say BFFD—big fat fucking deal. And that is what tonight's fundraiser will be. Hell yes, I'll be there."

"Okay, great. See you at the thing," Colleen says, and goes to get the rental car.

She stops at the restroom and, upon entering the vestibule leading to the stalls, sees J-Lock, looking lacquered, before the full-length mirror. She has a shoebox full of styling products on the chair beside her, and her face is fogged by hairspray, an old-fashioned brand with a net on the can.

"Hey girl," says J-Lock. "You caught me buffing up my bouffant. I keep this stuff in the drawer of my cube. A gal's gotta keep an emergency hair kit in the office."

She giggles as if Colleen should know what she means.

"Wow," says Colleen. "How retro. I didn't even know they still make that kind of hairspray, since it destroys the ozone layer,"

J-Lock laughs. "Yeah," she says, "Gosh, I guess I ought to buy myself some of those carbon setoffs."

"Offsets," Colleen says. "Carbon offsets."

She's about to add that J-Lock has her pollutants mixed up, but thinks better of it.

"Hey," she says, "thanks for the sleeping pill the other day."

She makes sure to walk out the opposite door as she leaves.

Colleen zips among the cabs and shuttles towards the Authorized Service Vehicles Only entrance at the airport. The professional drivers honk and flip her the bird, as per usual. She pulls into the private lot next to the terminal.

Allows herself to feel satisfied.

But as she kills the engine she gets a text from Hannah. The Senator's flight has had a mechanical problem and will be delayed. New ETA, 2:45 p.m.—nearly two whole hours to fend off the parking guards, one of whom is already eyeing her suspiciously.

Since she got the schedule so late in the game, she hasn't had time for worry to build. But now she feels it—the about-to-be-lowered-into-a-pit-of-tarantulas sensation of the Senator's approach.

Now that things have started going wrong, it's hard to know where they'll stop.

The parking guard lumbers over and demands ID.

He seems appeased when she flashes her Senate badge, but makes her flip the car around so she's parked tail-in, and later, when she asks out of boredom if she can dart into the terminal to pee, demands her keys.

Around three, Colleen is so absorbed in the book she's reading about the British photographer who pioneered motion picture projection that she doesn't see the Senator shuffle up to the passenger side. He has to tap on the glass.

"Didn't mean to startle you," he says as he buckles up. "You jumped about ten feet."

They pull away from the curb, and he tells her that aside from the delay, his flight was all right. "I gave up my seat and moved back so an old guy could sit next to his wife."

"That was thoughtful. Weren't you with Dot?"

"Dot was exhausted. High altitude in Denver."

"Oh no," Colleen says, then "Right, her lungs," then feels like a jerk for mentioning it—and wonders, too, if she should have said "lung."

"She was a real sport," the Senator says, "but we got her on an earlier flight. She's home resting. She'll be at the fundraiser tonight. How about you? How's that young man of yours?"

"Walter? He's fine."

"Are Dot and I going to be invited to your wedding one of these days?"

"That's sweet that you'd want to go," says Colleen, trying to mask her distaste for this question. "One of these days."

The Senator seems to notice anyway, but is too tactful to comment.

Instead, he asks if she's familiar with an independent band from Austin, Texas, named after a utensil. She says yes, theirs was the first twenty-one-and-over concert that she ever attended, and that she'd gone with Walter.

This pleases the Senator, who produces his MP3 player with the biblical fruit logo. Plays a song from his playlist by this band, one called "The Underdog," which avers that it is worth listening to everyone, no matter their status, and alleges that if a person harbors no fear of the title creature, then that person will not survive.

"I'm thinking this could be my new theme song," the Senator says. "Our favorite presidential candidate has been using a tune by another great band, the song about the fake empire. What do you think?"

"It's a good message," she says. "Absolutely. And the kids are into them," she adds, and the Senator laughs.

Colleen's to take the Senator straight to the interview in the Tower on North Michigan, at the radio station whose call letters, WGN, indicate that it is owned by the daily that styles itself as the World's Greatest Newspaper.

The Chief of Staff and Gina are waiting at the circle drive when Colleen pulls up. Gina whisks the Senator away. The Chief sticks his head through the passenger side window. "See you tonight at the thing, right?" says Colleen.

"Right," the Chief says, "but listen. You're taking us. I know, I know, you're not supposed to, since it's a political fundraiser. But we're running behind, and he can't be late. See you here in half an hour, and make sure you're ready when we are."

Before she can object, he's striding after Gina and the Senator.

The murky ethics of the situation trouble her less than the fact that it is almost impossible to wait in this driveway without getting a ticket. As soon as the Chief disappears, a parking attendant saunters up and tells her to roll it along. She flashes her Senate ID and the woman backs off, grudgingly.

At 4:35, Colleen sits listening to the Senator's voice, live on the radio, recapitulating the events of the Convention, when a man walks up. He's in plainclothes, but he wears an earpiece and a tough expression, so she can tell he's a cop. He leans into her window, mirrored cop shades all in her face, and tells her she has to "move this vehicle now, no ifs, ands, or buts."

The radio announcer is thanking the Senator. He'll be back outside in under five.

"So," she says, "I work for the Senator, and—"

"Now this ain't a game, miss, but I trump you there. I work for the Mayor, and he's about to be here any minute, and he needs to park here."

In real life, Senator trumps Mayor, Colleen thinks but doesn't say, because in this city, the Mayor trumps real life—is the guy who controls the police and the parking—so he gets to put his car wherever he wants, whenever he wants.

"All right, sir. But then where am I supposed to go?"

"You look like a smart gal. You'll figure it out. Take it for a spin around the block."

At this hour in River North, that'll take significantly more than five minutes, and she'll miss the Senator, and everyone will be livid that she fucked up such a basic task.

Her phone rings and it's the Chief of Staff. "We're coming down, babe. See you in two shakes."

"That was them," Colleen says. "They need two minutes."

"The Mayor's gonna be here in under one minute, and you need to move *now*."

Another black car has pulled up behind her, and its driver taps the horn approximately every two seconds. Colleen tries to ignore it.

"Sir, please," she says, speaking the first gibberish that comes to her mind, "You're stressing me out, and I am a bad driver as it is."

The cop looks at her as if she's gone full-on insane. "Uh, that ain't my problem," he says.

"With all due respect," says Colleen, "since you're not in uniform, may I please see your badge before I obey you?"

The cop shakes his head, pulls out a leather wallet.

And as she looks up, craning her neck, pretending she can't see, the Chief comes dashing across the plaza, Gina and the Senator following.

"Have a pleasant evening, officer," the Chief calls out as they pull onto Michigan Avenue. "Everything okay here, babe?"

Colleen's hands are shaking. "Sure," she says. "Everything's aces."

"That's my girl," says the Chief, and squeezes her shoulder.

And though she is grinding her teeth and trying not to scream or cry or both at the way her job lately has become a series of humiliating exclusions and petty altercations, she drives without incident to the front of the hotel and deposits the trio with a cheery "See you soon!" before delivering the rental to the nearest drop-off.

Walking the half-mile back to the hotel, she tells herself that she's not missing out, though the fundraiser started fifteen minutes ago. That she'll be late but fashionably so.

Her dress billows around her.

There's a chill breeze.

Summer absenting itself.

The coldness going well with the trend of her mood.

Riding the hotel elevator to the appointed floor is like leaving one America behind, and rising up, up, up into another.

The stratospherically wealthy one.

How appropriate to find that the ballroom's named after Versailles.

Gaping inequality is part of the theme. Pre-Revolutionary France the inspiration for the decor.

No signs. No ordinary fundraiser this. If you have to ask, you do not belong.

Andrew has texted her precise coordinates. She rounds a corner and receives his latest: "*nous sommes dans Le Petit Trianon.*" The placard at the door says that that is where she is. She pushes it open—dark wood, brass handle—and steps into a room whose carpet is plush and muffling, and where even some of the men standing on top of it have had obvious facelifts.

She is glad she brought her camera.

S he sees Palmira at the center of a circle of donors and knows she should go say hello, ask about the baby, but she can't bring herself to do it.

Each day, Palmira looks more processed, artificial.

Rich.

The other day, with nothing to do despite her willingness to do anything, Colleen looked up Palmira's salary on a site that tracks Congressional staffer earnings. She discovered it to be in the low six figures—almost thrice what Colleen makes.

The fact that many of her coworkers suffer the same ratio of pay inequality only makes Colleen angrier. She tries not to think too much about amassing money because it usually only leaves her frustrated. Then too she doesn't want to become as cash-obsessed or acquisitive as so many of her fellow Americans.

But she has, periodically, asked for a raise, and every time she has done so, Palmira has told her no, that there "isn't money in the budget."

Colleen noted how Palmira's salary seemed unaffected by any such constraints, rising consistently, quarter after quarter.

No doubt, part of it is the setting.

No doubt, part of it is the recession.

But looking at Palmira now, in her designer suit, champagne flute in her manicured hand, outsized diamond ring sparkling like the eye of a lizard, Colleen imagines her supervisor as the French queen who apocryphally posited that poor people should become cake-eaters.

Off with her head.

Colleen needs to find her friends.

She catches sight of Dot, tired but well-dressed in a tasteful matron gown, like the mother of a bride. Dot sees her and waves. Colleen waves back and smiles and feels a little bit better.

She locates her coworkers standing around a tall circular table. Lo'Kewell Benson is saying, "All politicians are phony."

"That's not quite fair," says Steve Moon Collier.

"Well, there's phony," says Colleen, "and then there's the need to divide your real self from your public self. You can't run for office as whoever you act like around your friends. You can't earn this job by Being Yourself. The Senator acts differently around all of us, too. When I'm driving, versus when Lo is. He never asks me about football."

"Driving him last week," says Lo, "he pointed out this hot girl crossing the street. 'There's a good-lookin' dish,' he said. He could never say that in public, but with me it's okay."

"Ha," says Andrew—because sometimes he does that, laughs by saying *ha*, like a comic book character. "He said that because he wanted to eat her up."

"I need a drink," says Colleen. "What's good here?"

"They've got an eighteen-year-old Scotch that's to die for," says Andrew. "It should probably be about twenty-five bucks a glass, but we get everything free." He offers to get her one.

Scotch smells to her like adhesive bandages, but she doesn't dislike it, and she wants something strong. The bartender asks Andrew who the drink is for, and he points at Colleen. The bartender motions her over and asks for ID.

"Terribly sorry," he says. "But we've been told to card everyone we think might be underage. The hotel doesn't want to risk even the minor scandal of interns drinking at such a major affair."

"That's flattering, but I've been old enough to have this drink for seven years now."

"This Scotch, however, is not old enough to drink itself," says Andrew.

"But this Scotch *is* old enough to go to college," says Colleen, "if it could afford to."

Walking back to the table, they run into the Chief. He has to be the only man in the room besides the Senator not holding a drink.

"I cannot get enough of you today," he says as he sees her.

She's wearing a black dress he says reminds him of a classical statue—very simple, very drapey—and a long double-strand of green vintage beads on a brass chain with faux seed pearls between them.

Whatever precious stone the beads are supposed to resemble, they aren't.

Sylvia, whose jewelry background makes her prone to excitement over such pieces, says they look like green grapes, and keeps pretending she's going to eat one.

The Chief of Staff keeps touching her as they chat, and the other attendees keep looking at the touches.

"It's so nice of these people, isn't it?" says Colleen.

"What do you mean?" says the Chief.

"For them to be so rich," she says, "so you and I don't have to."

S peeches at fundraisers are always extreme, so far off the record that you can't even see the record.

Choice cuts for the super-rich.

In the case of this fundraiser, the super-liberal super-rich.

The true believers who drank the Kool-Aid, except the Kool-Aid here is premium alcohol.

Colleen finished her first drink while talking to the Chief, and now she and Andrew circle for refills before the candidates take the stage. Lo's at the bar, too, already on his fourth.

Colleen is thrilled to be absolved of driving duty for the evening. It was ethically questionable, FEC-wise, for her to have dropped the Senator off, but it would be absolutely illegal, DUI-wise, for her to bring him home.

The Senator emcees, introducing each visiting Democrat.

The senior senator of New York goes first. The Senator introduces him with an anecdote about how the two of them, along with two reps, share a crummy townhouse on Capitol Hill when the Senate's in session. Kind of like a frat-house, he says.

The senior senator of New York takes to the stage and gives the crowd what they came for, a real stemwinder. He says "bawt" for "bought" and "yuge" for "huge." He declares that the current Administration has "transformed this great nation into a wounded giant, bleeding at the wrists." He warns that "we can't bring democracy to Iraq, because that's Western arrogance."

Next up, the female candidate running for the Senate in New Hampshire. She steps to the podium wearing a pink blazer. She talks about her state as being, per voter, one of the most expensive to win in the entire country, because of its smallness and its proximity to the Boston media market.

Catering staff cut stealthy paths, unobtrusive food ninjas, offering filet mignon, scallops, shrimp. Occasionally, Colleen takes one and hands it to Andrew, Lo, or Dézi. A short round woman in a tux with a platter and an accent tilts her tray towards the knot of them.

"What is it?" Sylvia mouths soundlessly.

"Goat cheese lollipop?" she says softly, and everyone grabs one.

"The most persuasive argument to run for office," the pink-blazered candidate explains, "is, *Your country needs you.*"

Is it? Colleen wonders. Is it, really? Questions effervesce in her brain like the bubbles in the champagne being passed out to toast the impending restoration of the "glory" and the "sheen" to this "tarnished country."

Next, a member of a Western Democratic dynasty who urges them to "vote for the cousin nearest you." He speaks of insidious Republican inroads, and describes the architect of the former Democratic Speaker of the House's defeat as "a man with an automatic weapon for a mouth and two stilettos on each shin who would stoop to anything to win."

Andrew grins across the room at an older woman who winks at him.

He motions to Colleen to borrow her notebook, jotting "cougar" therein.

The candidate cousins are attractive, Colleen thinks, in a teen-idol way.

They talk together about the importance of having each other, quoting the president whose nickname was Give 'em Hell: "If you want a friend in Washington, get a dog" and "The most important position in American government is not President or Senator, but Citizen."

Then the wrap up—the thanking of these citizens, these citizens applauding the cousins and themselves.

The Senator takes the mic, announces that dinner will be served in the next ballroom.

People begin milling either that way or into the night.

Ariana from Susan Scheck's office materializes at their table. "Susan was nervous," she whispers, "because this event had a target of over a million dollars. But we made the goal. Even in this economy."

Ariana flips her curly hair over her bare shoulder and glances at herself in the mirrored wall. "For those of you who haven't worked the campaign before," she says, "and as a refresher for those of you who have, the Federal Election Commission allows an individual to cough up up to $2,400 to each candidate per election. But they can give up to $30,400 to the national party per calendar year."

"Whooo-eee," says Sylvia, and Lo gives a whistle.

"Don't get too impressed," says Ariana. "There's a $115,500 overall biennial limit. The breakdown is $45,600 to all candidates and $69,900 to PACs and parties."

"I need to contact these people about my law school loans," says Andrew.

"Plus there are lots of ways to get around that cap," says Ariana. "You have your spouse donate—your darling husband, your doting wife, your loyal kids, your progressive relatives. Whoever. And there are plenty of people who give money to everybody—both parties—just because they have it. They treat it like an insurance policy: whoever wins, they'll be in good. They'll have gotten in on the proverbial ground floor by giving up to the ceiling."

C olleen thinks of the citizens in the city below, those citizens who could never afford an event like this, who would never even know it was happening.

She is surrounded by people who have spent to within a couple thousand dollars of her own yearly Senate Aide salary to be here. Lots of them spent this to attend and didn't even show up.

What will these citizens, these attendees, remember?

After the drinks, after the speeches, after the dinner?

Mostly atmosphere, she guesses.

Golden and glowing.

The atoms of the air becoming monetized.

The pleasing impression of being surrounded not just by like minds but a like class.

A quality of people, a quality of candidate.

A gist of having given well, and having done so in front of their peers.

Like going to church, but with more measurable influence.

The donors who paid only for the reception have dissipated. Those who paid full price have vacated the bar for the ballroom.

Colleen and her coworkers are seated in an antechamber where they can see, but not fully hear, the proceedings. The hum of the conversations, the clinking of the glasses, the knife-on-plate sounds, the cadence of further speeches.

Colleen looks around the table at her fellow bright-eyed non-persons as they eat their salads. Colleen eats the blood oranges, heirloom tomatoes, and arugula leaves, but gleans the prosciutto from her plate and passes it to Andrew, who says, "Mmmmmm, pig!" She signals to the server and tells him that she is a vegetarian.

There is more wine with dinner, and they all get drunker, and when next Colleen looks up from refilling her glass she sees J-Lock walking in, pulling a chair over and sitting between her and Andrew. The main courses arrive, and Ariana indicates they should bring a plate for J-Lock.

"Oh, I couldn't possibly," says J-Lock when the surf and turf is set before her.

"Why not?" asks Colleen.

"Andy and I had a big ol' lunch."

Colleen looks at Andrew who shakes his head slightly.

The other day, Colleen read an interview of an English supermodel, famous for being waifish with a wide cat-face. Her personal motto, the supermodel said, is *Nothing tastes as good as skinny feels.*

Colleen quotes this to J-Lock, and is frightened by the vehemence of J-Lock's agreement.

"And why aren't *you* eating your pasta, Colleen?" says J-Lock.

"Portabello mushrooms remind me of dolphins," says Colleen, "so I don't like to eat them."

Sylvia is gazing into the banquet hall, tapping her knuckles with a lobster fork. "It must be so strange to be Papa Bear," she says.

"How do you mean?" says Steve.

"To always have to be *on*," she says. "To always be so—in *front* of people. It must make you come close to being super-self-obsessed."

Colleen fears she is too tipsy to articulate what she wants to say, but tries anyway.

"To think about yourself all the time is to have no self," she says. "Because your self is not internal. It's relationships with others, and an interest in them. The Senator is not a single-minded fame-pursuer, he's a guy with interiority and exteriority who is capable of being fairly normal. This makes him less famous but more mysterious. That's why he's always kind of receding into the background, right? And why politicians don't seem to have real friends, so much as just allies?"

She can tell by the way everyone is taking a drink and avoiding eye contact that she hasn't made any sense.

J-Lock's debutante socialite skills tell her she needs to fill the silence. She tells a story she heard from a friend who worked for some Louisiana rep in college.

"My friend went to visit his district office one time," she says, "and right there in the waiting room he had this engraved oak sign, with a picture on it of this real curvy blonde wearing glasses. *You don't have to be ugly to be smart*, it said. It used to be in his office on the Hill, but there were a bunch of complaints, so he moved it back home. Isn't that crazy? It's so nice to work with all y'all, though. I was telling her that just the other day. Y'all manage to be so smart *and* so attractive."

In the forced laughter that follows, Colleen excuses herself.

The restroom is as opulent as the one in the Ryder video. She's been carrying the jump drive around, a tiny time bomb zipped in an inner pocket, in much the same way she used to imagine the President carried a "nuclear football" under his arm at all times, even in bed.

Locked in a stall, undies around her knees like cotton handcuffs, she knows she will not go back to the dinner.

She will leave without telling anyone good-bye.

Will pull a French exit, as Ethan calls it.

The silence here is a relief.

The only sound is the automatic air freshener squirting out scent, as if the room were farting spring blossoms at regular intervals.

She has not felt this depressed since she and Walter were in Tacoma, drifting yet trapped. The sadness melts her. She imagines herself as a chilled silver dish of expensive sorbet, like the kind Ariana said they'd be serving with dessert, temporary and deliquescing.

"I am so ridiculous," she says, and the acoustics of the empty bathroom make it echo, echo. "So ridiculous."

Colleen has sensed before, but fully realizes now: she will never be affluent.

She has always been okay with that, owing to her contempt for rich people.

Policy analysts treat poverty as though it is aberrant—a systemic malfunction in need of stamping out—and Colleen agrees with them, but she suspects in tandem that *wealth* is aberrant, and that the people at the fundraiser must have done something at some point, or their families must have, to seriously fuck somebody else over.

You do not get rich by being a just person, by thinking of

others as you would have others think of you.

You get rich by being like Palmira—by looking your workers in the eye and saying, "There's no money in the budget," and speaking the second half of the sentence, "for you," in your mind.

And yet, Colleen envies these people.

For the freedom they possess to make their own rules and to have those rules carry the force of law. For the privilege they enjoy to make their own mistakes and to have the consequences of those mistakes be so inconsequential.

Colleen, meanwhile, will remain at the middle—at the middle of the middle.

Unless she falls.

She has tried to rebel, to do her own thing, but what has that gotten her? Neither her parents nor most of her coworkers really get her, and she keeps her photography hidden from them—at least the kind that involves nudity. They know she's "creative" but only appreciate the pursuits that earn money.

This in turn makes her consider her lack of actual prospects.

She does not want to go into public relations, to enter the private sector, as Gina does, nor to become a lobbyist, Palmira's goal.

In any case, these more lucrative paths require official training and contacts, neither of which Colleen's experience, so ad hoc, has provided her. But even if she had the chance, she wouldn't want it. She does not want to sugarcoat the actions of amoral corporations, to present the selfish aims of moneyed interests as being for the greater good.

Some of her grad-school friends have told her, straight up, that they never thought she'd "end up like this," working for "The Man"—by which they mean the Senator.

Colleen disagrees.

She sees The Man as corporations, and the Senator, the government, as a buffer—a flawed one, but still—one that intervenes on the people's behalf, or could, or at least is expressly supposed to, unlike private companies.

But she can't see herself as a lifer, hopping from staff to staff, working for anyone on the Democratic side who will hire her, waiting for higher-ups to leave or die so she can grab their jobs.

She simply admires and wants to help this one unique Senator. The Senator and Dot are modest, living mostly off his Senate salary. A rarity, he is not bought and sold. He and Dot believe—truly *believe*—it is their duty to try to achieve something resembling social justice, not to treat everyone like a pack of animals, to live or die on their own.

So then, she wonders, what the fuck will become of her?

The phrase *If you're so smart, how come you're not rich?* has been running through her mind since she walked into the hotel.

She doesn't want to be rich. Okay then, fine.

But she *does* want to be important.

She wants to go to the Chief of Staff and invite herself over to show him the Ryder video. To be, suddenly, a critical component of the campaign.

She could do it, too. Right away.

But the timing would be bewildering.

Why now?

Besides, she knows—because she is wondering if she is too drunk—that she *is* too drunk.

She splashes cold water on her face, and makes her way to the elevators. The breath mints in the bowl by the exit are called "Petite Deceit." Colleen feels like an impostor for being here at all.

At street level, she wonders whether her coworkers wonder where she is, then gets a text from Andrew: "U ok? where did u go?"

"Had to get some air," she replies, still walking to the Red Line. "Going home now. Lates."

A burly guy in a leather jacket coming up the escalator whistles at her. Descending the staircase, she gives him the finger.

"L8r hater," Andrew texts back. She deletes it.

The train is full of wasted baseball fans who've been drinking since the victory earlier that afternoon. Their boozy bro bellowings are amplified by the train tunnel to an almost deafening cacophony of unintelligible speech. Not quite human, Colleen thinks, not quite animal.

The train ascends, and when they get to Belmont, a three-card monte team enters her car with green bottle-caps, a black felt-topped cardboard table, and a pea-sized red ball. Two of the men are black, one is white.

Colleen names them in her mind.

Visor Guy, wiry, wearing a visor, standing in the doorway.

Northsider, built like a side of beef in full team regalia, muscle going to fat, hat pulled low over pale blue eyes, tattoos edging from under the sleeves of his baggy jersey.

Scam-Master Jay, the keeper of the caps and cardboard.

They boarded the car together inconspicuously, far apart through separate doors, and ranged themselves throughout, Scam-Master Jay in the middle, where he keeps up a rap of non-stop patter. "Who's in, who's in? A game ain't no sin. If you're scared, go home to bed, covers over your head. Just watch the red ball, then make your call. Who's in, who's in?"

"Yo, man, I'm in," says Northsider, and everyone on the car watches him win! A hundred bucks!

Scam-Master Jay is distraught. He tries to convince him to go again, but Northsider doesn't budge. "Too rich for my blood," he says. "Let somebody else have a chance."

Some kid in glasses, sitting next to his college friend—on their way back to campus after the game?—says, "Okay, I'll try," and though he's confident the ball will be under the second bottle cap, he promptly loses his hundred bucks. "Bet a hundred, win a hundred," says Scam-Master Jay. "Lose a hundred, get a chance to win it back. You can break even, that's why they call me Even Steven," but the kid passes, and the team gets off at the Wilson stop.

"Who's got that many hundred-dollar bills on them?" a lady asks from her seat after they've gone.

Everybody left feels sorry for the mark. It was impossible not to feel played just by watching, like someone should have said, "Hey buddy, put away your wallet, there's no chance."

Colleen can't fathom why the kid couldn't identify it as a short con. Yet even as she sits thinking *how stupid*, she can't totally blame him.

She doesn't know why nobody else said anything either.

Politeness? Embarrassment? Fear of retaliation from the thuggy team?

Or maybe because everybody knows that they are not much better—all dreaming for some magic, some impossible payoff.

Every last one a hopeful sucker.

When she gets off the train, the kid and his friend are behind her.

"Hey man," his friend asks, "why didn't you try to break even?"

"Got bad luck once," the kid responds with his own pattery superstition, "you got it all night."

He still, Colleen marvels, doesn't grasp fully the extent to which he's been swindled.

14

To display photographs of your kids in your cube is considered a gesture of hope. Colleen hasn't got any, but this morning that's okay, because the office is playing host to not one but two three-dimensional babies.

An item broken simultaneously by the city's two major newspapers has led to an all-hands-on-deck meeting, including Palmira and Nia—and, because child care is tough to finagle on zero notice, their recently emerged offspring.

The scandal at hand?

Last March, the Senator—the "number-two Democrat in the Senate," as both papers pointed out—wrote a letter of recommendation for a staffer's daughter applying for admission to an elite high school.

Letters of rec are, at seasonal intervals, as thick as locusts around the office, so this was not, as Andrew would say, a BFFD.

But the fact that the Senator wrote the letter *after* the student was rejected from the academy in question made it more of a BFFD, at least in light of recent statewide investigations into the misuse of clout in the admissions process at selective-enrollment schools.

The letter itself is a study in the innocuous.

Boilerplate bereft of even the hint of arm twisting."I've had the pleasure," it read in part,

> "of watching _____ grow from a curious and sophisticat-
> ed nine-year-old into the sharp, well-spoken, and composed

young lady she is today, and I am confident that she will make a gifted addition to academic life at _____."

Redacted as it was before being handed over to the media, everyone convened in the Chief of Staff's office this morning knows it refers to Nia's daughter, Dahlia. But because the redaction had been lax by whoever was responsible for redacting it—aka, Gina—the papers had been able to identify the school as one very near the office.

Mascot: the Eagles.

Team slogan: "There's no pity in Eagle City."

The journalists, too, are pitiless.

"Senator Wrote Rec for Staffer's Subpar Student to Get into Elite Academy," reads the headline of one.

"Girl had been Rejected, But Principal Decided to Clear the Way," reads the subhead of the other.

Geez, what jackals!" says Sylvia, sitting on the arm of the black leather sofa. "Trying to make poor Dahlia sound dumb. How's she holding up?"

"Dahl knows she's no fool," says Nia. "I'm more upset than she is, and that's only because I don't want to embarrass the boss. She's supposed to tell all her new friends I'm a stay-at-home mom."

"As a mother," says Palmira, who has begun prefacing the majority of her declarations with this hallowed clause, "I find this so hurtful. Both articles bury the fact that the letter and Dahlia's admission do not in any way violate any policies or guidelines."

They are about to do a conference call with DC on how to respond, if at all, but they are waiting for Gina, who is running uncharacteristically late. Everyone has taken a turn holding at least one of the babies—Solomon and Esmeralda—except for Colleen and Steve Moon Collier.

"Kids are contagious," says Steve, arms crossed against his chest as Nia tries to hand him her son, "so I avoid contact."

Everyone laughs.

Nia passes Solomon to Colleen instead.

Colleen knows that her disinclination to hold the baby would not be as well received as Steve's, so she holds Solomon in a posture she hopes is not inept.

She gazes into his wide baby eyes, guileless and improbably blue. She says, "Nia, have you been using an eyelash curler on this baby?"

Andrew sits next to her, holding Esmeralda, who grins at him, a drooly smile, ear to itty-bitty seashell-shaped ear.

"You could water all the lawns in the city with that slobber," says Sylvia, daubing Esmeralda's face with a cloth diaper.

"It's a wonder they don't get dehydrated," says Nia.

"Ah-who's-a-cutie-patootie-beauty-wuvy-duvy-binkie-winkie-beddy-bye-boo?" says Andrew to Esmeralda, who squirms with wordless delight. "Babies love it when you say soothingly inscrutable things," he says.

The zest with which Palmira answers the Chief of Staff's questions—about feedings, about sleepings, about bowel movements—enervates Colleen.

Teenaged Dahlia she wants to talk about and with.

But these babies.

She looks down at Solomon, and kind of bounces him rhythmically.

Gina walks in pushing a rolling chair and sinks into it as she flings her backpack to the floor. "Let's get this show on the road," she says.

"Fire up the blower," says the Chief of Staff to Hannah, who dials DC.

Ryan Slattery is furious.

The Chicago office, he barks, should never have written the letter.

As Slattery rages, the Chief adjusts his top shirt button with one hand and makes a jerk-off gesture, stroking an air-penis located somewhere to the right of his face, with the other.

"I know you think it's time to unleash the ol' expletive-laced tirade," says the Chief. "But I'm going to advocate that the first thing we do is a whole lot of nothing."

"Ryder's already put out his own press release," says Slattery, "damning us to whatever circle of hell is reserved for people who abuse their influence for personal gain. He's going to ding us on the poll numbers."

"If he wants to act like a grade-A jagamuffin," says the Chief, "over a fully legal action to help a promising black student who is the daughter of a single mother on the West Side become a productive member of society and live her American dream, then who the hell are we to stand in his way? If Ryder wants to alienate himself from the entire urban constituency, it seems like we should let him."

And on the conversation goes.

Colleen looks around the room.

Nia and Palmira's midriffs are both flaccid, still kind of deflated, three months after giving birth.

Colleen glances to Gina for comparison, only to find she's been letting herself go, too.

The stresses of the campaign? Colleen wonders.

The conversation ends. The Chief wins out. Neither office will issue further statement. They will wait for the outcry to blow over, as it will within a day, the Chief predicts.

"You guys always know what's best, huh?" says Slattery. "But you may not know this: I got an email from the boss late last night. Dorothy's not feeling so well lately. They're discussing whether she ought to come out here, to be closer to him during the week, or if we should try to start getting him back to you as early as we can for the weekends. Heads up."

"Thank you for the warning," says the Chief, "but the Duke sent me that email, too. Talk soon."

He draws a finger across his throat.

Hannah disconnects.

Nice of you to grace us with your presence, Moretti," says the Chief to Gina, only half-kidding. "What the hell was the holdup?"

Generally snappy with the comeback, Gina presses her lips together and reaches into the pocket of her beltless khakis. She pulls out a sheet of paper folded into quarters and unfurls it, one-fourth by one-fourth by one-fourth by one-fourth. She holds it aloft and swivels side to side.

In grayscale in a field of black, curled like a shrimp, a fetus in the amniotic sac inside the press secretary.

The air is shattered by congratulatory shrieks.

Colleen feels instantly bad for thinking Gina had just been letting herself get fat.

"Oh my God!" says Palmira. "Look out! There's something in the water around here!"

Colleen pictures a black fluid coursing through pipes, like something a refinery might dump into the Lake, targeting hapless uteruses.

"Everyone in this whole joint's gonna be out on maternity leave before the year's through," says the Chief, hugging Gina. "What a racket."

"No, no, no," Gina says. "I'm not due until spring. We'll be in the clear by then."

"Now you and Walter have to get married," says Sylvia, "so you can be next, Colleen."

"There's a better chance of Steve getting pregnant than me," says Colleen.

Still in her lap, Solomon starts crying.

"Come on, Colleen," says Steve. "Where's your maternal instinct?"

"Can you please take him back?" says Colleen, passing Solomon to Nia.

"Okay, monster," says Nia, "I know you're hungry." She cradles him. "Let's go to my office and fire up Mommy the Milk Machine."

"It's going to kick in one of these days, Dugan," says Andrew, still holding Esmeralda. "Nobody can avoid their hormones forever."

"I never want to be a milk machine," says Colleen. She means it as a joke, but it comes out flat. "If I could be a father, maybe I might feel differently."

Colleen has been doing her best not to seem like a freak, but as Andrew will later tell her at lunch, "If that's your best, your best won't do."

Colleen can make eye contact with no one for a moment.

She fears she might cry.

The Chief is wearing one of her favorite ties, black with white-silver images of little grass huts and windswept palm trees.

Colleen wants to inhabit the scene.

To crawl in and escape.

To vanish into a beach chair with a frosty cocktail.

There are no babies pictured in the tie.

The Chief of Staff is correct. Ryder's numbers creep up an increment, but the Dahlia scandal never crystallizes. The rest of the week is underwhelming.

On Wednesday, Colleen notices that the callers checking the status of their open cases exhibit a higher-than-usual-degree of crazy. A World War II vet she's been helping to obtain a compromise offer from the IRS opens the conversation with, "I heard a nasty rumor that you broke the finger you use to call people back."

She tries to point out that he called overnight, and that she returned his call first thing this morning, but he is unimpressed.

"Go fuck yourself, madam!"

A few more like this and Colleen begins to detect a trend, which turns into a theory, which she shares with Andrew.

"People are more inclined," she says, "to yell at women over the phone because first, there is already a basic lack of equal respect. And second, this causes the yellers to believe their yelling will cause the woman to crumble because she's in a weakened position to begin with."

"Not everything can be explained by your bra-burning feminism, Colleen," says Andrew. "Maybe you're just rude."

"You're jacking me," says Colleen. "I know this. If you don't want to face the ugly truth, just say so."

"No, really," says Andrew. "Maybe you're not suited to the telephone. I'm naturally soothing in a way you could never be. My voice is like smoke for bees."

"Go fuck yourself," she says.

"See? That's what I mean."

"I wish you would *bee* gone," she says as his cell phone rings.

And a moment later, "Today," he says, "is your lucky day, Colleen. That was Nasrin calling from the Hotel Grand, demanding that I come over there tomorrow to work with her on a campaign project. Indefinitely. No longer must you suffer my gibes and taunts. Good-bye forever."

Colleen shows up at the regular office on Thursday and misses Andrew instantly.

She is drinking coffee out of a mug from the Jesuit university the Chief of Staff attended long ago, enamel emblazoned in yellow and red.

90% of your brain is developed by age 5. The heart is another matter.
At first this job made her heart flutter.

Lately she's flatlining.

Nothing better to do, she is dicking around online, reading the news, scrolling through an AP story that says a biweekly business mag whose motto is "The Capitalist Tool" has named Chicago the "Most Stressful Place to Live in the United States" for the second year running.

The low ranking is due to "crowding, poor air quality, a high eleven-percent unemployment rate and free-falling home values," which the article states "have created a cocktail of constant worry affecting many in the Windy City."

Colleen's comes from the sense that she is wasting her life and squandering her potential, as well as her suspicion that if the Junior Senator does not win the presidency, this already flawed world will hurtle even further toward total dystopia.

These reasons, she supposes, are too subjective.

Do not fit neatly into the magazine's metrics.

Too much heart, not enough brain.

S he notices Andrew online.

    Colleen: Why did Nasrin call you over to campaign HQ?

    Andrew: because they needed a heavy-hitter with brass balls to wrestle this thing to the ground.

    Colleen: Nasrin so did not say that.

    Andrew: It's b/c I'm a lawyer. We're doing debate prep. The Sen. is gonna face off with Ryder and we are making policy binders. Ryder's gaining in the polls and we need to kick ass.

    Colleen: I want to make binders! I want to help with the polls!

Andrew: You can't; you're a photographer by trade. This is for legal scholars ONLY

Colleen: But I am so organized. I feel seriously lacking in opportunities for growth.

Andrew: yes, well. Even over here, I think I suffer from insular dwarfing

Colleen: what does that mean?

Andrew: I saw it on a nature special. it is 1) when your species is on an island so you grow smaller each generation to adapt and 2) when your colleagues are jerks and idiots so it makes you regress instead of shine.

Colleen: even in the fast-paced high-stakes arena of the 2008 campaign?

Andrew: there is zero sense of urgency over here. it is spooky how calm it is. like a frozen lake

Colleen: where is everybody?

Andrew: they are here. There's just nothing happening. I don't think Steve ever does anything. I think he is just sitting in his chair wasting breath.

Colleen: What about the Chief?

Andrew: He gave me the tour today. You'd like it because we're on the fourth floor and the windows open and we get to have real fresh city air in our lungs all the time. The chief's big thing is that this is the perfect spot to watch girls go by; "everyone, with this amount of distance and distortion, looks like a great piece of ass" he said. But then a fat girl walked by and he goes "not her."

Colleen: Righty-o, Chief.

Andrew: my point, Colleen, is, you are not missing much.

Friday morning is so glacially paced that she and Dézi take an early lunch and go shopping. Window only, as they can't afford to buy anything.

They are on State Street, in a store whose name suggests that if you buy their flimsy, sweatshop-made runway knockoffs in yellow bags with "John 3:16" printed on the interior, then you will be able to remain perpetually at the legal age for drinking in America, when Colleen's cellphone rings.

It's the Chief.

His voice, insistent but calm, cuts through the electropop piped over the store's stereo system. The Rapacious British Oil Company has caved to their demands. The Senator wants a press conference this afternoon at 2:30.

"Ryder's going to have one, too," he says, "to steal the credit. We need to beat him to it, especially for the way he's been kicking us in the balls all week about the Dahlia thing."

Report back to the ranch posthaste.

Two hours later, here they stand, near the former airfield at Northerly Island, amidst the beach house and the restored prairie and the bird hospital and the unimpeded views of the planetarium and the adorable children frolicking in the water. And far off in the southern distance, the smokestacks of the Rapacious British Oil Company refinery belching pollutants into the August air.

"A little piece of paradise right here in the city," says the Senator to the Chief of Staff as they get out of the car.

Even though this is the Lake, the view is like a seascape painting from the nineteenth century. The outfits have modernized, but the attitude is timeless. Splashing kids and smiling bathers, pensive waders staring into the deep.

The light trickling through the clouds looks tricky. Late-summer sun has been warming the buildings gold, making the afternoon less clammy. The rays have faded to a dusty orange before the thunderheads roll in, muffling the shade to gray, with green at the edges.

Uncanny, unwell.

Andrew, driver for the day, tells them that a tornado watch is in effect for the county until five that evening, then pulls away to park.

They stand on the concrete terrace precipicing the sand in their summery best. The Chief in his seersucker suit, Gina in her tan one, Colleen in a linen skirt and white blouse.

Sudha, too, is dressed in ecru, clutching the press releases. Colleen had persuaded Gina to bring an intern, not so much because they need the help as because Colleen wants to keep handing out the hands-on experience.

Only the Senator is somberly clad in a slate-gray suit—wintry, as if inhabiting a separate season. He steps away from them and onto the strand, where he pauses, shoulders slumped for a passing second, a stately and professional lump of charcoal.

Bituminous pops into Colleen's mind, followed by *vulnerable*.

For such a big day for the team, the Senator looks alone, preoccupied.

Colleen would be tempted to go over and ask, *Are you all right?* but she does not have that kind of relationship with the man. Few people seem to.

"We're gonna look like a Wet T-shirt Contest if this storm catches us," says the Chief, raising his shades and gazing west.

Gina's curly brown hair stands more on end than usual, as if to better express her sense of foreboding. She is still mourning the loss of an expensive summer suit from a store that specializes in mail orders of "classic styles" made of "luxury materials"—Italian leather, cashmere, Czech glass buttons—and featuring "touches" that can't save the clothes from what Colleen considers their indefatigable blandness.

Gina's suit was wrecked last year under similar circumstances when she'd been caught in a downpour at an outdoor press event.

"I didn't have the receipt anymore," she tells them now. "Otherwise I'd have filed a reimbursement in DC. I'm still pissed. That thing cost hundreds of dollars."

Colleen looks south, past the Senator, to where the Lake makes its curve into northern Indiana.

For months now, both the State of Indiana and federal regulators, with the vigorous backing of senate candidate Ron Reese Ryder, have sided with the Rapacious British Oil Company's contention that their 1,400-acre refinery in Whiting lacks adequate room to upgrade the site's water treatment plant during the proposed expansion.

The choices, then, were clear: expansion and increased pollution (54% more ammonia and suspended solids dumped into the Lake) or no expansion at all.

The Rapacious British Oil Company's voluntary announcement this morning that it will no longer pursue this expansion is a direct result of weeks of protests, led by the Senator, by a coalition of local and state politicians, environmentalists, and average citizens unwilling to let more sludge be spewed into the largest single source of drinking water in North America.

A major victory of sorts—if you choose to define victory as the preventing of worse destruction than is already taking place—of public outcry and political will, without even the backing of federal law.

Notice of the reversal arrived around lunchtime, by fax to Gina's attention. The press release mentioned nothing about the Senator or the protests, the environmentalists, or the citizens. It will be up to the Senator to make this case.

Ryder will, predictably, muddy the waters, will hold a press event in his own North Shore district, will champion himself as a warrior in the fight to save the Lake, will ignore the disparity between his purported positions and his actions, will spin reality until it bears no resemblance to itself.

Colleen finds this hardly surprising but still disturbing.

More disturbing to her but equally unsurprising will be the media's amnesia that Ryder has had his anti-science head up his anti-environmental butt for months and is dragging it out now only because it's politically advantageous.

The wind picks up grains of sand on the cement and eddies them in teeny spiraling cyclones. The microphones threaten to blow over, so Colleen rests her handbag at the base of the rake. Wicked clouds keep massing to the west.

"Good thinking, Dugan," says Gina.

"They sell sandbags for that, you know," a TV-news cameraman says to Colleen.

"Do they sell them here?" Colleen says. "All I saw at the refreshment stand were hot dogs and pop."

The beach-combers gather behind the cameras. The Senator hoists himself up the stone steps and salutes to Gina. He centers himself behind the mics and convenes the conference early. "To spare you all the threat of the approaching storm," he says.

This flusters the horseshoe of reporters still forming around him. Political figures are rarely on time, let alone early, and almost never considerate.

"These are not just good lakes," says the Senator, leading with a line that's become a standard of his over the course of this fight. "They are Great Lakes."

The parents of the swim-suited children smile and clap.

"Shit," says Gina, hissing into the Chief of Staff's ear. "Some reporters are going to miss this entirely, and they're going to blame me. It's still fifteen minutes early."

"Nobody's gonna stand here long in a cloudburst, Trixie," he says. "Better to do what we can than not to do it at all."

The conference is over in under ten minutes, which is not to say the Senator hasn't made the most of it.

"Was it just me," Gina asks, "or did you hear him call, basically, for a new Clean Water Act?"

"Newer and stricter," says Colleen.

The Senator heads down the steps again and chats with the colorfully trunked and suited kids, summoned out of the choppy water by the lifeguard because it looks like lightning.

"Hi," the Senator says, "I'm your Senator."

"Hi, Senator!" the kids say back. And then, "Why are you here?" one of them asks, as the others monkey around for the cameras still shooting B-roll.

"To announce that we got the British Oil Company to agree not to dump more pollution in your lake," the Senator says.

"Yay!" scream the kids, and "Thank you!" and "You're not dressed for swimming!"

The Senator does some Q and A with the kids, asking them as many questions as they ask him, and by then it's 2:35, past when the event was supposed to begin, so he stands on the platform and repeat-performs the conference in brief for the pissy reporters who have showed up on time only to discover they're late.

They curse audibly, not even bothering to bury their swear words under their breath.

The story becomes the weather. Tornadoes! Warnings! The wind confirmed in a circular rotating motion!

The sky turns from green-gray to a purple-bruise, devouring

the few shreds of blue that remain. The effect reminds Colleen of the airbrush feature in basic graphics software.

She hands the Senate camera off to Sudha for safekeeping and documents the confusion with her own. A local network news anchor in a leopard-print top with shellacked blonde hair finishes with the Senator, then weighs in on the tornadic activity. She directs her cameraman to pan the skyline behind her.

Gum wrappers, leaves, press releases Sudha has lost flutter in the background. The only unmoving item in the landscape is the hair of the anchor.

Colleen and Gina pack up. Gina then hops into the car with Andrew and the Senator to make it to his next obligation. Colleen, the Chief, and Sudha are left to fend against the elements.

They make a break for it as the clouds erupt. The cabs disappear like yellow pills dissolving. The Chief is athletic, and not just for a fifty-something. He is categorically fast. Hobbled by their high heels, Sudha and Colleen struggle to keep up. Colleen feels hers stabbing holes into the grassy grounds of the museum campus, like the holes left after her dad would aerate the family lawn. She stops, hopping from one foot to the other, and removes them.

Sudha follows suit.

The Chief keeps on.

They make for the planetarium, all hope lost of not getting soaked, dodging the hailstones that have started to pelt them.

That was disaster movie-esque," says Colleen when she and Sudha join the Chief of Staff in the planetarium lobby. She leans against the glass door to force it shut. She is breathless and cold in the air conditioning, artificial wind as bad as the one outside, maybe worse, chilling her through her drenched clothes. They are surrounded by a crowd of beach-going unfor-

tunates, their sodden shoes squishing as they pace, their wet skin
goose-pimpling.

The lights flicker.

"The weather-stripping around the doors isn't worth a damn,
is it?" says the Chief as water pours in.

They stare outside as if the sheer focused power of their collective minds could make a taxi materialize. The Chief is getting
annoyed. Colleen goes to the courtesy telephone downstairs and
calls and calls. No luck. She returns to ground level and spots
the Chief as he scores the only taxi on the entire circle drive. It's
a minivan. He grabs her hand in one of his and Sudha's in the
other, and they run down the stairs and fling themselves inside.

Leaving the museum campus, Colleen feels elated.

This is what she likes, this is what she seeks—drama that is
physical, action that is exhausting, excitement that is experienced
together as a team.

She basks in the camaraderie.

"To the Loop," says the Chief. "Don't spare the whip and don't
skimp on the heat."

Before they make the turn north onto Lake Shore Drive, they
pull alongside one more frantic would-be passenger, a youngish
woman of indeterminate age—18? 28?—dyed-red hair, frumpy
black duffel, yellow shirt, and an inadequate purple jacket emblazoned with the logo of the NFL team from Minnesota named
after Norse barbarian warriors.

"Hey, baby," says the Chief. "She's kind of a looker in a wild
way."

This remark is not fatal to Colleen's beatific mood, but it
wounds a little.

"It would surprise me not at all if she turned out to be a serial
killer," Colleen says. "But it's so crappy out—let's let her in."

The girl says she's from Boston. She's going back today on the
bus system named after a dog breed bred for racing, or she wants to
be—there's only one bus every twenty-four hours. They offer to have
the cab swing her by the station before looping back to their office,
and she makes it in plenty of time for the four o'clock departure.

"If that's really what she's doing," says Colleen. "She's so cra-zy-looking, it's tough to tell for sure what she'll do."

"That's what I liked about her," the Chief says, in a wistful tone more appropriate for talking about someone he's known for fifteen years, not fifteen minutes.

The Chief's capacity to be nostalgic for the present is one of the main reasons Colleen tolerates his bullshit.

B y a quarter to five, Colleen has finished putting the press release up on the website, downloading the photos, posting the Hot Topic.

The Chief of Staff turns on his stereo.

"Time for the Going-Home-for-the-Weekend music al-ready?" says Lo Benson.

"Damn right," says Colleen, and feels, for the first time in a long time, like they've got something sorted out.

First the Chief plays a song written by a Jamaican regae mu-sician in 1979 circa his diagnosis with terminal cancer, based on a speech by a Pan-Africanist orator. Lo files VA cases and sings along faintly.

Colleen wants to believe that "None but ourselves can free our minds."

The lyric reminds her of the Junior Senator's line: "We are the ones we have been waiting for," which he got from the Afri-can-American novelist who wrote about the color purple.

This song is followed, as always, by the piano and harmonica ballad from the American singer-songwriter from the streets of New Jersey also known as the Boss. He's best known recently for practicing liberal politics, an early and ardent supporter of the Junior Senator's presidential candidacy, but this song, from 1975, is apolitical, all working-class striving, how he just can't face himself alone again, how the girl is scared that maybe they ain't that young anymore, of his faith that there's magic in the night.

Faint praise to the girl: "You ain't a beauty, but hey, you're alright."

"Goddammit, Dugan!" the Chief yells above the music. "Get your skinny ass in here. Now!"

She enters his office, about to ask what the hell she could possibly have done wrong, when he places his hand on her waist and guides her to the window.

"If I made this up," he says, "you'd say I sound like a clown. But would you look at that?"

Thirty-eight stories below, the storm has strewn tree branches across Jackson Boulevard. From this high up, they look like cocktail toothpicks, brown with crinkled green tops, knocked over at a party.

But that's not what he's gesturing at.

Above the Lake to the south, above the refinery in Whiting, a rainbow has spanned itself.

"It's like a Bible story," says Colleen. "God's promise never to let the Rapacious British Oil Company try to fuck us over again."

"Such a mouth on you," he says. "I'd tell you you should take a picture of it, but I know you probably have your own ideas, so I won't. I will take one of my own, though."

He prepares to snap the shot with his cell phone.

She begins to move, but he says, "No. Stay right there. You are involved."

"It's unreal," she says.

"It is," he says. "But here's some reality. There are going to be E. coli closings on all the beaches tomorrow. There was so much rain, the Water Reclamation District must have had to open the gates into the Lake to mitigate the flooding. And you know that water was untreated."

"I know," she says. "But we're still at it, right? We've got Great Lakes Cleanup Day on the twenty-seventh."

"We do."

They stand there listening to the end of the song and staring out the window and Colleen feels happy, so happy it's stupid.

She knows it's dirty, but everything seems washed so bright and clean that she half expects to see a unicorn leaping over the crazy rainbow.

She looks at the side of the Chief of Staff's face, and she likes the way he still likes things.

Still has faith, just not in God.

The way he values fun, well past the age where most men, most people, have lost that feeling.

The way he can take the shitty swirled in with the pretty.

Like, hey, it's alright.

15

By the Friday afternoon immediately preceding it, Great Lakes Cleanup Day has come together, fallen apart, come together, fallen apart, stayed apart, stayed apart, and come together again.

To blame: a variety of scheduling factors to which none of the Chicago staffers were fully privy which kept conspiring to have the Senator—on and off throughout the week—in DC, then Chicago, then Springfield, then DC, then Chicago again.

This morning, though, Gina had popped into Colleen's cube with bad news. She'd been looking for the Chief of Staff, but it was before 9:00 a.m., and no one else was in, so she settled for Colleen.

"Listen, Dugan, I'm glad I caught you. About Great Lakes Day."

"Yes," said Colleen. "Everyone's thankful it didn't fall through—the Aquarium, the Alliance, the Mayor's office. They think it's great that the Senator's going to roll up his sleeves and pick up trash with the common citizens."

"Yeah, regarding that," Gina said. "The day itself will still happen, of course. But it's looking like the involvement of the Duke is going to be scaled way back."

She handed Colleen that morning's front sections of the two hometown newspapers. "Senator Cashed Out During Big Stock Collapse," read one headline.

"Senator violated Insider Trading Laws, Opponent Alleges," read the other.

The stories were echoes of one another.

Congressman Ron Ryder had "caught wind of the scandal"

after reviewing the Senator's recently released financial disclosure statements. The Senator had "cashed out upwards of $100,000" worth of stocks and mutual funds, "just as US stock markets were beginning their plummet." The Senator did this "only one day after a highly secret closed-door meeting" with the Treasury Secretary and the Federal Reserve Chairman, who were outlining the growing financial crisis and urging Congressional leaders to craft legislation to aid tanking banks.

Buried at the bottom, the DC press office's response.

The Senator had simply done what countless other people did when they saw their savings vanishing.

The Senator did not, in fact, "cash out" anything, but merely transferred assets from one fund to another.

The Senator, in any case, had not capitalized on secret tips, since all the information the Treasury Secretary and the Federal Reserve Chairman gave lawmakers was made public the following day.

No mention that the funds the Senator had transferred his money to were performing worse than the funds he had transferred his money from.

"It looks like all he did was take money from his retirement account and move it from riskier funds to safer ones," Colleen said, skimming the articles. "Who cares?"

"Ryder cares," Gina said. "It's the Dahlia situation all over again. There's been no wrongdoing, but Congressman Asshole's going to flog it. We might have to pull the boss out of the limelight for the next couple days. Keep his head down and let it blow over."

Gina was telling Colleen this, not soliciting her opinion, and before Colleen could collect her two cents to toss in, Gina was on her way back to her office, trying to get the Chief on the phone.

At day's end, it has been decided by forces invisible and much higher up that Colleen will go to Great Lakes Cleanup Day on the Senator's behalf.

She will hand out press releases detailing his proposed Great Lakes legislation.

She will pick up trash.

She will not speak.

She learns all this while seated on the black leather sofa in the Chief of Staff's office, Gina and Steve Moon Collier in attendance, during a call with Slattery from DC, and it is hard for her not to feel taken advantage of, like they are saying, *We've gotten all the bang for our buck this issue has to offer, so we're pulling the plug.*

She knows Ryder is fighting dirty, but this seems cowardly.

Tonight, in Oxford, Mississippi, in the first of three presidential debates, the Junior Senator will face his Republican opponent—a Vietnam War hero with a face like a chipmunk who addresses his supporters and detractors alike with the insincere salutation *My friends.*

Colleen envies the people on the Junior Senator's campaign.

Their steady sense of busyness.

Their clear-cut mission.

"We have tomorrow sorted," says the Chief, "but the rest is so far up in the air we can barely see it."

"This is the right call," says Slattery. "To kill the trashfest, or whatever the hell they call it. No point putting him in front of the media until all the shit Ryder kicked up has settled. The reporters don't care about the bill. They'll want to ask questions about the boss's finances."

"Yeah, and the Aquarium does this as an ongoing thing," says the Chief, "as opposed to us. We just shoot a rocket into the air as high as we can and run like hell. We were honestly just glomming onto their event."

After DC has dropped off, Colleen can't help saying, "It baffles me why we can never make a plan in this office and stick to it."

"Colleen," the Chief says, "really. You can be so critical."

The others begin gathering their things, filing out.

"Everybody wait a sec," says the Chief. "Sit your butts back down. I want to be clear why the Duke is doing this. There are, as we've been discussing, a lot of factors, not least of which, frankly, is that we already got about as much mileage from the Lake as we're gonna get. And Ryder's trying to fuck us again, sure. But the big one—and this is the straw we hope will not break the camel's back—is that Dot is still not doing so hot. She was in and out of the hospital all last week. I know he wouldn't want me sharing this, so not a word leaves this room. I just want you to know that the Duke hasn't lost his spine."

Colleen feels asinine.

The Chief of Staff looks over, sees this.

There is a moment of seriousness as everyone contemplates the news about the Senator's wife.

"Plus," he adds, "I told him that Colleen here can handle the beach in all types of weather—the same soaking wet as perfectly dry. Everyone else looked like a drowned rat at that press conference at Twelfth Street, except for Colleen, who seemed to be dancing between the raindrops."

"You can save your oblique compliments," says Colleen. "You know I'll do whatever needs doing. But can you tell me one more time what exactly I am supposed to do tomorrow?"

"Just be visible," say Steve Moon Collier and Gina in unison.

"Are you still coming?" she says to the Chief.

"Unfortunately, no," he says. "I've had another important engagement arise."

"You'll get to see the Mayor, at least," says Gina.

"True," says Colleen. "Although the Mayor sucks the air out of every room, even if that room is the universe."

The Chief of Staff almost shoots coffee out his nose.

Back in Cube City, she phones Andrew at campaign headquarters and tries to convince him to go.

"How long will it take?" he asks.

"An hour or two," she says. "It's at North Avenue Beach, where we did the thing in May. Remember? We can ride bikes."

"No can do," says Andrew. "Palmira's rule. We only get comp time if the work takes at least a half-day. You're on your own."

"This constant disappointment," she says, "is starting to erode my unfailingly cheerful attitude."

"I know," says Andrew. "I consider every day I don't get churned under by my professional life a victory."

On the Red Line home, she calls Ethan up and tries to get him to join her, but he's already got a paying gig scheduled.

The train car is plastered with ads for a book by a bestselling author and motivational speaker, a buxom black woman with strobe light white teeth whom another motivational speaker calls "a rock star of personal growth." The book is about the Law of Attraction—how to "create the things in life you believed were out of reach."

What does Colleen want to create in her life? What does anyone want to create?

The answers posited by the ad seem uncreative. Money? Hot sex? A ton of friends? Why? Why not?

Colleen wants to create positive social change, to the extent that she can do so.

An extent whose aperture appears tighter the longer she's in the office.

And photographs, those too she wants to create.

She thinks of asking Walter to come to Cleanup Day tomorrow since she's sure he'd agree. But aside from fundraisers, it's weird to bring a boyfriend to random work events, as her experience with the Painters' Union taught her.

Her only option now is to go solo.

O, the loneliness of the long-distance Senate Aide.

She arrives at the beach a half hour before the event is set to start, as she would if she were advancing the Senator, owing, she figures, to the power of habit.

The sun is already high and hazy, drawing her eyes to the incompleteness of the buildings across Lake Shore Drive in the shroudy mist, solid at their bases but erased at the top, rubbed out like a sketch.

Though it is almost October and the air is getting crisper, the water is as inviting as it ever gets, having drunk in months of sunny summer days. Still plenty of sunbathers, volleyball players, disc tossers, bikini babes.

Colleen wonders if she hasn't contracted a kind of Stockholm Syndrome from the Chief of Staff.

She leans against the railing of the beach house and watches.

Spies the wide bottle-blondes in tank tops purchased from a fashion retailer formerly known as a purveyor of excursion goods but these days known for bare-chested male models and T-shirts for women with slogans across the tits like *I had a nightmare I was a brunette* and *Who needs brains when you have these?*

Tracks them as they pass with their small dogs—rhinestone collars, pink leashes.

Imagines Andrew or Steve Moon Collier here. Hears them utter their oft-made complaint against women who wear enormous sunglasses, sunglasses so big you can't even tell which girls are sexy and which are butterfaces.

Hears herself say nothing, because nothing is easier than arguing.

Habituating herself like this is less intentional than inevitable.

It would be ridiculous to do it on purpose anyway—out of any serious desire to appeal to the Chief.

He makes it clear a thousand times a day that for him, the best girl is always the next girl.

~

As Colleen watches, we watch Colleen.

We are waiting to see when she will see.

The system in which she labors is by its nature opposed to "differ-ence" of the sort she longs to make.

The system wants nothing more than to sustain itself.

To protect those within it who have accrued small measures of power.

Stasis is the system's raison d'être.

The mechanism of politics is wrecked, made unstable, by such difference.

It stifles it early and stifles it often.

~

Colleen spots the President of the Alliance for the Great Lakes checking in at the cleanup table.

Time to be visible.

She heads over with apologies for the Senator's absence, but her target is intercepted by a staffer from the mayor's office, a youngish woman with a severe face and a severer haircut—sharp blonde spikes. Ill at ease, Colleen stands to the side as the Alliance President raises a finger, sort of pointing at her, indicating she should silently wait.

Though she's met him half a dozen times, he doesn't seem to recognize her, but when he's finally ready to talk, he thaws out, gets eager at the mention of the Senator's name—is so glad to see her again, wonders how she's been, looks forward to meeting with her boss real soon, deeply appreciates all her hard work.

Colleen is relieved when the conversation is cut short by the arrival of the most I of the VIPs.

The longtime Mayor, son of the longtime Mayor known as Boss. Same first name, same last name, different middle initial.

He emerges from his motorcade of tanky black town cars, looking, as ever, every inch Da Mare.

As if typecast in the role of the elected leader of the Windy City in a Chicago-themed amusement park.

That trench coat, that fedora.

As if, at any moment, a tommy gun should appear somewhere in the background.

Florid and fuzzy-haired, the Mayor takes to the podium with his perpetually perplexed expression.

His speech is so stilted it is hard for Colleen to follow.

His accent is classic Bridgeport, nasal intonation and dipthonged vowels. "Basicky," he says, instead of "basically." Multiple *dats*, multiple *dems*.

Slated to speak for two minutes, he goes on for ten, then fifteen, his mispronunciations growing more and more pronounced. If she weren't so familiar with his style, Colleen would swear he had a head cold, or that he'd gotten drunk on the ride over.

"And dat's why," he says, wrapping it up, "dey gotta partner up, the private people and the public ones, the regular joes and the science experts, not just say 'government will solve it.' Thank you. Thank you."

Applause.

A few words from the Alliance President, an expression of sadness at the Senator's absence, an ingratiating nod at Colleen's presence, and the reporters ask their questions.

A phone rings—one of the Mayor's staffers', but none of them wants to admit they forgot to silence it, so it goes on ringing. Colleen tries to imagine it as a natural sound, like the softest rain.

The Mayor is done, then gone.

Colleen stays a while to help pick up trash, but she cannot transcend.

It is the epitome of anticlimax.

Fishing line, candy wrappers, plastic utensils. Aside from some really boring debris, the beach seems dispiritingly clean. She finds one prescription drug bottle, empty, and a flattened can that used to contain the champagne of beers, but large items like these are few and far between. The bulk of the litter is cigarette butts and the occasional crushed pack.

She digs up a solitary six-pack ring and tries to feel proud about possibly saving some seagull's life.

The volunteer collecting the bags thanks her with enthusiasm out of proportion to the small amount of good Colleen has actually achieved.

She feels herself blushing as she tells him, yes, she'll say hi to the Senator for him.

She paces to her bike and takes out her phone. Puts it back, then takes it out again. Because of their cautious pattern of chase and reject, chase and reject, she is reluctant.

Almost stops.

Then pulls up the Chief of Staff's number from her list of contacts.

Presses S*end.*

The photograph that corresponds to his digits is one she took in the summer of 2007, just after she'd returned from Tacoma. They were on their way to a fundraiser together in his green convertible, top down on Irving Park Road.

It was June, the solstice, the longest day of the year.

He should have been keeping his eyes on the road, but he had turned to look directly at her, his eyes behind his shades and the gap between his top front teeth on full display. She hates how everyone has identically perfect teeth these days.

He picks up on the first ring.

"Colleen!" he says. "Babe. To what do I owe the pleasure?"

His voice is gravelly as usual, from the two cigarettes a day he lets himself smoke. *Guilty pleasure*, he always says, and Colleen, if she feels like saying something winning, will reply that no pleasure is guilty—there's only pleasure.

"Are you busy?" she says.

"Not right at the moment. What's up?"

"I have something that's been burning a hole in my brain for a few weeks. I need to talk to you about it. Sooner, not later. May I?"

"Fire away."

"No," she says, "it has to be in person. I'm at North Avenue Beach. I could be there soon."

She expects him to hesitate, but he doesn't.

In the tone of his voice she can read nothing.

"Okay," he says. "Come on over."

As often happens to Colleen when she gets what she wants, she immediately wants the opposite. Now that she has been told she can make her way south to meet the Chief, she wants nothing more than to take herself north to home.

She forces herself south, past Oak Street Beach, around the perilous S-curve. The path is uncrowded, but to Colleen it feels hard to navigate, a thicket of apprehension. She cuts through the underpass at Chicago Avenue, the cool dark tunnel that runs beneath Lake Shore Drive.

The Chief lives in a hotel named after a Roman Stoic philosopher and statesman from the Silver Age of Latin literature. Or maybe, she thinks, after the tribe of Indians from the Iroquois League in upstate New York that white settlers decided to name after the Roman Stoic philosopher and statesman.

The place styles itself "an intimate escape, just a block off Michigan Avenue," a "quaint European-style boutique hotel with everything that you are looking for in a luxury downtown location."

Its neighborhood is Streeterville, along that mile known for being magnificent. Near the Water Tower and the Museum of Contemporary Art and the softball fields, where the Senate team plays on Wednesday summer nights against other vaguely civic teams, the Governor's office, the Junior Senator's office, the Park District.

The Chief and his wife own a house in Springfield, but he lives at this hotel under the extended-stay option in a furnished studio with weekly maid service. $1900 to $2510 a month, Colleen discovered one day looking it up online, more than twice what she and Walter pay, though a quick glance will tell you—the valets, the doorman, the black awning echoing the shadow of the iconic skyscraper named after the one among us with the biggest signature—it's very if-you-have-to-ask-you-can't-afford-it.

Colleen has heard about the Chief's living arrangement frequently. Dropped him off outside many times. Been in the lobby a few.

But never been in his room.

S he half-expects him to be waiting in the lobby, but he isn't.
Bike bag over her shoulder, she approaches the reception
desk.

The décor of the lobby strikes Colleen as unfortunate, beige
and busy. The interior is old enough that it could look vintage—
pleasingly old-timey—but as it is, it's merely nice-but-dated.
Faded, out of phase. Stuck in a vision of luxury from the '80s.

None of the tourists lounging in the jewel-tone floral print
armchairs are especially stylish, but nevertheless, Colleen feels
underdressed.

She's still wearing her bike gloves.

The woman at the desk says, yes, the Chief of Staff is expecting her.

She gives Colleen the room number and points her toward
the elevator.

This is both inappropriate—she'll have to go up to his actual
living quarters—and ideal—she'll need privacy to show him.

The air inside smells like stale perfume. Fruity chypres going
sour.

Colleen rides to the fifteenth floor.

Stepping off, it's hard to ignore the calculus here, the risk versus reward.

How wrong is it of her to be here in general—fraternization?
How wrong will he find the video? How wrong will he find her
for showing it to him?

It's so unsavory, and she's been waiting for this moment for
so long.

S he finds his room and is about to knock when the door un-
locks and swings open. There he stands. His eyes meet hers.
His snaggle-toothed smile.

Chops, she thinks. *He is licking them.*

"Nice place you got here," she says, though the carpet under his feet is blue and institutional, the sofas too stripy, the art too tepid.

"What can I say? It ain't much, but it's home," he says, taking her hand and leading her in.

He favors the same extravagant flower arrangements here as he does in the office. A vase full of glads stands erect on the kitchen table, a black and white baseball cap beneath it, like an odd still life.

"What's with the hat?" she says. "I didn't think you were a Sox fan."

"I'm not," he says. "But I got free tickets to see them play the Indians this afternoon, so I figured what the hell."

"That's why you couldn't come to Great Lakes Cleanup Day? Because the Sox are playing Cleveland later this afternoon? I feel betrayed."

"I've been debating which hat to wear. What do you think? This one," he says, picking up the crisp and uncreased team cap, "which clearly I just bought. Or this one that I got at the Modern Wing groundbreaking at the Art Institute?"

He puts the latter, well-worn cap atop his head to model it, and it's useless to stay mad.

He's a dick with a heart of gold.

In a red-and-white tattersall shirt.

Even when he's casual, he's never that casual.

"That seems more you," she says. "Why don't you just wear that one, if it's your trusty standby?"

"The truth is," he says, "and we both know it—I look good in anything. But the question remains: can I get away with wearing an art museum hat to a game full of South Siders, or will it get my ass kicked?"

"If your ass gets kicked, it won't be because of the hat," she says. "Or because that shirt makes you look like a picnic table."

"Dammit, Colleen. Always such a bitch. Have a seat and let me get you a drink."

She perches on one of the turgid sofas, striped and plump like an obscene piece of candy.

Notices there's no air conditioning.

It's early afternoon, but somehow being here feels like something that should be happening in the exact middle of the night. Solid darkness, equal on both sides.

Sticky, she thinks, because of the lack of AC, but only mildly. A ceiling fans swirls above, blowing strands of her hair that have escaped from their pins.

She sees herself in the mirror on the wall.

When she does this, when she checks herself out while trying to imagine what the man she is with sees, she thinks how she—how all women, perhaps—has been trained to consider herself as an erotic object, to find women's bodies sexy.

His bed is against the wall, in the same room as they are. Its duvet—loud with a geometric design—is reflected within the frame, its flaky gold paint.

They could see themselves in this mirror if they were to fuck there.

He brings two cut glass tumblers of ice water over, hands her one, and sits down next to her, very close. She thanks him, and remembers what Steve Moon Collier had said of the bikini babes at that press conference, which feels so long ago—that that was the first time the Chief had been around a scantily-clad woman in ages, and how the Chief had answered, sure, it was.

"Look at you in your bike gloves," he says. "You're just too much."

He strokes the palm of one, rubbing his fingers over the bumpy gecko ridges.

"I got them to look more hardcore," she says. "If I fall, I won't tear the shit out of my hands. I think it makes the other bikers take me a little more seriously."

"I thought it must be because they look so sweet."

Nonplussed, Colleen notices he's got the stereo on. An album by the legendary American singer-songwriter who adopted the name of a Welsh poet who advocated raging against the dying of the light. It's his Nashville album from 1969, the one where he sings through his nose in an affected croon.

Colleen is not prone to swooning, but she imagines letting herself.

She always looks forward, in this song, to the part where the singer goes, "You're the best thing that he's ever seen."

Colleen knows the Chief says coaxing things like this to everyone, but that doesn't make them not true. Does it?

"Stay while the night is still ahead," sings the singer.

"I love this album," she says finally, just to say something, although she really does.

"It's not my favorite, honestly, but it's got some decent tracks," he says. "I prefer the earlier stuff, from when he was working with Baez. Really early, like before they started putting the lumber to each other. Which, by the way, is almost always a bad idea. Almost."

And Colleen imagines again, for the millionth time, what it would be like to have an affair with him.

She bets, if they did, that it would be regular sex, relatively normal, made fun enough by being illicit.

That he wouldn't ask to fuck her up the butt, like most older, married, affair-having guys do, or so she gathers from her friends who have had such affairs.

She imagines that he would be neat and fastidious.

She'd slip one of his silk-lined blazers from his scarecrow shoulders, and before it hit the floor, he'd hang it over the back of a walnut chair.

The song gets to the part about how the man's clothes are dirty but his hands are clean, and this reminds her why she came.

"So," she says, "I've got a video I want to show you. Can we use your laptop?"

He cocks his head at this, and she can see his brain shifting gears—smoothly, imperceptibly, like the transmission in a really small and expensive car. He brings his computer over to the glass-topped coffee table in front of them.

She plays the video.

It feels twice as long as when she watched it with Ethan, which already felt like an eternity. It seems as though, no matter how doggedly he licks and sucks, Ryder will never be able to get the drunk businessman in the hotel bathroom to come.

But she can't take her eyes off the action on the screen—blue latex gloves here, pale red condom there—because she's afraid to look at the Chief.

She keeps wanting to laugh at inopportune moments, and as Ryder emerges at last from the stall and walks toward the bathroom mirror, she struggles to get a hold of herself.

It feels like they should be in a dark theater somewhere.

That famous Square in New York City, say, before the former Mayor cracked down and cleaned it up from seedy to seedless.

It feels like something Colleen should not be watching with her attentive boss, alone in his apartment.

"That," she says, removing the jump drive, "is what brings me to you today."

"I feel like I should have been watching that in the back of a pornographic book store," he says.

"I know!" she says. "Like at a peepshow. In a sticky booth or something."

"Very vivid, Colleen. Where did you get it?"

"A friend of mine," she says, then hedges, "from the photo community."

"It's that Ethan kid, isn't it?" he says.

"I'm not sure that where I got it from is the point. The point is, it's pretty compromising for an antigay, family-values candidate like Ryder. I thought it might be of use, or at least of interest, to the Senator."

The Chief exhales, rubs his palms over his thighs.

Thinks for a minute.

Says, "Our campaign strategy so far has been under the radar. Few ads, no announcements of endorsements, nothing. Unorthodox, I know. Springfield keeps asking if we should set up press events to declare stuff like the approval of the VFW or who-the-fuck-ever, and every time the answer is a big fat no. It's been crippling us for months. But we simply do not want to remind people that there is a Senate election of any sort in November."

"I understand that. But Ryder's being so *sleazy*. All those cheap shots—about Nia's baby, about Dahlia, about the Senator's finances. And getting in bed with the Oil Company over the Lake—"

"Oh, let there be no doubt," the Chief of Staff says, "the man is vile. But in those cases, we've been reactive. Taken the defensive posture. Have you seen us go on the offense even once this season?"

He pauses so long that Colleen worries the rhetorical question is not rhetorical.

"In spite of the conservative big talk," he says finally, "Ryder has a moderate voting record. But his temperament doesn't follow. He's known to require lots of handling. Kind of a prima donna. His own party was leery about throwing the full weight of their support behind him. Waited to announce any Senate endorsements until very late in the game. They eventually went for Ryder, obviously, but that was only after Ryder went to them and pitched a hissy fit. Why do you think that would be, Colleen?"

Colleen can see that this question is not rhetorical, and her lack of a ready answer flummoxes her.

"I don't like to get too hung up on other people's sexual predilections," he says. "But it's been a semi-open secret for a while, in certain circles, that Ryder is gay. In spite of the wife—now ex—in spite of the family values. Gay as a garden party. We keep expecting the true believers on his own team to turn on him—the real head cases, the foaming-at-the-mouth types. You've met these people, Colleen. Their notoriously shitty gaydar hasn't gone off yet, but one day it might. You play pool, don't you? Eight-ball?"

"Sure," Colleen says. "Sometimes."

"When you've got one of your balls sitting right on the lip of a corner pocket—real easy shot—do you knock it in? No. You leave it. That way you control that pocket. Hell, likely as not, the other guy will screw up eventually and knock it in for you. Look, we want to beat the living shit out of Ryder in November. But do we want to destroy him, so his name can never again be spoken in polite company? Or do we want to let him run for something else in a couple of years—governor maybe, or the Junior Senator's empty seat—knowing he could burst into flames at any time?"

He takes a slow sip of water.

"Don't we *want* opponents with self-destruct buttons? Think about it."

~

Colleen has begun to make out the faint outline of something.

It is a map. A map of a tiny region. A secret world.

It is a world inhabited by the Chief, and by those underlings he deigns, when necessary, to consult—the Ginas, the Palmiras, the Steve Moon Colliers, even.

It is a world we did not invent. Neither did we prevent it from flourishing.

It is a world some of us mastered, others were consumed by.

In this tiny region, this secret world, Colleen is a peon.

However flatteringly her ilk is treated, they are privy only to the merest of slogans.

However in-the-know her ilk think themselves, they are distinctly in-the-out.

It is only because of the fissures she has opened that the Chief of Staff has parted the veil.

And now—you can see it on her face—she knows what she will never know, has glimpsed what she will never glimpse, knows she is going nowhere in this field we devoted ourselves to cultivating, no matter how smart she is, no matter how hard she works, or how brave she is, or how kind.

This sliver of knowing has doomed her to that knowledge.

See how it hurts her to know this.

Yes, we saw it from the start, but we too hurt.

She had been raised to believe as her father still believes—that her ability to advance would be limited only by her own energy and ambition.

But that is the lie at the heart of all this.

Of course there is that other lie, the lie she's been telling herself.

That her actions have flowed only from clearest waters.

To aid the worthy. To vanquish the vile.

That lie.

~

Then again," the Chief says, "to be perfectly honest, the main reason we've been so circumspect in our handling of this is that nobody had any proof, and this isn't the kind of allegation you want to make with nothing to back it up. This dirty little movie changes the game. So now that we've got the goods, the question is, do we make a move?"

"I'm not interested in demonizing anyone for his sexuality either," says Colleen. "That's not what I meant, and that's not why I came here."

What she doesn't say is, *I'm just so fucking sick of feeling shut out.*

Instead, "If you'd rather, we can pretend that I didn't, and I can just leave."

She picks up her bag, but he takes her hand, makes her sit back down.

"No," he says, "now don't do that. My reaction is mixed also, because I don't want to nail anyone to the wall for being themselves. Even if they're doing something that's personally risky. Peace. Love. Acid. Hate war. Let people do what they like. That's my generation."

"It's mine, too," says Colleen. "Even more than yours. People under thirty in this country are the most tolerant generation ever. I'm totally sex-positive, and I wish everybody the best in terms of empowerment and satisfaction with their individual proclivities. But it takes a certain sociopathic personality to lead the kind of creepy double life that Ryder is leading. It's not a personality I like, or trust, or care to have as a viable candidate in my state. That's all. I just thought you should have the information."

"I hear you, Colleen," he says. "What's going to override everything here is the fact that the Duke likes to occupy the moral high ground. That's just his way."

"And that's admirable," she says. "But one of the things I've started to realize by working here is that being an asshole *to* an asshole might not make you an asshole."

"Your gift of gab has always been considerable," he says. "I'll take that under advisement."

"I shouldn't have shown you this. Just forget it. Never mind. It's like you're trying hard to make me feel weird, and it's working."

"Come on, babe," the Chief says, "don't say that. For one thing, you *have* shown me, and you sure as hell can't unring *that* bell. Jesus Christ, I'm probably going to remember Ryder smoking that guy's pole until the day I die. For another, it's not crazy to think that we might find ourselves in circumstances where we'll be happy to have this."

"You're only saying that to make me feel better. Don't worry about it."

"I don't have to say anything to you that isn't true," he says. "And this is true, Colleen, it really is: it is always a pleasure to have you around. Even though I don't know what, if anything, will come of this, you've done the right thing."

"I've got to go," she says, meaning it this time. "Or I'll make you miss the game."

"I always have time for you, Colleen," he says.

He is standing next to her.

He kisses her hand, placing his lips—warm, dry—to where the fingerlessness of the gloves meets the reality of her fingers. She pulls away, but he holds her by the wrist for a second longer—to show her, what? That she doesn't get to leave until he says he is ready.

Her leg muscles tense.

She is this close, *this close,* to drawing her knee up to land it—crunching and true—in his groin, when he squeezes her wrist one more time and lets go.

"Ciao, bella," he says.

It knocks the wind out of her, the force of her regret at not actually getting to knee him in the balls.

This evening at home, Colleen will post the catch of the day on her photo blog, which she's started using again now that she's not busy on the campaign like she thought she'd be.

A closeup of the Mayor clasping his hat to his head to keep it from blowing into the Lake.

She will post it captionless, titled only "Mayoral."

She will link to it on her social networking profile and get forty-eight positive comments.

Even her mom, who generally makes a point of "not getting" her photography, will call to say she likes it after Bridget forwards it to her.

Her dad will write from the Desert to say he likes it, too, and to "keep up the good work."

Within twenty-four hours, Gina will email Colleen and demand that she remove it, but will not say on what grounds.

Colleen will take it down, but will make the mistake of asking why.

Gina will reply with, "We'll talk on Monday."

Before this talk on Monday takes place, in private, as the most basic tenets of professionalism would dictate, Gina tacks it without warning to the end of an early-morning chat about political messaging they are having with the Chief of Staff and Andrew.

"About that snap you posted to your blog from Saturday's presser, Colleen," Gina says. "I thought we talked about that."

"We did," Colleen agrees.

"Then why did you do it?" Gina asks.

"We never decided I couldn't," Colleen replies.

Gina fake-laughs Colleen's last name—"Duuuu-gan"— stretching it into extra syllables to signify disbelief, and Andrew chimes in with, "It wasn't detracting from anything. Colleen still got plenty of solid shots of the Cleanup for the Hot Topic," and Gina swats him down with, "Was I talking to you, Eckhart?"

"I don't understand what the problem is," Colleen says. "If I'm in a position to take a photo without interfering with my Senate duties, then why can't I? You want me to sit in a car and wait for the Senator? Okay, I can do that, and shoot some images while I wait. Lo can sit in the car studying his law books. Nia can sit in the car texting Dahl. What difference does it make if I take some street shots?"

"We just don't want you to, Dugan," says Gina. "That's not why we pay you. And we damn well don't want you to put them on your personal website."

Colleen gives it her last, best shot.

"You pay me $42,000 annually. And that picture is from when I was working off the clock, all by myself, on a Saturday. It seems unreasonable to expect me to forfeit my entire life and personality for such a low price. A lot of what we encounter in this job is fascinating. It's unfair that I can never even think about chronicling it. What about the right of people to talk about what they do all day, and how they feel about what they do?"

Colleen wonders whether Gina catches her reference to the famous Chicago documentarian.

Gina doesn't.

The Chief of Staff does.

Winks a slow wink.

Weighs in finally with, "I don't know that we can prohibit Colleen from practicing her chosen art."

"Gina," Colleen says, in an attempt at rapprochement that is doomed from the start, "I respect your point. I know it wouldn't be right for me to use images of the Senator, or images of any of you guys. But the Senator himself loves that I'm a photographer. Every time I see him, he says, 'How go the snaps?' He asks me for camera advice. He refers to me in public as 'My on-staff paparazzo.'"

"He's not the authority on this one, Dugan," says Gina. "He doesn't always know what he should and shouldn't mind."

The Chief ends the carnage. "Gina, I appreciate your including me on this parley-vous. But you've said your piece. Colleen knows what's out of bounds. Let's move on, shall we?"

"I don't feel remotely resolved over this," says Gina. "But fine. Dugan, don't ever let me see you take a picture of the Senator that's not for our official use. And don't you ever, ever let me see any images of him on your website. Or at any of your shows."

"Scout's honor," Colleen says, and gives Gina the three-finger salute.

L ater that day, Andrew will lean into Colleen's cube. "I thought you were trying to get shitcanned, Colleen."

"I call bullshit on that entire conversation," she will say, not looking up from her work.

"What a surprise that is," he will say. "Sure, Gina wants to stand on your hands. Sure, she wants to exert mastery over her crummy domain. Sure, it's infuriating. But you need to be careful."

"What does she care, if the Senator's fine with my photography?"

"That's another problem, Colleen," Andrew will say. "That was dumb of you to bring up."

"Whose side are you on?"

"Yours, Colleen, but listen," Andrew will say. "The Senator is not your pal. He goes out of his way to make you feel like he is, but he isn't. It is always a mistake to think a politician is your friend. You are a friend to him, yes. You will be loyal, and you will sacrifice. But you will be sacrificed if necessary. Loyalty in politics only goes in one direction. So don't piss too many people off, because if you do, the Senator won't lift a finger to save you."

"Our Senator's different," Colleen will say. "Come on, Andrew."

"Your funeral. I've gotta go finish uploading the Hot Topic."

And away he will go, and back onto her blog will Colleen put the photograph of the Mayor clutching his fedora, but this victory will feel neither very triumphant, nor very final.

16

Under chapter 13-196-410 of the City of Chicago's Munici-pal Code, all residential units heated by a common heating plant must maintain "a minimum temperature of 68 degrees at 8:30 a.m. and thereafter until 10:30 p.m. and 66 degrees at 10:30 p.m. and thereafter until 8:30 am, from September 15 of each year through June 1 of the succeeding year."

Colleen can recite this ordinance verbatim from fielding calls each fall from constituent tenants, chilly and pissed about remiss landlords and -ladies.

This year it takes a while for the season to shift and cool, and the radiators in Colleen and Walter's apartment do not kick in with their ritual hammering until the sixth, the first Monday in October.

The first day of the new session of the US Supreme Court, Andrew points out.

To Colleen the radiators sound bestial, hissing like geese. She appreciates the clamor.

Fall is her most beloved season. All that showy gilded chang-ing, all that compulsory repetitive dying.

This year, though, it's almost too literal.

The change they can believe in, promised by the Junior Senator?

Yes, they want that.

The dying the Senator's wife might be doing?

No, they do not.

"You look just like Snow White!" J-Lock says when Colleen signs in on Thursday morning, later that week.

It's warm again.

The weather has been undecided—like the kind of voters Colleen doesn't understand. Less than a month before the election, how can anyone not have made up their mind?

J-Lock wears a sleeveless dress topped with a pastel cardigan from a tricot twinset. She looks like a petit four. Having gone unhired at any law firm, she has offered to stay on through the fall, and despite her less than lustered performance, Dézi has let her. One less person to train, one more set of menial hands.

Colleen doesn't know the name of the delicate intern womanning the second phone at reception. Sudha has been gone for a month, back to school, and though Dézi has done the usual orientation of the fall interns, Colleen is having a hard time motivating herself to get to know them.

Everything feels so contingent.

In her cubicle, Colleen wonders: had J-Lock meant it, or did she still think Colleen worth sucking up to after all these months?

In any case, Colleen is pale today, with an old-fashioned hairdo and a serious sleep disorder.

At first she told herself it was all right. She's a small person, and only takes half of one sleeping pill anyway. Or did. Now she needs a whole one. Sometimes two.

When the doctor prescribed it—she couldn't keep stealing J-Lock's—she and Walter mocked the warning label, a red sticker with a man whose cartoon eyelids hung half-mast. "May Cause Drowsiness."

No shit, ha ha.

But the "may" has become reality. Some nights it doesn't.

Andrew had warned her about rebound insomnia, but what can she do? The stillness and frustration, the stagnation of the campaign and the economy and her life.

Stuck in the constantly competing sense that everything matters, and nothing does.

J-Lock's compliment caught Colleen with nothing to say in response, so she asked how the phones were going. The intern next to J-Lock—a thin-faced redhead Colleen was sure the Chief of Staff would pick to be that session's pet—said everyone was calling to complain about governors, a none-too-surprising development.

There is the current Elvis-loving Governor to complain about, the Fortieth, the Democrat with the hair and the delusions who, in a few months' time, will find himself embroiled in two dozen federal corruption charges and ultimately impeached.

And there is the ex-governor, the Thirty-Ninth, the Republican with the Nobel Peace Prize nomination, the commuter of death sentences and emptier of Death Row, who since February of this year is better known as Federal Inmate Number 16627-424, convicted on multiple counts of corruption not only as Governor but during his term as Secretary of State, most notably for his "bribes-for-licenses" scheme which resulted in the deaths of the six youngest children of a Chicago reverend—burned alive when their minivan burst into flames after its gas tank was punctured by a semi whose driver happened to be the recipient of an illegally obtained license.

The Thirty-Ninth Governor is set for release from federal prison on July 4, 2013 but is requesting an immediate pardon from the outgoing Republican President, a gesture which sits none-too-well with the Senator's constituents.

"Blood for blood, huh," Colleen had said.

"What a brilliant way to put it!" the redhead replied, sucking up all the way.

Don't waste it on me, Colleen wanted to warn her.

N othing pressing to work on, Colleen decides to clean her cubicle.

A dim layer of filth films the cubes of her Cube City coworkers.

Andrew and Lo's work stations are not just cluttered—piled high with neglected casework in Lo's case, abandoned electronic equipment in Andrew's—but dusty, sticky.

She doesn't know how they stand it, and toys for a moment with the idea of tidying up for them—she loves to clean—but refrains.

She's not their mom.

The chlorine smell wafts across her nostrils.

Colleen likes to try on different emotions to see if she can inhabit them, and experiments with feeling sorry for the Thirty-Ninth Governor. Republican though he was, he did lots of good things in office, too, and he'll be 80 when they let him out of prison.

But she can't quite manage it, plateauing instead at intrigued-but-removed, considering him more as a thought experiment on unintended consequences.

Which deeds you can atone for, which deeds you can't.

P̲ost-lunch, she gets a text from Andrew.

He's in a rented minivan driven by Nasrin and the gang's all there—the Senator, Gina, Mary Dodge from DC, Steve Moon Collier, and the Chief of Staff.

They are bound for the Senatorial debate at a liberal arts college downstate, laden with precious binders full of the Senator's policy positions—also of every utterance Ryder has ever made about anything ever.

The college is in Galesburg, birthplace of the poet who called Chicago a hog butcher, a tool maker, a wheat stacker, a railroad player, a handler of freight.

Colleen would call Chicago a waiting room.

"Every time we see pretty colored leaves," Andrew's message

reads, "the Chief says we should call you. I think he misses you :)"

Colleen read somewhere that the emoticon may have been invented as long ago as 1862, in a newspaper transcription of a speech by the Sixteenth President.

She includes this factoid in her reply to Andrew to show that, even though she is not with them, she is still plenty interesting.

With a lot to think about.

She leaves a little early so she can hit the gym before she and Walter watch the debate on borrowed cable. The days are getting shorter, the dying light on the commute growing more dramatic. Jagged rooftops and leggy water towers, pigeon silhouettes against the sunset like silkscreens on a T-shirt.

Making dinner—a salad with spinach, hard-boiled eggs, and shallots—she thinks of the post-debate meal that will happen in Galesburg.

Jealous.

Not of the food, which will be greasy and disgusting, but of the conversation and the company. The Senator doesn't have much of an appetite before his appearances, but gets ravenous afterwards. She remembers the scheduling call resolving the details, the Chief of Staff asking, "What in creation could be open in Galesburg at 9:30 p.m.?" and Hannah saying, "I'll call the local pancake house. I'll tell them to hold a table and leave the griddle on for us."

The camera pans the audience, then tightens on the candidates. Petite and shifty, Ryder looks to Colleen like a ferret in a blood red tie.

"Couldn't Ryder be the villain in some melodrama, practically?" says Colleen. "Like if he had a mustache, he'd be twirling it evilly?"

"Oh, Colleen," says Walter. "I hate the guy too, but he looks like a standard-issue self-adoring jerk. Which is how pretty much all Congressmen look to me. Sorry."

The Senator opens with a nod to history.

Before taking the stage, he recounts, he was chatting with the president of the college, and he asked when the last time they had hosted a debate was. The college president said 150 years ago, when the soon-to-be Sixteenth President and his future opponent, the man known as the Little Giant, held the fifth in their series of seven brilliant and historic debates, right here on this very spot.

This is the first and only debate the Senator and Ryder are going to have, and it turns out to be neither very historic, nor very brilliant.

The Senator says more times than Colleen can count that he must "respectfully disagree" with his opponent. Ryder says the same, though he is less adept at sounding respectful.

Ryder praises the self-regulating benefits of "laissez faire capitalism." He blames the economic downturn on "the energy crisis" and proposes "more drilling." Healthcare, he warns, should never be "taken over by the government." Illegal immigrants, he demands, "need to be removed from the States."

And woven through it all, his "many years of service to this great country in time of war," which have prepared him to "serve the great citizens of this great state."

To Colleen, Ryder comes across as the world's hackiest hack, filling in the blanks with words that come from some *So You've Decided to Run as a Republican for the Senate* handbook. Red meat for the downstaters. It's always difficult for Colleen to know how anything goes over with anyone besides herself, but she suspects to those voters it seems that Ryder is winning.

The Senator's style is, to say the least, less sweeping.

The market that led to the present Great Recession, he says, had not only been allowed to run free, but to "go hog wild."

The current Administration's proposed privatization of Social Security, endorsed by Ryder and dubbed the "ownership society," is more about creating a "we're all in this alone society."

He rejects this aloneness, for "In the final analysis, we are stronger together."

And on and on, back and forth, like a protracted game of ping-pong, until all ninety of the allotted minutes grind by.

On TV, the Senator's face looks lumpy, eyes downcast, bags gathering beneath them. Attentive and thoughtful, he makes his listening face when Ryder speaks.

This face is never photogenic or attractive, but tonight it looks preoccupied, too, and far away.

Yesterday Colleen had checked with the Chief regarding the Ryder video—if maybe they should show it to the Senator. "The Senator's wife," the Chief had said, "might be dying. We can't show him gay porn right now."

Onscreen, the Senator looks shorter, like the weight of this worry is squishing him down.

Walter pushes the power button and unhooks the cable. This is the first time since the convention that the TV has been on, and turning it off leaves a lingering in the apartment, like someone has been there and left without warning.

Gone too soon.

October would mean a tighter tether, the Chicago office was cautioned earlier in the year. No travel requests, no time off, no casual days—nothing.

But the Senator has reduced his schedule for Dottie's sake, and Nia has sent the following email setting the staff partially free:

All—

Friday is a jeans day!! Dézi please let the interns know. Also, we have been given the green light to take vacation days in

the month of October. Any questions should be sent to me.
Yes We Can (wear jeans)!

—Nia

Fresh from maternity leave, Nia had sent the message because
Palmira, also back from maternity leave, will be out for the next
couple weeks, having agreed to a request from the Junior Senator's campaign to assist in rallying the Latino vote.

And so too, on this final day of this long weekend—stretched
to three days in honor of the quote-unquote Discoverer of America—have Colleen and Walter taken their leave, gone west to
Iowa, the final push, to canvass the backroads in search of the
Undecideds.

Cute Dubuque on an idyllic fall morning. The kind of perfect
Colleen can't help but refer to as September 11–perfect.

She was in DC for her senior year of undergrad when the
passenger plane crashed into the Pentagon, and the weather had
been incongruous in its flawlessness.

Crystal blue sky, cotton-ball clouds.

As was often remarked in the news coverage—that day and
for years ever after.

"These so-called Undecideds," Walter says, "just want
attention."

Colleen laughs. But some of them do seem to be shut-ins who
know how they'll vote and only want to talk. Like eighty-nine-
year-old Bernice, in a neighborhood like the one Colleen grew up
in. Lower-middle-class, three styles of houses, alternating 1-2-3
along the cul-de-sacs.

The pattern reminds her of her grandmother's quilts, and of
the three-color camouflage of her dad's desert fatigues.

Bernice lives on her own in a house that smells peculiar but not bad—camphor and onions, detergent and hand cream. She comes to the door in a sweater with bird appliques and food on her teeth—a boiled egg? cottage cheese?—and looks at Colleen and Walter inscrutably, responding with a clumsy pause to their scripted lines on behalf of the Junior Senator.

Perhaps she is hard of hearing.

Perhaps the unframed print of an oil painting of Jesus Christ and his disciples at the Last Supper behind her on the wall is omen to the sermon she is about to deliver on the Junior Senator's position on abortion.

But no, her smile flashes wide. "He's my guy," she says.

She is none too impressed with that Alaskan Governor, who's "too darn full of herself" and should "just go back to Alaska."

And Bernice is off and running, for a long, long time.

They extricate themselves in a way they hope is gracious and finish the block, but some of Bernice's loneliness has attached itself to Colleen, thin and fine and hard to brush off.

The endless doors on which they knock flicker by like a movie montage. Verité vignettes of other people's lives.

A couple in the middle of a marital dispute—the man pulling away in his sports car, two kids under ten in the backseat calling out, "Good-bye, Mom! Good-bye," his "Good-bye, Dear!" notably absent. His waving Colleen and Walter in. Their stepping forward only to find the woman, his wife, bathrobe pulled tight like she's just put it on, the pimple on her high forehead halfway covered by makeup she's been in the process of applying. Colleen asking, "Do you have a minute?" Her spitting out, "No, I don't. I have a wedding to get to."

Or the guy repairing his front stairs who mistakes them for Jehovah's Witnesses, then welcomes them with, "I wouldn't vote

Republican even if Jesus Christ himself was on the ticket."

Or the teachers with the Somewhere a Village in Texas is Missing Its Idiot bumper sticker who ask them for yard signs.

Or the mother and her college-aged son who agree with every plank of the Junior Senator's platform except for keeping abortion legal, who refuse to cave to Colleen and Walter's talking points about how creating a country in which children could be wanted would help more than hewing to a hardline ideology.

Or the couple who ask, "Doesn't he have black values? Isn't he a black man, going to favor black people and try to get revenge on the whites?" except with the N-word in place of "black"—a situation the Dubuque field office had warned was an outside possibility, but that Colleen and Walter could not have been fully prepared for.

Or the jerk in his station wagon full of kids (Wisconsin plates) who motions them towards the driver's side window and asks, "Who are you walking for?" then rolls his eyes and says, "Why?"

"A tax cut for ninety-five percent of all Iowans," says Walter.

"Not payroll taxes," the guy says. "My boss makes a million dollars a year, but he gives me a job. Poor people can't create jobs."

Colleen chimes in that she is not in favor of wealth concentrating at the top, nor does she believe that it actually moves down from the highest point, nor does she adhere to the philosophy that the worth of a human being should be calculated based on his or her ability to generate wealth over the course of a lifetime.

"You don't believe in trickle down?" he asks, incredulous.

The guy, neckless, his zillion kids breaking into pandemonium, says, "Your candidate is horrible on abortion. Do you realize that?" and Colleen says sorry, their definition of "horrible" differs, and to have a nice day.

"What was with that guy?" Colleen says after he pulls away. "Like we'd be all, 'Oh, thank you, sir. We drove four hours from Chicago and have bags full of literature for the Junior Senator, but you're right. The Republican candidate is the guy for us?'"

"He sincerely seemed to think he could change our votes, though. Which is kind of nice and democratic at its core," says Walter, and Colleen is reminded of why she loves him.

Colleen and Walter have knocked on 139 doors, and they get the sense that they've convinced at least a few people.

Back at headquarters, they tally their results, turn in their clipboards. A staffer invites them to help themselves to dinner—by which he means a soggy sandwich from a ham n' cheese croissant party platter. They say no thank you in favor of eating across the border.

They end up stopping in Galena, a town "named after the mineral form of lead sulfide, you know," says Colleen, who has not been here since she was a kid—the time her parents had brought her and her sister here because it was cheap to get to, and educational.

Eighty-five percent of the buildings in Galena are on the National Register of Historic Places, and Colleen and Walter eat in one of them, an Italian restaurant studded with a plaque and leafed—like everywhere else around town—with pamphlets about the one of our number whose face now graces the fifty-dollar bill.

He lived here for a while, and Colleen remembers hearing about him with the interns on their tour of the State Capitol this summer.

His life after the Civil War had seemed a series of public fuckups and political setbacks, but he managed to pull out the win in the end, destitute and dying of throat cancer, penning his life story so his family could survive off the book sales and royalties.

Yeah, Walter says, he can see why she would root for a guy like that.

Why Colleen would want to have faith in second chances—in second, and third, and fourth life acts.

W e are not sailing forward," the Chief of Staff says before scheduling call the following Tuesday. "We are barely keeping afloat."

He wears a black and white tie that looks like a chessboard. He and Gina are in low-grade dismay over the fizzling of the campaign. They are here to contemplate strategy, plan their next move.

As Dottie grows sicker, the Senator keeps canceling. Press conferences, speeches, even trips for the Junior Senator. Ryder's poll numbers continue to spider upwards. As an office, they are island-hopping from weekend to weekend, unsure how to pass the time until they reach the target: Election Day.

But perhaps, Colleen thinks, there is no real mainland?

"We've got a calendar that has October on it, and then that first fatal week of November," says the Chief as they wait for DC to join the call. "Then it drops off. There be monsters."

"I can't believe it's really, truly fall," says Dézi.

"I put on a jacket this morning and cried a little bit," says Hannah the Scheduler.

"And the tears froze," says the Chief.

Colleen looks out the window at the cold, cold Lake.

She heard at some conference on urban planning that views of the water are known as "blue ways." She forgets the term for views of the sky, but the view of the Lake is gray today.

A gray way.

The color of uncertainty, she thinks, then thinks, how pompous.

Ryan Slattery's voice barges onto the line—his usual combination of arrogance and nervousness.

Will the Senator go to Minnesota this weekend for the Senate campaign of a former late-night sketch comedy cast member? Neither DC nor Chicago has the answer. The first elected female Democratic senator from that state—the daughter of a sportswriter of whose work the Senator himself is fond—wants to know.

"And she wants to know yesterday," says Slattery.

"I'm afraid that still falls into the 'Who Knows?' category," says Hannah.

"All we *do* know," says Gina, "is come hell or high water, he has *got* to do a press event here in the state on Friday morning. To remind people he still exists. All right?"

"I'll give Dot a call," says Slattery. "See if we can't get her to say it's okay for him to leave her side for a split second."

"Only if it really is okay," says the Chief.

"Yeah, yeah," says Slattery, and switches subjects.

Colleen has developed a habit of checking her wristwatch for unavailable intervals of time, like days or weeks, and she does this now as she thinks of how far they have to go until the election—how far Dottie has to go, period.

She remembers last summer when she'd gone to pick the Senator up, and Dottie was standing in front of their building with him, teaching him how to take a photo with his Senate-issued smartphone. They hadn't realized Colleen had pulled up, and Dottie had struck a silly pose, twirling her umbrella like the star of that musical about the rain and singing in it.

A fter DC hangs up, they loiter, then kick around topics for Friday's press conference. Gina wants the Senator to talk jobs. The Chief says whatever he wants to talk about is fine, just get him in front of some goddamn cameras.

"We'll just hope no reporters bring up earmarks again," he says. "That was the part of the debate last week that hurt, when Ryder harped on pork. Pork this, pork that, pork pork pork. Jesus."

"Ooh, pork," says Sylvia, rubbing her belly, more like an elementary school teacher at story time than a Senate Aide. "I'm ready for lunch. A pulled pork sandwich—that would be luscious."

"We'll need to remind him to be prepared for that," says Gina. "And give him the heads-up that he'll probably be asked his opinion on all this ex-Governor pardon crap. With the media blitz about clemency, no matter the topic, somebody's going to want him to weigh in."

"*None of my fucking business* is his answer to that," says the Chief.

"If he sticks to the script," says Gina, "the presser will be cake."

Nia brushes her bangs aside with her pen. "Cake," she says. "Yum."

The Chief rakes the room with a *who-hired-you-people?* glare, and it occurs to Colleen, as it does periodically, that in the ten years that she has known him, she has almost never seen him eat.

For some reason, she admires that.

"My apologies for keeping you from your troughs," says the Chief. "You're dismissed."

17

If listening is an art, the Chief of Staff is a bad artist.

Walter is a good one.

Andrew is a fifty-fifty split.

The Senator possesses a gift for at least *acting* like a good listener, but he doesn't spend it on his staff. He expects their counsel, gets mad if it's absent. Hears it out, but only for the purpose of ignoring it better than half the time.

Standing in a small ballroom at a club across the street from the Federal Building, the one that calls itself a league, named after the Union of states, not of workers, Colleen cannot quite believe that the Senator is going to do the press event today when he so clearly does not want to.

Typically, such an event would be booked in a place pertinent to the issue being discussed.

Since today's topic is jobs, Gina would have had Colleen call up a local factory or business and imposed on them to host, to provide refreshments, even.

But the Junior Senator has been holding his stand-up press events here for months, and inspired by his campaign's simple elegance, Gina has decided to hold some of theirs here, as well.

Plus, as she and the Chief both know, they'd have a hell of a time convincing the Senator to go far afield.

After this, he's heading home to his darling Dot.

When Colleen got here with the equipment, she found the entryway flanked by doormen, beneath heat lamps that stay lit from fall until winter's end, and the requisite coat check, brimming with real furs.

Gross, thought Colleen, and then, because she was advancing the Senator, she got a dispensation to keep her cloth coat with her.

She gets called "Miss" and is treated by the men here with an elaborate politeness that is supposed to seem chivalrous but mostly serves to remind her that "ladies" don't belong. Women were not permitted to become members until 1987, when Colleen was seven.

People seem to be acting toward her with actions accompanied by adverbs.

They look her in the eye keenly.

They address her directly.

They show her kindly into the elevator before them and tell her warmly to please have a nice day.

Crystals droop from overhead fixtures like early-morning dewdrops from spider webs. Colleen affixes the Senate seal to the podium, watches the janitors rearrange the chairs.

With its patterned carpets and intricate molding, the room is usually dimmish and tawny, like being at the bottom of a glass of whiskey. But Gina has told Colleen to get them to crank up the wattage for the benefit of the cameras, which have begun to arrive.

A perk of having the Junior Senator on the campaign trail is that now the local media pay more attention to the Senior Senator. All the major TV and radio stations have said they'll be here, along with all the papers, a turnout unheard-of a couple months ago.

Tasteful paintings by famous masters space themselves at even intervals along the tall walls—oily, still wet-looking, like you could thumb them and move the colors around to your liking. Each has its own CCTV camera. Between some of them are faux Corinthian columns. Colleen is pretty sure they are Corinthian—the ones with the scrolls of foliage? Acanthus?

To the sides of each column hang wall-mounted candelabra, electric flames flickering. A pleasing room, well-conserved, apt for a conference about conserving and creating jobs.

The suit-clad League staffer assigned to assist her regales her with tales of the League. Its aura of tradition, its storied history. He tells her that once a year, amid the chandeliers and the Impressionist canvases, they used to bring in a ring and fight the Golden Gloves, and the audience members had to dress black-tie.

Somewhere in the building is a Monet, he says.

Wander the halls and maybe you'll find it.

The Senator arrives with Gina and the Chief, trailed by Andrew and J-Lock and two new press interns.

The Senator's lost weight and seems melancholy, but Colleen has to admit this makes him look better. Trimmer, not as bland.

Eating less, brooding more, his mind is elsewhere. He wears his disquiet like an outfit he hadn't intended to put on but can't take off, and it looks sharp.

He hands out the usual handshakes, then takes to the podium, thanks those present for being present, and proceeds to phone it all in.

Jobs jobs jobs.

The people want them.

The hardworking people of Illinois want them and so do their families.

We should give the hardworking people of Illinois and their families some jobs, some good jobs, some green jobs, and some jobs in manufacturing, and jobs that are jobs right here in Illinois.

Colleen sees Gina catch the Chief's eye. The Chief lifts and drops his slim shoulders. Gina returns the shrug.

The reporters cry like grackles, "Senator! Senator!"

As expected, not a single question about jobs. As expected, questions cribbed from Ryder's talking points.

And when those are exhausted, the usual potshots ensue.

Isn't our current governor a crook and why can't you or somebody stop him?

Do you really think that the Junior Senator can win the presidency in three weeks?

Adept but robotic, the Senator responds.

Gina looks at her watch, cups her hands around her mouth, and hollers, "Last question!"

A short, stocky woman Andrew calls the Shetland pony shouts, "Senator! How do you feel about the bid of the Thirty-Ninth Governor for a Presidential Pardon?"

Gina shakes her head once left, once right.

The Senator does not look at her.

He is about to make what they will later refer to as a snafu—emphasis on the -afu, as in "all fucked up."

At this very moment, the Thirty-Ninth Governor of Illinois, the man whose corruption led to the fiery deaths of six young children on a Wisconsin highway, sits in his cell in a country-club prison in Terre Haute. Each week, he's visited by his faithful wife.

The Senator stares at the squat reporter as if he hasn't understood the question, or understood how anyone could ask it.

Then his vague but statesmanlike expression curdles.

He reaches into his breast pocket, pulls out a piece of bleached white stationery.

"I've written a letter," he says. "To the outgoing President. Requesting clemency."

Flashbulbs pop.

The jaws of both Gina and the Chief of Staff drop. Caricatures of shock, like broken marionettes.

The Senator unfolds the sheet and reads—a sophisticated and philosophical statement on forgiveness and mercy.

The Thirty-Ninth Governor has lost his state pension.

He is old and ill.

There is every chance he will not survive to live with his wife.

His darling, his high school sweetheart, mother of his four kids.

Ever again, if the sentence stands.

"The bread of Justice," he reads, "must be leavened with compassion."

He is not, he wants to emphasize, requesting a pardon. What the Thirty-Ninth Governor has done is unpardonable, except by God the Father Himself. Rather, he is asking for a commutation of the sentence, so the poor old man can return to his family for his few remaining years.

Colleen sees the faces of the reporters in the gilt-framed mirror behind the Senator, mouths twisting down, minds turning against him.

The current Governor is under federal investigation for corruption. So is the young State Treasurer. The people of Illinois are embarrassed, angry, in no mood to cast forgiving eyes. More in the mood for an eye for an eye.

The Senator sees none of this, or if he does, does not care.

He quotes a Catholic religious leader who says that if forgiveness were easy, it would not be a virtue. He assures the people of Illinois that his request grows out of no political motive but rather a human one.

From where Colleen and the rest of the staff stand, this sounds like the no-shit statement of the year. Far from racking up political gain, this is suicide.

The Senator finishes reading the letter, folds the paper away.

The room stopped listening several principled rationales ago.

Gina throws herself between the Senator's body and the microphones, as though trying to take a bullet. "I'm afraid that's all we have time for today," she says.

But he edges around her, his brown eyes those of a cow to the slaughter, back to the mics.

The young reporter from the public radio station squeezes off one last question. Colleen recognizes him from last spring's North Avenue Beach presser, the guy with the Illinois tattoo on his forearm.

"But Senator," he shouts over the shouts of the others, "there are over 45,000 people presently incarcerated in the state of Illinois. The United States has the highest rate of incarceration of any country in the world. Countless members of our nation's prison population will die behind bars without ever having a chance to see their families again either. Should we let them out, too? Should we forgive them? How is this not favoritism toward a so-called elite? How can you honestly state that this is not an act of political cronyism?"

The room explodes in further flashbulbs, similar questions.

The Chief of Staff says the Senator has to go.

And they go.

The Senator lets himself be led from the podium. Copies of his letter, he says, will be provided to reporters as soon as possible. That is all he has to say on the matter.

Packing up the equipment with Andrew and the interns, Colleen thinks of Lo. She'll let him know what happened as soon as they get across the street.

In addition to veterans affairs and military issues, Lo deals with prisons—the prisoners in them and their families. From this instant on, he will be inundated with letters, calls, and emails on behalf of other convicted criminals asking the Senator for letters of clemency.

For their own personal slice from the compassion-leavened loaf of Justice.

The Senator, ever private, will refuse to make—will allow no one to make on his behalf—any mention of his own sick wife, his sorrow over Dot's deteriorating health, his own fear of growing old apart and alone.

No, Lo will have to tell them all, *no no no.*

This kind of forgiveness exists only for the Thirty-Ninth Governor.

Colleen, Andrew, and the interns arrive back on the thirty-eighth floor to a tableau that resembles an intervention on a daytime talk show.

Gina and the Chief of Staff stand in the hallway by Cube City, attempting to corral the Senator into his private office where they can talk him out of what they hear the Chief refer to as "this utterly phenomenal PR clusterfuck."

"Hey," Andrew says to the interns, by way of clearing the danger zone, "could you guys please go into the intern room and download the photos?"

They slink off, some eagerly, some reluctantly. Later Colleen will regret not paying attention to who among them lingered to eavesdrop. In her own intern days, she would have been one of those.

"If you draw the target around the bullet hole after you shoot," says Gina, "you never miss."

She's trying to make a point about messaging and damage control, about forming a plan, about spinning, about lemons and lemonade.

"She's right," says the Chief. "This is a tough spot, but nothing beats a fail but a try. What should we try, Duke?"

Lo, Steve, and Nasrin have come out of their cubicles.

The Senator does not notice.

He faces Gina and the Chief like someone who is about to puke, but who is trying to keep it together, trying not to not make it to the bathroom.

Then it's less like that.

He swallows.

Exhales, inhales.

He is like an animal, cornered, but prepared to attack.

A hippo, Colleen remembers. Cute at first, then you're dead before you know it.

"None of you get it," he says. "Do you? You people of *all* people. How *dare* you question me? How dare you not see that there are more important things in life than being ex*pedient*? Than making sure people *like* you?"

And then he loses it. Whatever *it* is—patience? composure? sanity? self-interest?—he no longer has it, and he no longer gives a shit.

Colleen realizes, as he screams at his staff for what may be the first time in his almost thirty-year career, she has never until this moment seen pure emotion from the man.

She has seen *real* emotion, yes. She would never say he's been faking it all this time.

But his feelings—his words, his actions—have always been ... controlled.

They have seen him troubled, they have seen him distant, they have seen him angry and they have seen him sad, but all those emotions were caught and filtered through the sieve-like mask of Senator as Distinguished Public Figure.

Eminently contained. Calculating. Rational.

They have never seen him this hurt, this raw, this ugly.

It is embarrassing.

Colleen is sorry, but she is embarrassed for the man.

It is like watching someone you admire get shamefully drunk and collapse. Like seeing them pick their nose, shit, fuck in front of you, not aware that you are watching.

It is something emotional, yes, but physical, too.

Humiliating and uncomfortable.

And you don't want to see it or know what it means, but you cannot turn away and you will never forget.

His mind has been running concentric circles around the

prospect of the permanent loss of Dot. He has been caught in this spiral, and now he is spinning out to where they can no longer touch or help him.

"Would you like me to arrange a cab to take you home, sir?" the Chief says when the Senator pauses, his deference as incongruous as the Senator's rage.

"No. No thank you. I am not going *home*," he says, biting into each word and snapping it. "I am going to the *hospital*. I can get there myself."

He twists toward his office to get his coat, his briefcase.

Colleen hears the semicircle of staffers, herself included, breathe out, a leaking tire sigh of collective relief. His eyes have punctured them. Now they can crumple.

Then he turns on the heel of his black dress Oxford, wheeling to face them one more time.

"I still don't think you see," he says. He is no longer screaming, but the voice he's using constricts their throats. "For me, there are more important things to worry about than my reelection. There ought to be more important things for all of you, too. I am leaving now, to go and be with my wife. I don't care what you tell people. I am gone. I am gone now, and for as long as she needs me. Good-bye."

Everyone is here to hear this. Nia has come out of her office. Even Agnes Lumley has made her way from the little southern clump of cubicles Andrew has named Siberia.

The back door slams.

The Senator is absent.

A wretched quiet settles, then breaks. There, in the wake of the Senator and his abdication, the Senator and his grief, they ask their questions, make their statements.

"What about the People's Work?" asks Nasrin, ever the idealist.

"What about our jobs?" asks Steve Moon Collier.

"It's a trajesty," says Andrew. "It has the majesty of tragedy."

"We cannot fix this if he will not work with us," says Gina.

"We need to prepare to get monster-fucking-trucked," says the Chief.

"I can't do this job," says Colleen. "I forgot how sad it makes me."

But she says it to herself, in her cube, where no one can hear her.

What she means is: always the cycle of sadness.

What she means is: always the tension between wanting to be a fool and do the right thing, and wanting just to push papers around and make cool jokes with your coworkers.

The Senator, she knows, has just been *so real*.

Fucked up as it is, she feels lucky to have seen it.

Yet his accusatory tone regarding their concerns about the political practicality of what he has done offends her.

Up until not even an hour ago, the Senator was one of the biggest practitioners of realpolitik in the country—guided by practical considerations more than principles or ethics.

Yes, he has principles and ethics. And decency, more than most. But first, last, and foremost, he has been, if one is honest, a hack—strong-arming colleagues who step out of the party line.

And as his staffer, Colleen is expected to do whatever she is asked—to hack hack hack away alongside him.

Her ideas on where to go are unwelcome, her volition nonexistent.

Her opinions on what to do are unrequested, she offers none.

She'll be told what to do once the higher-ups have decided.

The media shitshow has begun.

In stories all over the internet, blog posts and reposts, rags right-wing and left-, every wire service strung from coast to coast and beyond.

Colleen reads them all.

Ryder was contacted for comment even before the Senator had folded away his letter, which, of course, he supplied with glee.

"This is just the latest in a string of sleazy moves by one of Illinois' so-called statesmen. This lack of regard for human life sickens me, and it sickens the voters. How can he do this to those six innocent babies who never got the chance to grow up? This isn't about mercy! It's about one lying politician protecting another. His dishonesty—his hypocrisy—his corrupt and vile motives are patently disgusting."

Colleen thinks of the reverend's burning children, trapped in flames, banging their little hands on windows that would never open.

She thinks of the Senator's dying wife, of the career he is willing to trash in devotion to her, of what a luxury it is to be able to trash it.

She thinks of the Thirty-Ninth Governor of Illinois in his cell in Terre Haute, of his wife who visits him weekly, of the lavish trips they will never again take on dirty money.

She thinks of the thousands of prisoners in far less pleasant cells whose crimes had led to far less carnage.

Of the reverend and his wife and what it means to have a family reduced by sixty-seven percent in one instant on a Wisconsin highway.

Of the trucker, an undocumented worker who spoke little English, who just wanted work so he could feed his family, who likely knew nothing of the bribe paid in his name when he was handed his license.

She is about to close the window on the last of the stories she will read today when her eyes fall on the most recent comment: DEATH TO ALL GODDAMNED KILLER LOVING BABY KILLERS!!

And she thinks of how false emotions are one way of murdering a body politic, how sanctimoniousness is a form of murder, how manufactured outrage is a form of murder.

Not much longer, she tells herself, not very much longer.

Not this job where it's full steam ahead and damn the ideals.

Not just the ideals but the very underpinnings of the ideals.

Full steam ahead and damn the underpinnings.

She prints the story with the most odious Ryder quotes and brings it to Gina and the Chief. They are still sort of milling about, standing stunned in the hallway.

"Not to try to win the afternoon's award for most obvious news," she says, handing the story to Gina, "but we're already getting pummeled by Ryder."

"Yes, indeed," says the Chief. "We are hurtin' for certain."

"God," says Gina, glancing at the article. "That guy's an asshole at any speed, but this is happening fast."

"Thanks, babe," says the Chief. "We'll have a plan soon." He walks into his office, Gina behind him, door swinging shut.

By the end of the day there will be no plan.

In spite of herself, Colleen will judge them.

Nobody here has a fucking clue what they're doing.

She'll worry all weekend, though as Nia is fond of saying, this situation falls into the category: *above my pay grade*.

The Senator could lose the race over this.

She's furious at the Chief for not mentioning the Ryder video. If ever there was a time to make it known, wouldn't it be now?

Colleen can't put the pieces together because she possesses so few of them.

When she was in junior high, Colleen's mother was always trying to get her to read these mysteries, a series about a spunky girl detective who found secrets in old clocks, hidden staircases, lilac inns, shadow ranches.

Colleen liked the dry smell of the decaying paper, and she liked the idea that her mother had read these yellowed books when she was a girl, but finishing one always felt like a slog.

The books were written under a collective pseudonym. Over the decades, an untold number of uncredited hands worked from a general outline to produce and maintain the image of a girl who remained consistently strong, unswervingly heroic.

On an endless upward trajectory.

Wondering what will become of the Senator, Colleen feels like a teen detective who will never solve the final case, and will never grow old.

18

The Eisenhower, the 290, the Ike, whatever you like to call it, is experiencing heavy delays this morning due to a delivery truck accident and subsequent snack spill.

The public radio station that Colleen and Walter set their alarm clock to wakes them Monday with this report. Artificially flavored triangular corn chips cover the junction where the presidentially named expressway meets Congress Parkway, and cleanup crews have arrived on the scene.

Groggy, Walter asks, "What flavor of snack chip?" as the announcer says, "Eyewitnesses indicate that the chip involved is nacho cheese."

Colleen hears this story with relief.

Maybe, if something so stupid is getting so much coverage, the Senator's clemency request for the Thirty-Ninth Governor has played itself through the weekend news cycle and died a natural death. Fatal as they can seem, such mistakes sometimes drop like rocks into the center of a lake: ripples spread, but then the item sinks.

That is not the case today.

After the weather, the announcer plays the adenoidal audio of one Ron Reese Ryder scolding his opponent. "What this state needs now," he says through both nostrils, "is honesty." And, "My opponent's hypocrisy last Friday makes the people of Illinois sick." And, "We need to punish evildoers, not let them off scot free."

"Okay if I switch this off?" Colleen says, straddling Walter to reach the nightstand. "I'm going to hear enough of this at work all day."

Her finger has already pushed the button before Walter can say, "Sure, I understand."

The weekend polls that Steve Moon Collier hands to Gina and the Chief of Staff are troubling. He didn't make a copy for Colleen, but she can see as they flip through the stacks that the results are bad.

"What we're seeing," says Steve, "is a general antigovernment, anti-incumbent mood, and a huge bounce for Ryder."

"The Duke goes from being thirty-three points out in front—" says the Chief.

"To just five," says Gina.

A moment of silence.

"He needs to write us back," says Gina, "and please fucking advise."

"Don't take the snub personally, Moretti. I can't get a hold of him either," says the Chief. "Colleen, Steve, thanks. Keep standing by."

Sitting by, thinks Colleen, back in her cube, listening to the whirr of Nasrin's space heater across the aisle. Above the heater, Colleen catches the scrolling and clicking of Nasrin's mouse, and wonders if she's looking for a new job in light of the new data.

Whenever Colleen has the choice between doing something and doing nothing, she almost always goes for action. Dynamism, not stasis. You can never tell whether a choice is going to be genius or disaster, so you just have to go for it.

Or so she tells herself, studying the Contact Us page of the Semi-Scurrilous Lefty Blog that appears willing to publish almost anything.

Colleen reads it daily—which is fitting, since "daily" is in its name—but to date she has never given much thought as to where they get their "hot tips from a liberal perspective."

The file is too large to send over email.

First, then, a query.

For the anonymous email account she is about to create, Colleen considers using the name of a muckraking Danish-American documentary photographer, who published a book on economic disparity called *How the Other Half Lives,* before deciding that that's dumb.

She settles on "ConcernedCitizenIllinois2008."

"Dear Editor," she types. "No doubt you have heard the rumors that pro-family Republican Senate candidate Ron Reese Ryder is himself gay. . . ."

~

Colleen is about to experience a colossal fall.

Her descent will be both swift and hard.

But it will not be from grace. She, an earnest but low-level functionary, has not attained the heights of grace.

Will not.

Her fall is sad but compelling. Talent and enthusiasm squandered and wrongly applied is almost always, to a degree, compelling.

To a greater degree, instructive. If history repeating is instructive.

Colleen's doomed ordinariness, her brave and foolish misapprehension of her place in the world, is a primary factor in why we care for her.

Unlike so many of us, whose grace turned into highways, whose falls turned into libraries.

~

Colleen calls Ethan to invite him to their apartment for dinner that evening. He says yes.

She has to tell him what she's thinking of doing. Ask him if she should.

Ask Walter, too.

By the end of the day, "ConcernedCitizenIllinois2008" has received no response.

She tries to reason herself into patience: this close to the election, they must be avalanched with tips. It'll take a while to sort out the crackpots.

Second-guessing herself, third- and fourth-guessing, she rides the Red Line home, no longer feeling quite so steadfast.

From the alley, she enters their building's back courtyard, the automatic porch light clicking on, the moths flocking to it.

Don't do it, guys, she wants to warn them. *Can't you see you're embodying a self-destructive cliché?*

But they are just moths.

Over mole enchiladas—Walter's specialty—Ethan is thrilled when she announces what she's done (the query) and what she's thinking of doing (sending the recording) but unsympathetic to her doubts.

"It's *obvious*," says Ethan, knife banging on the table. "They write back, you overnight the sex tape."

Colleen looks to Walter, then back to Ethan.

"It's not that easy," she says. "I'm not a lone wolf in all this. I'm part of a team, an organization. You wouldn't know what that's like. It's not just the Senator and Ryder, or me and the tape. There are mothers and babies and—"

Strings connected to strings connected to other strings, she thinks.

Boxes upon boxes, cubes upon cubes.

"And anyway," she says, "how do I know that sending it will really end up for the best?"

"You don't," says Walter, thoughtfully setting down a forkful of black beans. "Instead of being all John Stuart Mill about this—trying to do the most good for the largest number—you've sometimes got to rock it Immanuel Kant style."

"What are you talking about?" says Ethan.

"Stick to a few core principles, and make peace with the fact that you can't predict what will happen after you act," says Walter. "Colleen, you believe in the truth. In not keeping secrets. In making sure everyone has all the information, so they can decide for themselves. Right?"

Colleen thinks about the things she has kept from Walter, and her chest tightens.

She nods.

"Okay, then," says Walter, "you send them the video. You see what happens."

He stands to gather the empty plates.

"If you can't do it," Ethan says, downing his wine, "I will."

Colleen says nothing to this, feeling much like the informant on the other end of the line in that movie about two Washington journalists who bring down a President and all his men.

Whose very silence was all the confirmation they needed.

Tuesday morning, not word one from the Senator. But when Colleen checks "ConcernedCitizenIllinois2008" after arriving at work, an editor has written to say that he finds the tip "of tremendous interest."

"Send it ASAP," he writes, "to the following address."

She forwards this to Ethan, with the subject line: "?!?!?!"

Scheduling call is usually full of camaraderie and shared purpose, plus major jacking and the wasting of time. Today it feels humble.

Colleen is sure her skin must be audibly buzzing with the knowledge of what might be happening, even as they wait here, but everyone else in the room seems numb.

In the wake of the Senator's breakdown, the situation is dire. It is Wednesday, and all Chicago staffers have been summoned into the Chief's office to catch any updates.

"This is so strange," says Agnes Lumley, standing in a corner, since there aren't enough chairs. "I can't believe it's come to this."

"Everything changes," says Andrew, standing next to her. "Who knows why? People used to feed tuna as trash to their cats. Now it's sushi."

From the black leather sofa, Colleen looks at her coworkers. They are all so alive, so present. The idea of them dying seems unreal, though of course they all will.

Ryan Slattery comes on the line. "What we know today," he says, "is that we don't know jackshit."

"Slight correction, if I may," says the Chief. "We *do* know that he and Dottie have asked all three of their kids to fly in as soon as they can, and that they are all arriving by early this evening."

"Not promising," says Slattery.

"No indeed," says the Chief. "But that's all we've got. If you don't have anything else, we'll bid you adieu."

Hannah the Scheduler disconnects, and Sylvia rushes into the silence that follows.

"I'm such a gabber," she says. "I'm so nosy. But can't you please give us an update on what's going on with Mrs. Papa Bear?"

"We have very little to say," says the Chief. "Not because we don't want to tell you, but because we don't know ourselves. Dot had an operation over the weekend."

"What kind of operation?" Sylvia says, persisting with questions Colleen is sure are on everyone's mind.

"It was her lung, of course," says the Chief. "But nobody's told us what exactly the operation entailed. We have also been told that she is having complications. The doctors are talking about performing another procedure this week."

"What's the prognosis?" says Sylvia. "She's going to get better, right? I mean, doctors these days. They know what they're doing."

Gina shakes her head, tight-lipped and grim as a medieval painting. This is partly because it is unseemly for Sylvia to be asking these questions, and partly because none of them know.

The circle of privacy has closed around the Senator and his wife.

"I know this is hard on everyone," says Gina. "But this is what we have to deal with. We can't overthink it. We just have to wait. And we have to respect the family's wishes."

"If you think too hard about anything," says the Chief, "you can get really scared."

Every eye turns to his, expectant to see how he'll finish the thought, how he'll make it all right, how he'll tell the team, *Hey boys, take a knee*—a favorite throwback to his high school football days. Ever the coach, hatching plans to win the unwinnable.

But he doesn't.

"That's all we've got," he says, running a hand through his whitening hair. "Go on. Get outta here."

It is Friday morning, and when Colleen's phone rings inside her bag as she's walking out the door to work, she half-expects to see an unfamiliar number: an editor at the lefty blog.

Impossible, of course. They don't know who she is.

The other half of her expects it to be Ethan. They have made no contact since Tuesday.

Instead, Gina's pixelated face glows from the display. She starts speaking before Colleen can finish saying hello.

"Hey Dugan. Gina here. Listen, Dot's still in the ICU. The boss can't make today's award ceremony after all."

Gina and the Chief of Staff had hoped to coax the Senator into doing one unfussy event this morning—stopping by the Aquarium to pick up a conservation award for his work on the Great Lakes.

A little grip-and-grin mixed with a dash of feel-good photo-op.

Then back to the bedside.

Colleen thought them irrational for even trying.

"Do you want me to call the director and let her know?" says Colleen, instead of *I could have told you so.*

"No, Dugan. I've already called her. I want you to throw on a suit and go accept the award on his behalf. If people ask, just tell them he's sorry, but there's an illness in the family. He expresses his heartfelt thanks and regrets, et cetera, et cetera."

If Colleen had a dollar for every set of condolences she collected at the Aquarium for the Senator, she wouldn't be rich, but she could afford to take everybody in the office out to lunch someplace fancy.

She props the plaque against the wall of her cube, gazes at the Senator's name engraved over the bronze outline of Lake Michigan.

"It's lucky that the shoulders in this city are big," said the bespectacled man from the federal agency established to protect the environment, who in the Senator's absence ended up as the main speaker, "because so is the responsibility."

The event was held in the "Local Waters" gallery. The backdrop was the *Zap! Electric Barrier!* exhibit—how to prevent invasive species from making their way from the Chicago River into the Lake.

The dinosaur-looking lake turtle in the tank next to Colleen stood floating on her hind flippers, as if she too were listening, neck craned from inside her heavy shell, the better to hear the ceremony.

This turtle, she knows from past visits, was rescued in the late 1980s after being hit by a car during her nesting migration. It took a year of intensive care before she was able to eat on her own. She is blind in one eye.

Animals connect you to the natural world is part of the Aquarium's mission statement.

As they both listened, Colleen felt connected to the turtle, even as she suspected the turtle might not reciprocate.

Ms. Dugan," says the Chief of Staff, and Colleen jumps. "Get the fuck into my office right now, if you please." His tone is as cool and dry as the hand he lays on her shoulder.

"Don't sit," he says. He closes the door behind them. "Do you see what is on my monitor?"

The lefty blog's start page. The bright orange headline shrieks: "Bathroom Tryst Could Blow Ryder Senate Bid."

"Oh," she says, swallowing her shock at actually seeing the words somewhere outside her own mind. "Well, look at that. Seems like good news to me. But—you seem not to think so."

"I submit to you Exhibit B," he says, setting the phone to speaker and playing a voicemail.

A man's voice.

Angry, breathless.

Identifying itself as belonging to Ryder's communications director.

"I thought we had a deal, you fucker," the voice says. "We were going to back off the clemency thing and run this campaign up to the end, fair and square. How dare you lie to my face? I know we've wound up on opposite sides, but I believed you were a man of honor. Look, I know you won't call me back, so I'll say it now:

fuck you. Fuck you hard. If you think we won't strike back with everything we've got, you're dreaming. It's on."

Colleen sits on the edge of the wooden chair across the desk from the Chief, suppressing both mechanisms of fight and flight.

"And finally," he says, skipping to another voicemail and pressing play, "Exhibit C."

"I don't know how you plan on explaining this X-rated blockbuster," says the voice of Ryan Slattery, "or why I've gotten three messages this morning from Ryder's press bitch saying how hard you double-crossed him. But I very much look forward to hearing all about it. You know where to call me. And you'd better call me. Fast."

The Chief of Staff steeples his fingers, presses them to his lips. He puts his hands in his lap.

His face looks like a papier-mâchéd mask of itself, badly drawn and ragged. It is hard to look at him as he begins to speak.

"The gentleman on that first call, Colleen, is my old college classmate. Not a buddy. An acquaintance. He started out lefty—progressive down to his shorts, like me—but he got a little wealthy and drifted right. Obviously. But on the basis of all the good times we had going to the same Jesuit university, we kept in touch."

He is looking past Colleen now, gazing out at the Lake.

"Earlier this week, I called him up. Asked him to lunch at the Union League. Said I had something he might like to see. After he took a look, he agreed that if he wanted his boss to have a career in public service for the foreseeable future, he'd get Ryder to lay the fuck off in these final weeks. Certain assurances were made. Certain guarantees."

He pauses, looks straight at Colleen.

"Now that those appear to have been broken—and now that it appears to him that they could only have been broken by me—he is pissed. And he is calling DC to say, 'Your guy in Chicago fucked us.' And DC, as you can see, has no goddamn idea what he's talking about. Consequently, they are also adopting the default stance of asking me what the fuck."

Colleen drills her focal point into the wall behind him, through the sheetrock and into Cube City.

The Chief of Staff is in deep shit. Okay.

Colleen appears to have inadvertently put him there. Less okay.

"So presumably you can see the tight spot your artsy-ass little friend Evan—"

"Ethan?"

"Fine. *Ethan* has put me in by sending the footage to this snotrag blog."

"Ethan didn't send it."

"Are you looking at the screen, Colleen? It's the top fucking story. It's got approximately one fuck-ton of comments. The thread is a shitbomb. Are you in denial?"

Through Cube City and out into the prairie.

"I sent it," Colleen says. "It was me."

The Chief of Staff blinks, squints at her, and blinks again, like he's looking at something blurry or far away. Colleen expects rage, which she has seen from him, but not confusion, which she never has.

He looks baffled, irritated, like a pirate captain whose trusty musket has misfired.

"If my arms were long enough," he says, "I'd reach over there and smack you. What the hell were you thinking, Colleen? *Were* you thinking?"

"I was thinking we needed to *do* something. Dottie's in intensive care. The rest of us are in limbo. I wanted to get the truth out. I couldn't keep looking at Ryder's face and listening to his lies. I wanted to be involved in the stupid democratic process. But all that's happened is more bullshit compromise. More backroom double-dealing."

"I had all this sorted out, Colleen. But now Ryder's people cannot be placated. They're going to be on the attack every day between now and November 4, and the Duke is down for the count and won't fight back. Do you see what you've done?"

He pauses, as if to reload.

"And I'm getting calls even angrier than that from DC. Of course I'm telling them I have no idea what this shithead is talking about. But Slattery has always hated my guts. He doesn't believe half what I say on a good day, so he sure as hell isn't swallowing this. I am double-fucked."

"What was I supposed to do with it?" Colleen says. "Nothing? Put yourself in my place. Could *you* have just sat on it? I mean, this isn't what I wanted to see happen, of course, but you could have just told me—"

"*You don't get to know,*" the Chief snaps. "Don't you get it? You are not a person who gets to know. That is not how this business or how *any* business works, Colleen. The escalator that you are on does not go there. I *don't* put myself in your place. You don't put yourself in mine. You don't get to call plays. This operation already has more quarterbacks than it can handle. What you do is, you show up, you do your job, you be pleasant and patient, you quit peeking over your goddamn shoulder all the time, and if you're going to get tapped for something higher, then someday somebody will tap you. That is what you do, and that is *all* you do. You don't get to *choose* how you're going to help us."

Colleen feels a wave of heat pass over her face, like she's leaned over a lit stove burner.

She thinks of Steve Moon Collier—aping the Chief, biding his time in his walled-off cube—and of Agnes Lumley—waiting, but for what? She wonders what they think about their lives, their careers.

She wonders why the Chief thinks he gets to be such a grabass and why he thinks *that* would never make her feel less than pleasant and patient.

"So just to be clear," says Colleen, "you're mad at me because I messed up your blackmail strategy?"

She knows she shouldn't provoke him.

In spite of everything, she has always admired him, ever since she was nineteen and an intern.

The way he styles himself as such a straight-shooter. The way he is who he is. The way he embodies what-you-see-is-what-you-get more than anyone else she's ever met in her life, besides her dad. The way he refuses to keep a shredder in the office, saying, *We don't play the game that way. I won't work in a place where anything needs shredding. You bring in a shredder, you get rid of me.*

Colleen had thought of him as a man with unlimited political pull, but for the first time she sees that he too is on the receiving end of exclusivity.

Like her, he has loops that he has been looped out of.

This truth blinds her for a second. A bare lightbulb, the fixture gone.

"Let me be frank," he says, his sharp face heavy, like leaded glass. "I have never been angrier with you, Colleen. I'm not sure where I expected to be at this point in my life. It's not exactly where I am. I'm almost sixty, you know. What's a guy like me to do?"

He smiles a little when he says this, as if it's intended as a joke, though it clearly isn't.

"I am, however, sure as shit this is not where *you* need to be," he says. "You're not even thirty. It's time to start thinking—where will you go? Because you can't stay here much longer. Slattery is gonna come down on me with everything he's got. He's going to tattle to the Senator, say I'm a loose cannon, try to make me take a fall."

But you are *a loose cannon,* Colleen wants to say, then says instead, "But Slattery is such a—" she thinks of an expression her dad might say—"a tin god. A paper tiger. A piece of shit. How can the Senator not see that?"

"What makes you think he doesn't, Colleen? Do not kid yourself that Slattery is not MVP, or that his ruthlessness has not proven useful to the Duke on many an occasion. Slattery is a bloodthirsty son of a bitch who's been trying to consolidate his power since he came on board, back when the Duke got elected to the House. He's not going to ignore this chance to nail my ass to the wall."

The Chief's face lightens.

"Now listen, Colleen," he says. "I'm going to keep cock-blocking Slattery as best I can for the next few days about how the fuck this all happened. But Colleen, princess, there are limits to how far I can go to keep your name out of this."

"I know," she says, then feels surprised, because she does know, has known for a while. "I don't think I have the passion for anonymity."

"No shit you don't, Colleen."

"But I don't think that you do either," she says, and wants to add, *Stop saying my name.*

"You've been doing a fine job, Colleen. Up until now, I mean. But you're not constitutionally suited to be a soldier. You need to go somewhere and try to be a general."

"You sound like Ryder with the military metaphors."

"Dammit, Colleen. Watch it. I'm still mad as hell at you. But you are not the sole owner of this fuckup. I understand that. It's not really anyone's. It's a mess. We'll have to wait and see what happens with DC. As for the rest, we'll stand back and watch how Ryder reacts. There's a very high likelihood he'll implode. I've told Gina this, but you should go talk to her, too. See if she needs you to do anything."

Colleen gets up to leave.

"And after you do that," the Chief says, "contemplate your parachute. Your exit strategy. Whatever they call it. All right?"

C olleen wants to say more, but isn't sure how.

For now, she's happier with what she did not say.

She didn't mean to hurt the Chief, but she has not said that she is sorry.

Colleen is forever apologizing. Thoughtlessly. Making nice, making peace, applying a mea culpa that means little to her as soothing balm to someone else's ego.

But not this time.

She is not sorry for what she has done. Why should she say she is?

She thinks for a second of what her mother would think, then thinks she cannot think that way. The perpetual state of self-reproach and self-restraint her mother inhabits—that she wants Colleen to inhabit—is not a state she can live in.

I may have hopelessly fucked my own career, she thinks, as she heads to Gina's office, and that of the Chief of Staff, but I have also, for the first time since I've come to work here, taken some concrete action to make the world more honest and just. And I've just seen how stupidly things turn out when you do that.

She wonders about the best way to balance out these debits and credits.

Personal growth, ruined careers, democracy, hypocrisy, the bad guys winning, the good guys losing, omissions and commissions, mortal and venial sins.

She shoves aside the terror she feels over the prospect of losing her job now that the economy has shit its pants.

She'll worry about that if—no, when—it happens.

Gina's on the phone, but as soon as she hangs up, she's giving Colleen orders.

"Tomorrow, 10:00 a.m. You, me, and Andrew at Ryder's presser responding to the video. He's holding it at the Vietnam War Memorial off the Chicago River. State and Wacker, lower level."

"Sure. Okay. He's not doing anything today?"

"Not unless you count scrambling," Gina says. "Issuing blanket statements through his people, like *I am so not gay.* And implausible denials like *That is so not me.*"

"Do you think it really is him?"

"Does the pope shit in the woods?" she says. "Come on, Dugan. You're the one with the trained eye around here. Have you seen the video?"

"I just watched it, yeah. But there's a lot of compression on it, isn't there? And it's pretty dark."

"Oh, it's him," says Gina. "The best part is that now that it's broken on the internet, all the other 'respectable' outlets are doing that thing they do where they pick up the story without really picking it up. Holding their noses and linking to the original source, going, 'Here's what some less reputable outlets are alleging, in case you're curious.' And, 'Here's where you can check it out if you're into that kind of thing.'"

On Gina's monitor, Colleen sees the screenshot that one of the city's two top dailies has pulled from Ethan's video. Tawdry and incriminating. Ryder's decline has been set in motion, and she's sure it won't be principled, it won't be graceful.

The reality of this does not please Colleen nearly as much as the idea of it had.

19

The next morning the sky is clear, but the wind howls off the river as Colleen and Andrew stand in the small plaza labeled Chicago Remembers, waiting for Ryder to convene his news conference.

The rushing air will create an irregular roar in the various mics. This, in addition to everything else, makes Colleen glad that this is not the Senator's event. Gina would inevitably blame the poor sound quality on Colleen and Andrew.

In this case, of course, unintelligibility may be Ryder's last hope.

"Where's the Chief?" Colleen asks, as Gina joins them at the edge of the crowd.

Gina's ashen face betrays no trace of the glee that played over its every feature yesterday, and Colleen tries to imagine why. Her stomach does a rollercoaster drop at the sudden thought that the Chief has been fired.

"I thought for sure he'd be here," Colleen says.

Gina looks at her as if she's asked the question in tongues. Colleen feels that much more paranoid.

"You didn't hear?" says Andrew.

"Hear what?" she asks, barely breathing.

"Colleen," he says, "Dottie passed away this morning. The Chief went to the hospital to be with the family."

It just happened, Colleen," says Gina. "Hannah had just started the calls as I was leaving the house. I guess it didn't get to you, yet."

Colleen feels the way she does when she's narrowly avoided an accident on the freeway—sick and wide-awake. Like her life has changed in an instant, or should have, though in fact not much is really different.

She pulls her phone—on silent for the conference—out of her bag and sees no missed calls. She pictures her name out on the scraggliest branch of the phone tree.

"I just—" Colleen says. "It's so sad. It's so—I wish I'd known. That somebody'd told me."

"Bad things happen to good people all the time, Colleen," says Andrew. "Dottie dying, you not being informed. If it makes you feel any better, J-Lock dumped me this morning."

"It doesn't, actually," says Colleen, and then, "Gina, is this going to be public knowledge? Dottie's death? Are people allowed to know?"

"DC's working on the statement," says Gina. "Slattery insisted it come from them. Very short, very succinct. It's going to be going out any minute, probably."

The writing of press releases often feels to Colleen like an empty exercise where Gina will look at what Colleen has written, and say "Now put it this way," followed by "Now put it back the way it was."

But their office should be the one writing the release about Dottie's death.

It's not a good sign that Slattery has co-opted it.

Colleen looks across the swelling knot of media and spectators. The event has attracted the typical cadre of far-right sloganeers sporting Uncle Sam hats—their messaging so disjointed it's impossible to tell whether they've gathered to support Ryder or to crucify him.

A man wears a foam finger that reads "U.S.A. #1! "on one hand while holding a "God Hates Fags" placard in the other. Next to him stands a woman waving a banner that says, "Can We Have Our Country Back? Yes We Can!" next to a man holding atop his shoulders a toddler clutching a "Don't Tread on Me" poster. The woman beside them—the toddler's mother?—holds an "Armed and Dangerous . . . With My Vote!" sign.

The reporters, you can tell, smell blood. Every news outlet—TV, radio, print—is here.

The public radio reporter with the Illinois tattoo emerges from the crowd, though today the tattoo is covered by a corduroy jacket. If the Chief were here, Colleen thinks, he'd be wearing his camel hair topcoat.

"Be right back," Colleen says.

She walks over and taps the reporter on the shoulder and whispers in his ear. He shakes his head, looks at Colleen, then nods. Colleen waves 'bye, and makes her way back to Gina and Andrew.

"Saying hey to your boytoy?" says Andrew.

Colleen doesn't even have the heart to tell him to suck it.

The news conference begins.

Ryder takes to the podium, joined by a blonde woman with a square chin. She is taller than he is by almost a head, including his ample hair, which gives him an extra inch-and-a-half. Sleek and streamlined, the woman wears jewelry that Colleen would describe as high-end museum giftshop—austere and geometric—which makes her appear even more intimidating.

Ryder, meanwhile, looks shorter than usual, with none of his straight-backed, ten-*hut* machismo.

Very shifty, very sweaty, despite the chill.

He lacks his signature black leather jacket, wearing instead a somber wool. He looks unwell, sniffling.

Or is he sniffing, Colleen thinks, detecting the smell of a public hanging?

Andrew starts taping.

"Who's the woman?" Colleen whispers.

"Human shield," says Andrew. "Ex-wife."

"He's dragged her back to his side for the conference," says Gina. "Props and stagecraft."

"Ten bucks says she's about to describe their vigorous hetero sex life in the most graphic terms imaginable," Andrew says. "Who'll give me fifteen to one? Anybody?"

~

Our own wives were a long-suffering lot. They sometimes encouraged us to remember the ladies, to be more generous to them than our ancestors were. We mostly ignored them.

They looked the other way while we had affairs with buxom blonde starlets.

Or they were lesbians, grateful to the affairs of state which occupied our separate lives.

Or they doted upon us as we doted upon them.

A woman invented the flag.

A few fought secretly in the American Revolution, the Civil War.

One first lady saved a famous portrait of one of us, and an original draft of the Declaration of Independence, from the clutches of an invading army.

But we who are telling you this story are all men.

All dead, all white, one hundred percent male.

Why are there so few founding mothers?

~

First up, the ex.

The woman's nails have been lacquered the darkest shade of red still distinguishable from black. Her hand grips the lectern with an unconscious tightness. Talon-like, a captured bird.

She reads from a brief statement which, Colleen notes, never overtly says, *My ex-husband is not gay.*

Just: "We divorced for a lot of complicated reasons, but we are still friends and it pains me to see a friend confronted with such nasty rumors. But I'm not here to speak for him. He can speak for himself. I am here to support him. And to ask that you please listen to him and support him. Congressman—soon to be Senator—Ron Reese Ryder."

Ryder leads with the same flimsy excuses he leaned on yesterday: the video has been doctored; neither of those two men in the restroom is me; it is shameful that a pack of liberal extremists would stoop to such smoke and mirrors to assassinate my character as a conservative champion of family values; war hero war hero war hero; rinse and repeat.

This litany exhausted, he looks down, pale and flustered, at his notes, then into the cameras, and it's clear he's no longer reading, that he's about to speak impromptu. Ryder's communications director—the Chief's old classmate, Colleen is sure of it—looks as though he wishes he had a cane, to drag his candidate off the stage, vaudeville style.

"People," says Ryder. "Let's not forget what this is really about. My opponent is a moral degenerate. He thinks any kind of sexual conduct—sex with animals, sex with little children—should be perfectly acceptable. I oppose that. And I believe that all real Americans oppose that. The party he leads is a pack of moral degenerates. They've proven it time and time again. They think that women should be actively encouraged to murder their unborn babies. They think that aliens who come here illegally and refuse to learn our language and adopt our values should be rewarded with cash and jobs and medical care. They cover up these crazy ideas in a banner they call *tolerance.* But I will not tolerate the compromise of Christian values! No one should tolerate it!"

At this, the crowd erupts.

The man with the foam finger jabs the heavens while God Hates Fags jiggles at his breast.

The woman beside him waves her banner so vigorously it reads, Can We Have Back? Can!

The toddler's hands have been commandeered by the man below him for some vicarious clapping, his Don't Tread on Me poster fluttering to the ground.

Ms. Armed and Dangerous is pumping her meaty fist in the air.

"People!" Ryder is shouting now, buoyed by it all, "This is no more than a conspiracy. A conspiracy by the liberal media, in collusion with gay extremists who will stop at nothing to promote their perverted agenda! My opponent is the biggest conspirator of them all, trying to turn attention away from his disgusting effort to win freedom for his criminal crony, the ex-governor!"

Cheers turn to boos, smiles to snarls.

"It's a blatant attempt to tarnish my reputation, which cannot be tarnished. People! I am a patriot. You all know why this is happening to me. Why they've taken these fanatical measures. It's because they regard me as dangerous. And I *am* dangerous. To enemies who would destroy the American way of life. I've flown planes. In the sky. Over war zones. To keep America safe. And with your undying support, I will continue to be a top gun for the interests of Illinois voters, and to do it in the United States Senate. Thank you! Thank you!"

Ryder basks in several seconds of applause.

The communications director strides in front of the microphones, his balding head glinting in the cold sunlight. "No questions," he says.

But the mass of reporters starts shouting them just the same, and Ryder shows no sign of stepping away from the lectern.

"I can't believe he's going to submit to this," says Andrew.

"He can be my guest," says Gina.

Without exception, the reporters' questions play variations on the theme: *how dumb do you think we are?*

Ryder's responses are just as unswerving. "I already answered that in my statement."

A sarcastic voice amongst the reporters asks Ryder whether it's possible he might be adopted—whether he might, in fact, have a promiscuous gay twin somewhere in town.

The communications director keeps clapping him on the back and walking off, then scurrying backward when Ryder doesn't follow.

This can't go on much longer.

Congressman!" the public radio reporter shouts. "Congressman, can I ask a question about your opponent's, um, moral degeneracy?"

Ryder's small face lights up, like he's just spotted a bouquet among all the hurled tomatoes. "Yes!" he says. "By all means."

"You mentioned the Senator's request for clemency for the ex-governor," he says. "It has been suggested that the Senator's request might have been prompted by his own family situation, which has caused him to be sympathetic to the ailing ex-governor. As you may or may not have heard, there are reports this morning that the Senator's wife has passed away after a lengthy and private—"

Colleen looks at neither Gina nor Andrew, but she can feel their eyes sweep from the reporter to her.

Apparently, nobody has heard this, yet.

Apparently, Slattery's press release must not be out.

A murmur moves across the mouths of the crowd.

The journalists are, for the moment, silenced, as they try to compute the changing of the game.

But for Ryder, there is nothing to compute.

"That's unfortunate," he says, "but irrelevant. There's no evidence that the Senator places any sanctity on the value of marriage, including his own, so I hope he will not use this—if it is true—as an attempt to curry favor with Illinois voters."

Even the placard-wavers grimace at this.

The public radio reporter persists.

"In light of the Senator's facing this personal tragedy," he says, "is there any chance that you would you like to temper your criticisms? Out of respect for your opponent's feelings?"

In the narrowing of his haggard eyes, Ryder's outrage is visible to all.

What is not visible to all, what is known only to Colleen and the Chief and the Chief's old classmate and to Ryder himself, is the personal betrayal he feels that fuels his rage. Nothing about this has been tempered for him, as he was assured that it would be.

But he can talk about none of that—not cutting the side deal, nor how he blames the Senator for a fatal double-cross.

Instead, he can only open his mouth—a sneer, an allegory of vengeance—to say, "I would be sensitive to the Senator's feelings if I believed he had any. But I believe that the Lord helps mete out justice in the world whenever he can. This may be a case of that. I leave you with the message that it is not enough to vote against my opponent and other degenerates like him. They have a complete lack of moral accountability."

He pauses, looks directly at the bank of cameras.

"They are fundamentally un-American, and they deserve to be stamped out."

His communications director looks poised to drag Ryder bodily away from the lectern, but Ryder goes willingly now.

Back up the stairs, into the waiting SUV.

The unspoken consensus even from this crowd seems to be: *Holy shit, the man is a nutroll.*

"Well," says Andrew, "*that* was an incoherent casserole of every far-right talking point ever."

"What kind of retort are we expected to provide?" says Colleen. She thinks of Nia's response to foam-at-the-mouth constituents: *Can't argue with crazy.*

"Now we get to compose some kind of *I am officially ignoring this person for the rest of the campaign* statement on behalf of the Senator, and we leave it at that," says Gina. "Ryder just turned this into a cakewalk for us. So it truly does not matter that the Senator is going to continue ignoring everything for a little while longer."

Colleen doesn't feel much contented—nothing like scoring the winning goal for her team.

More like a momentary satisfaction. Like she's just successfully balanced her checkbook, only to be reminded how broke she is.

She remembers the Senator, red-faced, screaming at his staff, *There are more important things to worry about than my reelection.*

She feels like they should do something uncalculated, non-opportunistic.

Perform some impractical gesture to indicate their sorrow.

Stop a clock, cover a mirror, drape something with black bunting.

Dottie is dead.

Instead she asks Andrew, "You taking the Red Line?" and he says, "No, the bus. I don't really feel like talking," and they say, "See you Monday," "See you Monday," "See you Monday," and go home by their separate and silent ways.

20

Colleen's mother kept her enrolled in the national scouting organization for girls from the time Colleen was five, when the girls were named after a flower, through age eight, when they were identified with a chocolate dessert or an elf—depending on your frame of reference—all the way to age twelve, when they were known as Cadets, but with the feminine suffix "-ette."

Each June, after school let out, the troop leaders piled the dozen or so girls into two station wagons, and although by sixth grade the Cadettes had come to deem pretty much anything to do with scouting or their mothers as terminally lame, for this remaining activity their enthusiasm never waned.

How they played the game: starting in the lead car, each girl took a turn flipping a coin whenever they came to a stoplight. *Heads* meant *right*; *tails, left*. After every girl in the lead car had flipped, the cars swapped spots so each girl in the second could have her turn. Navigating in this fashion, they proceeded from the elementary school parking lot in Woodridge to whatever eatery was closest to the last coin toss.

That year, on a road named in honor of the Twenty-Sixth President, they ate at a restaurant named after the seven diminutive companions of a fairy tale princess. Cartoon signage lit with small flashing bulbs! An old-fashioned soda fountain! Hamburgers! Milk shakes!

Colleen remembers this as she sits in her cube and tries to consider her career options, tries to imagine past next Tuesday.

From his field hospital in Iraq, her dad has sent her and Bridget a link to some article about successful people. Managers, high achievers, men and women in charge of things. Their common belief? The great degree of control they have over events and situations.

Colleen used to feel this way.

S he picks up her half-empty coffee mug and walks to the kitchen for a refill. It's early, still, and nobody else is in except interns.

She hears the telltale click of vertiginous high heels.

Almost turns back, but J-Lock, teetering by the coffeepot, spots her.

"Colleen! It's so great to see you."

"Is it?"

"Did Dézi tell you?" says J-Lock. "This is my last week. I got a job!"

"At a law firm?" Colleen says, trying not to sound incredulous. "Congratulations!"

"Not at a firm. Colleen, I'll tell you—I didn't pass the bar. And I couldn't make myself take it again."

Back and forth, like a rueful metronome, J-Lock slowly shakes her head.

"Right," says Colleen.

"Even if I *had* passed it," says J-Lock, "I'm not sure what I would've done. I've been working so hard and worrying so much about whether they're gonna *allow* me to do this thing, this thing that I'm just *dreading* having to do for the rest of my working days. I don't *want* to be a lawyer, Colleen! I couldn't see myself leading that kind of lifestyle. And honestly—" J-Lock, sheepish, lowers her voice, "I don't think anybody else can really see me in that lifestyle, either. You know?"

Colleen squirms a little.

"Oh, Colleen, sweetie, it's okay," says J-Lock. She gives Colleen's upper arm a reassuring squeeze. "I understand what people think of me. I mean, they don't think it for no reason, right? Lord, I have put a *ton* of work into making sure people notice me, see me a certain way. I'm real good at doing that. But once it's done, it's not easy to *un*-do. Oh, I could get a job, Colleen. The city's full of guys who'd make an offer just based on seeing *Luvabull* on my résumé, kinda just keep me around as eye-candy. Sweetie, I know *you* know what I mean."

It occurs to Colleen that she ought to take offense at this.

She and J-Lock are nothing alike.

But then she considers how J-Lock might think they are, and how other people might think they are, and how this, maybe, is why she always makes Colleen so ill at ease.

Do Gina and Palmira and Nia and Steve see Colleen as a valued member of the team, or as the Chief of Staff's plaything?

"Pretty much my whole life," J-Lock says, "ever since I was an itty-bitty thing, I've just *known* what people expect. So that's what I've always been. I don't mean *specific* people, I mean *everybody*. Pretty little princess. All-American girl. It was always so simple, like a billboard. And I *liked* it. But now I guess I'm starting to see where that goes. And it just seems so *small*, Colleen. So I've finally started thinking about what's really important. And I have to tell you, you have been such an inspiration to me."

Colleen looks at J-Lock's lowered eyes, heavily lined, and wonders if she is being messed with.

"Seriously?" she says.

"Sure. The way you work here, but you have your other life. Your photography. You seem to have a real healthy sense of what really matters. I kept visiting your website—the one Andy set up for you—and every time I do I think, *girl, if you don't at least try to do something else, you won't ever be satisfied.*"

"That's very wise," says Colleen.

"So I started applying for jobs I knew I truly wanted. And I got the one of my dreams! Me and Hillary are moving down to New Orleans. I'm going to work at the Louisiana Society for the Prevention of Cruelty to Animals! Do you know how many dogs and cats still suffer from formaldehyde poisoning from those post-Katrina FEMA trailers, Colleen? FEMA's your issue area, so I'm sure you do. There are still so many displaced pets down there. I feel called to help them, you know?"

Colleen has always assumed that J-Lock loves her dog in the same way that she loves her brand-name handbag with the LV monogram. She has also assumed that J-Lock either hated her, or did not think about her at all.

She feels ambushed, kind of, but J-Lock seems sincere.

"Well, if your vocation is calling," says Colleen, "you've got to pick up the phone."

"I *knew* you'd understand!" says J-Lock.

Colleen fears she's about to get hugged, but J-Lock holds off.

"When I first came here," she says, "and I met all you smart, talented, beautiful people, I was so excited! I really thought that this was where my real life was finally gonna start. But it's been a disappointment, Colleen. I don't mean the Press Team part. I really appreciate the way you made such a point of personally inviting me along to conferences and things. That meant so much to me. But I just thought—maybe this is silly—I thought, shouldn't we all be at least *trying* to change the world? Nobody here's trying. And if you *are* trying, then they don't really want to hear about it. I mean, you're all good at your jobs, and you all help people, but—I guess I just pictured this as a powerful place, where somebody can make a huge difference. Turns out, it's mostly just people trying to keep things the same."

Colleen feels unsettled by the fact that J-Lock is saying things that she's been thinking lately herself. It's a little like hearing the Constitution recited by a colorful sock puppet.

"Maybe that's what power always does," Colleen says. "Keeps things the same."

"Mostly," J-Lock says, "I guess I've learned that if you don't have it sorted real clear in your head—what you want for other people versus what you just want for yourself—then this is a bad place to be. I swear, Colleen, it's been making me a worse person. I thought working for the Senator would bring out the best in me, but the opposite has happened."

"I hope you don't feel like we've wasted your time," says Colleen. "Maybe it's as valuable to learn what you *don't* want to do as to learn what you do?"

She hopes she doesn't sound obnoxious, parental.

Hopes J-Lock won't notice how lame Colleen really is.

"Not at all, Colleen," says J-Lock. "Internships are supposed to help a gal figure out what to do with herself, right? God as my witness, I have figured it out."

Colleen tops off her coffee mug, raises it to J-Lock's to click them together.

"Cheers, Jennifer. It's been a pleasure to have you here."

"I hope you'll keep in touch, Colleen. I can't wait to see what'll happen to your career."

"Me either," says Colleen.

J-Lock giggles, but Colleen means it.

On her way past the Chief of Staff's office, Colleen finds him and Steve Moon Collier still standing in their trenchcoats, passing front pages from hand to hand.

Steve has bought himself a jaunty wool driving cap that matches the Chief's. One day soon, his transformation will be complete.

The Chief appears to find this sycophancy not sinister but flattering.

The daily that styles itself as the World's Greatest Newspaper has condescended to declare its endorsement of the Senior Senator.

"It has been decades since an Illinoisan held a leadership role in the Senate," Steve Moon Collier reads, his voice even more sarcastic than usual. "Yet even though he died in 1969, people remember with fondness the Illinois Republican who was the then Senate Minority Leader. Our current senior senator cannot be said to hold a candle to his predecessor, however—" and on to the end, where they suggest that though the Senator could use better role models, Illinois voters should vote for him anyway, since there's nobody much else available.

"Kind of a grudging and preachy endorsement, isn't it?" says Colleen. "I mean, *When the TV cameras are on, you can count on him to show up and whack a Republican?*"

"Sure," says the Chief, "but it's an endorsement all the same."

"We'll take it," says Steve.

"It's not like they've got a lot of attractive options, I guess," says Colleen.

The other paper, whose claim to fame is being the oldest continuously published daily, does the same, without the puffed-up history lesson, though they too lament the Senator's tendency towards partisanship—the adjective of choice here being "shrill."

Colleen concedes this point.

And she reminds herself that although neither of the papers truly knows the man, neither does she.

Sipping her coffee, Colleen visits the lefty blog and peruses the comments on the reticent story about Dottie's death. Even here, where vitriol and rancor are rewards unto themselves, the commenters display restraint.

Some address the Senator directly.

"We will pray for your wife, your family, and yourself. May God's angels protect her on her heavenly journey."

And, "I don't know that this will reach you. But I wanted to give it a try. What sadness in the midst of what should be a time of victory. I remember the early days in Springfield with you, and wanted you to know that I have followed your work and words from afar and for all these many years. My best love and regards to you and the kids. Our heart goes out to you."

And, "Our hearts are with you in this difficult time."

And, "You and yours are in our hearts and prayers."

Compassionate as the comments are, Colleen dislikes the expression "my heart goes out."

She pictures a big cartoon heart or a Mylar balloon or the Sacred Heart of Jesus hovering above Illinois, astrally projecting and somehow not causing people to crack up laughing or be grossed out, but bringing them solace.

Similar deal with "passing away."

She wishes it were passing, and away from here doesn't sound so bad.

But it's not.

It's just death, and once you are dead, you are done.

Yet she wants to tell the Senator something consoling, too, but there's nothing to say except "thinking of you!" so here she sits, waiting for inspiration.

She goes into her folder on the share drive, where she keeps personal photos.

Opens up one from the September fundraiser of the Senator and Dottie.

The Senator has taken Dottie's hand as they cross from the cocktails to the dinner. They are walking together through the opulent doorway. They are flanked on either side by dozens of donors vying to catch the Senator's eye.

But as Colleen snapped the shot, the Senator was looking only at Dottie, and she only at him.

The only two people in the entire Versailles suite.

D ugan!" says Gina from the cut-out cube doorway.

"Whoa!" says Colleen, jolting in her seat, instinctively toggling the screen back to the casework system.

"God, you're jumpy," Gina says. Her backpack is slung over

her shoulders, an open-topped cardboard box in her hands. "Got time for a project?"

"Sure," she says. "What's up?"

Colleen is as pleased as she is surprised by the prospect.

Since Dottie died, the office has been coasting and driftless, even more than before, but now the inertia is working in their favor. On Monday, Steve Moon Collier reported that Ryder's negatives were in the stratosphere, while the Senator's positives had climbed equally high. Nasrin has stopped job-hunting, and Mary Dodge is talking fondly of heading back to DC, post-campaign.

Sylvia bounces over, stands next to Gina, peers into the container.

"I hold in my hands," says Gina, "a box of sympathy cards to the Senator and his family." She thrusts the box towards Colleen, who finds it comically heavy. "Dugan, since you're the Press Team member with the bleedingest heart, the Chief and I are putting you on card duty. The Senator wants to respond personally to every single one of these."

"That Papa Bear has got such class," says Sylvia. "Who could stand to look through all these at a time like this?"

"Well, that's the situation," says Gina. "He can't get to these now. But he will when he's ready. Dugan, we need you to come up with some kind of system—a spreadsheet or something—so that after he composes himself, he can compose a reply, and we can make sure that all of these people get acknowledged."

"All right," says Colleen, sitting back in her chair to pull up a document. "I'll get started."

"No," says Gina. "You're going to want more space. There's two more boxes like this already, and it's only Tuesday. We're going to have you set up in the Senator's office. He's not coming in for a while, and you'll need the room."

For the rest of the week, Colleen sorts through condolences. She databases addresses from Illinoisans, current and erstwhile, who consider the Senator an old friend, who have never met the man but have seen him on TV, who tell him to stay strong and carry on for the sake of his great state and position of leadership, who say they go hollow when they contemplate his loss.

By week's end, Colleen too is empty. She wishes the cards would stop.

She does not cry, though.

Not until Friday.

First it's a couple of tears that drop and smear a couple of words, which makes her move the paper and cry even harder.

The Chief of Staff pokes his head through the open door. "Colleen?" he says. "What's the matter? I didn't have you pegged as a candy-ass."

"I can't even think of anything mean to say back to you," she says, "because this letter is too sad." She hands it to him. "She has the same handwriting as my dead grandmother."

The Chief reads aloud the spidery script on onion skin paper:

Dear Senator,

To start, my apologies for the tardiness of these, my sympathies, on the death of your beautiful wife Dorothy. I wanted to write to you right away, when I heard last Saturday, but I was in the hospital then myself. I am 84 years of age. But I was not there for me ~ it was my husband, Ray, of 59 years. You see, he had caught pneumonia. He died in my arms that Saturday morning.

Senator, I am not saying this to talk too much about me. I only wish to try to tell you: I think that I have an idea how you might be feeling. To lose the person who was by your side through all those things.

Enclosed, please find a small token of my condolences. A good friend of mine, a Roman Catholic priest, has taken parishioners of our Church on a pilgrimage to Jerusalem each year for the past four years. I am too infirm to participate, but when he returns, he brings me a crucifix from that city, blessed by him in a Mass he holds there.

I have put them all in this envelope here, one for you and one for each of your children in this very sad time. God bless you on Election Day, and on every day after. For Dorothy, if I may say, '*Requiscat in Pace.*'

Respectfully Yours,
Marie, a Voter

"Open the envelope," says Colleen.

Four small wooden crosses clatter across the glass top of the Senator's desk. They come to rest. They look accusatory, like *Why can't you do something meaningful?*

"Dammit, Colleen," says the Chief, and his eyes are shining too. "She underlines every damn thing the way my mother used to. It's too much." He picks up on one of the crosses, examines it. "You've done enough of this for the week, so take a break, all right? The Duke will understand."

"I will," says Colleen. "But before I stop, can we please write a *personal* personal note to this woman? And can we send it out right away, this afternoon?"

Putting down the cross, the Chief says yes, okay, he can see that this woman could probably use that.

So Colleen writes the letter, and the Chief signs it as the Senator, and this is what they tell her:

Dear Marie,

Thank you for sharing your sympathy and thoughts with me and my family at this difficult time. Your letter of condolence, with its story of your husband, as well as your gift of the crucifixes all the way from Jerusalem and blessed by your friend the priest, were a beautiful gesture of support.

I am grateful for your kindness. God bless you and your family, too, especially now, during your own difficult season.

Sincerely yours,
The Senator

It is Halloween. The eve of all souls. The celebration of the dead, both known and unknown.

Apropos, thinks Colleen, on the Red Line home, surrounded by costumed college kids, already partying. Such a death-filled week.

When she reaches the apartment, Walter greets her with more.

He heard it on the way home, on the radio.

The old Chicago author, whose real name was Louis, better known as Studs, nicknamed after the title character of a trilogy of novels, no longer read, about the spiritual degradation of an Irish-Catholic street tough beaten down by poverty, died today in his home on the North Side, at the age of 96.

Documentarian of the Everywoman and the Everyman.

Living proof that art might actually matter.

That the good fight might someday be won.

O you can't scare him, he's stickin' to the union, stickin' to the union, 'til the day he dies.

"I'm sorry," says Walter. "I didn't want to tell you, but you needed to know."

"Knowing is better than not knowing," says Colleen. "Even when the thing you need to know is shitty."

T'was the week before Christmas, last December.
　　End of day.

And all through the office, Palmira's pleas were met with wary ears. She needed someone, anyone, to run an errand. A last-minute gift to the Senator from Dottie.

"I need someone to go to this guy Studs' house and get some books signed?" Palmira said, sounding unsure whose house she was talking about.

Colleen practically knocked over her cubicle wall jumping up to say "I'll go!"

Her haste was in waste. No one else, so close to quitting time, was remotely interested.

"Who *is* this guy?" asked Steve Moon Collier.

Colleen threw on her coat and left it to the Chief to elucidate.

The Works Progress Administration's Federal Writers' Project, the McCarthy blacklist, the radio show he'd hosted for forty-five years, the publication of countless oral histories.

If she had tried to explain, she might have told them about his book on the Great Depression, how her parents had had an old remaindered library copy, how she'd read it when she was a kid.

Of how captivated she had been by the everyday people talking off the cuff about their everyday lives—about what they'd done to survive, the deprivations and humiliations they had faced, of how they felt about it all.

Captivated too that he got them to reveal it.

Later, as an adult, the part of the book that never failed to get to her was the interview he did with the unsuccessful 1936 presidential hopeful, who said of his tenure as governor of Kansas:

> Men with tears in their eyes begged for an appointment that would help save their homes and farms. I couldn't see them all in my office. But I never let one of them leave without my coming out and shakin' hands with 'em. I listened to all their stories, each one of 'em. But it was obvious I couldn't take care of all their terrible needs.

Colleen recalled this as the skyline was lighting its lights out-side Palmira's window.

Colleen had come here, to the Senator's office, because she had wanted to take care of people's terrible needs.

In the absence of the ability to do that, which was almost al-ways, she did her best to listen to their stories.

Palmira handed her a shopping bag containing four copies of the old author's new memoir, a book purportedly about himself but persistently about others, the ragtag cast that peopled his nine-decade existence. Colleen was to get one inscribed to the Senator, the other three just signed.

When Palmira handed Colleen the old author's address and the number of his live-in caretaker, it was like she was being handed an engraved invitation to the Prince's ball.

In a cab in the wintry twilight on her way to the home of a Chicago legend, an American hero.

The office, of late, had been anesthetized by the lack of work in the pre-Christmas monotony of a US Senator's office in recess. Even the Junior Senator's campaign was in a gloom. He trailed the female candidate by double digits. Iowa had yet to happen.

Colleen now felt energized.

She pictured a veil, a screen, a man behind a curtain, a palsied hand, wizened and clutching a pen in a claw-like grip. Would his signature be his, or would it be—like the Senator's most of the time—signed by a different hand?

The cabbie drove up Lake Shore Drive, the sky an orange-gray, the lake flattening into invisibility as they listened to a lite radio station that played only Christmas carols all through the holidays. Colleen wanted to tell the cabbie the story of her mission, but he spoke non-stop Croatian into his headset. Monsters of pop sang of drummer boys and decking the halls.

And then they were turning into the old author's neighborhood, rows of houses and three-flats with hard-to-spot numbers, some set far from the street on ample lots.

An icy driveway, a two-story house of brown brick with a privacy hedge at the end of it.

A middle-aged Filipino man greeting her: J. D., the assistant. He took her inside.

In the greenhouse front room, among a jungle of plants and books and a small flatscreen attached to a VCR/DVD player, the old author sat up in a reclining bed, raised to hold his skinny frame upright.

The man himself, in red footie pajamas and blue flannel sheets under a white hospital blanket.

The room smelled green like mentholatum, and the humidifier hummed, and there were two boxes of tissues by his bedside next to sundry syringes and bottles of pills. His hair was combed into a frizzled gray cloud, his brown eyes milky but with an impish gleam, like he was scheming great schemes.

"What's your name?" he said, sharp and demanding.

"Colleen!" she yelled.

Almost gleeful, he gestured at the accoutrements of his infirmity. "On top of all this," he said, "I'm deaf, too!"

J.D. placed the stack of books within reach of the old author.

"Is this for the Senator's wife? Or for the Senator?" asked the old author.

"For the Senator," said Colleen.

"Did he ask for it?"

"Yes," she said. "It was on his wish list."

The old author wriggled with pleasure, asked J. D. for a marker and a writing desk. Colleen watched, in awe of the caretaker's patience.

"What shall I write?" the old author shouted.

"Why don't you start and see what comes to mind?" J. D. said.

The room was hot—the old author's bones got cold—and Colleen felt a trickle of sweat beneath her scarf and sweater. She breathed in the chemical stink of the uncapped marker.

She was still standing while the old author wrote, not wishing to impose.

But then he barked kindly, "Have a seat! I'm not so fast as I once used to be!" and Colleen sat down in a rickety wicker chair, next to a wooden cane with a carved fish handle.

The old author wrote and wrote.

Colleen watched him, then looked around the room—the hardwood floors, the brass lamps, the walls so covered in books that it looked as though they were made of books, books-as-bricks. He had come from such modest beginnings in his mother's rooming house to such plenty. "I was born within two weeks of the Titanic sinking," he liked to say. "The Titanic went down, and I came up."

She studied his movements—thin wrists snapping the marker across the page with surprising spryness for a nonagenarian.

She asked if she could take his picture while he signed, and he said sure. Elated, Colleen documented the documentarian.

When he finished, he read to them in the radio voice of his bygone days:

> To My Senator and Every Other Sane Person: Senator, you are my #1 Political Figure in our society. Your policies, expressed & those unexpressed, & deeply felt may yet save our country of Tom Paine, Frederick Douglass, MLK & FDR. I—an agnostic—pray (get that?) that you & your policies prevail so we may have a world of peace, grace & beauty. With great admiration & affection, Studs.

J. D. reminded him to autograph the remaining three copies.

And then the old author was telling Colleen to tell the Senator hi, and offering to call her a cab, and she was saying, "Oh, no thank you. I'll save the taxpayers some dollars and take the train," though the real reason was that she wanted to be alone with the books, not talking to anybody.

The next day she got to work before anyone else.

She made a photocopy of the inscription, so that even after she gave the books back to Palmira, who would give them to Dottie, who would give one to the Senator, she could keep it forever.

The worst part," Colleen says to Walter, "is that now he'll never get to see how it all turns out."

The old author was an early supporter of the Junior Senator.

Colleen is not in the mood for costumes anymore.

But Walter convinces her they should still go to Halloween parties as planned, to take their minds off waiting for the election. He doesn't add that they are also waiting to see what will happen to Colleen's job.

So dressed up they get.

Colleen as a Mexican painter known for her self-portraits, with a drawn-on unibrow and a plush monkey on her shoulder. Walter as the painter's womanizing muralist husband, with a pillow stuffed under his shirt and a fake moustache.

And out they go.

On the sidewalk in front of their first party in Logan Square, a Mexican family out trick-or-treating crunches through the leaves, their three little kids in a line like ducklings. The youngest one, dressed as an angel with tinsel wings, points and yells out, "Hola, Frida!" and Colleen, happy for that moment, answers back, "Hola, mija!"

And after the parties, back home now, Colleen finds herself not drunk enough to fall right to sleep. It is unseasonably warm, so they leave the bedroom window cracked, kick the comforter to the floor. Exhausted, but out of sleeping pills, Colleen lies next to Walter, thinking.

"If this is a story," she says to the back of his head. "Would it be a tragedy? Because it keeps ending in all this death?"

Walter rolls to face her.

"Colleen," he says, "it's not over yet. We don't know what it is."

"The uncertainty is killing me," she says. "I don't know what to do between now and Tuesday. Fuck, I don't know what to do *after* Tuesday."

"In the absence of certainty about the world," says Walter, mumbling and sleepy, "you just have to keep being awesome. Of course, we are all already fucking that up. But there is a nobility, we have to keep believing, in the trying."

He starts to sing, slurrily, one of her favorite silly pop songs, the one about living just to find emotion, about don't stop believing, about the movie never ending, about going on and on and on and on.

He treats it like a lullaby, but he is the one to fall asleep first.

Colleen lies there a long, long time—thinking of streetlights, people—before she too falls asleep, just before dawn.

The Junior Senator's maternal grandmother, the one who helped raise him in Hawaii, dies on Sunday.

When Colleen's mother calls her that evening for their Sunday chat, she points this out.

"This is such a sad time, isn't it, sweetie?" she says. "The Senator's wife, that author you liked so much, and now the grandmother. But it's like they say, bad things come in threes, so hopefully this is it."

Colleen feels that whatever is afoot is more mysterious than that, but she can't articulate why.

She knows that both she and her mother are thinking of her dad in Iraq, and how, if it's a rule of three, he'll be okay. His latest email said they had heard they might be coming home in early December. The average deployment is eighteen months to two years, and by December he'll have been gone twenty-three months.

She hopes the Army doesn't push it back again.

Walter says that what makes the world mysterious is not any intrinsic quality that the world has, but rather the fact that your ability to perceive the world is limited, and that you are not always aware of those limitations.

So Colleen just says, "Yeah. Whoever they are, they may be right."

21

Before Dottie died, the Senator had been planning to have his own victory party.

Somewhere downtown.

Somewhere cheap, knowing Susan Scheck, who almost never even bothers to have food at solo events. Once she promised them a reception with "hors d'oeuvres," when what she meant was a single bag of wasabi peas and a bin of stale popcorn.

The Chicago staff had all planned to attend the Senator's party. They had to support their man, of course.

But it was the *real* party they had been despairing about—the rally for the Junior Senator, in the Park named after the Eighteenth President. How would they manage to make it to both?

But these days the Senator is not in a celebratory mood. His event has been cancelled.

And though they are sad for the reasons, the Chicago staff has to confess relief at being let off the hook.

The world is their oyster, waiting to be shucked with the two complimentary tickets to the Junior Senator's rally they will each soon have in hand.

I'm just glad we don't have to choose which party!" says Sylvia. "I mean, like woohoo, par-*tay* party. Not, like, political. Ya know?"

"We know, darling," says Nasrin.

"As always," says the Chief of Staff, patting Sylvia on the back. "Eltibani with her eyes on what's really important."

"It's going to be the stuff of legend," says Mary Dodge. "Everybody in DC would kill to be here."

"The party of the century," says Lo Benson.

"But is it going to be a victory party?" says Agnes Lumley.

"Better not be no pity party," says Nia.

"Damn right, Nia," says Lo.

"Agnes," says Nasrin. "Where's your positive attitude? Where's your game face?"

"I left them in my other slacks," says Agnes, and heads back to Siberia, prompting Mary, Nasrin, Dézi, and Sylvia to retreat as well.

"There's no way he can lose," says Steve Moon Collier, adjusting the hem of his new, navy, cashmere sweater-vest. "And the change is going to be permanent and irreversible."

"Could be," says the Chief, impassive, brushing an imaginary thread from his own sweater-vest, also navy, also cashmere.

"I don't know," says Andrew, from his cube looking at his computer. "What I *do* know is that there are people online offering—and I quote—'hour upon hour of mind-blowing sex' in exchange for tickets to the rally."

"Truly we are among the chosen few," says Colleen.

Are you lonely," Steve Moon Collier asks Andrew, "because your not-so-secret girlfriend has left us?"

"Whitlock, you mean?" says the Chief. "That gal is a few sandwiches short of a picnic. Did you have to pay her off to make her stay away, or what?"

"She's leaving to do something she really wants to do," says Colleen. "She wasn't that awful."

"What's with the about-face, Dugan?" says Steve.

"I just find it inspiring when people actualize their potential," she says.

"It's because Colleen wants to go, too, and do her photography full-time," says Andrew. "She doesn't actually like J-Lock any more than she used to."

"I've looked at Colleen's photographs," says the Chief, "and they largely confound me. Some of them are decadent filth, but not all of them. I would love to tell you they remind me of the kind of crap my silver-spoon college pals did to fill their draft-dodging days in Paris while I was in the streets facing down the National Guard, but there's more to them than that. They remind me of a Chinese opera I saw once. Really goddamn weird, and kind of boring, except that they're terrifying."

"The only thing Colleen's photos make me think of," says Andrew, "is how she needs to eat more fatty foods, like onion rings and pudding."

"Maybe you haven't noticed," Colleen says, "but I am actually right here in the room with you, where I am able to hear you talk."

The Chief of Staff is about to fire back, but his cell phone buzzes. He looks at the display. His jackal grin cracks and collapses. He walks into his office to answer it, slamming the door.

The future is swirling all about them now, pressing invisibly at the windows. Colleen doesn't want to think much about the future.

"Let's look at that polling site," she says.

Andrew pulls up the site, the one named after the number of votes that comprise the Electoral College. It calls the election for the Junior Senator by a generous margin.

"Look," says Steve, pointing to the screen that shows the Junior Senator's latest numbers. "He is so freaking popular, there is no way he can lose."

"Bud Light is the most popular beer in America," says Andrew. "Widespread popularity is only worth so much."

"All we know for certain," says Colleen, "is that people who work in politics their whole lives are dorks."

The Chief of Staff opens his door. "Got a minute to join me on a teleconference?"

"Sure thing," says Steve.

"Sorry, Collier," says the Chief. "I was talking to Dugan."

Colleen is never asked to join teleconferences.

T he main conference room has a TV so big, Colleen figures she could lie down inside it.

On it is the potato face of Ryan Slattery.

He's seated at the head of a conference table in the Whip office in DC.

Above and to the right of him, in a small-screen inset, is Colleen's own image.

She's seated at the head of a conference table in the Senator's office in Chicago.

Across from her is the Chief of Staff, who is nowhere to be found in the conference room TV.

This video conference, she realizes, is so she won't be able to say later that Slattery didn't have the class or the balls to do what he's about to do—face-to-face, so to speak.

The inset, she realizes, is because they think if she can see herself, she'll be less likely to break down.

On this, they are correct.

She can feel the panic and the sorrow that have been gathering in her gut and behind her eyes these past few weeks cool and harden.

Toward anger.

These two men—both from downstate, both self-made.
They could hardly be more different.

In manner, at least.

The Chief of Staff has cultivated a reputation as one of those magical, entrancing people, as adept at handling a softball as he is at handing a young lady into a taxi, a beacon in any political office's time of storm.

Ryan Slattery, weak-chinned and vindictive, shrill and quick to panic, has cultivated his own as a Grade-A asshole, adept at ferreting out threats both petty and existential, to himself in equal measure as to the Senator. Also in handing inferiors their own asses.

Since she was nineteen, Colleen has never had an instant of doubt about which man she identified with, whose professional manner she would try to emulate.

She is about to be told that she has chosen poorly.

Slattery starts off calm and polite.
All the better to eat you with, Colleen thinks.

"I want to begin, Colleen, by thanking you," he says, "for your years of service on the staff of the Senator."

Fake equanimity is a sharp knife, Colleen thinks.

The Chief of Staff is looking out the window at the Lake.

Colleen looks at her own face in the inset. Watching herself being watched.

Keep it together, she thinks. Do not cry.

"However," says Slattery, "as the Chief here has let you know, what you did with the video of Representative Ryder was unacceptable." Slattery's eyes shift slightly. "You *have* made this clear to Colleen, haven't you Chief?" Slattery's eyes shift back. "And, Colleen, you received the same training as everyone else—"

Training. Colleen stifles the impulse to burst out laughing.

Aside from the interns, who learn only the most basic tasks—the telephone, the copier, the fax machine, how to get lunch and rearrange binders—no one in the Chicago office receives any formal training on anything.

Colleen says nothing. She has not been brought here to account for herself.

"And, Colleen, you know as well as I do that Senate staffers are not allowed unauthorized contact with members of the media. You do not speak to anyone on condition of anonymity. You do not speak."

The Colleen in the inset presses her lips together.

The Colleen in the conference room watches her do it.

She clears her throat, unsure of how her voice will sound, but when she opens her mouth it comes out steady.

"I suppose the Chief told you," she says, "that my obtaining the video and my contact with the media had nothing to do with my employment here. I have not abused my position. The video would have come to me regardless"—not strictly true, but this is no time for nuance—"and as a citizen of the United States I would have done the exact same thing."

"Doesn't matter," Slattery says.

He purses his lips and clasps his hands, as if to convey his distress for her wrecked career, for the great American institution she has recklessly compromised, for the burden of his own solemn duty now that she's forced his reluctant hand.

The performance is grotesque enough for her to wonder if he's watching himself in his own tiny inset.

If it takes me years, Colleen thinks, I will get back at you for this.

But she knows even now that this will never happen.

People with power who value nothing above their own security are next to impossible to hurt.

"Like all of us," Slattery says, "you have served at the pleasure of the Senate. Now, Colleen, you have displeased the Senate. So it has been decided that you may no longer serve."

The passive construction obscures his active role in ruining her life.

"Taking away a person's livelihood is a pretty drastic decision," Colleen says. "Particularly in an economy like the present one. Particularly when that person has limited savings, owing to how little she is paid."

"Well," says Slattery, "maybe there's a lesson to be learned here, Colleen."

"Maybe," she says. "Like 'no good deed goes unpunished'? Or 'low-level workers get thrown out like trash'?"

This is really happening, she thinks. I am getting fired. It does not matter what I say, and no one can save me.

"Effective as of when?"

"Oh," Slattery says, as if stating something so obvious it need not be stated. "Immediately. In keeping with our standard practice. Even if you hadn't already demonstrated your willingness to disrupt Senate business through rash action, we'd require you to vacate the office right away. In cases like these it's customary to have the employee escorted out by Capitol Police, but in yours, I've asked the Chief to accompany you while you gather your personal belongings."

The small Colleen above Slattery's shoulder blanches, like someone has just raised a hand to slap her.

"You can't be serious," she says.

"Colleen," Slattery says, "I can assure you that the Senate is well within its rights to—"

"I'm not talking about rights," she says, as evenly as she can muster. "You're not seriously going to frog-march me out of here on the day before the election? I have friends here, coworkers. I've been a part of this. I've *worked* for this."

"I'm very sorry," says Slattery, "but it's simply not in anyone's best interest that you be permitted to maintain your position of trust. Consequently—"

"I would like to point out once again," Colleen cuts in, looking at the Chief, "that I have made no unauthorized disclosure of any privileged information that came from working in this office. Any sensitive information that I *did* gain here—such as, for example, the fact that the Senator's office got a copy of the Ryder video two months ago, or the fact that we negotiated with Ryder's people to keep it suppressed—I have kept strictly confidential."

Colleen has been careful to keep the threat out of her voice, but she has nothing to lose now.

"And I plan to keep doing so," she says.

The Chief's breath stills.

Slattery's beady eyes grow beadier as their pupils dilate. He has taken away too much too soon, has nothing left to threaten her with.

A long silence ensues.

The Chief speaks first, still looking out the window. His voice is soft.

"It would be better for the troops," he says, "if Colleen's departure could be postponed until the election is over."

Slattery lets out a peevish sigh.

"Fine," he says. "In light of current events"—his eyes shift again to the invisible Chief—"and morale in the Chicago office being so low of late"—and back to Colleen—"you will not be required to clean out your desk until first thing Wednesday morning. But you will *not* be permitted to log in to any Senate computer, or use the Capitol Correspondence system, or handle any casework files. If you are unable to find other tasks with which to occupy yourself, you are authorized to stay home. In the meantime, I will fax you the necessary severance info, and you can call HR about COBRA-ing your healthcare."

Colleen would rather go blind than call HR. She wants nothing more to do with DC. She wonders whether the village where Walter works can insure her as a domestic partner.

"We'll keep you on payroll until the end of this pay period," Slattery says. "That way everyone can start with a clean slate after Election Day, whatever the outcome. No need to thank me."

Slattery reaches up to disconnect the video feed.

The picture snaps off.

The sound of a door closing forever.

"I'm sorry, Colleen," says the Chief of Staff.

Colleen feels her sentimental education evaporate in the dry office air, air that has become more funereal than before. Colleen has a ridiculous urge to don a black veil, or to tie on a black armband.

The number one skill in her Senate skillset has been to act in a manner that is courteous but evasive. Now she is direct.

"This shouldn't be a hanging offense," she says.

"There is nothing to be done, I'm afraid," says the Chief.

"What am I supposed to tell people?" she asks, more of herself than the Chief. She imagines her desk empty and ransacked on Wednesday morning. She pictures her belongings in a cardboard box on her lap as she rides the Red Line home from the office for the final time. "What are you going to tell everyone?"

"It will be kept confidential. They won't be told anything. It's a private matter."

"But I *want* to tell them," she says. "I'm not ashamed. I want people to know what happened. Because I don't believe I've done anything wrong."

"That's your business, Colleen," he says, pushing his chair back. "Whatever happens next, though, I hope you believe me when I say that I wish you the best."

Watching him open the conference room door to leave, Colleen has the humiliating sensation of having misrecognized a stranger for a friend.

Walter is driving downtown from the village where he works to pick Colleen up in light of her having just been shitcanned.

He has promised not to breathe a word to her uncle.

Aside from Walter, she has told no one else, except Andrew and Dézi, both of whom were incredulous—more so that it was she who sent in the blowjob video than that she'd been fired for it.

"Way to go!" said Dézi.

"You should be a folk legend," said Andrew.

Going over the severance agreement that Slattery had HR fax, Andrew assured her that legally Colleen will be able to say that she resigned. "The Senate doesn't allege any official misconduct, so you're under no obligation to say that fuckface forced you out," he said. "Silver lining?"

Colleen can't bring herself to tell the rest of her coworkers.

She will not, she decides, tell her parents for a while.

She wishes she had a script for what to do next.

That society had some ritual for formally announcing this kind of idiotic turn of events.

Colleen passes the rest of the time waiting for Walter by going online under Andrew's login and figuring out how to apply for unemployment benefits.

O n her way out to meet Walter, the Chief of Staff beckons from the window of his office.

"Colleen," he says. "I need to say good-bye. I won't be in tomorrow. I'll be at the Hotel Grand, and then staffing the Duke in the Park for the rally. On Wednesday, everything's going to be different, one way or the other."

"Um," says Colleen, hoping her voice contains the exact right amount of bitchy sarcasm, "perhaps you recall from our recent teleconference that everything already is?"

"Politically, I mean."

"Different for the better in that case, I hope," she says.

"I think it will be," he says. "See you when I see you, babe. Thanks for everything."

She reaches for the door. He looks her up from foot to head.

Flat red shoes and the bruise on her white right calf, her overcoat too heavy for the warm day, unseasonable for November.

"Thank *you*," she says, "for throwing me under the bus."

"You did what you did," he says with a shrug. "I did what I did. We all lie down in the beds we've made. Listen, dollface, take it from someone who isn't really wired for this gig: you are not really wired for this gig. You're going to do great things, Colleen, but you're going to do them someplace else. I'll continue to follow your career with interest."

She feels his eyes on her as she walks down the hallway. She thinks about how fucked up it is that she'll miss this place.

Its assholery punctuated by flashes of brilliance.

On Wednesday morning, the day after Election Day, Colleen will clean out her desk and be gone again so early that not even the interns will see her.

She'll send an email to everyone explaining everything—the video, all of it.

Then, if anyone still wants to talk to her, which she doubts, they'll know where to find her.

When she walks out of the Federal Building for the last time, the sun is just barely rising over the Lake.

22

Election Day has been held on the first Tuesday after the first Monday in November since Congress said it ought to be in 1845. Those citizens wishing to exercise their franchise—all white, all male—had to make their way by horse to the county seat. The Tuesday date meant they could travel without disrupting the Sabbath or missing the traditional market day, Wednesday in most towns.

This has nothing to do with the way most people live now, but Colleen likes knowing this history, and she is telling it to Dézi and Agnes Lumley on Tuesday afternoon as they stand on the thirty-eighth floor of the Federal Building looking out the window at the park named after the Eighteenth President.

Colleen has been thinking of the Eighteenth President a lot today.

Not of his stellar military career, nor his fiasco of a presidency, but of his final days—of the swift and careful labor on his memoirs while he faced mounting debts from failed business ventures and certain death from terminal throat cancer.

The death brought on by her own failed ventures is less terminal but no less certain. She has spent her final day in the employ of the United States Senate emailing her CV and work samples to newspapers and magazines in search of stringers, and reconnecting with old photo colleagues via social networking sites.

In contrast to the Eighteenth President, her labors have yet to meet with rave reviews.

It is 4:00 p.m., and in the park across the street, a long line of hopeful ralliers makes a serpentine along Michigan Avenue.

Pointing to "that part of a beautiful woman where she is perhaps the most beautiful," an English printmaker from the Eighteenth Century whom Colleen had studied in undergrad said that the line of beauty must possess an S-shape.

At the time, she found his assertion arbitrary at best.

But now, this sinuous string of humanity makes her think that perhaps he was right.

It puts her in mind of her dad's honeybees. The trails they blaze to find food for the hive, the dances they dance to communicate their discoveries, the way they work together toward a common goal in harmonious understanding.

Colleen longs to lose herself in the crowd that winds and surges below.

Bobby Peacock comes up carrying a pink phone message slip. Colleen wants to tell him how much she's going to miss him. Same for Agnes. Same for everyone.

Even Palmira, she thinks, maybe just a little, and is shocked at the thought.

"We just got a call from Ryder's head press guy," Bobby says, "trying to get the number the Congressman will need to talk to the Senator tonight. Can you call him back?"

Bobby is asking Colleen because Gina, Steve Moon Collier, the Chief of Staff, and anyone else who matters are all at campaign headquarters, waiting out the results.

"Did he say *to concede?*" Colleen says.

"That part was implied," says Bobby, smiling.

It is 5:00 p.m., and the last one out locks up the office, and they all head to the bar at the base of the Board of Trade. The bar specializes in "margaritas" that everyone suspects are shots of grain alcohol tinged green with food coloring.

"*One and you're done* is the rule with these things," Nia always says, before downing three or four by the end of the evening, and tonight is no exception.

Dézi had been planning to use her plus-one for the rally on her boyfriend, but last week she caught him sleeping with her high-school best friend, and not wanting to waste the ticket, she offered it to Colleen to give to someone.

And so Ethan's with them now, thin and grinning, going a little swimmy along with the rest of Colleen's soon-to-be-ex-co-workers, and paying by way of thanks for Dézi's dyed ethanol.

Colleen has decided to stay sober. "If I'm going to get drunk," she says to Walter, "it's going to be on the Junior Senator's historic victory."

All around them, drinks get pounded and early returns flash on multiple TVs. Ethan and Colleen take pictures of the pictures, of faces at the bar reacting to the pictures.

The Senator is reelected in the blowout of all blowouts.

He sweeps all 102 counties in the state.

Ron Reese Ryder, who only weeks ago was closing in fast and hard, manages barely twenty percent of the vote.

Colleen has to keep reminding herself that the Senator is no longer her boss.

Standing in line usually has the opposite effect on Colleen, but tonight she gets the sense that time is speeding up, that they are hurtling forward, less like they're shuffling into the Park and more like they're being drawn inexorably through the world's most jubilant airport security checkpoints.

She pictures all the vague terrors of the last eight years—the elevated alert levels, the sleeper cells, the non-existent weapons of mass destruction, the war in the Desert her dad had been sent off to—being played backward.

It's a little after 8:00 p.m. by the time they make it through the final metal detectors, and states are already being called.

First, a slew of predictability.

Michigan, Minnesota, New York for the Junior Senator.

Kansas, Texas, Wyoming for his opponent.

They stream down the stairs and into the sunken basin of the park. Colleen holds the back of Walter's coat with both hands. The crush of people possesses an undertow, like the sea but not indifferent. Like an actively friendly sea.

Behind them, Dézi does the same to Ethan. They end up somewhere in the middle of the massive crowd, hundreds of thousands, and toward the back. They have an unobstructed view of the Jumbotron and an obstructed view of the stage where the Junior Senator will deliver his speech.

The four of them wear the lightest of jackets. Many people wear none. The day dawned warm and has stayed that way.

And then, the big states, the tossups, roll in.

Ohio.

Iowa.

For the Junior Senator.

And everyone knows—the cheers begin to rise and do not fall—tonight will be nothing like the doomed nightmare of 2000, the failed nailbiter of 2004.

"It's like the heavens are smiling on us here in this city," says Dézi. "Like our candidate is blessed, and we're going to win!"

Colleen locks eyes with Walter and then Ethan, but doesn't disagree. It really does seem that way. She feels a rush of nostalgia, even as it's happening. The windows of one skyscraper are lit up to spell USA in giant letters. The windows of another have become a glowing flag. Even the few faint stars she can make out above the city lights look like compatriots.

She can almost feel the presence, like she did as a kid, of people watching her from somewhere. She half expects to see their old faces staring down at her from above, but of course they aren't there. And even if they were, she's not sure what they'd be doing—silently rooting for her, like she's some kind of underdog, insomniac and jobless? For the Junior Senator? Or merely keeping dispassionate track of the results?

Colleen doesn't know.

She reaches for her camera, begins taking pictures.

The sky domes over, looking touchable, like fabric.

And then, the crowd erupts.

Colleen turns her camera to the Jumbotron.

California has been called for the Junior Senator, only seconds after its polls closed. Then Hawaii, Oregon, Washington.

And he is over the top.

Colleen clicks the shutter as the shining face of the Junior Senator's campaign photograph appears on the screen, above the words Projected Winner.

Colleen's phone rings, and it is her mother saying, "I'm watching it on TV, but I can't see you," and Walter says to tell her that they're "near the flag."

Though there must be at least fifty flags, her mother seems satisfied—her mother who didn't want her to be in the park anyway, afraid of the riots and the pickpockets and the terrorists and the assassins and the fights, but it's the most companionable crowd Colleen has ever helped to create, the kind of crowd where if somebody bumps you or steps on your foot, it's like, "Hey, don't worry about that, because we're all sharing euphoria."

She tries to explain this to her mother.

Tonight, she wants to shout, *I love my stupid country!*

"I'm finally living, for a minute, in the America I want to live in," she says instead.

"Good for you, honey," says her mother, and then, "Love you!" and then click.

The song in the video the Junior Senator's staff plays is by a band Colleen loves. They sing of a fake empire, with fluid piano and a fanfare of horns.

The Jumbotron flashes the faces and voices of a multiracial mix of Americans who talk about Hope and Change and Really Meaning It. And even though everyone present has seen this video a hundred times over the course of the campaign, they feel its fingers touching them right on the part that Colleen has to go ahead and call the heart.

"I know I'm being manipulated," Ethan says. "But it feels so right."

"Yeah," says Walter. "They're tugging our heartstrings, but they know just how."

A sudden cut, mid-video, to the former Republican candidate for the Presidency of the United States. A few mouths in the crowd screw up to boo, but then other mouths say, "Come on now," and everyone gets respectful.

"My friends," he says, "a little while ago, I had the honor of calling the Junior Senator of Illinois"—he waves his arms to silence the swell of boos in his own crowd of supporters—"to congratulate him on being elected the next President of the country we both love—"

And soon his speech is done, and the Junior Senator is taking the stage with his beautiful wife and his beautiful daughters, the nation's beautiful new First Family.

He looks celestial.

Like he is the moon behind bulletproof glass.

And the crowd, tidal, is surging toward him.

Colleen and Walter lose Ethan and Dézi in the watery sweep forward.

Even we can barely keep our line of sight on Colleen.

Tomorrow morning, hours before dawn, the free paper Colleen will read on her final commute to the Federal Building to clean out her desk will write that "the first black president hails from Chicago, Illinois, USA."

"We split the atom," it will read, "invented the skyscraper, reversed a river, linked a sprawling continent by rail and air, butchered the world's hogs, rose from the ashes of an historic blaze, rigged a World Series, raised graft to an art form and all but trademarked the political machine. We masterminded the scandal of 1919. But today, we can be proud.

"We can be proud today."

Tonight the sky above the park is dark.

A no-fly zone.

Only the little squiggles of police helicopters hover there. Colleen can barely hear them over the crowd's roar, chopping the air.

And rising above it all, the Junior Senator's—the President-elect's—words.

"If there is anyone out there who still doubts that America is a place where all things are possible, who still wonders if the dream of our founders is alive in our time, who still questions the power of our democracy, tonight is your answer."

A tangible tremor—Colleen is almost knocked down by it.

A sudden job loss is like a sudden death, and since yesterday she has cycled nonstop through the five stages of grief, all at once and in the wrong order.

But in this moment, for this instant, she is living in a world where certain nouns are capitalized. Adversity. Romance. Chance. Death. Love. Hope. A world she has always longed for, where things actually matter.

"It's the answer spoken by young and old, rich and poor, Democrat and Republican, black, white, Hispanic, Asian, Native

American, gay, straight, disabled and not disabled. Americans who sent a message to the world that we have never been just a collection of individuals or a collection of red states and blue states."

I should keep doing my life, Colleen thinks. But I should do it better.

"Because of what we did on this day, in this election, at this defining moment, change has come to America."

It suddenly strikes her that "All I ever wanted" may be the saddest construction of any sentence, but also the best.

"The road ahead will be long, our climb will be steep. We may not get there in one year, or even in one term—but America, I have never been more hopeful than I am tonight that we *will* get there."

He speaks to Colleen as he speaks to everyone, as if she is already her best self, which makes her want to be worthy of that.

She remembers, as she is meant to remember, arcs and history, remembers marches from Selma to Montgomery decades before she was born, hears another man's eloquence in this man's. "The arc of the moral universe is long," she hears, "but it bends toward justice."

The Junior Senator has finished speaking.

Colleen is no longer thinking, as she has been since her recent occupational disasters, *I am fucked and futureless.*

Instead, she turns to Walter and screams so he can hear her, "This is it!" with everything she's got.

Tomorrow we might all wake up and hate each other again, Colleen thinks as they walk through the throngs, and with them, taking picture after picture.

But tonight, she thinks, this is the story, and you *get* this story. This is the story you get tonight, she thinks.

And you are not here as a functionary.

You are here as yourself. You are here as a witness.

And who knows, years from now, decades even, people might look at these images and say, *Yeah, for one night it was like that.*

And it could be like that again, they might add.

And maybe, she thinks, if they aren't too far gone, it could be like that all the time.

Colleen looks to the horizon, or where the horizon would be if she could see past all these people.

She squints as if she were going to take its photograph.

She tries to see the curve curving.

Herself and everyone on it.

Little moving points on a fixed orbit toward a shared destiny.

Published in 2014. First Edition.

Printed in the United States on acid-free paper.

Fifth Star Press
1333 West Devon Avenue, Suite 221
Chicago, Illinois 60660

Distributed by Small Press United.

20 19 18 17 16 15 14   1 2 3 4 5

ISBN: 978-0-9846510-9-2

ALSO BY KATHLEEN ROONEY

Reading with Oprah: The Book Club That Changed America

Oneiromance (an epithalamion)

That Tiny Insane Voluptuousness (with Elisa Gabbert)

Live Nude Girl: My Life as an Object

For You, For You I Am Trilling These Songs

Robinson Alone

ACKNOWLEDGMENTS

Rose Rooney Super—thank you for representing the future in a way that's concrete and unsentimental.

Beth Rooney—thank you for flattering photos and extensive visual documentation.

Megan Rooney—for sisterhood (is powerful).

Chris Weiher—thank you for the film-making and general goofballery.

Abby Beckel—for publishing partnership and expert advice.

Kari Stuart—for agentry.

Elizabeth Crane Brandt, Jonathan Evison, Bayo Ojikutu, and Christine Sneed—for being stellar examples and inspirations.

Ryan Crawford, Christen Enos, Daniel Maidman, Jason Skipper, and Kimberly Southwick—for early read-throughs, thoughts, and commiseration.

Elisa Gabbert and Liz Hildreth—for constant or near-constant electronic contact.

Sheryl Johnston, Jennifer Musico, Dana Kaye, and Anne Whealdon—for helping me get out there.

Eric Plattner—for the vision to see this story as it needed to be seen and for the time and for the tirelessness.

My DePaul students—for your hard work and for the opportunity to work hard.

My Roosevelt students—for the same.

Ian Morris and Jason Stauter—for making this book a thing in the world.

Martin Seay—for everything.

ABOUT THE AUTHOR

Kathleen Rooney is the author of six books of poetry and nonfiction, including *For You, For You I Am Trilling These Songs*, *Reading with Oprah: The Book Club that Changed America*, and *Robinson Alone*, winner of the 2013 Eric Hoffer Award in Poetry. From 2007 to 2010, she worked as a U.S. Senate Aide. A founding editor of Rose Metal Press, she lives in Chicago. This is her first novel.